HELLSPARK

by

Janet Kagan

Hellspark © 1988 by Janet Kagan
Hellspark Afterword © 1997 by Janet Kagan
Uhura's Song Afterword © 1997 by Janet Kagan

HELLSPARK

An MM Publishing Book
Published by Meisha Merlin Publishing, Inc.
PO Box 7
Decatur, GA 30031

Editing & interior layout by Stephen Pagel
Copyediting & proofreading by Teddi Stransky
Cover art by Kevin Murphy
Cover design by Neil Seltzer

ISBN: 0-9658345-2-2

http://www.angelfire.com/biz/MeishaMerlin

First MM Publishing edition: January 1998

Printed in the United States of America
0 9 8 7 6 5 4 3 2 1

Table of Contents

This one's for Eileen Enquist, Lincoln Park Volunteer Hose Company No. 2, Bob Lippman, Warren LeMay, Tom Cleary, and Danny???, David G. Hartwell, and Rick Sternbach—all of whom came to the rescue—

THANK YOU ALL!

and for Susan and Gardner, fellow alumni of the hottest writers' workshop in the history of sf; Chris, who had the "unique perspective"; and Ricky, as always—
with love

Sometimes I think if it wasn't for the words, Corporal,
I should be very given to talking. There's things
To be said which would surprise us if ever we said them.

—Christopher Fry, *A Sleep of Prisoners*

A Note on Orthography:

I have chosen to follow GalLing' usage: italicizing the term *layli-layli calulan* and capitalizing it only when it begins a sentence. This should serve as a constant reminder that what appears to be a name is rather a designation. *Layli-layli calulan*'s name is unknown to any but a very few of her most trusted intimates. Her world of origin bears the designation (not the name) Y, meaning (very roughly) both "sound of strength" and "source of strength."

Again following GalLing' usage, I do not capitalize the Jenji title "swift-" except where it begins a sentence.

—MLL, ed.

Prologue: Lassti

South of base camp, a daisy-clipper skimmed through the flashwood, buffeting the undergrowth into a brilliant display of light. Its beauty was lost on swift-Kalat twis Jalakat. The dazzle was merely one more distraction that might prevent him from finding some trace of Oloitokitok, the survey team's physicist—he had been missing for two days now.

Swift-Kalat, a small slender man with a ruddy complexion and, normally, an easygoing temperament, punched the daisy-clipper's comtab as if it were to blame for Oloitokitok's disappearance. The weighty silver bracelets that on his homeworld of Jenje would have chimed his status here clashed and jangled. The sound only served to remind him that such expertise was useless in the situation he faced, and he jammed the bracelets almost to his elbows to silence them. When he addressed himself to base camp, his voice was clipped with exhaustion and anger.

"Swift-Kalat and Megeve," he began, identifying himself and his companion, "we have completed the search of sector four." He paused to choose his words with care. In his own language, he would have had no hesitation; his own language would have included in any statement the warning that he was neither suited to this task nor physically reliable because of his weariness. In GalLing', he was unable to speak with such accuracy. He found himself limited to saying: "We've seen nothing we are able to interpret as an indication of Oloitokitok's presence." His eyes flicked to the right, seeking a denial from Timosie Megeve, the Maldeneantine who piloted, but it was as futile as asking the loan of a Bluesippan's knife. He received only a glare of anger and frustration.

"Nothing in sector four. Acknowledged." The answering voice was low and weary, despite its careful control: it was that of *layli-layli calulan*, the team's physician—and Oloitokitok's wife. She went on, "Dyxte says there's another storm, a bad one, coming up fast in your area. Return to base and get some rest."

The small screen on the pilot's side lit to show the projected path of the storm. Frowning at it, Timosie Megeve opened his mouth as if to voice an objection, but before he could even begin, *layli-layli* added, "Doctor's orders."

"Acknowledged," said swift-Kalat wearily. He thumbed the comtab off and closed his eyes.

"She's right, I suppose," said Megeve. "We've been searching for nearly twenty hours." He ran a cream-colored hand through a tangle of gray curls, dropped it to his thigh, and stared at it unseeing. "We're both so tired we'd likely miss a drab-death's-eye if somebody dropped it into our laps. —And if we miss something we *should* spot, we're worse than useless."

What Megeve spoke was true, swift-Kalat knew, but he also knew that rest would not come easily: even Oloitokitok's disappearance could not drive the sprookjes from his mind.

Megeve shifted forward, glared at the instrument panel, then thrust out a hand to tap a nail against an indicator. He said something in his own language that was clearly a curse and tapped it again before returning to GalLing'. "One equipment failure after another," he said, still growling. "This wouldn't have happened if that transceiver hadn't failed on us."

"This wouldn't have happened if Tinling Alfvaen had been here," swift-Kalat countered, surprised to find that the statement approached the proper degree of reliability even in GalLing'.

"Who? —Oh, your serendipitist friend." With a second disgusted snort, Megeve gave up on the indicator and guided the daisy-clipper forward, following the snaky curve of the river back to base camp. "Maybe, maybe not. A serendipitist isn't all-seeing, you know."

Swift-Kalat made no response, but the thought worried him further.

Allowing three months for the letter he'd sent with the last supply ship to reach Alfvaen and another for Alfvaen to act on it, the polyglot he'd requested was at least four months overdue. Perhaps he had misjudged—not Alfvaen—but Alfvaen's culture, which was so alien to him. Perhaps her custom prevented her from assisting him. Swift-Kalat had worked with people of differing cultures long enough to be aware that one culture's truth was not necessarily another's.

He called from his memory the image of her smiling face with its exotic pale skin, sharp features, eyes a striking green. She was beautiful to him, but it was her eyes that held him always, even in memory: the fierceness of her eyes when she believed in something or someone. She would have believed the message he'd sent because *he* had sent it. Even custom could not have prevented her from acting on it, as custom would not have prevented him from aiding her were their situations reversed.

If not custom, then what had delayed her?

He formed the truth for himself: his real fear was for Alfvaen's safety. Perhaps the disease she had contracted on Inumaru was more severe than she, or he, knew.

The shock of the discovery jerked him back to reality. To his added surprise, he found that Megeve had turned the daisy-clipper to a new heading.

"What is it? Can you see something?" Swift-Kalat looked out, forcing himself to alertness.

He saw only a small stream, still swollen from the noon storm. A lush growth of drunken dabblers bobbed and weaved in the rumbling water; at every surge their dead-black leaves came alight with veins of eye-burning amber, the precise shade and glare of an antique sodium light. Beside them, smug erics danced, churning and whirring — each pale white leaf edged, each silver stem spined, with a harsh glitter of actinic blue. There was no sign of Oloitokitok. Blinking to clear his eyes, swift-Kalat turned to Megeve for explanation.

Megeve listened to a faint roll of thunder and said, "I make it twenty minutes before that storm hits here. That means we have enough time to reach your blind and change the tapes. There's always a chance they may show some act of the sprookjes that the captain can credit as intelligent."

It was a faint hope and both of them knew it, but swift-Kalat accepted it gratefully, and Megeve went on, "I know you're concerned about the sprookjes. So was — *is* — Oloitokitok."

Despite the immediate correction, Megeve's use of the past tense chilled swift-Kalat. GalLing' was an artificial language and it did not have the same accountability as Jenji, but swift-Kalat still reacted sharply when someone misspoke in such a matter.

It affected Megeve almost as strongly. He and Oloitokitok had been close companions since the beginning of the survey. He took a deep breath and went on, "Oloitokitok wants to prove their sapience as much as you—and he's bought them a reprieve. Kejesli won't send his status report while a member of the team is missing. I only wish it hadn't happened this way."

Megeve turned the daisy-clipper across country, threading it through the flashwood, where the turbulence of its wash whipped the Shante damasks from pure white to ripples of silver and stirred the blue-monks mistily alight. To their right, a row of smoldering pines went from black to the dull red glow of embers that had earned them their name. As the craft rose to avoid a deadly Eilo's-kiss, swift-Kalat pointed to a vast, gaunt stand of lightning rods, black and limbless spikes that rose to astonishing heights. "About thirty meters to the right of that," he said.

Megeve brought the daisy-clipper to a hovering stop in the small patch of flashgrass swift-Kalat indicated and asked, "Shall I go in closer, or will that disturb your wildlife?"

"You wait here," responded swift-Kalat. "I'll be quick." He folded back the transparent membrane, but was stopped by Megeve, who said, "Remember? We're back to Extraordinary Precautions."

Swift-Kalat had indeed forgotten. To lose a team member this late in a preliminary survey implied a danger that had not been catalogued. Until Oloitokitok was found, the team was to take the same precautions they had their first few months on Lassti.

The first and foremost of those precautions was to seal his 2nd skin. He popped his epaulets to draw out his hood and gloves, laying them across his knees. Once the epaulets were closed, he shook the hood open and coiled his glossy black braid into it; pulling it tight over his head, he ran a finger about his neck to seal it. Even where there was no need for life support canisters, the habit remained; gloves came second because they were clumsy enough to make sealing the hood difficult.

As Megeve double-checked the seams for him, swift-Kalat found himself wondering how much good Oloitokitok's 2nd skin might be doing him. Even a carefully sealed 2nd skin was no proof against electric shock—and shock was Lassti's major hazard.

"Sealed," Megeve pronounced.

Swift-Kalat thanked him and slid the few feet to the ground, buffeted at a slight slant by the daisy-clipper's ground effect. Around his ankles, flashgrass whipped violently to and fro. Like so many of Lassti's plants, it tapped energy from motion piezoelectrically, discharging any excess as alternating flickers of vivid green and white light. Swift-Kalat paused a moment to tune his hood, shielding his eyes from the ever-increasing dazzle the oncoming storm winds raised within the flashwood, and then plunged into its riot of light.

He pushed through a stand of solemnly chiding tick-ticks, thinking as he did so that it was too bad the 2nd skins MGE supplied its employees weren't sophisticated enough to damp his other senses to this world as well. Squat hilarities cackled, competing noisily with the tick-ticks for the attention of a swarm of vikries, Lassti's version of the bumblebee.

Some hundred yards in, he reached the clearing where he had erected his blind. Here, flames-of-Veschke and penny-Jannisett unfurled their deep red and copper leaves. Both species used the more conventional method of photosynthesis, and against the storm-brought brilliance of the background they looked almost black—and deeply restful. He breathed a sigh of relief at the quiet.

And then stopped in his tracks. The clearing should not have been so still, even in the absence of thunder or roar of rain.

The first time the survey team had stepped into this clearing, those small, golden-furred creatures had shrieked out. Oloitokitok had shrieked back at them, startling everyone as much as the creatures themselves had. Laughing, but defiant, Oloitokitok had explained that in his tongue they seemed to be saying, "I don't believe it! Not for a minute!" "I couldn't let it pass without comment," he had added. "I had to tell them to believe it."

On each subsequent visit swift-Kalat had paid to the blind, no matter what precautions he had taken, the flock of golden scoffers—for so they'd become in the surveyors' common tongue—had shrieked out their incredulity at his presence.

Now, there was no flash and beat of wings, no scornful shrilling. The only sound was the distant chiding and cackling of plants.

In the uncanny stillness, a sudden whiplike crack against his ankle made swift-Kalat start. He looked down to find he had brushed against a small blue-striped zap-me. The zap-me fed on electricity and obtained it by startling small animals that used a charge for defense. Swift-Kalat did not respond in the desired manner: he gave no shocks. As he watched, the plant patiently reset its whip-tendril to await a creature that would.

Something gold lay at the base of the zap-me; swift-Kalat knelt for a closer look.

It was a golden scoffer. Its bright fur was unmarked, but it was dead. Three more were scattered a few feet beyond. All dead.

A flicker of motion partially hidden behind his blind caught his eye. For one brief moment, hope rose to sting his eyes. *Here? Oloitokitok here?* But before he could shout a query, he saw a flash of scarlet, and a different hope stifled any sound from his throat.

A sprookje!

Swift-Kalat forgot the golden scoffers, forgot the oncoming storm. *A crested sprookje!* Afraid to disturb it by rising, he moved only his head, craning awkwardly for a better look.

It was humanoid, but neither parody nor deformation of human. It was instead exotically beautiful: tall, slender, and deceptively fragile. Like its fellows at base camp, it was covered with short feathers, subtly patterned in shades of brown. (After dark or in the dim light of an overcast, swift-Kalat knew, the feathers would emit a ghostly light.)

This sprookje, however, was a type that the survey team had not seen since their first contact with the species nearly three years ago. It was superbly crested in scarlet, and its long, smooth neck rose from a swirling yoke of red and blue feathers.

It knelt on both knees, over something shiny that was hidden from swift-Kalat's view by the art-nouveau tracings of an arabesque vine. Its head dipped rapidly — once, twice, three times — but swift-Kalat was unable to see what it was doing.

At last the sprookje stood and turned to face him. Enormous golden eyes stared at swift-Kalat from the sharp-featured, scarlet face. It opened its beaklike mouth as if to speak, but made no sound. Its tongue glowed an ominous red. Then, feathers ruffling, it backed slowly away and vanished into the flashwood.

Swift-Kalat realized that he had been holding his breath. He exhaled with a sigh and rose, just as a rattle of thunder recalled the need for haste.

Cautiously, he pushed through the heavy underbrush to see what had so interested the sprookje. A large object with the sheen of plastic lay beside his blind, reflecting bloody red the flames-of-Veschke it lay among. Scattered around it were a dozen more dead golden scoffers. For a long moment, his mind fought identification of the object.

He closed his eyes. The golden scoffers were scavengers. When swift-Kalat opened his eyes once again, he saw that Oloitokitok was dead. In death, Oloitokitok had silenced the scoffers once and for all.

Megeve and swift-Kalat found Oloitokitok's daisy-clipper on the far side of the stand of lightning rods. They lifted the remains of his body into it and Megeve switched the hovercraft to *follow* mode. This bitter parody of a funeral cortege—the only rites Oloitokitok would have until the cause of his death had been ascertained—arrived at base camp on the edge of the breaking storm.

Torrents of rain dimmed even the field of flashgrass. It distorted into unrecognizability the tiny crowd of surveyors who huddled grimly at the main gate. Only *layli-layli calulan* seemed sharp-edged, in focus, as she came forward to take charge of the body.

No one could find the words to speak to her. A moment later, the crowd disbanded in total silence. Swift-Kalat sat in the grounded daisy-clipper and watched them all go.

Wearily, he gathered up his specimen bag and fought through the thick red mud of the compound to his cabin.

He taped a record of his sprookje-sighting while it was still fresh in his mind; then, unable to sleep, he took the dead golden scoffers from his specimen bag and spent the next few hours dissecting one. His exhaustion had at last caught up with him. He put the second small corpse to one side and played back his report: the voice that issued from the recorder sounded chilled and shaky.

The thunderstorm passed and the rain settled down to a steady drizzle. He fastened the cabin door open—he wanted company but he was too tired to seek it out—and his sprookje entered. (At least, he assumed this one was "his"; like Gaian cats, each of the sprookjes in camp seemed to favor a particular person.) It was not the company he had hoped for but, unlike most of the other surveyors, swift-Kalat didn't mind the sprookje. His inability to communicate with it was troublesome; its presence was not.

It shook rainwater from its feathers with a controlled shiver.

Swift-Kalat rubbed his eyes. "Don't drip on the floor," he said. As always, he spoke to the sprookje as if it might understand.

The creature rubbed its own silver-blue eyes and blinked at him. "Don't drip on the floor," it said, its Adam's apple bobbing; and

15

swift-Kalat was again disturbed to hear the shakiness in his own voice, this time captured by the sprookje.

It parroted everything he said with the same accuracy and retention as his recorder, and only the beaklike shape of its mouth made its mimicry imperfect.

Swift-Kalat sighed.

The sprookje did likewise. Then it looked down at the table and saw the golden scoffer. It leaned over and opened its mouth.

"Hey! Don't do that!" said swift-Kalat sharply.

The sprookje echoed both his words and his tone and went on as it had intended. Swift-Kalat caught a quick glimpse of the sprookje's "sample tooth"—the single retractable needlelike organ that was ordinarily concealed within its beak—as the sprookje nipped the golden scoffer.

It was an irrational response, he knew, but the sharp thrust of the beak, the bite, always seemed aggressive. The first time they had seen crested sprookjes, van Zoveel had stepped forward to attempt to communicate with them. He had been examined and bitten. Everyone assumed he was being attacked. The resultant commotion had driven the sprookjes away.

Now he reacted not only to that, but to the thought of the dead golden scoffers as well. Eating Oloitokitok's flesh had poisoned them, as eating from the humans' garbage dump had poisoned the scavengers near base camp. With considerable relief, swift-Kalat remembered that he'd been bitten by the sprookje when it first arrived at base camp, with no ill effects to either of them.

The sprookje lifted its brown cheek-feathers slightly, as if in surprise; then it walked away, out the door and out into Lassti's brilliant dusk. Swift-Kalat was too tired to follow, too tired to wonder at the sprookje's behavior. He sank into his chair, closed his eyes, and lay his head on his arms just for a moment...

When he awoke, it was to the sound of thunder and the spray of rain streaming through the open door. Stiffly, he crossed the room and drew the opaque membrane closed. Reflected patterns of dull yellow light made him turn to the computer in the corner—he donned his spectacles and reluctantly called up the message the computer was holding for him.

The image of Ruurd van Zoveel, the survey team's polyglot, sprang into view. Van Zoveel was a large, solidly built man with a smokewood face, shaggy dark blond hair, and shaggier sideburns. Even seated before his computer console to tape a message, he was in constant motion. His gaudily beribboned tunic rippled with his agitation. He spoke Jenji without a trace of accent, however, and he spoke it with a high degree of reliability. Swift-Kalat closed his eyes and found comfort in the sounds of his native tongue that he did not find in the content of the message.

"*Layli-layli calulan* has finished the autopsy: she concludes that Oloitokitok died of heart failure due to severe electric shock. I saw what I took to be burns on his chest and shoulder. His locator had been fused; Megeve says in that condition even Oloitokitok's death wouldn't have set it off. The captain concludes that Oloitokitok startled a shocker—"

At that, swift-Kalat found himself frowning. Several of the indigenous predators used an electric charge to stun or kill their prey but the idea that a live-wire or a blitzen would mistake Oloitokitok for prey seemed out of keeping with what he knew of the habits of the creatures the team had dubbed shockers. A charger, perhaps? Unlikely in that area of the flashwood...

"—Or perhaps was simply struck by lightning. The captain has therefore lifted Extraordinary Precautions."

Something in van Zoveel's voice made swift-Kalat open his eyes. Van Zoveel brushed his sideburns anxiously, then he swallowed hard and finished, "There will be no final rites—at least, no public ones. *Layli-layli calulan*'s culture restricts death rites to the surviving family, in private."

Apparently, *layli-layli* had broken one of the taboos of van Zoveel's culture. For the sake of understanding, swift-Kalat would have to look into the matter.

With visible effort, van Zoveel composed himself. After a moment, he said, "That's not what I called about. I must speak to you, swift-Kalat, as soon as you've rested. Captain Kejesli wants my formal decision on the sprookjes."

To swift-Kalat's surprise, van Zoveel abruptly switched to GalLing' and went on, "I apologize for switching languages on you, swift-Kalat, but I can't say this in Jenji without creating an untruth: I believe that Kejesli wants the sprookjes found *non*sapient. No! No, it's not even that—I think he wants this survey over and done with, and it doesn't matter to him how sloppily he goes about it. It doesn't matter to him what the sprookjes are as long as we decide *now*."

Again, he made the effort to compose himself. Then he added, "Please understand that this statement has no reliability whatsoever, it's only the feeling I have. But I must discuss my report with you."

The tape beeped end-of-message and then there was nothing to see but cabin wall. Swift-Kalat took off his spectacles and continued to stare at it. Even in GalLing', and even with van Zoveel's careful disclaimer, the words were chilling. They could do the sprookjes no good. He did not want to face van Zoveel for fear of the further harm the man might do with his words.

To postpone the unpleasant duty as long as he could, he ate, telling himself throughout that van Zoveel's words in GalLing' could have no adverse effect on the sprookjes' situation. That, in fact, he knew that reliability was an aid to understanding only; that it was only superstition that it had an effect on reality. Having reassured himself somewhat, he showered as well, rebraiding his hair while it was still damp. There was no point in waiting for it to dry: it would only get wet again as he crossed the compound to van Zoveel's cabin.

The thunderstorm had not let up. He stood on the sheltered step of his cabin for a long time, reluctant to venture into the storm. Thunder rattled, numbing his ears; a sheet of lightning whited out even the red mud of the compound.

For a long moment, he was deaf and blind. He blinked furiously to clear his eyes, shielding them with a raised hand from ensuing flashes as the lightning repeatedly struck the stand of lightning rods that grew only two kilometers from camp.

When at last he found his vision returning, swift-Kalat could no longer distinguish between the dazzle of the Lassti flashwood and that in his own optic nerves. He drew an angry breath and plunged into the pouring rain. All around him sparks flew.

CHAPTER 1
Sheveschke, on the Rim of The Goblet

Wind rose to sweep the great bay known as The Goblet, where the Sheveschkem fleet gathered to honor Veschke, patron saint of thieves and traders, and to be blessed by her priests. The hissing light of torches along the wharf shaped and shadowed a hundred small craft, all alive with whispered sounds as if they shared the festival excitement. Ironwood hulls groaned and ropes creaked to the pulse of the waves; pennants and ribbons snapped counterpoint in the wind. They spoke of a thousand more ships beyond the acrid blaze of torchlight.

The same wind brought the wood-smoke of the festival fires, the tang of keshri bark, and the warm, rich smell of great cauldrons of stew.

It was the sailing wind of Sheveschke, and it whipped through Tocohl Susumo's red-gold hair and sent her moss cloak streaming about her. Her 2nd skin glistened over her tanned flesh like rubbed-in oil, reflecting the sparks riding the wind.

She was tall and spare, and she acknowledged her kinship to the captains of these tiny craft with a nod that, on another world, would have been a bow. Momentarily caught by torchlight, her eyes flared gold.

Beyond the bay, a thousand extra stars bejeweled the clear, cold skies of Sheveschke, their light splintered and spattered by the rowdy waves of Shatterglass Sea. A thousand extra stars—the Hellspark traders come to pay their own respects to Veschke, to have their ships blessed, side by side with the tiny skiffs and the sleek schooners of Sheveschke.

Tocohl Susumo looked up at the sky, into constellations old and new. (Where are you, Maggy?) she subvocalized. (Here,) came the response, and a tiny arrow appeared against the night sky, projected on Tocohl's spectacles, to indicate a new star at the tail-tip of the smallest Lunatic Cat.

Tocohl smiled her satisfaction, then leaned against the ironwood railing and said, (Now play back the message from Nevelen Darragh.)

19

(Your adrenaline level has dropped two points in the last five minutes. Playing Nevelen Darragh's message would only raise it again,) said Maggy; and Tocohl imagined a plump and prim Trethowan attempting to speak Jannisetti without using any taboo words.

(Cheeky,) Tocohl said, (don't argue with me.)

(I can't argue.)

Not half, you can't, thought Tocohl, amused; then she subvocalized again, (Play back the tape.)

This time Maggy made no objection.

There was no image, only the voice of a stranger. Her words were crisp, formal, and legally binding: "Tocohl Susumo is hereby notified of case pending judgment and enjoined from her proposed run to dOrnano to answer the charge of Tinling Alfvaen." A single bell-like note sounded. The crisp voice said, in signature, "Byworld Judge Nevelen Darragh," and then there was silence, except for the night sounds of the bay.

Tocohl drew her cloak tightly to her, not for warmth—that was amply provided by the 2nd skin—but for gesture, as a cat lays back its ears in preparation for a fight.

(Your adrenaline is up to—)

(Shut up a minute and let me think.) Tocohl breathed deeply and, reminded of the Festival of Ste. Veschke by spicy odors, decided that she did not need the Methven ritual for calm.

She was more puzzled than angry. A byworld judge dealt with cases where two cultures met and clashed—tourists who got themselves in trouble through ignorance of local customs, for example—or cases where no world claimed jurisdiction, in deep space or on worlds without a charter.

Tocohl shifted to Jannisetti and said, (As far as I know, I haven't stepped on any cultural toes lately,) turning the Sheveschkem cliché into a Jannisetti obscenity.

(Is that funny?) Maggy asked.

(I thought so; how did you know?)

(You smiled.)

In Jannisetti, a smile was limited to the face, so Maggy was apparently reading the implants at Tocohl's ear and throat rather than feedback from the 2nd skin. Tocohl touched the spot just before her ear and smiled again, but she could feel neither the transceiver nor play of muscle. She frowned slightly without meaning to.

Maggy said, (Then why are you worried?)

Tocohl grunted. (It could be about that "farm equipment" we sold on Solomon's Seal; two of the people I dealt with were third-generation Siveyn, and Tinling Alfvaen is as Siveyn as names come. —To be honest, Maggy, it could be about a lot of things, but *that* would worry me.)

(I don't understand. The manifest said "farm equipment" and that's what we delivered.)

(Maggy, this is a little difficult to explain: they expected arms.)

(Then why would they request farm equipment?)

(To make the shipment seem legal.) To forestall the inevitable question, Tocohl said firmly, (Yes, Maggy, the shipment we made was entirely legal, but we didn't deliver what the customer wanted.)

(I don't understand. If the shipment was legal—)

(What kind of charge could they bring? Price-gouging, as much as I hate to say it. They paid a lot more for farm equipment than they intended to. And serves them right.)

Maggy made no response. This was apparently beyond her and it was clear she felt it better for Tocohl's adrenaline level that she not inquire further.

Probably just as well, thought Tocohl, though it led her to wonder just what files Maggy might be checking in that silence. To distract her was a hopeless task, Tocohl knew, so she merely said, (How do we find Nevelen Darragh? Skip the map.) The projection vanished as quickly as it had come. (Give me verbal directions for the quickest route to Veschke Plaza.)

(That would take you through an area the Sheveschkemen consider highly dangerous after dark.)

(Fine,) said Tocohl. (Perhaps I'll have a chance to work off some of that extra adrenaline you're so concerned about.)

There was a pause, almost of resignation, then Maggy said, (Turn right and follow the Rim of The Goblet.)

Tocohl set off as directed. The silver filigree of her cloak streamed behind her and the lightness of her stride gave no evidence of her unsettled thoughts.

Here and there, she eased her way through crowds of merrymakers overspilling from waterfront taverns onto the wharf. Her captain's baldric brought her a spate of invitations which she reluctantly turned down or set aside for another time. Twice, laughing, she pulled stray hands from the pouch slung at her hip. "Clumsy doesn't honor Veschke," she chided the would-be thieves.

Twenty minutes later, Maggy turned her away from the Rim and into the narrow, dimly lit streets of the Old Quarter.

Tocohl did not slow her pace. One of the minor pleasures of having first-class equipment, Tocohl thought, was that she needn't worry about stubbing her toes on cobblestones. She might trip and crack her head, for her hood lay softly cowled about her neck, but if her toe struck stone the 2nd skin would spread the impact to absorb it and spare her the bruises.

She reached an unlit square, and Maggy said abruptly, (Trouble.)

Tocohl stopped. In the starlight, she could see only the constricted alleyways and the cramped stone houses and shops typical of Sheveschke.

Across the square, a solitary figure—a fisher, to judge from his rough-woven clothing and the pronged knife thrust into his belt—lounged against a stone doorpost. He straightened and whistled shrilly but made no move toward her.

(What trouble, Maggy?) she asked.

(Three people fighting in the alley.) Maggy pointed to the pitch-black opening to the right of the whistler.

(Push my vision two points,) said Tocohl, and the scene brightened and sharpened. Around the edges of the spectacles, Tocohl's peripheral vision darkened in contrast. It was as if she looked down a tunnel of light, the end of which was whatever object she focused on.

Three dim figures clashed in the alleyway. Two were Sheveschkemen and, like the whistler, wore fishers' garb. The third was undoubtedly an off-worlder; over the sheen of her 2nd skin she was dressed in a combination of styles from several different planets—what Hellsparks called worlds' motley. Not Hellspark, for she wore no baldric. Tourist, then.

She fought well, outnumbered as she was, but her movements were slow and broad. Drunk, thought Tocohl, her timing's off—and that's the standard surveyor's 2nd skin, not much help in a brawl. She's going to lose this fight.

Tocohl didn't much like the odds. (I'm going to pull rank, Maggy; watch my back.) Unclasping her moss cloak, she let it drift gently to the ground.

Few people in the Extremities would argue with a Hellspark captain on whose good will their interstellar trade depended, but Tocohl took the elementary precaution nonetheless. The deceptively simple action exposed all of the sensors in her 2nd skin but those still covered by her captain's baldric, and Maggy could work around those easily enough.

She started across the cobbled square heading for the alleyway. But the whistler stepped forward to meet her. His knife flashed upward in a swift, glittering arc.

Tocohl had no time to be surprised: she shrugged gracefully and the blade missed its mark. Before he could recover sufficiently to thrust at her a second time, she slammed her edged hand into his wrist and the knife jarred away, clanging on the cobbles.

The Sheveschkemen called a warning to his companions and backed away from the mouth of the alley, scrambling after the knife. Tocohl had no intention of letting him rearm. She followed—with two long strides and a lightning kick that took him squarely in the chest just as he bent for the knife.

Her 2nd skin absorbed the impact. Tocohl felt only a mild twanging sensation from foot to thigh but the whistler slammed against brick wall, cracked his head, and crumpled forward, unconscious.

Tocohl's back tingled. (Roll!) said Maggy, and a sandbag blow struck across her shoulders. But for Maggy's warning, Tocohl would have been thrown off balance. Instead, she somersaulted and twisted, came up back to the wall to face a second assailant.

This one too held a knife but he stared at his weapon dumbly. With Maggy to see it coming, the force that would have enabled the knife to pierce her had been transferred instead along the warp and woof of the 2nd skin; and because she had rolled forward at the crucial moment, it was unlikely she'd even have a bruise from the attempted stabbing.

There was one further advantage: his disbelief gave Tocohl the few seconds necessary to regain her breath and charge. The Sheveschkemen's nerve broke. He gave a sharp squeak of panic, dropped his knife, and fled.

Tocohl wasted no time following him; she rounded the corner into the alleyway—and stopped short. The third Sheveschkemen was gone, and so was the off-worlder.

(Overlay infrared,) Tocohl snapped, and a line of ghostly red footprints appeared, drag marks trailing them. The prints steamed away even as she watched, and she followed at a run.

Deep into the alleyway, the prints brightened and led to a narrow door. Even with her vision pushed for available light, Tocohl might have missed it—it was flush with the alley wall—but in infrared, the door's outline was unmistakable and the misty heat patterns told the rest. The Sheveschkemen had dropped the off-worlder, fumbled for the latch, then dragged her inside...

Once again sounding prim, Maggy began, (Breaking and entering—)

Tocohl cut her warning short. (It's festival. Read up on it.)

(If you're going in,) said Maggy, changing tactics, (put on your gloves so I can protect your hands.)

Tocohl gave each hand a sharp snap downward. Her neat cuffs unfolded and met just beyond the tips of her fingers. She gave Maggy a moment to individuate the 2nd skin between fingers, then reached for the latch and swung the door inward.

Maggy adjusted the spectacles so smoothly that Tocohl was not blinded by the unexpected glare of electric lights.

The fisher, a woman almost as tall as Tocohl and twice as massive, wrapped twine tightly, viciously, about the off-worlder. She looked up at the noise, grunted, and threw a shiny object.

Tocohl swiftly drew the door to, and the object struck it with a thud, splintering wood where Tocohl's head had been the moment before, then crashed to the floor and rolled away. It was a heavy copper sap that fishers used to kill their netted catch.

Still using the door for partial cover, Tocohl kept her eyes on the Sheveschkemen.

Then the fisher's eyes flicked once to the left. Warned by the movement, Tocohl leapt to the left even before the Sheveschkemen.

The fisher's knife lay beside a skein of netting twine. Tocohl swept it from the ironwood table seconds before the fisher's full weight struck her. Tocohl staggered back, but stayed between the fisher and her knife, and blocked two punches in rapid succession.

Then she saw an opening, whipped the edge of her hand across the fisher's temple. Maggy was good to her promise: the 2nd skin stiffened and Tocohl felt bone crunch beneath the blow.

The Sheveschkemen fell, first to her knees, then onto her face. Tocohl stepped aside and, without taking her eyes from the fisher, knelt for the knife.

Cautiously she rose and stood looking down at the fisher's prone body. After a long moment, she let out a sharp breath. (How's my adrenaline level now?) she asked.

(Still high, but dropping,) Maggy answered, impervious to sarcasm. Tocohl grinned in relief and turned her attention to the off-worlder. The small woman was still unconscious and breathing with difficulty. Tocohl first removed the crude gag and blindfold, then set to work on the rough twine with the fisher's knife.

Over her 2nd skin, the off-worlder wore a kilt of charcoal gray, black boots, and a fringe bodice of blue and silver. Silver threads laced through her jet-black hair, which hung in double braids over either ear. Taken singly, the styles might have identified her world of origin, but together, they gave Tocohl no clue.

Nor did her face. Her features were angular but gentle, and her skin was shockingly pale in contrast to her hair, except for the burns on her cheeks caused by the force with which the fisher had gagged her.

Her breathing gradually became normal.

Tocohl sliced through the last of the twine, and the woman slumped forward. Tocohl caught and eased her gently to the floor. As she did so, the braids fell away from the off-worlder's ear and exposed two bright bits of cloisonné: earpips.

(Definitely a surveyor,) Tocohl said. (Surveyor-grade 2nd skins are fairly common but earpips aren't. On holiday, I suppose, though this is an odd place for it.) She bent for a closer look at the earpips.

The first identified the woman's profession as serendipitist, which caused Tocohl to raise an eyebrow. To those who believed in espabilities, and Tocohl did, a serendipitist was one who brought luck to herself and those around her. This is serendipity? thought Tocohl; if so, it certainly takes a peculiar form.

The second pip was a medic alert. (Maggy, what does this mean?) She raised the emblem slightly to give Maggy a clear view.

(The wearer suffers from Cana's disease—)

(In layman's language, please,) said Tocohl, to forestall a spate of medical jargon that would be of no practical use.

(—A parasitical infestation that acts like a superyeast,) Maggy continued. (It converts sugar into alcohol. Cana's disease can be controlled in the human but not cured. Under stress, the victim appears to be—is—drunk.)

(Contagious?) said Tocohl.

(If it were, I would have said so. The parasite undergoes alternation of generation and is only transmissible through a blood-sucking mammal native to Inumaru, in the system of which it is a symbiont.)

(Sorry,) said Tocohl, reacting more to tone than content. (Is there anything I should do for her?)

(She'll have her own medication for that, and I've sent for a doctor.)

The woman stirred and, without warning, struggled violently from Tocohl's arms. *"Laiven!"* she gasped, *"laiven la'ista!"*

Siveyn, thought Tocohl, and responded in the same language. "Gently. The wild beasts"—she used the literal meaning of *la'ista*—"have had their claws pulled." Tocohl offered the fisher's knife, hilt first, as proof.

The Siveyn blinked pale green eyes at her, and touched the knife lightly but did not take it. Then she relaxed with a long shuddering intake of breath.

Torchlight flickered through the darkness beyond the splintered door. Tocohl came to her feet, stepped across the Siveyn, ready for more trouble.

(Police,) said Maggy. (When the lookout called for help, I did too.)

Tocohl relaxed, made a reassuring motion to the Siveyn. (I didn't ask for police,) she said, (or a doctor, come to think of it.)

(You didn't say not to call them. Was I wrong?)

(No, you did just fine.) Tocohl walked to the door and waved broadly to the little knot of uniformed Sheveschkemen who filled the mouth of the alley. "In here," she called in Sheveschkem.

She glanced at the splintered door and said, (Thanks, Maggy. If you hadn't adjusted my spectacles, I wouldn't have seen that coming. You saved me quite a headache!)

(You're welcome,) said Maggy primly. (Next time, though, pull up your hood too.)

The police doctor stooped to the fallen fisher. "She'll live," he said; and, without a further word, he crossed to examine the Siveyn.

The stumpy lieutenant in charge of the local authorities grunted sourly. A brusque wave of his hand brought two officers to guard the fisher. Then he turned to Tocohl. "Captain, may I have a word with you in private?"

"Of course," said Tocohl, and the two of them stepped into the alleyway. Tocohl leaned against the rough stone, beneath a freshly kindled torch.

"Lieutenant t'Ashem," he said, offering his hand.

His voice held no accent, but his stance did: Tocohl judged him a northerner still unused to southern kinesics, despite long residence. Instead of grasping the hand, she touched palms, northern-fashion, as she gave her own name. His eyes widened slightly, but more than enough to confirm her judgment, and she knew she had added one more minor embellishment to the Hellsparks' reputation.

He went on quietly, "May I hope, Captain, that you won't hold the wasters against us?"

"Wasters? Ah!" said Tocohl, "that explains the electric lights. I had wondered about the absence of Veschke's candles." The wasters—the Inheritors of God, to give them the name they used for themselves—were a fairly recent but widespread religious sect. Arrogant and troubling to most authorities, because, put simply, whatever they did was right. A more severe case of "God is on my side" than most of the usual religions. "—No, Lieutenant, they cause you more than enough trouble on their own. Why should I add to it?"

The lieutenant looked relieved and went on, "Then you won't mind telling me what happened?"

"Not at all. See for yourself." Tocohl removed her spectacles and handed them to the Sheveschkemen. (Maggy,) she said as he donned them, (run back the visual from where you warned me of trouble to the lieutenant's arrival.)

Obviously, the lieutenant had had previous experience with a first-person replay. He placed one hand firmly against the stone wall for physical reference; and only twice did he react involuntarily, the first time as Tocohl somersaulted, the second as the fisher threw her sap.

The younger of the two guards joined them. Tocohl thumbed her earlobe for silence, and he waited patiently beside her.

After a moment, the lieutenant removed the spectacles to frown at her. "Are you in need of medical attention, captain?"

"What? —Oh, the knife blow. No." Tocohl turned to show him an unmarked back. "I have a fondness for first-class equipment, even in 2nd skins. This is a stripped assault version." She didn't bother to mention that Maggy had made a considerable improvement even on that; what she had said was quite sufficient to take him aback.

"Very expensive!" he said.

"Very good trade," she corrected him with a grin, "—and that is, after all, my business!" It actually drew an answering smile from him. She reached out to collect her spectacles, saying, "Now you know as much as I do. Shall I make you a copy of the tape?"

"You needn't bother," said the lieutenant, "I know the third one." His smile turned grim. "I won't have any trouble finding him." Remembering the presence of the younger man, he suddenly said, "Well?"

The guard said, "They jumped her just outside the Shavam Inn and dragged her here. *She* assumes they meant to rob her."

The lieutenant looked swiftly at Tocohl and said, "She's not Hellspark, then?"

"No," said Tocohl, evenly, "she's from Sivy. Robbery seems unlikely, even from the Inheritors of God. Given that I found her bound and gagged, kidnapping would seem their goal. But why her? I guess we'll have to ask the fisher what it was all about."

The lieutenant grunted. "That's like asking a Bluesippan for his knife. The Inheritors of God don't explain themselves to heretics." He scowled and shrugged.

The Sheveschkem shrug, southern or northern, took one hand only, and—even as performed by the stumpy lieutenant—it was an eloquent mime of a man who tests the weight of an object with a bounce and, having found it unsatisfactory, discards it over his shoulder in disgust.

"Still," Tocohl prompted.

"Captain, we've had any number of incidents from the wasters in the past few months. Most of them unaccountable. Something stirred them up, and the usual sensible restraints don't apply. It'll be a pleasure to put a few of them away. Take it from me, this is just another bunch of wasters doing what they feel like at the moment. They break the law to prove the law does not apply to them. Random violence is almost a sacred act to a waster." He scowled more deeply.

"At any rate," he finished, "you and your friend needn't miss any more of the festival on their account."

He stalked to the doorway, pausing on the threshold to pick up the copper sap. "A souvenir," he said, and tucked it into the loop on Tocohl's baldric designed for just such a purpose. "Use it on the next waster you meet. God may not be on your side, but I certainly will."

Taking it for a sour joke, Tocohl smiled, but her smile vanished as she entered the lighted room. The second guard was giving a finishing touch—a boot to the ribs—to the unconscious fisher. The Siveyn, moved to the fisher's pallet and still being probed by the Sheveschkem doctor, watched and shivered visibly.

"That's enough," snapped Tocohl, and the guard looked up, startled and angry. Seeing her captain's baldric, however, he backed away from the fisher and began to make apologetic noises. They were noises only; none of his anger at Tocohl's intervention had gone.

Tocohl turned. "I'm sorry, Lieutenant, but that's taboo to the Siveyn. And I can't say I much like it either. If you can't control yourselves any better than the wasters can, could you at least wait until I get her out of here?" Between the insult and her baldric, that ought to put a stop to any further beatings.

The lieutenant took in the severity of her disapproval and gestured brusquely again. The guard muttered and retreated, but not before he had spat once on the fisher and said, bitterly, "Hull-ripping waster."

"I agree with his sentiments," the lieutenant said, sighing, "but not with his expression of them. His actions aren't taboo here, but they do make more work for the doctor."

He stopped abruptly. "Wait a minute," he said. "Taboo to a Siveyn? The Siveyn fight duels over anything—they'd fight about a theft at festival!"

"They duel, yes, but a duel is rigidly codified behavior. No Siveyn would dream of striking someone without first exchanging the proper ritual insults with him or her. Anything else is *la'ista*, the behavior of wild beasts; and that's the attitude that puts your officer there socially on a par with the waster."

He still looked puzzled. "Lieutenant," Tocohl went on, "she can challenge people all day long on Sheveschke, but she won't fight a duel unless she runs into another Siveyn. A challenge is one thing—but you simply don't attack unless you get the proper ritual responses."

She could see he still wasn't understanding. "If you went for Veschke's fire, and the priest didn't say, 'For Veschke's fire, one must shed blood,' would you continue with the ritual?"

"No, of course not. It wouldn't be properly done. It would be worthless... Ah, you mean fighting is somehow worthless to her without the proper responses."

"That's it. Nothing more than wild beasts. And it can't be done on that level. Besides, this Siveyn is more cosmopolitan than most; she's worked with a survey team and, judging from the fact that she hasn't challenged anybody yet, that's made her very tolerant."

The Sheveschkem doctor looked up as they approached and addressed Tocohl. "No concussion. She'll have a headache, but she'll owe it more to her celebrating than to the wasters."

(Maggy, find me a real doctor.)

(Does Geremy Kantyka qualify?)

The name gave her a start; Geremy was one of the few who'd heard the story of the "farm equipment" for Solomon's Seal. (Geremy's in town? He'll do nicely, yes.) Aloud, she said to the Sheveschkem doctor, "Thank you." Then she added, including the lieutenant in the query, "Is there anything else, or may we go?"

"Unless your friend wants a judge," said the lieutenant, "we'd prefer to treat this as a local matter."

Tocohl bent to the Siveyn. Extending her right hand, she laid her left palm up, fingers lightly curled, in the crook of her elbow and repeated the lieutenant's offer in Siveyn.

The small woman's green eyes focused with difficulty. She glanced obliquely at the guard who'd kicked the fisher and said, "I'd rather leave." Then her eyes fell on Tocohl's outstretched hands. "You s-stopped them?" Only the slight hesitation in speech betrayed her drunkenness.

"Yes," said Tocohl. "I apologize for the appearance of *la'ista*—my own as well as the officer's. Sheveschkem ritual is not Siveyn ritual, bur Sheveschkem ritual was satisfied."

The Siveyn took a deep breath. "I see," she said and rose, bracing herself on Tocohl's proffered arm. "As the Hellspark s-say"—like most Siveyn, she pronounced it *Hell-spark*— "'When on s-Sheveschke, be a s-Sheveschkemen.' Your apology is unnecessary, and you have the thanks of Tinling Alfvaen."

Tocohl frowned. (Maggy, *Tinling Alfvaen?*) Tocohl missed a sentence or two as Maggy responded, for her ear alone, in the crisp voice of Nevelen Darragh, ("... to answer to the charge of Tinling Alfvaen ..."), then in her own voice went on, (That is the name of the only surveyor of the twelve who contracted Cana's disease on Inumaru who was of Siveyn origin.)

(You might have told me.)

(You were busy. I didn't want to interrupt.)

(Anything else I should know?)

(She was also the only one of the twelve to lose her job with MGE after that survey.)

When Tocohl snapped her attention back, Tinling Alfvaen was saying, scornfully, " — And Multi-Galactic thinks I've lost my serendipity!" She gave her head an impatient shake that sent her braids flying. "If I'd lost my serendipity, I'd never have been rescued by the only other Siveyn on Sheveschke!"

"I can't speak to other circumstances, but I'm not Siveyn."

"Oh?" Alfvaen paused at the threshold to face Tocohl; she blinked her pale eyes in an effort to clear them and frowned slightly. "Oh!" she said, after a moment, "You're Hellspark, then."

"Yes. Susumo Tocohl, and pleased to meet you, Tinling Alfvaen."

Alfvaen released her arm and made the Siveyn formal greeting. "That's the same thing," she said warmly.

(She didn't recognize my name.)

(You didn't recognize hers, at first,) said Maggy reasonably.

Alfvaen wobbled and Tocohl caught her again. (She's getting drunker the longer she stands here,) said Tocohl. (*That* might explain her lack of recognition.)

Tinling Alfvaen raised a hand level with her throat, palm out, fingers splayed. It was one of the few gestures that GalLing', the universal pidgin, recognized as necessary.

"No," said Tocohl, "you haven't caused offense. Do you have medication with you?"

The Siveyn looked startled. "Yes-s," she said and began to pat the pockets of her kilt, her hands clumsy with haste.

She drew out a small box and gouged at it with her nail — then, exasperation in her sharp features, she handed it to Tocohl. "Would you please ... ?"

Tocohl opened the box, and Alfvaen took a pill and gulped it. "I'll be fine in a minute," she said. "How did you know?"

"Your earpip," said Tocohl. "Which direction are you headed?"

Alfvaen inhaled deeply. "I was on my way to Veschke Plaza, to meet Judge Darragh at the main festival fire."

Tocohl smiled wryly. "That's where I'm going. I'll accompany you, if I may."

"Certainly! —Are you a judge, too?"

The Siveyn's innocence was mystifying. "No," Tocohl said, "a high percentage of the byworld judges may be Hellspark, but a high percentage of Hellsparks are not judges."

Alfvaen frowned and, for a moment, Tocohl thought that the Siveyn had at last recognized the name. But when she said nothing about it, Tocohl concluded that she had only been reacting to the Hellspark tradition of alternating the pronunciation of their world's name: first *Hell's-park*, then *Hell-spark*.

Like most, Alfvaen came to the conclusion she had misheard and let the matter pass, saying instead, "I s-see. Most of the judges I've met have been Hellspark; I guess I do expect the reverse to be true as well. —You're a trader, then, or is that also a s-stereotype?"

Tocohl tucked a thumb beneath the black and gold leather of her captain's baldric and drew it slightly forward. "I'm a trader, here for the festival. My ship was blessed this morning. And you?"

"I came on an errand for a friend." Tinling Alfvaen seemed steadier, stood straighter now. She took several more deep breaths, and gestured a readiness to be on her way. As she followed Tocohl through the alley to the square, she added, "And if it hadn't been for you and Judge Darragh, I wouldn't have made it this far."

That only added to Tocohl's mystification. She stopped to pick up her cloak in passing. From the scent of it, she knew it had been trampled. Bruised, it was always aromatic, but this time it was pungent. Probably by the guard with the demonstrably heavy feet, she thought, snorting with disgust that owed more to the guard than the condition of the cloak.

Alfvaen said, "Your cloak was damaged? Perhaps you'd allow me to replace it."

"You couldn't. There's only one like this on Sheveschke; customs insists. Don't worry, it'll grow back." With a critical eye, Tocohl spread it in the torchlight. "In fact, it's due for a trimming."

"Grow back? Trimming?"

"It's a moss cloak. Not moss, to tell the truth, but an epiphyte, a real plant. If I don't trim it regularly, one day it will burst into spectacular bloom, seed, and die." She swirled it across her shoulders, clasped it, then pointed the direction Maggy indicated. "That way—and go on with your tale. I didn't mean to interrupt."

Alfvaen continued as they walked, "I s-short-hopped my way here, taking whatever transport I could find when I could find it. While I was on Jannisett, waiting for someone headed this way"—she grinned with embarrassment—"would you believe somebody s-stole my boots and I was arrested for indecent exposure?"

Tocohl laughed. "I believe it. A Jannisetti friend of mine once invited me to her private club, where all the members went barefoot and thought themselves very wicked!"

"Yes," said Alfvaen with a smile, then more seriously, "but if Judge Darragh hadn't happened along, I'd still be in jail."

They came to a broad avenue, lined with torches and bustling with people. The air was smoky and pungent; pottery shards crunched beneath their feet at each step.

They pushed through a knot of people, past a woman in the uniform of the local police, and Alfvaen shivered. "Perhaps you could explain something?" she said, over the noise. "I did read the standard tourist guide before I got here—and the captain of my last survey was Sheveschkem, so I was chamfered for Sheveschke, as well." It was a chamfer's job to teach one the basics of someone else's culture, to avoid any embarrassing or potentially fatal incidents. "He must not have done a very good job: I honestly thought theft was legal during the festival."

"In a way. If you're caught, you have to return what you've taken. But there's no punishment, aside from the razzing for clumsiness your friends hand you for the next six months. —Of course, taking more than someone can afford to lose is considered bad form."

"Then why did the police—" Unable to express her distaste, Alfvaen finished with a gesture.

"You're confused by a mistranslation," Tocohl said. "Veschke protects those who steal by verbal artistry or legerdemain. Skill is all. Anyone who uses brute force—violence or the threat of violence—is no thief by Sheveschkem standards."

"So those three weren't under Veschke's protection? I see, *dastagh*"—now that she had sobered, she came remarkably close to duplicating the Sheveschkem word—"means something like 'thug'?"

"No, the woman who attacked you was beaten for being an Inheritor of God. Among other things, they believe that their god gave them dominance over all the other species, and that they're entitled to use them, even wipe them out, as they choose. As a philosophy, it's enough to give an ecologist high-gold fever. *Dastagh* is the current derogatory word for a member of the sect; it means 'waster.'"

The avenue opened onto a great hexagonal plaza, edged with torches and ablaze with the light of a dozen ritual fires, each attended by a glory-robed priest and her acolytes. Alfvaen stopped short and gave a wordless exclamation of delight.

(Wait here,) said Maggy, (Geremy's coming.)

Tocohl was content to wait and, like Alfvaen, drink in the scene. Although she often attended the Festival of Ste. Veschke, the solemn joy around the fires in Veschke Plaza still elated her.

Despite the crowd's chatter and the crunch of broken pottery, here it was always quiet enough to speak in a normal tone of voice, so the traders, both Sheveschkem and Hellspark, gathered to exchange tales and songs.

A ripple of Apsanti water-music drifted through the smoky air and the laughter, to be picked up by someone around another fire and tossed back as dolphin song. A black-haired priest threw a double handful of keshri bark into the central fire and the air grew pungent.

A handful of Sheveschkem youngsters watched Tocohl and Alfvaen for a moment. After much giggling and gesturing, the smallest of them was urged forward to, shyly, offer Alfvaen a circlet of braided fair-sea-blues. Alfvaen glanced at Tocohl, who responded, "If you'll wear it and if you have some small off-world token you can give in return, you'll make it a festival they'll talk about for the rest of their lives."

Alfvaen lowered her head to accept the gift, and catching the child's arm before he could dart away, she said, "All I have is a brass coin from Jannisett. That's not very—"

"It'll do fine."

Alfvaen looked at Tocohl dubiously, then dipped into an overpocket for the coin. Tocohl stepped an inch closer to the child, familiar distance here in the south, and said in that language, "She offers you the Jannisetti truth-coin. The people of that world believe that while one holds this under the tongue, one cannot lie."

The child looked from Tocohl to Alfvaen, his eyes very bright and very wide. "Is it true?" he asked.

Tocohl shrugged, Sheveschkem fashion. "At any rate," she smiled, "one will learn that even truth can be bitter in the mouth."

"Oh!" said the child. He took the coin, kissed Alfvaen's hand, and dashed back to his friends, who huddled excitedly about to see what he'd been given.

"What did you tell him?" asked Alfvaen. Tocohl translated. When she'd finished, Alfvaen said, "But won't they be disappointed when they learn there is no such thing?"

Tocohl grinned. "Being conned by a trader at festival is more an honor than a disappointment. —And don't be surprised if, the next time you're here for festival, someone tries the line on you. The Sheveschkemen never let a good con go to waste."

The oldest of the three children waved an arm at Tocohl and called, "In Veschke's honor, Hellspark!"

Tocohl smiled and bowed to the child. Then she translated for Tinling Alfvaen, adding, "That is the polite way of saying she doesn't believe a word of it, but, since this is Festival, she'll let it pass."

A thin, wiry man with woeful eyes pushed through the edges of the crowd. He grabbed Tocohl and swung her around in an enormous hug. *"Geremy!"* She thumped him joyfully on the shoulders, then shoved him out at arm's length for a better look.

He was, as always, a walking work of art. The stylized waves of a darkened sea surged rhythmically around his 2nd skin to break and spray at the unchanging bulk of his equipment pouch; a handful of sparks blew past, trailing their reflections in the dark waters. The design was locally generated by a microprocessor in the suit itself.

"Very nice," said Tocohl, turning him around to follow the course of the sparks as they blew beneath his baldric and reappeared on the other side. "Very nice indeed."

(I could do that with your 2nd skin, if you like,) Maggy said.

(I'd like, but Geremy wouldn't. I promise, I'll explain later.) Aloud Tocohl said to Geremy, "Is that really a Ribeiro?"

"It is, and when Ribeiro took the commission, she said she'd been thinking about the subject for a long time." He folded his arms (along them stylized waves crashed soundlessly) and eyed her with suspicion. "Maggy said you needed a doctor, but you look disgustingly healthy to me."

"For the Siveyn here." Tocohl drew Geremy around the two

large merrymakers who hid Alfvaen from his view, but before she could begin a formal introduction, Geremy said, "Alfvaen? What happened?"

"She took a very nasty beating," Tocohl said.

Geremy backed off a pace and looked with hurt astonishment at Tocohl. "You?" he said, once more in Hellspark. "Listen, Tocohl, about that judgment—"

"She knows no more about it than I do," said Tocohl, then caught the import of his first reaction. "Geremy, don't be stupid. I haven't changed *that* much since the last time we worked together!" She gestured at Alfvaen: "Please, look her over."

Chastened, Geremy shifted back to Siveyn to offer his professional services.

"Your pardon, Geremy, but I've already been s-seen to by a doctor," said Alfvaen.

"I know. Maggy told me he was a quack—honestly Tocohl, I don't know where she picks up these words!"

(Any good dictionary has them,) Maggy said.

Tocohl laughed and repeated that for Geremy's benefit. Then she added, "I'd feel more comfortable if Geremy assured me of your health, Alfvaen—then we'll see to finding Judge Darragh."

While Geremy went professional, Tocohl excused herself to approach the festival fire. All the curious events of the past few hours vanished from her mind, pushed away by heat and flame and the sound of shattering pottery...

The priest's glory robe was orange velvet—the highest of her sect—and she wore the firecrown of her office with surpassing dignity. Tocohl dropped to one knee before her, spread her arms wide, and spoke the ritual words: "I come for fire."

"For Veschke's fire, one must shed blood," responded the priest.

"As it must be, let it be."

The priest sketched Veschke's sign in the smoky air above her head. "Rise then, and choose."

An acolyte held a tray of pins before Tocohl. Each bore a different emblem at its head: the pin of remembrance, the pin of dreams-come-true, the pin of smooth tongues...

On impulse, Tocohl chose the pin of high-change: its emblem was a face in flame. She dropped a coin in its place. The remaining pins jangled suddenly. Tocohl's hand shot out to steady the tray and she looked into the acolyte's startled eyes and gave a reassuring sign.

The youngster was unaccustomed to the Hellspark penchant for risk—a glance at the priest's face confirmed this. The priest drew the girl away to speak quietly to her.

And Tocohl stood alone before the fire. As she held her right hand high, the 2nd skin fell back into a cuff. She lifted the pin of high-change—it flashed as if of its own accord—and a great drop of blood welled from her fingertip. She shook the drop onto the broad circle of cast iron in the center of the fire, where it spat a moment, then was gone.

"Veschke's fire," she said softly, "taste my blood that you might hunger for it, that you might seek it out and devour it. Burn me to the bone and lift my living ashes into the sailing wind to light the way for those who come behind. As Veschke's sparks fly with the wind, let me follow."

CHAPTER 2
First Judgment

Tocohl made Veschke's sign, turned, and walked away from the fire, her hands and face still burning from the blistering heat. Only then did she realize that Maggy had recited the ritual words with her.

(So,) said Tocohl, (we share the pin of high-change.) She used the Hellspark *tight-we,* the pronoun reserved for two or more acting as one.

(Did I do wrong?)

(No. We share our fortune, as usual.) Tocohl laced the pin of high-change into a tuft of her cloak.

A second acolyte gestured her to the cauldron of stew, where she turned away a bowl, having eaten earlier, and accepted a ritual cup. The stew was thick and savory, and she finished quickly, then dashed the red clay cup to the ground. It shattered with a satisfying crash. By the end of festival week, the cobblestones of the town would be grouted with the rough red dust of a hundred thousand such cups and bowls. Like the other captains, she'd carry the dust aboard her ship and count it Veschke's blessing. Though luck had little to do with it, she thought. The soles of her 2nd skin were still covered with it—Maggy had been reading up on her subject indeed, or she would have cleaned them.

(Well done, Maggy,) she said, pleased.

(Thank you,) came the reply, then: (Geremy and Alfvaen are twenty paces from your right elbow. Thirty if you walk around the cooking fire.)

Tocohl turned her head to line her sight with her right elbow. As the crowd eddied, she saw Geremy and Alfvaen and a third Hellspark beyond one of the small cooking fires. She strode to join them.

"Well?" she demanded of Geremy.

"She's fine," he responded, "aside from a case of Cana's disease: that leaves her—"

"Slightly tipsy at the worst possible times; I saw. Though in this crowd nobody will notice." Tocohl pointed. "Pass the flagon and we'll all catch up."

The woman holding the flagon offered it with a smile.

She was old, thought Tocohl, with admiration. She had a face worn into comfortableness, seamed and tanned; her hair was fine and white. There was a mischievous look about her brilliant blue eyes to which Tocohl took an immediate liking. She smiled back and accepted the flagon, to find the woman had exceptional taste in dOrnano wine as well.

Alfvaen lifted her hands in the Siveyn formal gesture, fringe trickling from her arms, and said with affection, "Tocohl, this is Judge Darragh Nevelen. —Judge, this is Susumo Tocohl, the woman I was telling you about."

(Geremy,) Tocohl said, for Maggy alone. Her glance swept from Geremy to Darragh and back again. (Alfvaen had nothing to do with those charges. It was *Geremy!* I'm going to have him for breakfast—)

Maggy interjected, (Cannibalism—)

(Right after I'm done with the judge here,) Tocohl went on, overriding Maggy's attempt to warn her of the illegalities of cannibalism.

"Your pardon, Alfvaen," said Tocohl aloud. "Do you understand the language of Dusty Sunday?"

"No," said Alfvaen, and Tocohl continued, "May I speak it in your presence without giving offense?"

Puzzled, Alfvaen nevertheless granted her permission, and Tocohl shifted her stance to the language. So did Nevelen Darragh— the woman was good, thought Tocohl.

Judge Darragh slid her spectacles into her hair. Tocohl did not follow suit. On Dusty Sunday, wearing one's spectacles in conversation was a deliberate insult. It said plainly that one would rather be listening to someone else, watching someone else. Nevelen Darragh flushed a vivid scarlet.

When the red had reached the very tips of Darragh's ears, Tocohl added coolly, "Madame, I expect an explanation; I do not, of course, expect it to be adequate."

Nevelen Darragh stared hard at Tocohl for a long moment— then, with a burst of laughter, she bowed her appreciation.

Geremy said, "I told you she was good, Nevelen."

"The incident on Solomon's Seal told me that, Geremy. But she's better than you know." Judge Darragh laughed again. "You haven't been on Dusty Sunday recently, I take it?"

"Not for ten years," Geremy said mournfully.

"Then I'd better tell you that what your friend just did was the exact emotional equivalent of 'In Veschke's honor.' She smiled again at Tocohl: "I'm pleased to hear there are no hard feelings."

Glancing sidelong with mock menace, Tocohl said, "I haven't had my shot at Geremy yet." She took a long pull from the flagon of wine and contemplated him, measuring him until he squirmed with discomfort. "Perhaps some other time," she said at last, "when he's least expecting it."

More woeful of face than ever, Geremy said, "I'm sorry, Tocohl. Maggy wasn't letting anybody through to you. I was the one who suggested that a judgment might override her orders."

"I'll bet you told her it was business," said Tocohl dryly.

Geremy looked abashed. "I didn't talk to her; Garbo did. And you're right, the message said business."

"If you'd put your money into your equipment, instead of on your back"—Tocohl's finger traced the path of the sparks briefly along his arm—"your computer wouldn't be so damn dumb and it'd do more than deliver messages verbatim."

She raised the flagon again, then passed it to Geremy, who hesitated before taking it. "Oh, Geremy ... In Veschke's honor, then." At that his eyes brightened within his sad-clown features, and he accepted the wine to drink deeply his relief. "All right," Tocohl went on, "let's talk business and be done with it so I can get back to celebrating."

"Your business is with Alfvaen," said Nevelen Darragh.

Tocohl crossed her ankles, seated herself beside Tinling Alfvaen, and said in Siveyn, "Were you aware, Alfvaen, that you'd called for a judgment against me?"

Alfvaen, startled, splayed a hand at her throat. "I have no quarrel with you, Tocohl."

"Nor I with you," said Tocohl. "Someone"—two quick thrusts of an elbow indicated a choice of Geremy Kantyka or Darragh—"owes us both an explanation."

It was Judge Darragh who spoke. "Tinling Alfvaen came to the Festival of Ste. Veschke to find a glossi. As Geremy explained, the judgment was a way to contact you, nothing more."

Maggy made a pinging noise. Tocohl held up a hand and said, (Yes, Maggy?)

(The judgment has been canceled. There's a formal statement. Do you want to hear it?)

(Not necessary,) said Tocohl; aloud, she said to Alfvaen, "All right. I'm here. What is it you want of me?"

"You're a polyglot?" Alfvaen asked.

"Glossi," Geremy corrected, "—from an old, old word meaning 'speaker of tongues.' There's some evidence that an espability is involved, and if it is, Tocohl's got it."

"Your pardon, Tocohl," said Alfvaen. "You are a glossi?"

"Yes, although Geremy exaggerates. As far as I know, I have a good ear and a good eye, not an espability."

Alfvaen looked at her intently, then said, "You were tricked into coming to meet me. I apologize and I will fulfill any ritual you think just."

Tocohl gave a reassuring smile. "It was only a theft at festival, as the Sheveschkemen say, and Geremy's theft at that." From the corner of her eye, she saw Geremy flinch quite satisfactorily. To Alfvaen, she added, "You gave no offense, I take none."

"Then please hear me out." Alfvaen leaned forward.

"I'm listening," said Tocohl, surprised by the small woman's sudden urgency.

"When I was with Multi-Galactic Enterprises," Alfvaen began, "I spent a good many years working with swift-Kalat twis Jalakat of Jenje—perhaps you've heard of him?"

"Yes—considered by some to be the best survey ethologist in the business, considered by most to be 'crazy as a Hellspark.' Go on."

Tinling Alfvaen did. "Swift-Kalat is three years into the survey of a world named Lassti. He has reason to believe that the planet has a sapient life-form and should be declared off-limits to exploitation and colonization. The problem is that the survey team's polyglot—I don't think I'd call *him* a glossi, Geremy—hasn't been able to make sense of the language."

"After three years?" sad Tocohl. "That is odd. So MGE wants to hire a glossi?"

"No," said Alfvaen, "swift-Kalat does. He'll pay your fee."

Maggy made a querying noise.

"Let me think a moment," Tocohl said, and explained to Maggy, (It's not illegal for him to hire outside talent, especially not with a byworld judge involved, but MGE certainly won't like it!)

(Do we care?) Maggy asked, using *tight-we*.

(No, not about MGE's likes and dislikes. But MGE has a good deal of power on some of the worlds we trade on, and they could make our lives considerably more difficult. Suppose we do prove sapience — then MGE has wasted three or more years of a survey team's time without any return; and that they'd like even less!)

(So the system works against proving sapience?)

(In a way, yes. You can't prove sapience without proving a species has a language, but the MGE polyglots are damn good, usually, and regulation is strict. For the most part, I'd say it's honest — though you could probably quote me chapter and verse on *honest* mistakes that have destroyed cultures.)

(Should I?)

(Skip it. I can think of a couple of nasty examples myself. Maybe we should take this job.)

(Maybe?) said Maggy.

Tocohl smiled. (You're getting awfully good at holding up your end of the conversation!)

(Thank you,) said Maggy, primly.

(Maybe,) Tocohl repeated. (Swift-Kalat is the survey team's ethologist. That, and his "swift" status, give him a lot of credence, but I'd be happier if the polyglot had asked for a glossi.)

(I have forty-three files that quote swift-Kalat as the highest authority on ethology. Would you like a random sampling?)

(No, I concede his expertise. Let me find out more.) Tocohl said aloud, "Stepping into that kind of situation is asking for trouble, whatever the outcome."

Tinling Alfvaen said, earnestly, "Tocohl, swift-Kalat is Jenji. The Jenji don't lie." That was conventional wisdom on many worlds, but to Alfvaen the belief seemed to go beyond convention to a personal conviction. "I've known Jaef for a long time —"

Tocohl raised an eyebrow and said, "That you're entitled to use his soft-name is proof of that." (And proof of a strong bond between the two,) she added for Maggy's benefit.

"— And if he says the species is sapient, I believe him," Alfvaen finished, "but you must help him prove it." She reached into a pocket of her kilt and drew out a folded piece of gold paper. Without a further word, she offered it to Tocohl.

Tocohl took the paper, unfolded it. The startling boldness of Jenji script seemed to leap from the page: three lines and the signature, *swift-Kalat twis Jalakat of Jenje.*

"Geremy," Tocohl said quietly as she refolded the paper and returned it, "are you free to take a cargo of winterspice and tapes to dOrnano for me?"

Geremy turned. "What do you say, Nevelen—can you spare me for a few weeks?"

So Geremy was acting as the judge's aide, Tocohl thought. That explained much. She would have withdrawn her request, but Darragh spoke first: "I haven't been to dOrnano for years, Geremy. I'll go with you."

Geremy turned again to Tocohl. "After festival?" he said.

"Of course," Tocohl replied, and because it was Geremy, their dickering was pro forma. In only a few moments they had snapped fingers to close the deal.

Alfvaen's face lit as she realized the import of this exchange. "You'll go!" she said and looked down at the paper in her hand. "He told me this would convince the kind of person he needed. I don't understand why, but I'm glad."

Tocohl said, "To say 'I know' in Jenji, you must specify *how* you know. You have a choice of degree—firsthand experience, inference, hearsay, to name just a few of the options—and each tells your listener how reliable you think your information and why. That, in turn, reflects on *your* reliability. The language is also backed up by strong cultural penalties for using the wrong degree, and a religious belief that you may, by lying, inadvertently create a truth that would do no one any good."

Tocohl touched the edge of the paper in Alfvaen's hand and went on, "He tells me here that he has in his hands an artifact, and from this artifact he deduces the presence of sapient life—anyone might have written that in any language. In Jenji what swift-Kalat wrote is very complex and very precise. The degree of his surety is so high that if I were MGE, I'd pack up the survey team and go home."

"In three sentences?" Alfvaen unfolded the paper and stared at it in wonder.

"Four," Tocohl said. "He signed his name—and that puts his status on the line. If he's wrong about this, he'll be forced to drop his 'swift' status. And that's the social equivalent of your going into your hometown and admitting to *la'ista*."

Alfvaen's eyes widened still farther. "He's *that* sure?"

"He's that sure," Tocohl said, but before she could say anything further, a group of Sheveschkemen passed and their cheerful singing momentarily brought conversation to a halt. The song was a lengthy and awe-inspiring detailing of Ste. Veschke's sexual adventures.

One gorgeously drunken woman in the green leather baldric of a trading captain leaned down, her slim hand on Geremy's shoulder. "You look too solemn," she told him, "Veschke made a merry blaze even when she burned!" She pointed to the flagon in his lap; "Drink to Veschke!" she commanded over the singing.

Geremy raised the flagon, clinked it against the captain's. She said, grinning hugely, "Veschke was a Hellspark!"

Geremy shouted his laughter. "To Veschke, then!" he said, and took a long drink. Then the Sheveschkemen passed on, still singing as they went.

Tocohl turned back.

Alfvaen had drawn up her knee and wrapped herself disconsolately about it. Her green eyes were dark and sad.

"Alfvaen," said Tocohl, "is something wrong?"

The Siveyn answered slowly. "I didn't know how strongly he felt about the situation. I should have. I should have! Tocohl, you've never even met him and you know more about him than I do!"

"No," said Tocohl, "you believed him. Fancy words and fine phrasing are necessary only to convince strangers."

"Yes, but—" Alfvaen raised her small hands and grasped air. "I have to learn the words as well." She fell silent, but her hands remained clenched.

After a moment, Darragh said, "There's another matter of language, Tocohl. Before you accept this job, you should know what happened on Jannisett."

Keeping a watchful eye on Alfvaen, Tocohl said, "She told me. She was arrested and held, until you straightened the matter out."

"She was expertly framed," Nevelen Darragh said, "—and the man who framed her was a *crayden*."

Tocohl stiffened in surprise. She said nothing, but Nevelen

Darragh's expression was all she needed to confirm that she'd heard correctly.

"I see," said Tocohl, and she laid her hand on Alfvaen's shoulder, partly to comfort, partly to draw Alfvaen from her preoccupation. "What are your plans, now that your message is delivered?"

Alfvaen stared at her, uncomprehending. Then she blinked as if come into sudden sunlight.

"A moment ago, I had none," she said. "MGE dropped my contract after Inumaru. —I don't blame them much. Even I find it hard to believe that catching Cana's disease could be serendipitous."

She reached across and caught Tocohl's wrist. "Take me with you," she said. "Teach me the words I need."

"I was hoping you'd say that," said Tocohl. "MGE may have doubts about your serendipity, but I don't. You know how to deal with members of a survey team," she paused, then added, "and you might be safer on Lassti than anywhere else."

"Safer?" Alfvaen asked. "I don't have the words to understand that, either."

"You need just one: the Jannisetti word *crayden*. It is an exact translation of the Sheveschkem *dastagh*—waster. As the Jannisetti say themselves, 'Once a thing happens twice, you must think about it three times.'" Tocohl stood. "Geremy, I'm sorry to break up your evening, but could we get that cargo transferred now? Under the circumstances, I'd prefer to leave immediately."

Despite its value, the cargo was small and compact. Even Nevelen Darragh pitched in to help, and the transfer of tapes and winterspice went quickly. As a courtesy, Tocohl registered her new destination with Sheveschkem traffic control, giving the coordinates Alfvaen had received from swift-Kalat.

"I'll bet traffic control loved that!" said Geremy. "I take it the captain of the survey team is Sheveschkem?" he asked Alfvaen. The naming of a new world was often the captain's privilege.

"Yes," said Alfvaen. "What's so funny?"

"*Lassti* means 'Flashfever,'" Geremy explained. "It's a local disease—as common on Sheveschke as a cold—characterized by bizarre visual effects."

"It's like being slugged in the side of the head and seeing sparks,"

Tocohl put in. "I know. I had it once."

Geremy went on. "The very religious call it 'the Fist of Veschke' and would say Tocohl had been punished for her many sins."

Tocohl waggled a handful of fingers at Geremy insolently, then got on with the business of rearranging the interior panels to create a cabin for Alfvaen.

"—That must be some planet!" Tocohl finished.

Maggy pinged for attention. (Two passengers for Flashfever,) she said.

(Passengers?) said Tocohl in surprise. Only rare circumstances would take people to a world still under survey. Visiting was inadvisable, not illegal, and one stayed only as long as one's transport stayed. Transport stayed at the discretion of the survey captain.

(Let's have a look at them,) Tocohl instructed. (Put them on the screen.)

Maggy complied. A man and a woman, Sheveschkemen, appeared on the small screen. Both wore severely cut green jumpsuits, lacking any adornment. The expressions they wore were equally severe.

The woman spoke in GalLing'. "Captain Susumo? We wish to book passage to Flashfever for the duration of your stay."

That should have been icing on the cake. Tocohl's expenses were already covered by swift-Kalat. Two passengers would double her profit—and yet Tocohl did not immediately reply. Something about the two disturbed her. Then she suddenly had it: here were two Sheveschkemen prepared to leave their planet before the end of festival and neither wore a pin of any sort. Neither had gone for Veschke's Fire!

(Not worth the risk,) thought Tocohl and only realized she'd subvocalized when Maggy said, (What risk?)

(The Inheritors of God don't participate in "pagan" rituals. In fact, I imagine they'd find Veschke particularly hateful. She burned for her refusal to give Sheveschke's coordinates to exploitive second-wave colonizers,) Tocohl explained briefly. (I won't risk having Inheritors aboard while Alfvaen is with us. She's been attacked twice. The first time on Jannisett, when she was framed. The second we interrupted. One could deduce that the attacks were escalating.) She said aloud, "You'll have to find other transport. I'm taking no passengers this trip."

"What about the Siveyn?" demanded the woman.

Tocohl glanced coolly around. Only Geremy was within range

of the visual pickup. Beside the stow-webbing, Alfvaen looked at the screen with surprise and started forward. Nevelen Darragh stopped her with a swift hand on her shoulder.

Geremy, the best of accomplices, shrugged one hand at Tocohl and looked puzzled. Tocohl turned back to the Sheveschkemen. "What about *what* Siveyn?" she asked, with an innocence of expression she'd been practicing since the age of two.

Unlike Geremy, the woman was no actor. Realizing her error, she inhaled sharply and turned from the screen in an effort to hide her self-reproach.

Her companion elbowed her aside and began, in a conciliatory fashion, "A friend of ours at traffic control said you'd registered for Flashfever, Captain, and he said something about a Siveyn, so we naturally thought he meant you were taking passengers..."

(*Ping!*)

(Yes, Maggy.)

(You said nothing to traffic control about Tinling Alfvaen.)

(I know. Later, Maggy.)

The Sheveschkemen finished, "... Perhaps we were given the wrong ship, then." The woman had disappeared from view, and the man glanced off-screen, paused, then said, "May I ask your destination, Captain?"

"My destination is Flashfever," said Tocohl. There was no point in lying—the woman was probably double-checking now.

"Then it's only a matter of the fee," said the Sheveschkemen. "I'm sure we can arrange something that will satisfy you."

"No passengers," repeated Tocohl.

The Sheveschkem woman returned, angry. "I see no reason for you to deny us passage," she said. "We will ask for a judgment!"

Nevelen Darragh stepped into visual range. "Ask then," she said, "I am Byworld Judge Nevelen Darragh, and I will consider the problem. I must, however, point out that it will probably be a waste of your money: in all but the most exceptional circumstances, the captain has the ultimate say in what occurs on her vessel, whether it be fishing ketch or starship."

Nothing had prepared Tocohl for the professional Darragh. The transformation reminded her of the first time she had seen a Bluesippan dress dagger drawn, the sudden startling realization that the dagger was fully practical. The judge was layered steel, glittering and razor-sharp. Tocohl was impressed.

The two Sheveschkemen were equally impressed and more than a little unnerved. They made hasty private consultation. When they turned the sound on once again, the man said, "It is, after all, the captain's privilege. If she wishes to lose income ..." He shrugged and went on. "Will she agree to carry a letter for us?"

"Of course," said Tocohl instantly. There she had no choice. Automated message capsules were expensive, so the only reasonably priced interstellar communication was through traders. Mail was always accepted.

And the refusal of mail could cause a judgment that would most certainly detain Tocohl and might well go against her.

Perhaps that was what the Sheveschkemen had in mind. At any rate, he seemed disappointed at her agreement, but said, "We'll send it up on shuttle."

"Make it soon. We leave within the hour."

The image vanished.

Nevelen Darragh said, "I wouldn't wait, Tocohl."

"I wasn't planning to," Tocohl said with a smile. "Thanks, though."

Nevelen clapped Alfvaen on the shoulder, turned to Geremy and said, "Come on, we're wasting valuable festival time!"

They walked to the hatch, where Geremy wrapped Tocohl in a farewell bear hug. "Say hello to Bayd and Si for me, will you?" Tocohl said into his shoulder. "Tell them I'm sorry I missed them and I'll see them next year for sure." She tucked a tape into his equipment pouch and patted it as she stepped back. "Tape for them. See they get it."

"I will."

Nevelen Darragh looked on, then fixed her piercing blue eyes on Tocohl one last time and Tocohl again sensed the steel behind them. "One question, Tocohl."

"Question, yes. Answer? Ask and we'll see."

Darragh laughed but her eyes did not change. "Why did you take farm equipment to Solomon's Seal?"

At that, Tocohl laughed. "Because that was what they needed."

"That's the answer I expected. It's been a pleasure meeting you." She gave a Hellspark two-finger salute and hustled Geremy through the port.

The inner hatch closed, and Tocohl led Tinling Alfvaen forward to ship's control.

CHAPTER 3

The ship's control was a spacious room bright with telltales and—because it also served as captain's quarters—tapestries, a hammock, a jumble of paintings, and Tocohl's small but treasured collection of hardbooks.

(Hop to, Maggy,) said Tocohl, (let's program that jump—)

(I have a message from Geremy.)

Settling herself at the control console, Tocohl said, (Tell me.)

Maggy complied in Geremy's own voice: (Tocohl, I'm not the one who told Darragh about Solomon's Seal. I swear it.)

(Interesting,) Tocohl commented.

When she said nothing more, Maggy said, (Geremy said goodbye to me, too.)

(Shouldn't he have?)

(The judge didn't.)

(The judge was never introduced to you. I'm sorry, Maggy, I must be getting forgetful in my old age.)

(You are only 103. If you are forgetful, it has nothing to do with old age.)

(That was just an expression, Maggy.)

Alfvaen took the seat Tocohl indicated, then glanced at Tocohl curiously and said, "I have no wish to intrude, nor to violate a Hellspark taboo, but you seem to be listening to something. Judge Darragh and Geremy often gave the same impression."

(This time I won't forget, and you can practice your Siveyn, Maggy.) Tocohl tapped the spot just before her ear and said aloud, "No mystery and no taboo: I have an implanted transceiver." She made the formal Siveyn gesture and said, "Alfvaen, may I introduce Lord Lynn Margaret—*lord* is a title, something like *swift-*, but its use is not obligatory in this case. Maggy, Tinling Alfvaen."

Maggy, as prim in Siveyn as she was in Hellspark, said, "I'm very pleased to make your acquaintance, Tinling Alfvaen."

Her brow furrowed, Alfvaen half rose to survey the room. Puzzled, she said, "And I yours, Maggy—but where are you?"

Maggy chuckled. "All around you," she said.

Tocohl sat down to the controls. Her fingers danced over the keyboard, then paused as she said, "I like that chuckle—where did you get that?"

"It's yours; I changed the pitch to match my voice range. Did I use it correctly?"

"Perfectly," said Tocohl. Her fingers danced a second time. "What made you decide to use it?"

"You smiled," said Maggy, once again.

Alfvaen's features went from total bewilderment to sudden comprehension. "You're the ship's computer? —But you sound human!"

"I'm not," said Maggy, "I'm only a top-class extrapolative computer with a larger memory bank than most."

"You needn't say *only*," Tocohl commented, checking a bank of indicators. "It doesn't seem applicable to you."

"All right," said Maggy. "I'm a top-class extrapolative computer with a larger memory bank than most."

"That's better." Tocohl glanced over her shoulder to address Alfvaen: "If you find talking to a disembodied voice bothers you, Maggy can always activate a small mobile."

Alfvaen thought for a moment. "That's not necessary; I'll get used to it."

"Will you please correct me?" Maggy asked.

Tocohl gave two final taps to the keyboard, straightened, and turned to face Alfvaen. "Her Siveyn consists of a basic grammar and an enormous vocabulary to plug into it. She's had no practical experience in conversation and she wants you to correct her usage. She learns like a kid does, except that she only needs to be told once. Anything you tell her she stores for later use; her entire program undergoes constant revision.

"—I think it helps to tell her when she does something right, too," Tocohl grinned, "like that chuckle."

Alfvaen looked around her again. "I'll be glad to help, Maggy."

Tocohl said, "Treat her as if she were a friend looking over your shoulder. Believe me, unless you tell her not to, she is always looking over your shoulder!"

"I will not violate Siveyn taboos," Maggy said. There was a moment's pause—obviously supplied for esthetic reasons—then she added, "Alfvaen, I have a large selection of Siveyn literature. I can read or display it to you anywhere in the ship. All you need do is ask."

"How will I know if I'm interrupting your duties?"

"That's no problem. I can do several things at once." As if to demonstrate the truth of that, Maggy pinged and announced, "Jump programmed, Tocohl. Ready when you are."

"Ready," said Alfvaen. Tocohl turned back to her console and said, "Then let's go, Maggy."

Ordinarily, Tocohl would have done the programming herself, using Maggy only as a double-check, but that was merely a matter of keeping her hand in. Since they were in something of a hurry, she let Maggy do it and set them on their way. Then she went through the programming herself for the practice.

Interstellar flight was mostly a matter of long days of waiting, punctuated by an occasional flurry of programming the next hop. Flashfever, by Tocohl's estimate, was a hop, three steps, a hop and a skip away. First hop accomplished, Tocohl worked out the first of the three steps, then, satisfied to find that Maggy had opted for the same route she would have, she swung her chair.

Alfvaen, she saw, had temporarily chosen to address Maggy as if she were hidden in the blank screen on the far wall. Not a bad choice, that, since it contained one of the sensor banks that Maggy used to watch the control room.

She was saying, "I'm sure I wasn't drunk enough that my ears were playing tricks on me. It sounded as if Tocohl said, first, 'Hell Spark,' and then, 'Hell's Park' when she talked about her people."

"She did," said Maggy.

"But which is it?"

"That's a state secret," said Tocohl.

"That's a joke, Alfvaen," Maggy said, her prim tone making it sound much like a child's confidence, "Tocohl told me."

Tocohl grinned. "So it is, but you're entitled to use the joke too, Maggy."

"All right, but Alfvaen wants to know. She wants to get it right."

"I accept your reasoning," Tocohl said. "Alfvaen, the correct pronunciation is to *alternate* the two pronunciations—to use first one, then the other, even in the same sentence."

"How odd. Why?"

"For the same reason anybody does anything in any language: because."

"That's not enough reason," Maggy said, sounding primly offended.

"I know, Maggy; but that's all the reason there is in most cases. In the case of Hellspark, well, since that was originally an artificially created language, there's a bit more reason. The alternation I think was intended to remind you of the need to be flexible in language. If so, it's failed in a way. I can no more use two Hell's-parks followed by a Hellspark than some people can learn to alternate them every time. So I don't think it achieves the desired result, but it's retained as a joke all by itself—even *without* the 'state secret' line."

Alfvaen added thoughtfully, "Every Siveyn I ever met pronounces it hell-spark. I suppose that's *because*, too."

"Hell-spark *means* something in Siveyn, while hell's-park is only nonsense syllables. One tries to make any new word fit the parameters one is accustomed to. When I speak Siveyn, I pronounce it hell-spark, too."

"You didn't that time," said Maggy.

Tocohl considered this. "Had I been speaking Hellspark to you, Maggy, while I was talking to Alfvaen?"

"Yes."

"That would account for it, then. A holdover from language to language. Tell me if you catch me doing that again. It's bad practice." This last was directed at Alfvaen as well.

Speaking very slowly and very carefully, Alfvaen said, "But I'd like to try doing it anyway, even if it's bad practice for a Hell-spark. It seems common courtesy to pronounce 'Hell's-park' the way a Hell-spark would." Her green eyes lit with pleasure. "That's not easy!"

"No, it's not," Tocohl agreed. She rose, crossed the room to hang her cloak near the best source of light, and said, "If you can hear it and, better still, do it, then I think I have a good pupil. That is, if you're still interested in a crash course in Jenji, Alfvaen?"

Alfvaen came to attention instantly, so eager in manner that her words were unnecessary. She said them anyway, "Oh, yes! Please!" then looked momentarily worried. "I haven't much to pay you, not after passage."

"Passage is for acting as my liaison with the survey team. As for payment for language lessons … if you're helping Maggy with her Siveyn, I'll consider it even."

(She can pay you by teaching me?) Maggy inquired privately.

(Anything you learn is to my advantage. And it has never seemed right to me to charge for such a basic tool as language.)

(I think I understand.)

Alfvaen began, "Does Maggy—is that all right with you, Maggy?"

"Of course," said Maggy, this time aloud. "If I learn Siveyn, I can help Tocohl."

It was so much like a small child's absolute assurance that Tocohl couldn't help but smile. "That's settled, then," she said. "We might as well get started. On your feet, Alfvaen."

Alfvaen looked at her with surprise.

"Up," Tocohl said. "You were expecting the basics, weren't you? Well, they aren't *hello, good-bye, please, thank you,* and *Where's the bathroom?*"

"They aren't?" Alfvaen came immediately to her feet. "Jenji is *that* different from Siveyn?"

"Not in the sense you mean," Tocohl said, "but Hellspark language lessons always start with the proxemics and kinesics of a new language. The earliest of the old Hellspark proverbs is 'The dance is sweeter than the song.'

"Let me give you a practical demonstration." Tocohl glanced down, indicated a broad yellow stripe that halved the tapestry beneath their feet. "Stand with your toes touching that. If at all possible, I want you to remain with your toes touching that, and I want you to tell me what you're feeling while I talk to you."

Alfvaen, despite her puzzled look, arranged herself carefully. Tocohl took a step forward and greeted her formally in Siveyn. Alfvaen responded instantly in kind.

"Look at your toes," Tocohl said.

"Still on the line, but I ..."

"Bear with me. How did I greet you?"

Alfvaen gave this some thought. "I'm not sure I understand your question, Tocohl. You greeted me as if you were Siveyn, you know that."

"Aggressively? As if I were a long-lost friend?"

"Neither. As if you were ... Tocohl. Just as you are."

Tocohl pursed her lips slightly. "All right. Keep your toes on the line. I'm going to do it again." This time the language she chose was Jannisetti, and it required a step backward on Tocohl's part to greet Alfvaen formally.

Alfvaen had clearly learned her *hello, please*, and *thank you* in Jannisetti, for she responded in good kind to the greeting. Her accent was impeccable, but she stepped a full two inches across the line. "Toes," said Tocohl. Alfvaen looked down, her eyes widening in astonishment.

"Why did you step forward?"

"I don't know," she said, stepping back to stare at the line as if it had somehow moved from under her.

"Try again," Tocohl said. Alfvaen fixed a corner of her eye on the line and readied herself visibly. Again Tocohl greeted her formally in Jannisetti, and again Alfvaen moved forward. This time, however, she caught herself in midstep.

With great deliberation, she set her foot back, glared at Tocohl, and responded to her greeting in clipped tones. Then suddenly her anger was gone, lost in the interest she gave to her feet.

"First lesson," Tocohl said. "Why were you angry?"

"You backed away from me, as if I were diseased." She was still staring at her feet.

"No," said Tocohl, "I did not. I greeted you in exactly the same way in both Siveyn and Jannisetti."

"But you didn't, Tocohl. In Jannisetti, you—" She closed her mouth abruptly. She stared up at Tocohl. "On Jannisetti, they *all* backed away from me!"

"Are you that offensive?" Tocohl grinned at her. "I didn't think so."

"You thought so in Jannisetti! You backed away! Why, Tocohl?"

Shifting back to Siveyn, Tocohl said, "I'll show you the emotional equivalent of what you did to the Jannisetti in Siveyn. Try toeing that line through this ... !" she challenged. Once more, she greeted Alfvaen in her own language. While the words were formal, her movements were not—instead of the requisite one step forward, Tocohl took two.

And Alfvaen instantly backed away from her.

Tocohl waited patiently where she was, making no further move that could be interpreted as aggressive.

After a long moment, Alfvaen again looked down at her toes, taking in the distance she had moved from her mark. She said, "You came at me!"

"And why do you suppose the Jannisetti all stepped back?"

Alfvaen stared at her feet in an embarrassed fashion. "Oh, Tocohl," she said at last, "do you mean that every time I said hello — and thought I said it in a friendly way in their own tongue — I was ... jumping at them the way you jumped at me?"

"I'm afraid so, yes."

"'But why didn't someone *tell* me?"

"Because it's one of the hardest things in the world to tell. You interpret both spacing and gesture on a subconscious level as you've been trained to interpret them by your culture. In fact, there are at least six different sets of proxemics and kinesics on Sivy alone, and you'd be hard put to get one of the others correctly. The fact that, to the ear, you all speak the same tongue, makes it all the more liable to misinterpretation."

Alfvaen sat down, put her chin in her hand. After a long time, she said, "I've seen it, and I didn't know what it was. And if it's that difficult between two people who've known each other all their lives ... Tocohl, perhaps I've misinterpreted Jaef altogether."

"I doubt it, or you'd be calling him 'swift-Kalat' like the rest of us. He gave you his soft-name, Alfvaen; that's a very good indication of how he feels about you." For Maggy's benefit, Tocohl added, "And I'd say you felt the same way, even though you had no soft-name to give in return."

Tocohl knelt to look her straight in the eye. "You have a good ear, and you can catch on quickly to the visual aspects." She grinned. "And you have a better motivation than most to learn. I'd bet money you can get all the basics on a conscious level by the time we get to Flashfever. If you're willing, that is ... ?"

"Willing?" And once again, Alfvaen was on her feet. In three steps, she'd set her toes once more against the broad stripe in the carpet. "All right," she said, "show me how it works in Jenji. I swear I won't move an inch."

Tocohl laughed. "You probably will — but by next week you won't."

In fact, it was the rigidly codified rules of dueling that gave Alfvaen her greatest asset in learning the proxemics and kinesics of Jenji. Tocohl could explain certain uses of space between two speakers in terms of the very precise movements of the duel, codifying them in Alfvaen's mind.

All in all, Tocohl was pleased with her pupil. Even now, as she fairly crackled with anticipation, Alfvaen spoke in Jenji and carefully maintained the proper polite distance. Tocohl knew it was no easy task for her—on Alfvaen's world, physical closeness implied intimacy.

"I mean no denigration of your teaching ability, Tocohl," she said, "I am only afraid that *I* will forget my lessons-s. If I s-stop thinking about it, I will s-step back." The emotional stress had brought her slurring back.

Tocohl's hands moved swiftly as she manually brought the *Margaret Lord Lynn* into geostationary orbit above the survey camp; Maggy flashed confirmation. Tocohl said, without looking up, "Take a pill and don't worry. I'll let you know when you can stop thinking about it."

(Something is bothering her,) Maggy said privately. (What's wrong?)

(Nothing we need worry about, Maggy,) said Tocohl in the same mode, (I'll explain it later.) Aloud, she said, "There we are. Good to know my brain hasn't atrophied. Now see if you can raise Captain Kejesli."

She glanced briefly at the serendipitist and wondered why she'd ever thought those quick green eyes pale. "Your pardon if I speak Sheveschkem?"

"What distance do I s-stand for that?"

In Jenji, it was not a joke, but Tocohl grinned back at her. "Stick to Jenji," she said. "The usual survey team is so diverse that no two members speak the same language. Don't confuse the issue."

Maggy pinged for attention; "I have Captain Rav Kejesli," she said. Tocohl pointed to an area of the screen.

A face appeared in the indicated spot, dwarfed by the full-screen display of the stormy atmosphere of Flashfever. Tocohl shifted her attention to take in Rav Kejesli. He was a stocky man with gray eyes and a worried expression. His long dark hair was elaborately beaded and clicked with each movement of his head. A festival pin glittered in his vest lapel—a pin of remembrance, in the northern style.

Tocohl made the northern gesture of greeting and introduced herself.

"Yes, yes," Kejesli responded. He returned the gesture automatically but he spoke in GalLing', his voice impatient. "You came because of Tinling Alfvaen?"

"No. I came at the request of swift-Kalat twis Jalakat of Jenje."

"What is it you want?"

"Your permission to land, and proper coordinates for a skiff."

"Permission denied," said Kejesli.

The words chilled her, even as Alfvaen gripped her arm convulsively. Permission to land on a planet this late in survey should have been a formality, Tocohl knew. She gripped Alfvaen's hand, answering convulsion with firmness, and waited, frowning slightly, for the bad news.

"Quarantined? Are you quarantined? Whatzh—what has-s happened?" Alfvaen demanded of him, the shock of his refusal making her slur violently despite every effort to speak plainly.

Kejesli jerked his head violently, starting a stormy rattle. "No, Alfvaen! Nothing like that! We're taking normal precautions. Everything is all right!" He closed his eyes and rubbed his hands across them as if suddenly he were very tired.

He said at last, "—No, everything is not all right. We lost Oloitokitok. But, Alfvaen, swift-Kalat is fine. There is nothing to worry about."

"Then why won't you let us-ss land?" demanded Alfvaen.

"It is my prerogative." His hand came up, the Sheveschkem shrug.

There was a single sharp movement to her side and Tocohl turned. Alfvaen stood, rigid, her right arm shoulder high, her forearm parallel to her chest. The fringe shivered with the tension of her body. "*This* is your choice, then! Look on me, child of fools!"

She had spoken in Siveyn, but it was clear from Kejesli's horrified expression that he knew what had happened. Tocohl addressed Kejesli brusquely in his own language, as if translating Alfvaen's words: "Your whim prevents her from fulfilling her obligation to swift-Kalat. She will challenge you if you do not reconsider your action. She's angry enough to do it, too. And if she goes to a full challenge and you don't give her satisfaction, you'll never be able to work with a Siveyn again. And she'd have judgment on her side; there would be no recourse. Is it worth that much?"

Kejesli jerked his eyes away from Alfvaen. "Veschke's sparks, no!" he said. "How—?"

"How do you get out of it?" Tocohl finished for him. "—Reverse your decision." Kejesli frowned and Tocohl switched back to GalLing'. "It's *not* your prerogative, Captain," she said. "We have mail."

For Kejesli to refuse the delivery of mail for anything short of the planet-wide quarantine he had just denied was unthinkable, and he accepted the excuse Tocohl provided him gratefully. "In that case," he said, "you have permission to land."

Again in Sheveschkem, Tocohl said, "Say to her, This is my choice: that you and I clasp hands and drink together." Kejesli did so, and although the words came out slightly differently in GalLing', the effect was good enough. Alfvaen slowly lowered her arm and turned her back to the screen.

"Well," Tocohl interpreted in Sheveschkem, "you're not good enough to drink with, but she'll forgo the fight."

Relief washed his features. Without taking his eyes from Alfvaen, Kejesli went on, "If you'll link with our computer, Captain Susumo, we'll transmit the coordinates you need. I suggest that you wait out the storm. Lightning is hazardous in a skiff—or any other small craft, for that matter."

"Then give me coordinates for a class 13 trader, if you will."

He complied. When she had acknowledged receipt, he said, "I'll send a daisy-clipper to meet you as soon as the storm passes." With one last worried look at Alfvaen, Kejesli broke contact.

Tocohl programmed her landing. While Maggy checked her figures, Tocohl responded to the survey computer's customs queries. The only item of interest was her moss cloak, and since no other moss cloak was present, customs okayed it. It always pleased Tocohl that her cloak was a one-to-a-world item.

Then she leaned back and waited quietly.

At long last, Alfvaen turned back. "My apologies," she said formally, in her own tongue, "I thank you for your assistance. I had no cause to challenge. I should know Kejesli better by now. He does what he thinks MGE expects of him and nothing more."

"I'm afraid nothing is that simple. Someone on this world must have passed the word to have you delayed," said Tocohl, "and Captain Kejesli is as good a suspect as anyone else."

At Alfvaen's shocked look of denial, Tocohl said, "Just bear it in mind." Her hands danced and the image of Flashfever swelled. "Now, I promised Kejesli mail and mail he shall have," she grinned. "Go write a letter. —And just in case Kejesli tries to restrict us further, specify hand delivery to swift-Kalat."

Alfvaen went to write a letter. Tocohl's hands danced again on the console. (Now, Maggy,) she said, (in answer to your question: Alfvaen finds swift-Kalat sexually attractive—judging from the way Kejesli spoke, that's no secret. She wants to learn his language in order to be more attractive to him. She's now afraid that she'll do it badly and ruin her chances of a relationship, or of learning that he doesn't return her feeling.)

(Oh,) said Maggy. (—So Alfvaen will tell him she loves him and fight a duel with her closest friend and win and be cruelly wounded?)

(Wait, wait!—Veschke's sparks, Maggy, what *have* you been reading?!)

Maggy's recital of what she had been displaying for Alfvaen lasted through planetfall. (Maggy,) said Tocohl, firmly, (we're going to have to have a long talk about fiction. I think you still misunderstand its purposes: fiction is a lie for entertainment, it's a lie the listener willingly accepts for the sake of something else.

(Alfvaen reads formula fiction. Each book, as I'm sure you've noticed, follows a set pattern, and the delight of the reader is in the variations on the theme—while the theme fulfills certain basic emotional needs. Alfvaen's a romantic: she wants to see duels fought and won at great cost for great passion.)

She broke off as Alfvaen returned, her letter prepared. Clipped to her belt was one of Maggy's handhelds, striped diagonally with gold and purple for easy identification. Alfvaen touched it lightly and explained, "Maggy s-said to ask you if I might carry this s-so s-she could talk to me."

Tocohl gestured her permission. "That's for voice transmission only—remember, Maggy does listen unless you tell her otherwise." She looked slightly away from the Siveyn. "Maggy? Why don't you activate an arachne and poke around on your own as well?"

"You didn't tell me to," said Maggy.

"I'm telling you to, now. Check that construction in your Siveyn grammar: it indicates a nonobligatory suggestion or request."

Planetfall accomplished, Tocohl gathered her cloak about her and led the way to the cargo hold to await local transport. Maggy pinged for attention almost immediately, and relayed a message: "Move ass, Hellspark!" said a deep, cheerful voice. "This lull won't last forever, and I've an allergy to lightning!" The words were GalLing' but the delivery was pure Jannisetti.

Tocohl glanced quickly at Alfvaen's feet. Yes, the Siveyn was wearing boots. That left only Tocohl indecent by Jannisetti standards. (Maggy, I need boots—red ones,) she added quickly, knowing that Maggy would ask. From the soles of her feet to the top of her calves, her 2nd skin turned a dark red, with stitching in all the appropriate places and a darkening of shadows to suggest thickness. (Thank you. Now let's "move ass" like the lady says.)

Maggy popped the hatch. Tocohl whistled her wonder and thrust her head through for a better view. Truly, this world had been struck by the fist of Veschke!

The broad grassland below was alive with light. As the spray-laden wind rippled through it, it flickered and flashed in response. Beyond, some two kilometers, the grasslands gave way to woods—and the woods themselves winked jewel-bright lights. The air was so pungent with ozone it stung her nostrils; lightning flashed, brief and spectacular, into a far-off group of stiff black structures.

A daisy-clipper edged in, cutting off her view of the shimmering world and substituting that of a broad brandy-dark face. Still in wonder at Flashfever itself, Tocohl had enough to spare for the remarkable piloting that brought the pilot virtually nose-to-nose.

The Jannisetti woman stared back at Tocohl and then, suddenly, grinned hugely. "Good," she said, her satisfaction plain, "you pass. Wait until you see it by night—it's a Port of Delights and a firework display all rolled into one! Now, pull your eyes back in your head and let's get the hell out of here."

Tocohl stepped lightly from Maggy's hatch into the daisy-clipper and held out a hand to assist Alfvaen. Without taking her eyes from the landscape, Tocohl made a circle of her arms. The arachne squatted on its long, spindly legs and leapt. (Close the hatch, Maggy,) she said, settling the arachne's fat round body on her lap and adjusting the legs so she could see past them.

"Buntecreih," said the Jannisetti, turning the daisy-clipper around and settling into a low fast skim toward base camp, "but everybody calls me Buntec. —The arachne won't last long here; you probably should have left it on board your ship.

"You've heard of electric eels? We have electric mice, tigers, buzzards, you name it. Corner any wildlife around here and you're in for a shock, literally." Buntec's voice turned abruptly grim. "We just lost a man that way." —Tocohl touched her forehead in acknowledgment, and Buntec went on, forcing herself to a lighter tone. "Half the wildlife, plant or animal, on this flashy planet uses electricity for defense or offense—and one good zzzzzzaaap! from an Eilo's-kiss will fuse your arachne solid. Either that, or a tape-belcher will get it."

"Tape-belcher?" said Alfvaen, and Buntec laughed. "That's right. The first time we saw one was when it *swooped*"—she demonstrated expressively with the hovercraft, and Tocohl clutched at the arachne to keep it on her lap—"down and scarfed up a tape recorder. Thought about it a minute, gave a horrendous belch, and barfed it right back up again. And if you think this *sounds* disgusting, wait until you see one!"

(Maggy, you're not to wander around until we get you full descriptions of these things. Maybe losing a mobile doesn't hurt you, but until somebody invents a cheap superconductor, replacing it takes credit we could better spend other ways.)

(For more memory, you mean?)

(You're getting greedy, aren't you?) Tocohl grinned.

(Yes,) said Maggy. There was a pause, then she added, (Was that the right response?)

(Very. On the nose. Now cut the chatter and let me find out what's going on here.)

Buntec was commiserating with Alfvaen in no uncertain terms. "Yeah, I heard they dropped you after Inumaru. SOP for the s.o.b.s. Kejesli was on that one, too, wasn't he? And he didn't make any objections?"

Buntec set the craft down with an abruptness that Tocohl expected to be followed by a hard jolt—it wasn't—and answered her own question. "Naw, he wouldn't. Too worried about his own hide. I never saw such a rattlebrain!" She lifted her chunky hands from the controls, cracked her knuckles, and twisted around to face Alfvaen. "And I'll bet you thought that noise was just the doohickeys in his hair! No, I tell you, it's three loose thoughts in an otherwise empty container."

"Maybe you're right," said Alfvaen. "He didn't want us to land, and I don't think he'll let us stay."

"I fixed him." Buntec tapped her nose with self-satisfaction. "I figured from the rattling he did when he told me to pick you up that you were the last person he wanted to see, ever." Alfvaen flinched, but Buntec went on, "He may not want to see you but the rest of us do." She emphasized her point with a finger-tap, this time to Alfvaen's nose. "So I jogged his brain a bit on that count … and I made a few calls on my way out to get you. Half the survey team is waiting for you in the common room—let Old Rattlebrain try to throw you off planet with us around!"

She turned to take in Tocohl as well and added, "And wait'll the other half finds out about you, Hellspark! He'd better let you stay: we're all sick of looking at each other. With what we've just been through, we need the diversion." For a brief moment, her face darkened as she added, "Another two weeks of nothing but sprookjes and I'll tip darts and hunt Vyrnwy."

Tocohl raised an eyebrow at this last, but Buntec only spread a flattened hand and said, "Better a little harmless excitement, I say. —And I say you'll stay if I have to peel Kejesli and roll him through a field of zap-mes."

A sudden gust of wind brought a torrent of rain. "Shit," snapped Buntec, "me and my big mouth. Now we'll have to run for it. Follow me!" and she was off, with Alfvaen at her heels. Tocohl dropped to the ground, the arachne under her arm, and stopped, transfixed. Water sheeted on her spectacles—and Maggy compensated for the remaining distortion—as she stared up into the flash-filled sky, her ears filled with the roar of the rain.

"Hey! Hellspark!" Buntec roared over it. "I said move ass, I meant move ass. This is only the leading edge. From here on it gets worse!" A chunky hand grasped Tocohl's, and together they raced through the field of flashgrass to the thick red mud of the compound.

CHAPTER 4

Swift-Kalat clamped his jaw shut, unable to respond to Ruurd van Zoveel's polite overtures in GalLing'—they served only to renew his memory of what van Zoveel had so misspoken. Without a word, he took the towel van Zoveel proffered and focused his attention on drying himself from his dash through the storm. Again, he told himself that GalLing', being an artificial language coined for trade, had none of the reliability of Jenji. Again, he found it difficult to believe.

It wasn't until van Zoveel addressed him in Jenji that he was able to answer at all. Hearing the Jenji forms calmed him slowly. He chimed his bracelets in polite response, mildly surprised when van Zoveel did not follow suit. Of course, he thought, Zoveelians wear no status bracelets, but it disturbed him nonetheless. Even the youngest child makes the arm motion...

Their conversation continued in Jenji. The sound of it was enormously welcome but swift-Kalat found himself more and more discomforted. Something in Ruurd van Zoveel's manner disturbed him enormously; it never bothered him when he spoke to van Zoveel over the comunit but, here, in his presence ... If only the man would sit down! swift-Kalat thought. For all his courtesy, van Zoveel seemed always to back away, and swift-Kalat felt obliged to follow.

Instead of sitting, however, van Zoveel paced nervously, his beribboned tunic fluttering. He offered a glass of dOrnano wine, as if the occasion were one for celebration; and swift-Kalat accepted, knowing it was not, but grateful because the acceptance took van Zoveel to the far side of the room.

Van Zoveel's furniture was plush and as gaudy as his clothing. Swift-Kalat chose a plump red and blue pillow near a low table and sat, piling smaller red and yellow pillows to support his elbow as he'd seen van Zoveel do. It was far from comfortable, but it was better than following van Zoveel around the room.

Van Zoveel returned with the wine and handed him a sheaf of hardcopy as well. "That's my report," he said. "That is what I will have to give the captain. I thought perhaps you should read it."

"I need only read your conclusion." Swift-Kalat sat up to take the report. He leafed through to the final page. It read as he'd expected: *"The sprookjes have no language as far as I am able to determine."* He slapped the report closed and dropped it onto the table with more force than he'd intended.

Van Zoveel, pouring the wine, jumped; wine splashed. He finished the pouring carefully and wiped away the droplets. "I'm sorry, swift-Kalat," he said, not looking up, "I am unable to say otherwise."

This time the absence of van Zoveel's status bracelets—or at least the movement that would have set them ringing—struck swift-Kalat more forcefully.

"Something on this world is sapient." Swift-Kalat snapped his forearm sharply; his own bracelets rang emphasis of his words.

"Something has your reliability in its favor. I explained that to Captain Kejesli but the captain hasn't the ear to hear the distinction. —And I am unable to match your certainty. I am unable to say otherwise," he repeated.

"I made a formal application for a second polyglot, but Kejesli denied my request. My record is too good, he said—*too good!*—and he did not wish to go the additional expense of sending an automated message capsule." He spat, startling swift-Kalat (who had only read of and never seen the Zoveelian expression of utter disgust) with his vehemence, and finished. "There is nothing further I can do."

A peal of thunder rattled the wine glasses. Swift-Kalat put out a hand to steady his but did not drink. "I thank you for your trouble," he said. "I did not know you had gone so far—"

"Ruurd?" From the comunit, Buntec's deep voice broke in.

Van Zoveel excused himself and activated the screen. "Could this wait, Buntec?" he said. "I have company."

"No, it can't. You gotta come sweet-talk the captain in his native croak," Buntec said. "You remember Tinling Alfvaen? She's here—"

Swift-Kalat came instantly to his feet. Unable to restrain himself, he clapped his hands sharply above his head, bracelets clashing triumph. He strode to join van Zoveel.

Buntec acknowledged him with a wave. "She's here with a Hellspark," she said, repeating the words that had been lost to swift-Kalat's joy. Then she went on, her indignation rising in proportion to their enthusiasm, "Old Rattlebrain tried to keep 'em from landing. Now

64

he wants 'em off planet just as soon as they've delivered their mail. But we need 'em—we need *something* after the trouble we've been through!—and native croak always makes a difference, Ruurd. You know that!"

Van Zoveel began a polite refusal, but swift-Kalat said, "We'll come." He turned to van Zoveel and said, in Jenji, "Would you accept the assistance of a Hellspark polyglot?"

"Yes, of course! —Of course, we'll come!"

There was no need to translate for Buntec. The screen was already dark.

Hellsparks made Rav Kejesli uncomfortable.

As a young man on Sheveschke, Kejesli had haunted the streets at festival time looking for the traders to the thousand worlds. He'd found them no different from anyone else he knew. Oh, they dressed differently, that was certainly true, but they spoke Sheveschkem, they acted like Sheveschkemen. They were a disappointment.

It had taken Kejesli fifty years to make his first jump away from Sheveschke—in search of real differences—and there were the Hellsparks again. Only this time, they were not like Sheveschkemen; they were like Jannisetti, Apsanti, Bluesippans, or like the Yns, the Zoveelians, the Maldeneantine. They were more alien than he could have imagined—or could accept.

He shuddered. What would this one be like, surrounded by a survey team composed of such variety?

Bad enough dealing with so many aliens. He accepted that as part of the job: the Comity insisted that as many cultures as possible be represented on a survey team—to widen the scope of its knowledge and to broaden the range of its available working data. Besides, a planet Sheveschkemen loathed—this one, for example—might well be attractive to natives of some other world.

But to throw a Hellspark in on top of it all? How would she choose which culture to be?

Perhaps this Tocohl Susumo would simply be *Hellspark,* whatever that might be. Kejesli was not sure he wanted to know.

In any event, he was not about to allow her to interfere with his career. MGE would not approve of an outsider meddling in one of its surveys.

He poured himself a second cup of winter-flame from the warming pot, then hesitated. For a moment, he thought to join one of the conversations scattered about the common room but he had already overheard one such and its topic was Tinling Alfvaen. That was not one he had a desire to discuss. He returned to his seat in the far corner of the room.

A tooth-jarring clap of thunder signaled that the storm had broken in earnest. His hand jumped, winter-flame slopped red and gold across the tabletop. Involuntarily following the sound, he glanced at the ceiling. A wave of vertigo made the base of his neck prickle. Forcing his glance down, he wiped away the sudden sweat—then used the same cloth to mop the spilled winter-flame, trying to concentrate on the action alone. Buntec and Alfvaen and this Hellspark had not yet come. The thought that they too might meet the same fate as Oloitokitok …

The more he tried to tell himself that other survey captains had lost team members, the more he felt responsible for Oloitokitok's death. This was his third survey, and the first time he had lost a surveyor … unless one counted the twelve that had contracted Cana's disease. No, he wouldn't count them—they lived and Oloitokitok was dead.

A shout of laughter jarred Kejesli from his thoughts. He looked up in time to see Buntec, Alfvaen, and Tocohl Susumo burst through the door, spattering water about them. The membrane slapped wetly behind them, and the Hellspark laughed again. Her evident joy in Flashfever's weather made him suddenly angry.

After greeting the startled Vielvoye cheerfully, she placed an arachne on the ground beside her, dried her spectacles and replaced them, and reached up to twist water from her hair. The arachne unfolded a set of improbable stilt-like legs and immediately began to explore, but Kejesli could not take his attention from the Hellspark. Their brief conversation by screen had not prepared him for the intensity of her presence.

She strode to the center of the room, her silver cloak trailing rivulets of water. There she stopped. In a single turn that focused the attention of every surveyor present on her, she seemed to him to take in everything, and to pronounce judgment. He waited, terrified of the verdict.

Om im Chadeayne, the team's geologist, was suddenly on his feet. "Hellspark!" he said. "Hellspark, what news?" He crossed to her in a few quick strides and stood before her, his hands on his hips, his head cocked expectantly upward. Om im was tall for a Bluesippan, but he came only to this woman's elbow.

Tocohl Susumo held out a palm. "News for news," she said.

"Hah!" said Om im, touching a finger to his brow. "Yes, payment there will be. Always payment for a Hellspark. But first, a cup of winter-flame." He snapped his fingers at Vielvoye, who was nearest the warming pot, and Vielvoye scurried to bring a fresh cup.

The Hellspark looked at the cup, and then at Om im, warily. "— And the payment?" she said. Om im clapped his hands, drew them expressively down to indicate the space she occupied. "Your presence, Ish shan, is more than sufficient pay for a cup of winter-flame."

The woman bowed low, sweeping the ground with the edge of her cloak. "Tocohl Susumo is my name," she said.

Om im returned the bow with equal extravagance. "Om im Chadeayne of Bluesip," he said, taking Kejesli by complete surprise. He had thought them old friends from Om im's initial reaction.

The crowd continued to converge on her, as excited as children with a new toy. Everyone wanted a look. Not everyone, he corrected— Buntec was talking earnestly into a comunit, and she was probably passing the word, something she did well. Now only he and John the Smith had not joined the crowd.

John the Smith, Kejesli recalled, was from one of the Navel Worlds, close to the main centers of civilization. Those worlds no longer needed the independent traders, not the way the people of the Extremities did. Obviously, John considered himself too sophisticated to court Hellsparks. Kejesli was mildly annoyed at the thought.

Another burst of thunder combined with nearby movement caught Kejesli's eye, and he turned to find the arachne poised beside him like a hunting farrun that had found its quarry. He stared back at it, surprised that it did not leave when its inspection was completed. A moment later the Hellspark stood before him, and the arachne was once again on its way.

"With your permission, Captain?" She gestured at the chair facing him. Her gray cloak, still glinting silver droplets, cascaded softly about her as she sat. She pushed back a tangle of red hair made darker by Flashfever's downpour.

The tangle caught momentarily. Only when she had tugged it free did he see the cause of the snag: a pin of high-change was thrust through her cloak!

His first thought was that she must be mad—only the desperate would choose to take that risk—but for all his sudden stare he could find nothing desperate in those gold eyes, and nothing mad either. Instead he found something disconcertingly familiar. He had seen those gold eyes somewhere—

He found himself fingering the pin of remembrance in his vest lapel. He had worn it not for Veschke but for remembrance of Oloitokitok.

The Hellspark's gold eyes followed his fingers. He knew she could tell from the pin's design that it was four years old, that being the last time he had attended the Festival of Ste. Veschke. She smiled, indicating the pin. She was Sheveschkem at that moment. "Don't worry," she said, "I've tracked in enough of Veschke's blessing from this year's festival to cover us both." Thrusting out a foot to show him that it was covered with red mud, she went on, "I assure you only half of that is local."

Surprised to find that it did reassure him, he looked at her face again—and realized why she had seemed so familiar. He had seen those gold eyes a thousand times in his youth, smiling triumphantly from an icon that depicted Veschke's burning ...

He suddenly wished for John the Smith's sophistication—or his ignorance.

Where else but on a survey where his ship had not been blessed, where else but on a world *he* had given the ill-omened name of Flashfever, could all these things coincide? The death of Oloitokitok, Alfvaen (deny it as he would, he was responsible for the twelve of Inumaru as well), and this woman with the pin of high-change. Veschke was renowned for her sense of humor.

He fought the imagery: all he had to do was send a report to MGE and he could leave this world. He made a conscious effort and his hand dropped from the pin of remembrance.

Tocohl Susumo smiled at him again. She raised her cup, made Veschke's sign with her left hand, and said, "To Veschke!"

"To Veschke!" he repeated, without intending to, and drank with her.

By the time Tocohl rejoined Alfvaen, the crowd had doubled in size; Buntec beamed at this result of her handiwork. Amid a cheerful pandemonium of greetings in a dozen different tongues, Tocohl spoke quietly to Alfvaen in Siveyn, "We have a local day's grace. Speak to your friends—perhaps they'll put some pressure on Captain Kejesli for us." Alfvaen set to the task, drawing aside first one member of the survey team and then another.

Om im poured Tocohl another cup of the scarlet and gold drink, then, as if he were the aide of a prince, he presented the surveyors to her one by one.

(Maggy, keep a file of faces and names.)

(I always do,) Maggy responded as Tocohl greeted each surveyor in his or her native tongue with due respect to ritual. To Dyxte ti-Amax, she bowed; to Vielvoye ha-Somol, she respectfully tipped a nonexistent hat; both were Tobians but *ha* and *ti* spoke different languages. Hitoshi Dan, she greeted with a soft version of a whistle that had originally developed to be heard for several miles. And to Timosie Megeve, the Maldeneantine, she raised her left hand, crossing it with her right. Before he could reply, Alfvaen suddenly reappeared at Tocohl's side.

Pointing to the doorway, Alfvaen said anxiously, "There's swift-Kalat."

Tocohl laid a reassuring hand on her shoulder. In Siveyn, to avoid offending Buntec, Tocohl said, "Toes. Don't move: let him come to you. And stop worrying—he'll appreciate your attempt even if your execution isn't perfect." Unobtrusively, she took the added measure of placing a set of her own toes where Alfvaen would stamp them if she backed away from swift-Kalat. It was an old Hellspark technique for helping a child remember her proxemics.

"Swift-Kalat," Om im announced, smiling up at Alfvaen, "I can hear him chiming this way." His smile faded before her obvious anxiety. After a second's consideration of the problem, he reached for Alfvaen's elbow, with the clear intent of escorting her, as shy as she might be, to swift-Kalat's side. Tocohl, blocking his hand with her own, said softly, "No." He gave her a curious look but drew back his hand and patiently folded his arms to wait with them.

Of the two approaching men, Tocohl thought, the smaller would be swift-Kalat: his skin was a rich glowing red, almost the color of Dusty Sunday glass; bracelets gleamed the entire length of his forearm, jangling cheerfully. Tocohl had never seen a Jenji with quite so many. (Up to his elbows in silver,) she said.

(What?)

(Jenji expression for very, very smart,) she explained. (Now I see why.)

The other man, dressed in a tunic flamboyant enough to coin a Jannisetti phrase, was unmistakably Zoveelian.

The crowd parted just enough to let the newcomers through. Quietly, in GalLing', swift-Kalat said, "Alfvaen, I'm so glad you've come. I'm so glad you're safe." Then he strengthened his words with Jenjin emphasis, snapping his forearm down so sharply that his bracelets clashed and rang as he moved closer.

Alfvaen had learned her lessons well: as he passed the point Alfvaen's culture considered the proper distance for general talk and closed into the comfortable position for his own, Alfvaen tensed slightly but did not step back. Right down to her toes, she greeted him in perfect Jenji. "I am so glad to see *you*," she said, snapping her bare arm down for emphasis of her own.

There was no chime of bracelets, but swift-Kalat more than amply compensated for the lack. His sharp intake of breath told both Alfvaen and Tocohl that Alfvaen's attempt was a complete success. Swift-Kalat's eyes and smile widened in delight.

Alfvaen smiled back shyly and, with this encouragement, went on to make proper introductions. She assumed, Tocohl saw, that Ruurd van Zoveel spoke Jenji as well as she. The polyglot *spoke* excellent Jenji, but that was all; he was clearly ignorant of both proxemics and kinesics. Tocohl automatically switched to Zoveelian to reply to his greeting and then returned to GalLing' out of courtesy to Om im.

"We have a day," she said.

Swift-Kalat looked at Alfvaen in distress, and van Zoveel exclaimed, "A day! What can you do in a day?"

Tocohl smiled. "Change Captain Kejesli's mind," she said.

"It can be done, Ish shan." Om im craned toward the door and said in his own tongue, "If Buntec was willing to call Edge-of-Dark, her feelings run high on the subject."

Tocohl followed his look to the latest arrival and raised an eyebrow in surprise. No worlds' motley for this woman! Her 2nd skin was an unavoidable exception and that was transparent to minimize its intrusion. Everything else about her was pure Vyrnwyn high-born, from the feathered crown interwoven in her black hair to the tips of her fingers and toes, polished dark green to match her victoria ribbon.

That made sense of Buntec's threat to tip darts and hunt Vyrnwy. Buntec might have been able to deal with bare feet—but the outright perversion of polished toenails would have tried the most cosmopolitan Jannisetti.

Tocohl said, "Now that's what I call getting off on the wrong foot."

The joke stood in Bluesippan and Om im laughed appreciatively. Then he said, "We were chamfered by a moron. He gave us each a stack of hard-copy and told us to read it. With some people, that's not sufficient."

He glanced again toward the door, "We've tried to talk to Edge-of-Dark, but ..." He threw up his hands and, still in his own tongue, added, "I tell you, Ish shan, with the exception of the old-timers, this team gets on together about as well as flot and eggri."

Tocohl grinned: in Bluesippan mythology, the battle between flot and eggri was responsible for the second destruction of the world. "How long has it been since she's visited home?"

"A good ten years," he answered. "Why?"

(Maggy?) Tocohl said privately, raising a finger to hold off Om im's question. (Look through your records and pull out some stills of Madly of Ringsilver—pick only those where the background is blurred— and hold them until I ask for them.)

By the time she had finished speaking to Maggy, Edge-of-Dark had joined their company, but Om im's look told Tocohl quite clearly that his question was not forgotten, simply postponed.

With much solemnity and ceremony, Om im presented her. Tocohl took the hand Edge-of-Dark extended. She kissed it formally, said, "I am indebted to Om im Chadeayne for his kindness in making you known to me."

"I too am indebted to Om im Chadeayne," Edge-of-Dark responded. In GalLing', she went on, "It is a pleasure to be in discriminating company once again. Like most of your people, your dress is decidedly eccentric"—she eyed Tocohl's moss cloak with jaundice— "but your manners are unfailingly impeccable."

Tocohl laid a hand on her breast and inclined her head. GalLing' suited her just fine for this minor bit of business. "I imagine this must be a great trial for you," she said. "I see you have not been back to Vyrnwy for, oh, five years at least."

"Almost ten years, now. —How did you know?"

"Come now! Styles do change." Tocohl laughed, "If you think my dress eccentric, you should see what high-born Vyrnwy wear these days!" Tocohl gestured at Edge-of-Dark's clothing and said, "Not that I suppose it matters much—this is perfectly suitable for surveying."

Edge-of-Dark flushed as deep a red as swift-Kalat. "Tell me," she said, "describe it to me."

"I'm not much at description. I could show you some pictures, if you'd like."

"I would," said Edge-of-Dark eagerly and Tocohl finished, "To-morrow, then … if Captain Kejesli grants us the time. (Maggy, we're going. Bring the arachne.) Today I am here on business and I must deliver my messages."

Still flushing, Edge-of-Dark offered her hand again, this time to take hasty but formal leave of Tocohl. Sparing only the briefest of embarrassed glances for the others, she hurried to the door and out into the thinning veil of rain.

"Little bugger's really rude today, even by her standards," Buntec said. "Wonder what bit her ass?"

Om im stared thoughtfully, first after Edge-of-Dark, then at Tocohl. Touching a finger to his brow, he gave Tocohl a delighted smile. "Ish shan always was an ass-biter," he said in his own tongue. "Unless I miss my guess, Edge-of-Dark will not be seen until she is once again in fashion—and the fashion will include shoes."

"Boots," corrected Tocohl and grinned impishly in response, pleased that she could accomplish that much at least.

Om im made a deep bow. "You shall have fair payment, Ish shan, *that* I promise you!"

Maggy's arachne pricked its way through the crowd just as Tocohl bent to return the bow. Mistaking her intent, the arachne leapt into the crook of her arm, to settle itself there like a Gaian cat. Tocohl laughed once as she straightened but, again face-to-face with swift-Kalat, she said soberly, "Now, swift-Kalat, you and I will have a word or two."

Swift-Kalat found it hard to withdraw his attention from the behavior of the arachne; the ethologist in him was fascinated. No adult could have mistaken Tocohl's bow for an invitation—its controller was evidently a child.

But Tocohl was correct, the two of them had business, and the glance the Hellspark gave van Zoveel made it clear that simply speaking in Jenji would not be sufficient privacy.

"Of course," he said. Reluctantly, he released Alfvaen's hand, and gestured Tocohl to follow him. Privacy was difficult to arrange on Lassti, or perhaps that was only his perception, after three years with the same forty people in the same small compound. He did not even think of his cabin as private in that sense, it was too familiar. Too many of those people had been within its door. So he drew aside the membrane and looked out. It was still raining, but the storm had passed, the danger from lightning with it.

He led her out into the rain, his boots squelching in the mud at every step, taking her only a few feet around the side of the common room building. Lightning still played above the stand of lightning rods beyond camp; his ears rang with it. He tapped the wall behind him. "If we speak quietly," he said, "we are alone. All of the buildings were heavily soundproofed the second week of our stay."

Tocohl twisted her head, agreeing to the place. Swift-Kalat breathed a sigh of relief; with the one gesture, she had somehow become someone he could talk easily to.

"We will discuss your fee," he said. That was another area where he lacked expertise, never having dealt financially with a Hellspark.

She lifted a finger no. "Alfvaen and I have done so," she said. "The fee we agreed upon is 2,000 G, contingent of course on my being permitted to stay."

That was singularly low for an open-ended task the like of this, of that much swift-Kalat was sure.

"It was clever of you to send a Siveyn," she went on before he could protest, "whether the cleverness was intentional or not. It's impossible to dicker with someone who takes one's first price as fixed. I don't rob babies." She snapped her wrist with such authority that he almost heard the weight of her status on this subject.

"It was not intentional," he said.

"*Never* tell a trader that!" She countered with a smile—and again snapped her wrist to give ring to the command. "In fact, the next time you call someone a liar"—he jerked at the unexpectedness of the obscenity—"put him to work: let *him* deal with the traders."

She phrased it so adroitly that he could object to neither the words nor the suggestion. And in that moment he would have risked his status on the statement that Alfvaen had found him the one person who could tell him without fail whether or not the sprookjes had a language. He smiled. "I accept your fee and your contingency. And I shall consider your suggestion."

"I see I pass," she said, smiling back. "To business then: when you sent your message to Alfvaen requesting the services of a Hellspark glossi, did you tell anyone of your intention?"

That seemed an irrelevancy but, from her manner, it was not. "Yes, I told Oloitokitok. He was concerned about the sprookjes"—she exposed a bare arm to indicate her unfamiliarity with the term—"that is the name van Zoveel gave the disputed species. He was concerned about the sprookjes, as I was, so it was natural to mention what steps I had taken."

"When you sent your message, were others sent at the same time? If so, do you know by whom they were sent?"

"Others were sent, yes; by whom, I do not know. Investing in an automated message capsule was unnecessary, for I made the decision at the time of the last supply ship. It would be little risk to assume that everyone sent messages at that time."

She raised a finger. Thoughtfully, she said, "No confirmation, then."

The words disappointed him. He had hoped for an explanation of the queries. But if she was not ready to speak about the subject, there was little he could do, except ask again in GalLing'. After van Zoveel's misspeaking, he was not about to risk that.

"Are there any Inheritors of God among the survey team?"

"I do not know."

"How did Oloitokitok die?"

Again, he said, "I do not know. It was reported to me that *layli-layli calulan* believes he was electrocuted by a live-wire or a blitzen." He used the GalLing' terms for both; they conveyed some sense of the menace of the creatures.

"Do you accept this?"

He realized, to his own surprise, that he had told her the fact had been reported to him, not that it was generally accepted, as indeed it was among the remainder of the survey team. She waited quietly while he reconsidered his own thoughts. At last he said, "I think it unlikely: neither of the creatures has ever ventured into that particular habitat of the flashwood, in my experience. Their prey and their modes of behavior argue against it."

"What then killed Oloitokitok?"

"The third possibility is lightning. It is as unlikely as the first two."

"What special knowledge did Oloitokitok possess? What was his area of expertise? Could he have known something about the sprookjes that no one else knew? I am asking for conjecture, only: no conclusions on your part are necessary."

"He was on record primary engineer, secondary physicist, tertiary botanist. Shortly before he disappeared, he was excited, it seemed, although I am no authority on Yn. He told me at that time that I need not worry about the sprookjes. I inquired, but he would speak no further."

Tocohl Susumo stared at him thoughtfully for a few long moments. At last she said, "Nor may I, as yet." She turned, ready to head back to the others.

"Wait," he said. "Can you judge the sprookjes' sapience?"

"I am only one. I will do my best, given the circumstances."

His query was ambiguous, he realized. She had taken it to mean in her capacity as byworld judge, and she had graciously reminded him that a judgment of sapience required at least four such without calling his status to question. It left no doubt in his mind as to hers; were she Jenji she would ring as loudly as he.

She wiped streaming rain from her face. "Now, let us see what we can do in the small time allotted to us."

Swift-Kalat raised a finger in agreement, although it meant returning to the presence of van Zoveel. He had the sudden thought that he was perhaps ascribing sapience to the sprookjes largely because he was more comfortable with them than he was with the survey polyglot. Tocohl Susumo could make all the difference. At least, he might learn to his own satisfaction the actual state of the matter.

CHAPTER 5

Tocohl had given considerable thought to the matter while they rejoined the others. That a Jenji of *swift-* status had made the assumption that she was a byworld judge surprised her no end. It had taken considerable verbal maneuvering on her part to avoid calling his reliability into question without an outright lie of her own. Now the conversation could in retrospect be recalled with no disgrace to either speaker. She only hoped she could handle the sprookjes as well.

Swift-Kalat had offered his cabin for their further discussions. Typical of survey living, it was still a cut above standing out in the rain. Small, stamped from a single mold, it had been carefully personalized. While swift-Kalat searched for an additional chair and found a pillow for van Zoveel, Tocohl set Maggy's arachne in the middle of the floor. Maggy promptly unfolded it and began a careful inspection of the surroundings. Tocohl did the same, with special attention to the holograms (they were originals, and very fine) and the tyril, a small flute-like instrument of red porcelain.

"Alfvaen," said swift-Kalat, "I worried that something had happened to you when you were so long in coming."

Alfvaen began, "You had cause—"

But before she could finish, Tocohl interrupted. "Your pardon, swift-Kalat, Alfvaen. We have little time, and a great deal to discuss." Tocohl had no intention of letting Alfvaen bring up the matter of the Inheritors of God until she knew more about the members of the survey team. It was also something she was likely to misspeak about in swift-Kalat's estimation.

"Yes," Swift-Kalat said. "Please sit." The two women followed the invitation, but van Zoveel made as if to decline.

"Sit," said Tocohl, firmly. She had not failed to note swift-Kalat's uneasiness with van Zoveel or its cause. "It's one of my cultural taboos," she added with a smile.

The polyglot stared at her. "I thought the Hellsparks didn't have any cultural taboos."

"Anyone who says she has no taboos is a fool. —Please," she indicated the pillow to her right and van Zoveel obliged. Swift-Kalat looked relieved.

"Now," she went on, "tell me about your creatures; or, better still, show me one."

"I can't," said swift-Kalat.

Van Zoveel said, "The sprookjes leave the camp during the thunderstorms. They won't be back until the rain lets up, if *then*." The big man's brow furrowed. "I am unable to speak to them," he said. His hand slapped his thigh. "I'm not stupid: I've puzzled out three nonhuman languages during my career with MGE—and yet I feel stupid now! I've tried every tongue I know, but all the creatures do is parrot!" He thrust two fingers in swift-Kalat's direction. "Don't ask me about the sprookjes, ask swift-Kalat!"

Such had been Tocohl's intention in the first place, and without hesitation she turned to him. He said, "I'll show you." A moment later, he handed her a large orange fruit and a knife.

"That's a native plant," he said, "and it's an artifact."

"A biological artifact?"

"You'll see. Cut it open."

Tocohl sliced the fruit in half, then in quarters, then in eighths— it was pulp all the way through. No seeds. If it had no seeds, how did it propagate? "Runners?" she asked; but, as she expected, swift-Kalat said, "It has none."

Tocohl said, "Then why doesn't MGE accept this as initial proof that something on the planet, not necessarily the sprookjes, is capable of creating an artifact?"

"I was not hired as a botanist."

"That makes you no less knowledgeable," Tocohl said.

"To Kejesli, it does," said Alfvaen. "When I worked with him before, he considered a person's primary specialty his only specialty."

"Ah, and the team botanist?" asked Tocohl.

"He considers Flashfever wildlife so unusual that anything is within the realm of possibility—that we simply haven't found this plant's particular mechanism yet."

Tocohl gazed down at the slices of fruit spread on the surface of the table. "But you say artifact."

Emphasizing his words with a clash of bracelets, swift-Kalat said, "I say artifact."

"They're too curious not to be sapient," said van Zoveel. "They are interested in everything."

"So's Maggy," said Alfvaen abruptly. She pointed: the arachne was opening cupboards.

"Cut that out, Maggy," said Tocohl. "That's impolite. You should always ask permission before you open a closed door." (—At least, if you're doing it in public,) she added, *sotto voce*.

Tocohl gestured. "Come over here. —I apologize, swift-Kalat. When you told us your house was ours, Maggy interpreted it in Hellspark. That's the language she knows best."

(You lie!) said Maggy.

(Polite, social,) Tocohl told her, (but take care not to call anyone a liar aloud in the presence of a Jenji. Now, come apologize.)

The arachne made a skittering dash for the spot Tocohl had indicated. "I'm sorry," said Maggy, using the vocoder in the fat body.

"Don't apologize to me, apologize to swift-Kalat. You know enough Jenji for that."

The arachne dipped slightly before swift-Kalat and said, "I apologize if I have given offense. I intended none." Tocohl recognized the phrasing as her own, pitched to match Maggy's voice.

Alfvaen delighted at their surprise. "Magic to a Hershlaing," she said to Tocohl. Tocohl smiled.

(Hershlaing?) Maggy asked privately. Tocohl said, (Hershlain is a mythical world so far off the beaten orbit that the Hershlaing consider any advanced science—even striking a match to light a fire—to be magic. Introduce yourself, Maggy, and give them an idea what state-of-the-art is.)

Before Maggy could begin, a tall creature pulled the door membrane aside and stepped, its feathers silvered with rainwater, into the cabin. It was a beautiful thing. Tocohl stared at it in wonder, and it stared back at her.

At last, she let go her breath. "Sprookjes—fairy tale creatures," she said. "Now I understand their name."

Maggy's arachne walked slowly around the sprookje for a better look. The sprookje turned to follow the movement; it showed no hesitation in turning its back to the humans.

Tocohl rose, only the soft rustle of the moss cloak betraying her movement. Van Zoveel caught her arm. "They bite," he said, quietly.

"Everyone on the team has been bitten once."

"Have there been any ill effects?"

"No, but I didn't want you to be startled."

Maggy had completed her circle and the sprookje was brought face-to-face with Tocohl. The two of them stared at each other. The creature's brown and gold feathers gleamed and whispered as it took a step closer.

Tocohl held her ground. When the sprookje stopped, she slowly and deliberately rolled up her cuff and lifted her arm to bring her hand a scant two centimeters from the beaklike mouth.

The sprookje accepted the invitation and bit, its head flashing forward with startling suddenness. Tocohl flinched but made no outcry—she was more surprised than hurt, for she hadn't been snapped at by the potentially nasty beak. It was exactly like being stabbed with a pin.

She brought her hand slowly back to inspect the wound—yes, a mere pinprick.

"Buntec calls it their *sampling tooth*," van Zoveel volunteered. The sprookje now walked around Tocohl in the manner of the arachne's inspection.

Alfvaen gave a sharp cry of warning. Tocohl turned swiftly to find the sprookje drawing back. "I thought it meant to bite your shoulder," Alfvaen explained. "I'm sorry I startled you."

(Maggy? What happened?) asked Tocohl; and Maggy replied, (It bit your cloak; from the trajectory, that was all it intended to sample.)

"Alfvaen," Tocohl said aloud, "are you willing to try an experiment?"

"Yes, of course."

Tocohl unclasped her cloak and tossed it into the Siveyn's arms. "Put that on," she instructed, "then come out here and do exactly as I did."

Alfvaen followed her instructions to the letter, even to letting the sprookje complete the distance, as she had previously done with swift-Kalat. With the same deliberation Tocohl had used, she lifted her hand, and, as expected, the sprookje nipped. Tocohl watched the entire procedure as closely as she could. (Maggy? Did the sprookje's cheek-feathers puff out, or was it my imagination?)

(No imagination—want to see?)

(No, I want to confirm that they didn't when the sprookje nipped me.)

(Confirmed,) said Maggy.

The creature circled Alfvaen slowly. Tocohl kept her attention close, curious to see what it would do about the cloak. After a moment, it seemed to have completed its inspection of her. It had completely ignored the moss cloak.

Then the sprookje's beak flashed forward—Alfvaen yelped in surprise. Rubbing her wrist, where the sprookje had bitten her a second time, she said accusingly to van Zoveel, "You said everyone had been bitten once! I thought you meant only once!"

"He did!" said swift-Kalat. "You are the first to have been bitten more than once!" He was echoed word for word by the sprookje.

One could easily develop a stutter from speaking in the presence of one of these creatures, thought Tocohl; it was like listening to oneself on a two-second delay.

Tocohl was struck by another oddity: the puzzling fact that the sprookje echoed *only* swift-Kalat.

Swift-Kalat seemed to have learned to ignore it. He came toward Tocohl excitedly, "And the cloak! Why would it bite your cloak?"

The excitement was too much for the sprookje. Even as it repeated swift-Kalat's words, it backed hastily away, its cheek-feathers now unmistakably puffed.

"Quietly," said Tocohl. "—That's a moss cloak," she explained. "Your sprookje can obviously tell the difference between living and nonliving. It didn't bite the arachne, after all. And it lost interest in the moss cloak having bitten it once."

She glanced at the pinprick on her wrist. "I think 'sample tooth' is dead on. —As for Alfvaen, *Alfvaen tastes different than the rest of us!*"

"Of course," said Alfvaen, "I have Cana's disease!"

"Yes," said Tocohl. (Maggy,) she added privately, (tomorrow morning, if necessary, I will have a violent attack of an unidentifiable plague, probably from having been bitten by our fine feathered friend over there. If I have to get this planet quarantined to gain time, I will!)

Sunrise on Flashfever met the omnipresent rainclouds with a rare brilliance. From within swift-Kalat's cabin came the sweet, silvery sound of the tyril. Tocohl leaned back against the door frame to appreciate them both before returning her consideration to the compound.

Any creature's behavior is affected by its environment. Like most survey camps Tocohl had seen, this was utilitarian. It was standard operating procedure to sterilize an area of ground for base camp. Here, the result was thick red mud everywhere. Tocohl thought it odd that no walks had been built, either at ground level or higher. The uniform, nondescript cabins (a small town of them—privacy was a very real need when some forty people had to spend two to ten years together) stood partly raised from the mud on stubby stilts.

Only one of these had been personalized on the exterior. It was painted a lavish blue and decorated with Yn mystic symbols of white and gold. Two pennants hung near the door, drooping heavily with rainwater. That must have belonged to the dead man, Oloitokitok, she thought.

A sprookje splashed through muddy puddles to stop some distance away. Seemingly attracted by the sound of swift-Kalat's tyril, it cocked its head to listen, but made no attempt to mimic the spritely dance tune. After a while, it knelt, pressed its hands into the mud. She wondered what it might be doing.

The sprookje's presence reminded Tocohl that she was ill—ill with something unknown but not debilitating enough to require bed rest. With Maggy's assistance, she chose a handful of symptoms and set to work initiating them.

By the time she was done, the sprookje also had finished its task, if indeed it had been at one, and stood gracefully. It ran long fingers through the feathers on its knees and shook away some of the clinging mud. Tocohl blinked at it but, for a moment, she could not see clearly.

Still dazed from effort, she was dazzled by the flashwood that ringed the camp, pressing at every length of fence, as if offended by and yet drawn to the barren space within. Its glitter made the camp more stark by contrast.

As her vision cleared, she saw that the fence was barbed wire, not the electrified barrier favored by survey teams. When the dance tune came to an end, she peeled back the membrane and asked swift-Kalat, "Why barbed wire?"

Swift-Kalat laid his tyril aside and joined her in the doorway. His glittering bracelets and the sun raising iridescent highlights in his black braid shamed the compound as much as the flashwood.

"So much of Flashfever's wildlife uses electricity as an energy source that an electric fence only attracts trouble. Buntec suggested we try that sort. It works quite well."

"I see," said Tocohl.

She judged it time to act, and because swift-Kalat was Jenji and had the traditional reputation for truthfulness, she decided to let him draw his own conclusions. She raised her hand to her forehead and, looking puzzled, let the blood drain from her face as if she might faint.

"Your hand," he said, and caught her wrist to examine the pinprick she'd received from the sprookje the night before.

The area around the puncture was an angry red and slightly puffed—a matter of dilating the local capillaries. Once done, Tocohl could maintain it indefinitely without strain, despite the effort of concentration it required to initiate.

It had the desired effect. Swift-Kalat pressed gently but firmly at the edges of the swollen area; his fingers left whitened marks. Tocohl winced. "The doctor must see this," said swift-Kalat. Without releasing her hand, he drew her across the compound to the blue cabin. He struck a chime.

"You may enter," said a regal voice from within.

The survey team's doctor sat cross-legged in the center of the room, on a blue mat ornamented with designs of power. Her mouth was broad and rich with hidden smiles, the fine lines at the corners of her eyes could only have come from laughter. Her whole face was designed for joy—and yet she did not smile. Her dark eyes brimmed with anger, although it was not directed at Tocohl or swift-Kalat.

She was plump and deceptively well muscled beneath that plumpness. By swift-Kalat's standards she was, no doubt, overweight; but Tocohl, who was already thinking in Yn, took her on her own culture's terms and found her beautiful.

In her lap lay the rich glitter of a koli thread with its fantastical tangle of knots. Around her lay a chalice, three silver knives, and a strawlike pile of jievnal sticks: she was preparing to enter deep mourning. Tocohl was glad she had decided to act quickly; to interrupt mourning would be risky, even for her.

Tocohl raised both hands in greeting and, as the woman lifted her head and hands to reply in kind, all of Tocohl's hopes for a quarantine vanished. Two long scars slashed across her left cheek and on each index finger she bore a bluestone ring. The doctor was an Yn shaman.

"I am *layli-layli calulan*," she said, in a cool, quiet voice.

Tocohl inclined her head a fraction of an inch and responded, "I am *the tocohli susumo*." To give one's true name to an Yn was to give that Yn power over one. Accordingly the Hellsparks had, from the very beginning of their trade relationships with the Yn, convinced them that no Hellspark name was more than a title, the equivalent of the designations Yn women gave to others. She also took the liberty of ascribing to herself the sound of power, the tiny phoneme *i*, which gave her status, though nothing like that the doubling *i* gave *layli-layli calulan*.

"You lie," said the shaman, in GalLing'.

Swift-Kalat took in his breath with a hiss. His braceleted arm came up as if to ward off a blow, but Tocohl caught it and quieted him with the sharp negative tap of a finger.

To *layli-layli*, she said solemnly, "As do you."

(I don't understand,) said the voice in Tocohl's ear. (Check a tourist guide to Y and I'll fill you in later, Maggy.)

Tocohl turned to swift-Kalat. His forehead was beaded with sweat. "It is a ritual greeting," she said. "I apologize for the mistranslation."

Swift-Kalat jerked his head from one to the other. "In my culture," he said, "it is an insult of the highest order."

"I am aware of that. I said, 'mistranslation,'" Tocohl repeated. "The Yn word means both 'lie' and 'dream'—it only becomes a problem when you try to pick an equivalent in GalLing'. There is no equivalent in GalLing', but 'dream' is much closer to its emotional meaning."

She could see him make a visible effort to replace his emotional reaction with an intellectual one. Then he pointed to Tocohl's swollen hand. "She was bitten by a sprookje," he began.

Tocohl interrupted. "Your pardon, swift-Kalat, but I must speak to *layli-layli calulan* alone."

Gratefully, swift-Kalat accepted the dismissal.

When he was gone, *layli-layli calulan* said, "You are not alone with me."

Tocohl was startled. Either *layli-layli calulan* was sharp-eyed enough to have seen the muscle twitch that signaled her subvocal exchange with Maggy, or she was relying on her shaman's espabilities.

"No," admitted Tocohl. She tapped the implant. "My partner, the *maggy-maggy lynn* listens as well."

Because she now spoke Yn, Tocohl used the *my* that signaled personal relationship rather than property, which in Yn culture included males as well. That was how she thought of Maggy, she realized, as both her partner and female. She had also translated *lord* into the Yn doubling, quite unintentionally giving her equal status with *layli-layli* herself. She made a mental note not to introduce Maggy as a demonstration of state-of-the-art after all.

Instead, she said, "I would introduce you properly, but *maggy-maggy* has no facilities for speech except through me. If you wish to greet her, please do. She will acknowledge the introduction through the vocoder in her arachne later."

Layli-layli calulan made Yn formal greeting to Maggy.

When she was finished, Tocohl crossed her ankles and sat before the Yn shaman. She held out the "injured" hand. Her ruse was still worth the try, but it was not worth upsetting swift-Kalat if she was found out. "I was bitten by a sprookje last night. This morning ... well, it's infected, I think, and swift-Kalat tells me that's never happened before."

The shaman lit a jievnal stick and its piney odor filled the small room. She thrust the slender rod into her hair, took Tocohl's hand gently in her own. For a moment, her dark eyes looked puzzled, then she said, "You did this to yourself? To my knowledge, there is no one in the survey team who could have done this for you."

"Could have done what?" said Tocohl with puzzled innocence.

Layli-layli calulan's dark eyes lit suddenly with amusement, and Tocohl dropped her gaze before that knowing scrutiny. "All right," she said, "I was trained in the Methven rituals."

"You are an adept," said *layli-layli calulan*.

"Not adept enough."

Layli-layli released Tocohl's hand and twisted the bluestone ring from her left finger. The rings, by Yn tradition, prevented the accidental release of power. In reality, Tocohl suspected that the rings only worked because the Yns believed they worked — many espabilities needed a channel or focus or, in this case, a control.

The shaman held out her right hand and Tocohl laid her swollen wrist across the waiting palm. The tip of *layli-layli*'s bare finger touched her injury with feathery delicacy.

Just for a moment, for the pure devilment, Tocohl concentrated on maintaining the dilation of the capillaries. Dark eyes met the Hellspark gold, and a trace of smile touched the corners of *layli-layli calulan*'s broad mouth. Then the heat in Tocohl's wrist cooled, the swelling began to subside.

Activated by *layli-layli*'s espability, Tocohl's cells found their normal pattern and set about to regain it. Against the shaman's gift, Tocohl had no chance of maintaining the artificial illness. The red faded to its original shade. Soon only the pinprick remained, and that too was healing rapidly.

Layli-layli calulan replaced her ring and said, "You too believe swift-Kalat. So did Oloitokitok." She took up the koli thread from her lap, and as she spoke, her fingers added knot after intricate knot to its tangled glitter.

"Long before you dreamed your first dream," *layli-layli calulan* began, in the manner of a mother telling a tale to a child, "there was a man named Oloitokitok who was not like other men. He thought and dreamed like a woman. He dreamed a dream so strong that it took him to a world no woman's eye had ever seen..."

Listening to the Tale of Oloitokitok, Tocohl heard much that someone unfamiliar with Yn culture would have missed. The Yn were so gynocentric that only in the last hundred years had their men been taught to read. For Oloitokitok to have achieved as much as he had, he must have been very special indeed.

He had agreed with swift-Kalat's assessment of the evidence, and he had chosen to gather evidence of the sprookjes' sapience on his own. Although *layli-layli calulan* confirmed swift-Kalat's observations about Oloitokitok's manner on the day of his disappearance, Oloitokitok had told no one, not even *layli-layli,* what he planned to do or where he planned to go.

Tocohl wasn't surprised. To the members of the survey team, Oloitokitok may not have been a token male but, in his own mind, he may have thought himself so. Given partial evidence in favor of the sprookjes' sapience and a belief that no one would credit his opinion, he had quite likely chosen to gather such overwhelming evidence as to present a *fait accompli* that would force belief.

Now what evidence he might have had was lost with him.

As if echoing Tocohl's thoughts, *layli-layli calulan* said, her voice harsh, hurt, "The dream was lost with Oloitokitok." With that, she grasped the free ends of the koli thread and gave a slow, steady pull. One by one, the glittering knots unraveled, until she held only straight bare line shining coldly between her outstretched hands. The tale was ended.

Tocohl gave a sharp upward jerk of her chin. "No," she said, "I keep the dream." She gestured at the string. "It's true a single koli thread leaves no knots, but, alive, Oloitokitok would have knotted his thread with the beings of this world. Despite his death, it is still possible if you wish it."

Layli-layli looked hesitant. Tocohl wondered how important Oloitokitok had been to her. Looking down, she once again saw the chalice, the knives, the jievnal sticks. This time she registered them properly. *Layli-layli calulan* was preparing to go into deep mourning—something only done for women, never for men.

When she looked up again, *layli-layli* placed her palms together, ring on ring, and said with quiet defiance, "He was my mate." She used the *my* for relationship.

Tocohl held out both her hands, the strongest symbol of understanding and agreement available to her in the Yn mode, and clasped *layli-layli calulan*'s wrists in her own supporting grip.

Swift-Kalat was only partially relieved that Tocohl Susumo had sent him away. He needed the time to put his thoughts in order. The last time he had heard someone call another a liar in GalLing', the ensuing fight had resulted in a death, so he was well aware of the potency of the word even in its unreliable GalLing' form. To hear it used as a greeting was more than he could handle. He found himself envying the Hellsparks their ability to deal with such rupturing of their social order. Having at last settled his thoughts on the matter, intellectually if not emotionally, he now wished he were back inside *layli-layli calulan*'s cabin, listening to the conversation between the two.

"Jaef! Jaef!"

Even though the sound was distorted by the shout from across the compound and a peal of far-off thunder, he knew it had to be Alfvaen. Of all the surveyors, she alone knew and had the right to use his softname. She raced toward him, heedless of the muddy water she splashed with every footfall.

Breathless, she drew up beside him—too far away, some small portion of his mind noted—and said in GalLing', "Jaef, Kejes-sli's-s readying an automated message capsule ... He's s-sending the report to MGE now!"

It was deductively true: beyond her swift-Kalat could see the other surveyors coming from their cabins to gather before Kejesli's quarters. The final report was a matter of ritual, requiring the presence of all those responsible. Except that Oloitokitok would not be present.

Still staring up at him anxiously, Alfvaen swayed suddenly. He shot out a hand to steady her, remembering as he did so that stress aggravated her condition. "Your medication, Alfvaen," he said. She focused with effort on his face, then her eyes widened in an exaggerated manner and she reached for her pouch. He waited only long enough to assure himself she could stand on her own, then he released her arm to ring the chime beside the door to *layli-layli calulan*'s cabin.

He did not wait for an answer. Instead, he thrust his head inside, to find *layli-layli calulan* and Tocohl Susumo with their hands clasped.

"Will you help?" Tocohl asked *layli-layli calulan*. Wanting to hear the answer as much as she, swift-Kalat held his tongue. *Layli-layli calulan* said, "By quarantining Lassti? That would give you time, not necessarily understanding."

She said no more. Swift-Kalat felt he must make the urgency of the query clear. "Alfvaen tells me that Captain Kejesli is preparing an automated message capsule for MGE *now*," he said.

Tocohl jerked her head back to stare at him. Releasing *layli-layli calulan*'s hands with a few murmured words in another language, Tocohl rose smoothly to her feet. *Layli-layli calulan* remained as she had been, her stare holding Tocohl in place.

She said, "Should I help creatures that were responsible for Oloitokitok's death?" Spoken as it was in GalLing', the question was directed at him as well, but he had no answer. The question itself was unreliable.

Again Tocohl dealt with the matter on a level he himself would not have been able to. She spoke one word only; the word was, "No."

Catching him by the elbow, she ushered him out, stopped momentarily in her tracks to scan the compound, said, "Ah: Kejesli's quarters?" When he confirmed that, she touched her fingers briefly to the ornate pin at her throat. "One more try," she said, pausing to give Alfvaen a reassuring smile, then she squared her shoulders and strode across the compound, her cloak swirling like heavy mist in the light rain.

Swift-Kalat put his arm around Alfvaen's shoulder, as much to comfort himself as to support her, and led her in the same direction. At the edge of the crowd, he heard Tocohl bark rapid-fire some dozen or so words, each with the sound of a different language to it. Heads turned in succession, and the crowd parted to let her through.

Without Tocohl's skill at linguistic manipulation, swift-Kalat and Alfvaen found themselves stayed at the edge of the crowd. "I must get her to teach me that," Alfvaen said, giggling despite her overall anxiety.

"Teach you what?"

"I only recognized the Sheveschkem 'Cheap tattoos!' but I'll bet all the others were the same—whatever a waiter says to negotiate a crowd with a tray of hot dishes."

He stared down at her, fondly at first, appreciating the joke as she had found it, then he raised his eyes to stare into the distance, deep in consideration.

Tocohl had found something in *layli-layli calulan*'s last phrase that she could answer, and that fact still concerned him. Could the question be answered in Jenji? Could it even be *asked* in Jenji?

He tried framing it carefully in his mind: *Should I help creatures that were responsible for Oloitokitok's death?* But *death* in GalLing' was ambiguous; it could mean "natural death" or "accidental death" or even "murder."

Murder, he thought. He patted Alfvaen's arm absently and released it, to pace away from the noise of the crowd to follow the thought. He himself had told Tocohl the causes given for Oloitokitok's death were unlikely. "What then killed Oloitokitok?" she had asked.

That was a question that indeed could be framed in Jenji... one to which he would very much like an answer.

CHAPTER 6

The ceiling in the captain's quarters had been lowered to conform to Sheveschkem spatial standards—no doubt to the extreme discomfort of most members of the survey team, thought Tocohl. Generations of sailing had left their mark on Kejesli even here, as a need to keep the ceiling within reach. Nothing better sustained balance below deck in stormy seas than a flattened palm against a ceiling. Under the circumstances, Tocohl had to suppress her own impulse to reach for the ceiling. "Captain," she repeated, "all I'm asking is a few months' grace."

Alone with Kejesli, she automatically followed his lead and "danced" Sheveschkem, despite the fact that he spoke GalLing' and she replied in kind. She spoke in GalLing' because Kejesli refused to speak Sheveschkem with her. She wished it weren't so; she might have been more convincing in Sheveschkem. She continued, "If you send your final report now ..."

Kejesli tightened his grip on his desk, as any Sheveschkem captain might grip the bolted furniture for support. "Hellspark, you can stay as long as you wish. Half the survey has made a point of requesting your continued presence." He was clearly not pleased about that. "If you find evidence—beyond swift-Kalat's sleight-of-tongue—that the sprookjes are sapient, you can always appeal to the Comity's courts."

Tocohl's hand swept to one side, a derisive gesture on Sheveschke. "It would take years in court—and by then irreparable damage may have been done to the sprookjes, to their world. Veschke's sparks, man, will you be responsible for genocide?" She shot the word at him, and he flinched.

Just for a moment, Tocohl thought she had struck home; both knew how Veschke would take such an act. —Then Kejesli stiffened and said, "I don't know they're sapient."

"That should be sufficient reason to allow us more time."

Kejesli's knuckles whitened. "I rely upon what my people decide; and, in this case, all their evidence points to nonsapience."

"*All?*"

89

"We hire people to do specific jobs in specific areas. They have done them." His beaded hair swung to the side, past stiffly set jaw.

No Sheveschkem sea captain could have said that: in an emergency, the cook lowers the mainsail. Tocohl frowned, and saw Kejesli suddenly for what he was. He was a man trying not to be Sheveschkem, without conscious knowledge of what being Sheveschkem actually entailed. He spoke GalLing' but danced Sheveschkem; he wore worlds' motley, but lowered his ceiling. Not comfortable with the cultures surrounding him, he was no longer comfortable with his own, so he substituted the rule book for culture. *If I can give him a way out by the rule book ...*

Under her scrutiny, Kejesli once more gripped the desk. "I would like to oblige you," he said, "one should always be obliging to Hellsparks ... but in this case I cannot. The thunderstorms have already left us behind schedule. Now MGE has pressed me for a quick decision."

He loosed his grip on the desk and rose. He did not reach for the ceiling; the storm was over as far as he was concerned. He had reached his decision. Tocohl knew she had lost the battle.

As he showed her to the door, it occurred to her that he had, at least, agreed to let her remain on Flashfever. Here, it might still be possible to follow Oloitokitok's lead, and present a *fait accompli*.

Perhaps because of her silence, perhaps because, for him, the emergency was over, Kejesli's manner softened. As he drew the membrane aside and stepped into the wan sunlight, he said, "Come, Hellspark—for you it is only a theft at Festival. For me, it is a good deal more."

She did not reply. If her oblique appeal to Veschke's good opinion had not worked, then the only way around him was by the rule book. Her quarantine ploy would have worked—could still work. A glance at her hand showed redness remaining; it would take her only minutes to reestablish her spurious infection, with *layli-layli calulan*'s assistance.

Tocohl plunged through the crowd that had gathered outside Kejesli's quarters in anticipation of the ritual that marked the end of their job. Alfvaen, swift-Kalat, and van Zoveel turned anxiously to her, but she brushed them aside absently. "I can stay," she said, "but the report goes."

The news brought a mixed reaction. Swift-Kalat turned abruptly and walked a short distance away, anger and disappointment stiffening his gait. Tocohl automatically caught Alfvaen's arm to prevent her from following him: an angry Jenji is, by definition, unreliable. He would not appreciate her company at the moment. Still without conscious thought, Tocohl drew Alfvaen along with her.

Watchful, the shaman stood quietly apart, a jievnal stick laced through her hair. Her eyes followed the sprookje that wandered among the humans. Only *layli-layli calulan* had the power to grant the sprookjes a stay of execution, Tocohl thought. Would she?

Thrusting Alfvaen forward—a talisman of serendipity to influence a shaman—Tocohl folded her arms across her chest and stared long and hard at *layli-layli calulan*, willing her to speak.

"Tocohl Susumo!" swift-Kalat's voice and instantaneous sprookje-echo rang with such command that all, Kejesli included, turned to him.

Caught by his tone, Tocohl responded formally. "Yes?"

Swift-Kalat's bracelets flashed as he leveled his arm at the sprookje. The sprookje, feathers ruffling, imitated his gesture with frightening accuracy. And, as swift-Kalat spoke, it echoed word for word: "I accuse the sprookjes of the deliberate *premeditated* murder of Oloitokitok. Will you agree to judge?"

At Tocohl's side, Alfvaen gave a short, sharp gasp. Tocohl caught her shoulder and gave her a look of silent command. Alfvaen held her tongue.

"Yes," said Tocohl, "I agree to judge."

Maggy pinged furiously for attention and, when Tocohl ignored her, said, (The penalty for impersonating—)

(I know, Maggy, now just shut up.)

"You can't," said Rav Kejesli. It came out like a plea. "The sprookjes would have to be sapient in order to commit murder."

"Yes," said Tocohl, "they would." She could not help but grin. "I will first be obliged to make a judgment on the sapience or *non*sapience of the sprookjes. Would you be kind enough, Captain Kejesli, to have your team put their files at my disposal?"

For a long breath, Kejesli said nothing; his face had the look of a man in great pain. Then, slowly and almost implausibly, he smiled.

"In that case, I will hold my report until you have made your judgment." His eyes shifted from her face to the pin of high-change in her cloak. "—In Veschke's honor!" he finished.

CHAPTER 7

Forty-two members of the survey team crowded the common room with excitement, jostling each other and speaking in whispers. You'd think, and Tocohl did, that surveying an uncharted planet would be enough excitement for anyone, but obviously it was not so. News of a judgment, coupled as it was with the accusation of murder, stirred even the oldest and most blasé of the team members.

Tocohl scanned the crowd for the reactions of those she had already met. Om im had been accorded a position in the front, in deference to his size, and he grinned at her and winked broadly, gesturing across the room to Edge-of-Dark. To her costume of the night before, the programmer had added a second victoria ribbon, this one pale green, which crossed her breast at right angles to the first, and tall laced softboots of Ringsilver fashion. Tocohl flashed a wink at Om im; her pictures of Madly had worked.

Captain Rav Kejesli made a grudging formal introduction and the room became silent but for the monotony of rain.

"By now," said Tocohl, "you've all heard that the sprookjes have been accused of murder; and most of you realize we've an unusual situation on our hands. In essence, in order to judge the guilt or innocence of the creatures, I must first know *to my own satisfaction* whether or not they are sapient." The whisper of noise became a surprised chatter of voices, and Tocohl raised a hand. "Wait and hear me out."

When the noise quieted once again, she continued, "I know that your primary specialists all seem to have reached the conclusion that the sprookjes are not sapient, but I would like to keep an open mind on the question. Some of the secondary specialists are not so convinced, and a secondary specialist is not mere backup. Survey teams were designed to have as many talents and specialties available as possible, and I believe that the original intent was to take advantage of the synergistic effects among the surveyors as well.

"So I'm asking for your cooperation in an experiment. Let us for the moment forget authority. If anyone has anything to say on the subject of sprookjes, I want to hear it. I don't care how wild it is, I don't care if it's totally out of your field of expertise—I want to hear it anyway. I'll even listen to anecdotes about the sprookjes." She flashed a grin at Om im. "Story for story," she finished, to add a bit of a bribe for their effort.

Once more, she scanned the group—surveyed the surveyors, she thought with a smile. By virtue of the novelty of the situation, she'd get her cooperation and then some. As for slighting the primary specialists—each primary specialist had a secondary or tertiary specialty; given the chance she offered, they'd be delighted to show off.

"One last thing," she said, "before I send you all off to dig out material for me. Has anyone here fallen on Pasic?"

There was a titter of amusement—obviously some had.

It was John the Smith who pushed forward to say, "Pasicans are the closest things I've ever met to the Hershlaing in the flesh. They're as nontechnological as they come, at least within the known human realm. They don't even have, oh—matches or flints!"

Within the known human realm, Tocohl observed with satisfaction, you're thinking already.

"True," she said aloud. "Now, a Pasican once told me the difference between himself and an orival—that's a small native animal. 'An orival does not know how to put branches on the fire when it is dying, therefore a Pasican is human and an orival is an animal.'"

It brought a chuckle of superiority from the crowd. Tocohl waited for it to pass, then she said, "I may not be human to a Pasican."

That got their full attention. Spreading her cloak for the added drama of the gesture, she went on, "My 2nd skin provides me with all the warmth I need. My spectacles can push for available light. A fire is of no particular use to me. Not knowing I must prove myself human in this one fashion, *I may let the fire go out!*"

"See here!" It was John the Smith again, and this time he was angry. "Are you saying that the sprookjes may be so advanced—"

Tocohl said, "No. I'm saying that they may be so *different* that we don't recognize one of their artifacts when we get our noses rubbed in it... I'm saying that even *Homo sapiens* within historical time have had difficulty in proving their humanity to other *Homo sapiens*. I'm asking that you all consider the circumstances in which you would be hard put to prove your sapience, especially if you were unaware that you were being tested."

#

Enlisting Buntec and a daisy-clipper, Tocohl and Alfvaen made a quick trip out to the *Margaret Lord Lynn*. Maggy, for once giving no warnings and predicting no doom, taped Tocohl's subvocalized message on the way and waited with open door when they arrived.

Buntec stowed their belongings in the daisy-clipper amid cheerful obscenities and colorful blasphemies. And Alfvaen said, in Siveyn, "You told me you weren't a judge."

Tocohl said quietly, "I lied to you."

"But why? We'd only just met; you had no reason to lie to me." The small hand flew lightly outward, dismayed.

"No offense intended," said Tocohl easily. "I like to keep in practice. In Veschke's honor."

Tinling Alfvaen frowned up at her, as if squinting into the sun. Tocohl could almost read the thoughts as they rippled through the Siveyn's mind: anger, then suspicion, and, finally, concern.

"All right," said Alfvaen. "You lied to me. No offense taken."

Alfvaen would keep her own counsel; but the concern in the Siveyn's green eyes did not fade.

Buntec bellowed from the hatch, "All stowed! Let's move— Flashfever looks about to do its act again!"

As they sped toward base camp, Alfvaen maintained a pensive silence as Buntec cajoled and cursed the daisy-clipper along its way.

Behind them, the *Margaret Lord Lynn* rose solemnly into the sky and disappeared. Tocohl watched the ship go, and answered Buntec's query with an economical, "Geosynchronous orbit. Better for communication."

"Oh," said Buntec, "if I'd known you had one of those top-line computers, I'd've stuck around to watch. You have an implant too?"

"Yes," said Tocohl, and Buntec said, "Before you run out on us, give me a guided tour, will you? Talk about technological toys ... !"

Tocohl grinned. Not only did Buntec have a passion for technological toys but, Tocohl suspected from the way the Jannisetti handled the daisy-clipper, she was a gifted player as well. She hadn't seen any research on the subject, but, she'd always suspected that there was an espability relating to machinery that was kith and kin to the more common "green thumb." A "metal thumb," perhaps; whatever it was, Buntec was a prime example. "If you'll keep Maggy's abilities to yourself for the duration, Buntec, I promise you a chance to talk to her yourself."

"Talk to her? *That* top-line?" Buntec raised her eyebrows, simultaneously demonstrating her pleasure by raising the daisy-clipper in a neat arc as well. "A nosy-poke computer?"

Tocohl laughed; she'd never heard the Jannisetti term for a computer of Maggy's capabilities, but she was willing to bet that was a literal translation. "A nosy-poke computer," she repeated, "that she most certainly is."

(Should I resent that?) Maggy asked. Tocohl couldn't help but repeat the query for Buntec's benefit.

"Resent it?" said Buntec. "Shit, no! Wow! And hello there, Maggy! I meant it as a compliment."

(Tell her thank you for me.)

Tocohl relayed the message.

"You're on, Tocohl. My mouth is stitched shut. But I do warn you there are a couple-three smartasses in the crew might spot a nosy-poke faster than me."

"Just don't give them any help."

(Stabilization of orbit in three minutes,) said Maggy, sparing her the details. (I launched the message capsule, and it should reach Sheveschke in about six days, unless something goes wrong.)

(Fine,) said Tocohl. (Now if Alfvaen asks you whether or not I'm a judge—though I doubt she will—if she does you are to tell her that I am.)

(You want me to lie?) Maggy somehow managed to sound outraged.

(That's it exactly. I want you to lie.)

(I can't lie.)

(Nonsense. Of course you can. That's a direct order, so I'll have no more of your lip.)

(Suppose Captain Kejesli asks his own computer: it won't lie. I tried to talk with it, and it's too *stupid* to lie.)

(Nicely phrased, Maggy. —And no doubt it does contain a list of byworld judges. In which case it will contain the name *Tocohl Sisumo*.)

Maggy made a rude noise, and Tocohl almost choked with laughter. (That's your father,) said Maggy. (That won't help at all.)

(The rude noise,) said Tocohl, (was not quite appropriate, but I'm glad you've added it to your repertoire—at least, I think I'm glad. In any event, if Kejesli sees Tocohl *Si*sumo, he'll assume it's a lousy transliteration into GalLing'. Stop worrying, Maggy; Kejesli would stand for a higher garble-factor than that.)

(That's not what I'm worried about,) Maggy said primly.

(Okay, okay. But keep your worries to yourself,) Tocohl finished, and turned her attention back to Buntec, who said cheerfully, "Gossip away. Don't let me interrupt. *Move ass*, you dopes!"

This last was shouted out the window, as Buntec steered the daisyclipper into the compound, spraying all those who hadn't turned and run with a comprehensive layer of red mud. Directly opposite swift-Kalat's door, Buntec grounded the daisy-clipper with feather lightness.

"You're not interrupting," Tocohl said. She slid from the craft, caught at the door frame abruptly. "Watch your step," she cautioned, "it's slippery out here."

"Always is," said Buntec. "Makes a *fine* mess of things, doesn't it?" She landed beside Tocohl with a splash. "I've been thinking," she said as she snatched luggage from the daisy-clipper, "swift-Kalat says he's got a biological artifact—Hitoshi Dan says it's not an artifact, but he can't figure out how it propagates, right?"

"Right," said Tocohl as she took her parcels from Buntec. "What do you have in mind?"

"Suppose," said Buntec, hefting the last of the parcels herself and following them up the steps into swift-Kalat's quarters, "Suppose we just assume it's an artifact and go from there. Where does that get us?"

"Good question: by Comity standards, we've got to prove the sprookjes have language, artifacts, and art or religion. It could be argued that language is an artifact—and has been, in fact. As I recall, both dolphins and whaffles whistled by on the strength of their poetry. And that," said Tocohl, dropping her bundle, "means that art and artifacts overlap as a category."

"So all we have to do is prove to our *mutual* satisfaction that the sprookjes are sapient," Buntec observed. She glanced about and, failing to find a spot to stow the parcel she carried, raised an interrogatory hand at Alfvaen. "*All*," snorted Alfvaen, misunderstanding the query.

"What I'm getting at," Buntec said, handing the Siveyn the parcel and turning again to Tocohl, "is that perhaps we should assume all their artifacts will be biological. We haven't found anything else, after all."

Tocohl stopped in the act of stowing to give Buntec her full attention. "You think we should be looking for *other* biological artifacts?"

"Why not?"

"Why not, indeed," Tocohl agreed. "Do you have anything particular in mind?"

"I came straight off the farm." Buntec grinned and lifted a foot. "That's not mud you see, honey. —We had our share of gene-tailored crops and animals. Now that's a biological artifact right there, but it's not one you could spot. But even with all the high-order stuff we did the basics. Grafting is about as basic as you can get, aside from the simple switch from hunting-gathering to genuine agriculture."

"The sprookjes appear not to have made that switch," said a new voice.

"Neither did dolphins," said Tocohl. She looked at Buntec questioningly.

Beckoning in the newcomer, Buntec said, "Timosie Megeve, Tocohl Susumo, and Tinling Alfvaen."

Timosie Megeve was Maldeneantine, from the severe wine-red of his oversuit to his earpips, held as they were by a thread about the cap of each ear—Maldeneantine frowned on violation of the body. His GalLing' held a slight but distinct accent, as did his hands, held close to his body as he spoke, making his gestures tight and spare. "Please, go on. I hadn't meant to interrupt—"

Buntec swung her hands wide, encompassing all three of them in the arc. *"You* think of cultivation as nice neat rows and the same sort of plant in each row, but you can get much better results in some cases by mixing plants. Using a second crop to keep out weeds or pests, or to nitrogenate the soil. Why bother with nice neat rows?" She turned to Tocohl. "Maybe the sprookjes don't *like* nice neat rows."

"Maybe not," Tocohl agreed. "I admit that's a possibility; one I hadn't thought of." Choosing a spot of rug, she crossed her legs and sat, to consider the problem. "Let's find out what they *do* like. Do you think you could spot a graft?"

"Bet your ass I can spot a graft, if I can find one new enough! I plan to start immediately." Buntec hauled over a chair and sprawled her chunky body into it, immovable. As if on cue, rain roared against the roof in earnest.

Alfvaen, still stowing her belongings, glared up at the sound and said, "Immediately isn't possible on Flashfever, is it?" She brought her eyes down to bear on Tocohl, where the glare softened to resignation. "I wish there were something we could do *now.*"

"*Now*," said Buntec, "Tocohl can tell me all about cosying up to Vyrnwy." The pronouncement drew a startled look from Timosie Megeve. Buntec waved an arm at him: "Edge-of-Dark got decent. If there's anything I can do to keep her decent, I'm for doing it. Bet your ass it's worth the trouble to me."

"… Cameras on!" said Kejesli.

A blurring of motion as the camera swung upward, and a moment before the image focused.

Another voice said, "Don't make any sudden moves; you'll scare them."

Three tall sprookjes filled the center of the frame, taller than the ones in camp by perhaps a foot, if the stand of tick-ticks was any guide. They craned their smooth flexible necks forward, and their cheek-feathers ruffled. No sound came from the humans off-screen, only the glasslike tinkling of frostwillows graced the tape.

Then one of the sprookjes took a step forward, its gold crest and multicolored yoke brilliant in the patch of sunlight. "Hello," said van Zoveel's voice; and the sprookje spread its hands (as van Zoveel had done) as if to show them empty of weapons.

The sprookje said nothing.

"Hello." said van Zoveel again. "They have hands, Captain. They may have a language."

Tocohl had the eerie feeling that the sprookje *was* speaking, or lip-synching to van Zoveel's words. This was the fifth time she'd watched the tape and hearing it through her implant didn't give the location of the sounds.

Maggy abruptly cut off the tape, thrusting Tocohl back into a jolting here-and-now as a shattering clap of thunder reverberated through swift-Kalat's room. The cup of winter-flame leapt in her hand and spilled across the table.

"My apologies, Ish shan," said Om im from the doorway.

"Not your fault," said Tocohl. "The thunder caught me by surprise, not you. I had hoped I'd grow accustomed to it after two days of continuous racket." She grinned. "That's not to say I don't like it, but a week of unending high would wear anyone out."

Om im Chadeayne bowed, dripping, and came to settle himself in the chair across from her. "I know. I suspect that's one reason we've had so much trouble with personnel on this survey."

Tocohl wiped winter-flame from her stack of hard-copy and gave him a sidelong questioning look.

"Ionized air," he explained. "It evidently has the same effect on Hellsparks as it does on Bluesippans. I've seen a couple of studies that show it to be an activator of sorts: creative people get more creative, and nuts get nuttier."

"Have you mentioned this to *layli-layli calulan?*"

"Yes," he said, "but she knew about it—there are certain advantages to shamanism. She says there's really nothing she can do, short of tranquilizing everybody, and—"

"She wouldn't advise that either," Tocohl finished. She leaned forward, folded her arms on the table. (Maggy, have you got anything on that?)

(Let me look,) Maggy said, much to Tocohl's amusement, and then there was silence. The pause was clearly provided for esthetic reasons, leaving Tocohl to wonder how Maggy would time its duration … by the length of time it would take a human to access the information from her by keyboard, perhaps?

She focused again on Om im. "Sorry," she said, for her moment of inattention.

"Don't be. It's worth consideration. Be aware that it might lead you into rash action."

Maggy broke silence, but only to comment, (It already has.)

(Swift-Kalat gave the sprookjes a chance. Ionization or no ionization, it would have been worth taking him up on it. What's done is done, Maggy; there's no point in nagging me about it.) Aloud, Tocohl said to Om im, "You think this ionization effect is responsible for the disturbances among the survey team?"

"Only partially," he admitted. "As you noticed, we were chamfered by a moron. But a number of us have worked together before, and I'm seeing edginess I've never seen. Take Kejesli: I've worked with him on two previous occasions. He's not a great captain, but he's a good one ordinarily. Now nobody wants to talk to him."

He drew his knife, considered the blade thoughtfully. There was no menace in the action, it was simply one of those things a Bluesippan will do when he wants to think. Reflecting in a blade, they termed it.

"No, I'm wrong," he said, tapping the flat across his palm, "nobody wants to talk to him unless he comes to them—or will meet them in the common room. I don't know why, but there it is."

"I can answer that one," Tocohl said. "The lowered ceiling in his quarters makes most of you mildly claustrophobic."

"Come now, Hellspark. You're right that he's lowered his ceiling—and that's unusual now that I think of it—but *I'm* hardly likely to bump my head ... !"

Tocohl chuckled. "That has nothing to do with it. The ceiling in your own cabin is a good three feet higher than the one in Kejesli's. It's a matter of what you're comfortable with. Am I to understand that Kejesli's quarters on previous surveys have had higher ceilings?"

"Now that you mention it, yes. Are you seriously telling me that's why nobody wants to visit the captain?"

"Yes, the low ceiling makes you all uncomfortable ... even if you aren't likely to bump your head. The point is, that low ceiling makes him comfortable, and if what you say is true this is the first survey he's felt he needed that. Perhaps that's his reaction to the ionization stress."

"Perhaps. But I think the haft of the matter is more likely what happened on Inumaru—or more properly what happened after Inumaru.'"

"Were you there?"

"Yes, for both." He frowned. "A lot of people were plenty angry when he refused to back Alfvaen, when MGE canned her."

"You?"

"No, not really. I agree with him that contracting Cana's disease hardly seems serendipitous. It was the rest of us he was trying to protect, after all. But ..." Again he gazed into the fine blued blade of his dagger. "But. Who knows, maybe there was a serendipitous reason that she caught it with everyone else"—he tilted the blade toward her—"you see my point."

"I do. I also call your attention to the fact that she and I are *both* here now."

"Your presence, Ish shan, is certainly worth the trouble," he acknowledged. He spread his hands in offering. "What can I do for you today?"

"Today you can tell me about Oloitokitok, and about the sprookjes," she said. "I've seen the tapes; now I need some on-the-spot reports."

Om im tilted his head slightly to the side and said slowly, "Now, the moment before the cameras went on, one of the sprookjes—the one that gestured at van Zoveel—was tearing up a thousand-day-blue."

"*That* wasn't in any of the reports," said Tocohl.

"That's why I mention it: you said you wanted any information related to the sprookjes. —It probably wasn't mentioned because sprookjes don't eat thousand-day-blues."

"They just tear them up?"

Om im grinned. "No. That's what seemed worth mentioning. On that occasion, I found a recently pulled patch of earth and the shredded remnants of the blue, but since then I've seen perhaps a hundred sprookjes pass by an equal number of thousand-day-blues without paying them the slightest attention. Which is a little hard to do. The tapes won't give you an idea of the smell of a thousand-day-blue either—it's *raunchy*."

"Interesting," said Tocohl. "Not very enlightening, but filed and noted." A flash of light crackled outside the membrane, and Tocohl waited out the thunder before speaking, then said, "Go on."

"The fact that the sprookjes have hands was what made van Zoveel so excited. You should have seen him!" Om im Chadeayne's eyes sparkled. "Perhaps you did: that sprookje was like his reflection. But, as you saw on the tape, those sprookjes didn't say a word and when van Zoveel got close, the sprookje nipped him. Everybody overreacted and the sprookjes got frightened and disappeared into the flashwood. Nobody followed; we were all too concerned about van Zoveel."

Shifting forward in his chair, the Bluesippan continued. "Van Zoveel came to no harm, except for the reaming out Kejesli gave him for ignoring safety rules. Evidently the sprookje didn't either, because they went on nipping everybody they came across." He smiled. "After a while, the pinprick became Flashfever's badge of acceptance."

"But that came later?" asked Tocohl.

"That came later, when the parrots had moved into camp. —I wasn't around the second time van Zoveel tried talking to the sprookjes, so you'll need another eyewitness."

Tocohl filled in from the tapes she'd seen: van Zoveel had used his vocoder and tried high frequency, thinking perhaps that the sprookjes might be that one-in-a-thousand species that heard only in the upper ranges. The sprookjes had heard it, all right—heard and run!

"I *can* tell you," Om im raised his voice as a gust of wind outside brought a particularly heavy crash of rain against the north wall, "*why* they ran. We'd made some tapes—including the high-frequency range—of general flashwood noises. That's not as easy as you might think: we had to hang the tapers from poles or all they'd have picked up was *tk-tk, tk-tk, tk-tk*." He made the appropriate scolding face to accompany the sound of the paired tongue-clicks.

Tocohl grinned. "So that's why they're called tick-ticks—you named them but no one else on the team can do the tongue-clicks."

"Yes," said Om im, "I should have left well enough alone, but you've heard them yourself and you know they sound like a chiding parent ... !"

He grinned back before taking up his tale once more: "We—Buntec and Megeve and I—were taking advantage of an hour's sunlight. You'll find everybody does that here, sits outside and spreads her feathers for drying. We were studying our tapes, but *outside* in the middle of the compound.

"And all of a sudden, the ugliest thing you ever saw—and believe me, I've seen some ugly things in my life—I've fallen on Stuckfish!—swooped out of the sky and ate the taper.

"It sat for a moment—it didn't turn bilious green because it already *was* a bilious green—but it gave two resounding belches and vomited up the taper. Then it flew away, cursing, or so I assumed from its tone. Timosie cursed just as much over the loss of his taper, but Buntec and I must have howled for twenty minutes. It was at least that long before we could tell the rest of the team what had happened."

He leaned forward, his expression turning serious. "But tape-belchers, we later found out, are nothing to laugh about. Megeve got a nasty slice taken out of his side when he got too close to one's nest. Even tape-belchers don't like tape-belchers: they tear each other up constantly."

Tocohl had seen hard-copy on that too. Evidently the tape-belchers were territorial and held that territory beak and claw, especially against other tape-belchers. According to swift-Kalat's notes, the taper-eating incident had probably been sparked by a recorded challenge of another tape-belcher that the live belcher had taken for genuine.

Om im gestured at her cup. "I know where swift-Kalat keeps his supplies. Would you like a refill, as long as I'm getting myself a cup?"

"Please," said Tocohl. As Om im crossed the room, she said, (Maggy? Are you getting all this?)

(Of course,) said Maggy. (He's right about the ionization stress effects. It could be enough to account for your lack of sense.) Tocohl breathed a sigh. (But probably not,) she said. (Let's hear the short version of what you've found.)

It took no more than a minute from Maggy's choice of quotes and displays for Tocohl to see that the exhilaration she felt was not merely an emotional reaction to Flashfever's gaudy displays of lightning but a genuine physical reaction to the ionization of the air. (I think,) she said, (I can probably tone down the effect a little with the Methven rituals.)

(Then do,) said Maggy, (or who knows what you'll claim to be next. And I'm not sure I approve of lying. You did say not to lie to Jenji...)

(I didn't. Not precisely. I said I'd agree to judge—I never said I was one.)

There was something akin to a muffled snort. Tocohl squinted, as if she might see the speaker if she looked hard enough into her spectacles. (That's not *my* snort of disapproval, is it?)

(No, it's Buntec's. Does it match the rest of my voice? Did I use it correctly?)

(Yes, and yes again,) Tocohl said. Deciding it was time to change the subject, she added, (What are you up to?)

(You mean what is the arachne doing?)

(Mm. Yes. Even Hellspark doesn't have the proper words to cover all possible situations.)

(Exploring the perimeter. Would you like to see?)

(Please,) said Tocohl, and was rewarded by a portion of the arachne's eye-view of barbed-wire fence, no doubt the most interesting area in Maggy's opinion.

Heavy rain lashed a grove of frostwillows into a frenzied display of light. Their ordinarily sweet tinkling sound had become a disturbing one of shattering glass that could be heard even above the rushing downpour. Something slithered past in the foreground, and as it passed through a clump of flashgrass, Tocohl saw that it was a lizard-like creature, as brassy as penny-Jannisetts.

(You might show that tape to swift-Kalat,) said Tocohl. (I don't recall having seen that particular animal in their files.)

(You're right. They don't have a picture of that one.) Maggy had evidently checked while Tocohl was speaking. (They should,) she added primly.

Tocohl chuckled. (Perhaps they know enough to come in out of the rain; you and the lizard-thing don't.)

(The storm is not yet overhead. The arachne is in no danger.)

(No offense,) said Tocohl.

(None taken,) said the voice in her ear, and Tocohl said, (Perfectly put. And, Maggy, you're making good choices about what needs an immediate response and what can wait.)

To this last, Maggy made no response, but the vision of the camp perimeter vanished. Om im set a second cup of winter-flame before Tocohl and reseated himself, cradling his own cup for its warmth, an unconscious response to the dankness of the weather.

"Thunderstorms," he said, "are a time for talk. There's not much else to do on this world during one except drink winter-flame and cavil about the weather."

"I wish the sprookjes felt that way," said Tocohl, "about talking during thunderstorms, I mean. It's been two days now and I haven't gotten to talk to a sprookje—or gotten one to talk to me. What do they do during thunderstorms?"

"Nobody is willing to brave that"—Om im flourished a hand in the direction of the door; a flash of lightning gave the gesture more emphasis than he had intended and he rubbed his fingertips in delighted surprise—"in order to find out."

Before Tocohl could open her mouth to comment, he said firmly, "If you're going to suggest arachnes and other robot probes, Ish shan, be assured we thought of that. And we promptly lost five of them to Flashfever's wildlife, most of which either gives electric shocks or feeds on them.

"As long as yours stays within the perimeter, you probably won't lose it, unless it gets hit by lightning, but I wouldn't risk it outside if I were you." Om im paused, then went on, "And as for getting the sprookjes to talk to you when they're around, don't feel neglected. I'll finish my eyewitness account and you'll see what I mean."

"Do," said Tocohl, and raised her cup.

"After the episode with the high-frequency sounds, none of us saw much of the sprookjes, except an occasional glimpse in the distance that might have been one. Then, one day about six months later, a handful of the brown ones showed up in camp."

Once again, he drew his dagger. He peered critically at the blade, then drew a whetstone from his pouch and began to hone it, comfortably matching the rhythm of his words to the motion. "The ones that came to camp are all brown and all smaller than the crested ones. I never thought about it before, but I suppose the camp sprookjes are younger, or a different sex?"

"There are speculations to that effect in the hard-copy," said Tocohl, "though I did notice that no one did an anatomical study."

Om im stopped honing, shocked. "When half the survey team thought they were sapient? No way—"

"I only meant no one had found a dead sprookje to autopsy. You give me an undeserved reputation for bloodthirst."

"Sorry," said Om im, "I intended no offense. The situation makes us all a little edgy one way or another."

"And you lean toward defending the sprookjes. Why?"

This time the Bluesippan looked not so much shocked as surprised by her words. "You know," he said, "I do think along those lines, but I'm afraid I haven't any idea why I do."

With a faintly puzzled air, he went back to his story—as if he were listening for some clue to his own attitudes. "After the handful, more and more trickled in, and three months later, we had one apiece. Now I had better be specific…

"For the exact date, I'd have to check my records, but it was late afternoon and I was sitting on a stool I'd brought outside, 'drying my feathers,' as I said before; and there was a sprookje, staring at me with those great solemn eyes of theirs. So I said hello. And *it* said hello—"

"Just a minute, Om im. In what language?"

"In GalLing'. It was too tall for a Bluesippan, after all. At any rate, I was stunned and it was stunned, or gave a good facsimile thereof. Finally I said, 'I'm pleased to meet you,' and went on to introduce myself. I got about halfway through my self-introduction before I realized that the sprookje was parroting me, word for word, inflection for inflection. I was so surprised I stopped midway through my name, and a second or two later, that's precisely where the sprookje stopped.

"By this time a couple of other people had come over, slowly, of course, so they wouldn't frighten the creature. So I tried again. This time, I introduced Buntec. And the blunted sprookje kept pace again, just a little behind me.

"But when Buntec spoke, also in GalLing', it was as if she didn't exist at all. And that, children, is how your uncle Om im acquired his sprookje." The Bluesippan's puzzled look was replaced by an ironic one; his narrative had failed to give him the clue he'd been seeking.

"If it's any consolation," said Tocohl, "I didn't find anything either."

Om im lifted his gilded eyebrows and raised his cup to her. "Sharp as Tam shan's blade! You come by your reputation honestly, Ish shan."

"Hah! You established it in your own mind when you chose that nickname for me." She leaned back, then said, "I believe you have payment coming. What do I owe so far?"

"I think," he said slowly, as if in an effort to keep his voice light, "that you have more than repaid me. You're right: I believe the sprookjes are sapient. Strongly enough at least to know they must be given a chance. The chance is yours."

Tocohl met his eyes with practiced misunderstanding.

He laughed, his eyes merry beneath his gilded brows. "No, Ish shan," he said, "that won't help. My Hellspark may not be the best, but I can tell a hawk from a handsaw when I hear it in your tongue."

It took Tocohl a moment to understand … In the Bluesippan translation the words were identical but for a *si* and a *su*, the difference between her name and her father's.

By the time she had grasped his meaning, she knew she had no cause for alarm. His dagger was on the table; he slid it, hilt-first, across to her. "My blade is at your service, Tocohl *Su*sumo," he said. "That is the least I can do for Oloitokitok and for the sprookjes."

She laid her hand across the hilt, accepting his service and his silence.

CHAPTER 8

A kiss on the hand is worth all this? thought Buntec incredu-
lously as she looked down at the table spread with Vyrnwyn delicacies.
She didn't recognize any of these foods, but the Vyrnwyn obviously
considered the visual side of eating at least as important as the flavor.
Spread before her were a dozen separate plates, each a different size—
here a delicate gold paste heaped high in a black bowl, topped with a
sprinkling of something round and rosy; there, on a pale blue plate,
semitransparent slices of something pure white arranged in the shape,
yes, in the shape of a frostwillow.

Buntec stared at each wonder in turn... When she found her
voice at last it was to say, "They're beautiful, Edge-of-Dark, beautiful!
Surely you don't expect me to *eat* them!" Realizing this might be mis-
understood, she added hastily, "If I *eat* them, they'll be *gone*. Shouldn't
we at least take a picture or—!" Her arm flung wide, as if of its own
accord, to encompass the entire display.

Edge-of-Dark smiled. To Buntec's surprise, it was not the
patronizing smile she'd seen so many times before but a genuinely
warm and open smile that suited her rich features so perfectly that
Buntec was overwhelmed.

"Perfection never lasts," Edge-of-Dark said. "We eat them
because they are beautiful. If they weren't, we shouldn't bother."
Smiling still, she added. "We differ so much, you and I, I was unsure of your tastes in food. I'm glad to know that I am already partially correct."

Buntec hesitated, unwilling to disturb that luminous image of
frostwillow.

"That one," said Edge-of-Dark, "is eaten with this"—she indicated one of the three unfamiliar utensils that lay before Buntec—"and
I won't know if you like the way it tastes unless you taste it. Please."

Buntec raised the little gold-pronged implement Edge-of-Dark
had indicated and, taking a deep breath, speared a piece of "frostwillow."

In that brief moment, she found the time and the honesty to admit to herself that if Edge-of-Dark's wearing boots could mean that she felt so relieved, then perhaps a little hand-kissing *could* make all the difference to Edge-of-Dark.

The "frostwillow" was cold and crisp and delicately spicy. She couldn't tell if it was animal or vegetable, but she reached for a second piece and found Edge-of-Dark smiling at her again.

Edge-of-Dark, her hand poised over a pile of flamboyant red and purple curls on a striped platter, said, "These are to be eaten with the fingers. The ... uncertainty is part of the appeal." She demonstrated, dipping one of the curls into a bowl of gold paste.

By "uncertainty" Edge-of-Dark clearly meant that of getting curl and paste down the gullet instead of plopped into her lap. Buntec smiled back, intrigued by this new aspect of the Vyrnwyn programmer. Fashionable clothing seemed terribly important to Edge-of-Dark; to see her risk splattering it was a double wonder.

Following Edge-of-Dark's example, Buntec dipped one of the red curls into the gold paste. "I still don't see," she began, but the paste was as uncertain as Edge-of-Dark had implied. Seeing it about to drip, Buntec tilted the curl first one way, then the other. When that did no good, she hastily caught the spill with her other hand. "—Oops! I'm sorry, Edge-of-Dark. I don't know a thing about Vyrnwyn table manners. Did I just cheat? Will you be offended if I lick my palm or—?"

"Ordinarily one doesn't begin that until much later, after one has had a good deal to drink. 'Cat-drunk' we call it, because the Gaian cat has such fastidious manners even though it cleans itself with its tongue. You're a beginner, Buntec, so that's a different matter altogether. If you'll have some wine, we'll consider it to be in good taste," Edge-of-Dark said, then added, with the caution the question deserved, "As far as I know, I don't have any taboos having to do with dinner. But I'm not sure. I never realized that *I* speak with an accent until the first time I stayed in—well, a very different part of my country on my own world. —Do you have any table manner taboos that *I* should know about?"

The two women considered each other warily, each afraid of her own provincialism. Then Buntec grinned and held up a chunky hand. "Do you like dOrnano wine?"

"Yes," said Edge-of-Dark in a puzzled fashion, and Buntec went on, "Then I have a solution: the first of us to spot one of her own culture's food taboos gets treated to a bottle of dOrnano wine—to be shared with the other, of course."

"Of course," Edge-of-Dark said.

Happy with this solution, Buntec took a sip of wine, then licked the paste from her palm. "In good taste is right," she said. "This is better than good." She also caught some taste of the Vyrnwyn game: the paste was heavily laced with brandy, potent even without the blackwine that complemented it.

"Mm! No way *this* perfection will outlast my appetite!" Buntec reached for another curl, a purple one this time. "Well, I was going to say: I still don't see how you can put so much artistry into something so perishable."

Edge-of-Dark poured herself another glass of blackwine. Gesturing left with the decanter, she asked, "Would you find that too perishable to bother with as well?"

Buntec followed the gesture: on a low rectangular table in the far corner of the cabin sat a flattish container filled with a variety of local plants. She was momentarily surprised that she had not seen it before, until the thought occurred to her that perhaps it was intended to be seen only from this point.

The design—for design it was, she realized—caught her eye and held it: three rich red-purple leaves from a flames-of-Veschke, their spear-head shapes rising from the container, each higher than the last; a single intricate piece of arabesque vine bound them loosely and wove its way down to a tiny knot of penny-Jannisetts...

Like light sculpture, but done in plants! Buntec had never seen anything like it. She rose, intending to take a closer look.

"No," said Edge-of-Dark, "it is to be seen from a distance; we call that *naoise*-style."

"Is it something you invented?"

"No, of course not. Flower art isn't done on your world? It's very common on mine. Not everyone is good at it, but everyone does it."

Buntec, her attention torn between the flower art and the food, said, "Jannisett's a farm world. We grow a lot of plants inside, especially the flowering ones, but nobody ever thought of doing anything like that! And it sounds to me as if you're talking about more than one *kind* of flower art, like different schools of light sculpture."

"I wasn't, but there are. Within each school, there is a viewing distance factor. For example, *joliffe* flower art, no matter what school, would be something we'd place in the center of this table, to be viewed at this particular distance; *joliffe-che* would be a composition to be seen from all sides at this distance."

Buntec said, "You must be a grand master, or whatever is the appropriate term."

"Thank you," said Edge-of-Dark, "but I'm scarcely more than an occasionally inspired amateur. If you like that, you really should see the works of Shadow-Blue or Spite-the-Devil. They *are* grand masters!"

Edge-of-Dark lifted one of the as yet untouched plates of food and offered it; Buntec took some. As she chewed it slowly, trying to figure out what the aftertaste reminded her of, Edge-of-Dark said, "Flashfever opens up a whole new world of flower art. If only I could find some way to keep frostwillow or flashgrass or Christopher-bangs fresh, the sounds and lights would add a completely new dimension to a piece! But that's hardly as simple as putting penny-Jannisetts in water..."

"But that should be easy!" said Buntec.

"*Easy?*"

"Sure, all you'd have to do is—" Buntec, excited by the idea herself, launched into a highly technical description of how it could be done. Somewhere in the middle of it, she realized that Edge-of-Dark wasn't following her. "Sorry," she said, "it is easy, though. I'll make you some little things you could kind of plug the frostwillow or whatever into. Movable, so you can put them in the right place." She swung her broad hand, "And for the drunken dabblers, we can build a fountain—recycle the water but move it fast enough to keep them alive and healthy."

Grinning, Buntec spread flattened hands. "I think I'd better calm down. I'm not paying the food the attention it deserves. I'm sorry if I sound like a little kid who's just discovered outdoors." She looked again at the work of art that graced the corner table and shook her head in amazement. "I never saw botanical art before and it's—" The thought struck with the force of a blow. Unable to complete the sentence, Buntec let her jaw drop and stared...

"Buntec? Is something wrong? You have the oddest look on your face. Is the food all right? Buntec!"

"Wrong!" said Buntec, hard put to keep from bellowing the news: "Everything's *perfect!* Everything's *wonderful!* We're geniuses, you and I!"

"What are you talking about?"

"Edge-of-Dark, think of the damn sprookjes—swift-Kalat has that fruit without seeds. He says it's a biological artifact. Well—*hell!*—if the sprookjes have biological artifacts, what kind of art do you suppose they'd have?"

Grinning, Buntec waited. Edge-of-Dark did not disappoint her—the Vyrnwyn's face lit once more in that beautiful glowing smile—and she whispered back, "Biological art. Botanical art. Flower art." Astonishment mingled with delight, Edge-of-Dark half rose, "We've been looking for the wrong things! We must tell everyone ... !"

"Down, girl," said Buntec, "first things first." Choosing another red curl, she scooped paste and, this time, brought it to her mouth without incident. "Well," she said, grinning in triumph, "as you say, perfection never lasts ... but it sure oughtn't go to waste! First, we eat—*then* we wise up the yokels!"

CHAPTER 9

With the storm now raging overhead, Maggy judged it time to move the arachne out of danger. As the discussion she monitored through Alfvaen's hand-held made it clear that swift-Kalat intended to dissect one of the golden scoffers, her choice of shelter was obvious. She couldn't watch and record the dissection through the hand-held, only through the eye of the arachne.

She scratched politely at the entrance to swift-Kalat's cabin; behind her a flash of lightning made her acutely aware that human politeness was often at odds with survival. She stored that observation to look into at some later time, while she attempted to calculate the effect of an unannounced entry.

Alfvaen saved her the trouble by splitting the membrane. "Hello, Maggy," she said, "come on in." A second jagged fork of lightning ripped through the air behind her. Having been invited, Maggy bent the arachne's legs and sprang it to safety. There were only two mobiles, after all, and she wouldn't be able to watch a thing if something happened to this one—at least, until she could send another down.

"Hello," Maggy said in return, responding from the hand-held. "Is that correct, Alfvaen? I thought in GalLing' you say hello only when you first meet. Or is that a holdover from Siveyn custom?"

Alfvaen glanced down at the unit on her hip and made a noise that Maggy tentatively interpreted as not understanding. To test the interpretation, she elaborated, "I've been listening to your discussions for some time now."

"Oh," said Alfvaen—in a tone that conveyed sufficient confirmation for Maggy to tag the previous noise as understood. "You're right. But you haven't said anything through the hand-held for hours, so I thought you'd gone away." She cocked her head to one side and stared directly at the arachne. "I guess I'm not used to the fact that you can be in two places at once. The arachne makes your presence more visible somehow, solider, if you know what I mean."

"No," said Maggy, "I'm sorry, Alfvaen, but I don't understand."

Swift-Kalat, who up to this point had merely watched the two of them, said, "The human eye is automatically drawn by the movement of the arachne. Were the arachne still, and silent, we would be inclined to forget your presence, as Alfvaen did with the hand-held monitor."

"Oh," said Maggy, employing the same tone she had heard from Alfvaen only moments before. "The arachne seems more of a discrete entity?"

"Yes, that's it," said Alfvaen. "After all, it's dripping on the rug."

Clearly, that was construed as impolite; yes, except when she was very excited, Tocohl toweled off carefully on entering a shelter. "I'm sorry," Maggy said, dipping the arachne in the bow of apology Tocohl had taught her, "I hope I haven't given offense."

"None given, none taken," Alfvaen said, "but let me find something to dry you off with."

Given Alfvaen's greeting and explanation of it, given also the way Maggy's voice seemed to startle Alfvaen whenever it issued from the hand-held, given this new use of 'dry you off' that unmistakably meant the arachne, Maggy concluded that it was convention to think of the mobile as the whole.

Accordingly she said, this time using the vocoder in the arachne, "If I understand you correctly, you would be more comfortable if I spoke from here?"

"I would," Alfvaen admitted. "It's not so much of a surprise that way. —Ah." She pointed and swift-Kalat, who had been watching their exchange with evident interest, turned, reached for a towel, and brought it to Alfvaen.

Kneeling, Alfvaen held it out. Maggy sent the arachne to her as gingerly as its mechanisms would permit, to avoid further dripping. When it was within reach, Alfvaen said, "May I?"

Tocohl would have categorized that as Dumb Question. "I can't do it myself," Maggy said, but because it was Alfvaen who asked, she simultaneously checked the odd usage. Concluding that Alfvaen had intended to be polite, she immediately added, "Oops. You meant to be polite, didn't you? I'm sorry again, Alfvaen."

"No offense," Alfvaen said as she toweled the arachne briskly.

"Yes, I meant it to be polite." Maggy turned and tilted it to expose its various surfaces. Scraping mud from its legs, Alfvaen said, "Stop being sorry, though. Your use of 'oops' was absolutely perfect."

She cast a quick glance upward at swift-Kalat. "Maggy learns," she explained, "so it helps to tell her when she does something right, not just when she does something wrong. Just like any kid." She smiled directly at the arachne's lens. "In fact, like most, you get a rather low-angle view of everything. Why don't I put you on the table where you can see something besides feet?"

"Yes, please. If swift-Kalat won't mind?"

"I don't mind—" swift-Kalat began. Alfvaen lifted the arachne. "Where would you like to be, Maggy?" she asked.

"Where I may watch and record swift-Kalat's dissection of the golden scoffer."

Alfvaen set the arachne on the table, giving it a clear view of the small furry cadaver. Maggy shifted it slightly, to avoid obstructing swift-Kalat's work with its shadow, and settled the arachne with its legs folded.

"Maggy," said swift-Kalat, "I would appreciate some information."

"I have tapes of an animal not in your computer's memory," she offered, "I recorded it in the flashwood at the perimeter of the camp. I will transfer them if you wish."

"You *are* in two places at once!" said Alfvaen.

"Four places," Maggy corrected, to set the record straight.

Swift-Kalat said, "Yes, I would like you to transfer your record, but I meant a request for specific information from you."

"I'll answer as reliably as I can."

"Please understand that I mean no offense. I do not know what culture you belong to or I would avoid the known taboos."

"Hellspark, I think," Alfvaen said.

"Yes, that's right," Maggy confirmed, "Hellspark is the culture I'm most familiar with. I have a good working knowledge, Tocohl says, of the Jannisetti, the Sheveschkemen, the Holyani, the Dusties—"

Laughing, Alfvaen held up her hands. "Enough, Maggy. You're *definitely* Hellspark." To swift-Kalat, she added, "Her Siveyn is very good, and her knowledge of Jenji is better than mine—she has the vo-cabulary at her command; I don't."

"I can look things up faster than you can, Alfvaen, and I don't have to worry about where to stand."

"You're sweet, Maggy."

"Am I? Tocohl says I'm a pain in the butt."

"It is possible to be both."

"Oh," said Maggy, and filed that for future reference. "What information do you request, swift-Kalat? I apologize for having strayed from the subject."

He paused. Maggy recognized this only because Tocohl had given both her and Alfvaen training in the timing of responses in Jenji. This was, for Jenji, too long a pause; Maggy inferred that he was having trouble framing his question.

At long last, he said, "Maggy, how old are you?"

That was an oops, thought Maggy, that implies he thinks I'm a child, and a Hellspark one too. Tocohl had told her not to tell people she was an extrapolative computer, but this was a Jenji asking, and Tocohl had also made a point of telling her not to lie to Jenji. Tocohl was busy or she would have asked Tocohl what to say. As it was, she balanced odds one way, then another, and decided that swift-Kalat had hired them both. So she shouldn't lie to him, even if she had permission to lie to Alfvaen about the judgeship. Alfvaen was likely to correct his impression, anyway, so Maggy had better find a way to do so politely. She took a nanosecond more to search through all she knew of the Jenji...

Alfvaen said, "Oh, no! Maggy's n—"

That *would* have been impolite, the way Alfvaen was headed. Maggy interrupted, "I was manufactured eight standard years ago, thirteen and a half Jenji, but Tocohl says I'm only three standard."

Alfvaen closed her mouth, peered curiously at the arachne. "Why *three* standard, did she say?"

Maggy would have replied with Tocohl's own words had they not been in Hellspark. Instead she translated: "Because that's when I started mouthing off."

Tocohl sat at a large table in the common room, Om im beside her. To another Bluesippan, the blade offer and acceptance needed no announcement; that he sat at her left hand and thus guarded her unprotected side would have been enough. The surveyors took it for simple gallantry.

As a handful of others, among them John the Smith and Rav Kejesli, approached the table, Tocohl said softly in Bluesippan, "Don't let your instincts run away with you, Om im. I won't take a parting of blades for a threat—at least, not yet." She had asked him about the Inheritors of God but, to his knowledge, no one on the team was a believer in the faith. Aside from that, she was not yet ready to jump at shadows.

"I know, Ish shan," he said, "and John the Smith will be the first. I guarantee that, and I guarantee my own judicious behavior."

"Good," she said, "I can't stand the sight of blood. —Why John the Smith?" But the question came too late for Om im's answer for the party was already in hearing.

John the Smith promptly answered the question in his own way by attempting to draw a chair between Tocohl and Om im. He was Sobolli—of course!—his status accorded him a place to the left of the one he addressed. Om im took it well; as promised he did not take the action as a threat, he merely closed in on Tocohl and doggedly refused to relinquish his position to John the Smith.

"Here, John," said Kejesli—he was at least partially aware of the problem, Tocohl noted—"Beside me." With poor grace, which Kejesli was unaware of, John the Smith once more rounded the table, this time to "outrank" his captain.

Tocohl mentally wished the team's chamfer the Death of a Thousand Butts. To put a Sobolli, guaranteed to approach on the left, on the same team as a Bluesippan, who took a left approach as threat was to court disaster. Not to mention severe injury to the Sobolli... She found sweat beading her forehead and wiped it away.

Om im chuckled. In Bluesippan, he muttered, "If I haven't killed him for blind-siding me yet, Ish shan, I'm not likely to today. I think I mentioned we were chamfered by a moron..." In GalLing' he said, "The Hellspark's in search of sprookje tales. I promised her each of us had one of her own, certainly to the acquiring of her own personal sprookje."

"Do we!"

That was Kejesli reaffirming his status by taking the first word, and telling the first tale. When he had finished, a half a dozen others told their own in turn, but the end result was no new information about the camp sprookjes. In every case, the experience had been almost identical to Om im's: each sprookje had begun to mimic one surveyor— no apparent reason for the choice, no apparent understanding of the words echoed, and no sprookje echoed more than one surveyor.

"And," contributed Hitoshi Dan, the team's botanist, when he had finished his own acquisition tale, "they don't speak unless they're spoken to. They never volunteer a word. In fact, you don't know if the sprookje's 'yours' until you say something, and then you wish you hadn't."

"Wrong," said Om im genially.

Just as genially, Hitoshi Dan splayed his fingers before his throat. "Never insult a man with a knife," he said. "I did forget: my small sharp-edged friend there can tell the sprookjes apart before their echo gives them away."

Jabbing both thumbs at his temples, John the Smith made a scoffing sound. Luckily, both Om im and Hitoshi Dan took notice only of the scoffing sound.

"True, John," Om im said, "I've gotten to the point where I can tell which sprookje is whose."

"He can. Ask him sometime as they come into camp," Hitoshi Dan said, but he shifted his gaze from the Sobolli who so clearly disbelieved to Tocohl, who assured him with a tap to her nose that she planned to do just that.

To Tocohl, Om im explained, "Each of the sprookjes has its own face and its own personality. I can tell you which will mimic whom. But Dan's right that they never speak unless spoken to."

Then, once again turning his attention to John the Smith, he said, "Homo sap is essentially lazy. He looks at two cats and he says all cats look alike. Or he'll go so far as to acknowledge that one cat is striped and the other isn't, but he'll only acknowledge gross differences."

He rose with an easy arrogance, as if the act of standing proved his point. "People look at me and say, 'Ah, a Bluesippan!'—I am forced to say, no, that's not sufficient. I'm Om im Chadeayne, I am myself." He paused, then, "I am different than you are but I *am* an individual. I am informed by my culture and my world but I am not defined by it."

Very true, thought Tocohl, or you would have drawn on John the Smith. Even that is unlikely to have made an impression on him.

As Om im resumed his post (to all appearances settling himself easily back into his chair), John the Smith said, "But that's hardly the question here. We're talking about sprookjes and they aren't—" he broke off suddenly.

"Yes?" said Om im, and the Smith looked embarrassed.

"You were, perhaps," said Om im, "about to add, 'and *they* aren't human,' were you not?"

"Yes," the Smith admitted.

"But that's a question we have yet to decide," Om im said. "You see? I'm not faulting you in particular, John. It's a language problem in more ways than one. Assuming the sprookjes have a language, then we're having trouble with their language and with our own as well."

Confident now of his ability to retain his audience, Om im paused to sip his winter-flame, then continued, "You call them all sprookjes, which defines them in a certain way—and limits your ability to think about them. I'm not much better: I think of them as John's sprookje, swift-Kalat's sprookje, and so on."

"All right, Om im, but calling them human won't make them human."

"True, but calling them *non*human or *in*human will set limits on our perceptions of them. —Tocohl, you see what I mean?"

"Perfectly," said Tocohl. "You took one look at me and made up your mind that I fit your image of Ish shan—a legendary giant from Bluesippan folklore," she added for the benefit of the others around the table, "who was known for her ability to outwit the gods. So, from that moment on, anything I did in your presence became highly charged: my successes will be more than successes, my failures will be more than failures. All this through no fault of mine. Being thought more than human has problems all its own."

Having taken Om im's audience from him, *she* paused for a sip of winter-flame before continuing. When she resumed, it was to say, "Take van Zoveel for an example. He named them sprookjes. To him, they're fairy tale creatures, something from a story for kids. Surely that affects his image of them."

Hitoshi Dan stabbed the air for attention. "Your point is well taken, but what do you suggest we do? Shall we call them 'native humans'? —Must we, in order to see them as human?"

"I don't know what *human* means," interjected John the Smith, "especially after Tocohl's story about the Pasicans. Human is itself a highly charged term!"

"Human means *like me*," Tocohl said.

"Human means having art, artifacts, and language," Rav Kejesli corrected sourly. "That's the legal definition."

"Which," said Tocohl, smiling, "is nothing more than a complex way of saying *like me*."

For a brief moment, Kejesli tried to stare her down, but still smiling, she met his stare with her own level gaze, and at last he touched the pin of remembrance. "For the moment, I'll grant it," he said.

Touching her pin of high-change in acknowledgment, Tocohl went on, "Convince enough people—and I use that term loosely—that any given species is enough *like them* and they may even find a way to circumvent the legal definitions. Witness the dolphins. Perhaps it was just wishful thinking on the part of *Homo sapiens*, but dolphin song was judged an artifact. Personally, I think *Homo sapiens* wanted so badly to ally itself with such a graceful, gentle, and talented species that cheating was the obvious answer." She drew her hands close about her wrists.

"I don't begrudge the cheating, certainly." She smiled. "It gained for *Homo sapiens* a greater humanity in that other sense of the word."

Hitoshi Dan smiled wistfully, as if in remembrance. Evidently he'd had some contact with the Gaian dolphins. "Perhaps we're using the wrong term," he said, "if it's a language problem. Perhaps *sapient* or *HILF* would be less loaded?"

"In GalLing', yes," said Tocohl, "but how many of you actually *think* in GalLing' rather than translating automatically into your homeworld's tongue? The Yn word for *sapient* translates literally as 'she who speaks.'" She gestured toward Rav Kejesli: "And the Sheveschkem term means 'sparked' or 'enflamed'—though neither GalLing' word quite captures the imagery of the original."

John the Smith said, but with a slight smile, "You have an admirable talent for confusing the issue, Hellspark."

"That wasn't my intention; I meant merely to break down the boundaries to some extent, to show you how flexible reality is when compared to our means of *expressing* that reality."

There was a long moment of silence. Tocohl scrutinized the faces of those around her: Kejesli scowled, John the Smith looked thoughtful. In fact, to Tocohl's satisfaction, thoughtful looks predominated. At last, Hitoshi Dan broke the silence. "All right," he said and—as if in positive answer to a question—rose and strode away.

His departure signaled a general turnover of those assembled. Most of the deserters, Tocohl felt confident, were off to think over what she and Om im had said. Only John the Smith and Kejesli, still scowling, remained.

"What else can we tell you about Flashfever," Om im prompted. "What else might be of help?"

"Tell me what's so valuable about this world," said Tocohl. "You're the geologist—is there anything that might make Flashfever especially interesting to colonists or exploiters?"

Kejesli's scowl deepened, but this time was not directed at her. When he unwittingly touched his pin of remembrance, she knew he too was thinking of the sort of exploiters who had burned Veschke.

"Not from my end," said Om im. "Flashfever has the usual supply that you'd find on any previously unexploited planet in its category; a colony wouldn't have any lack of resources, certainly. But ores aren't worth the cost of export, and so far I haven't turned up any unusual gemstones that would be."

"Not gemstones," John the Smith snapped suddenly, "forget gemstones, Tocohl. This is one of the most valuable planets ever surveyed!"

Kejesli jerked to face him, eyes widening in surprise at the Smith's sudden animation. A quick yank brought the Smith's chair an inch closer to Kejesli: the Sobolli meant to convince. When what would have impressed another Sobolli only made Kejesli kick his own chair the same inch backward, John the Smith turned his attention back to Tocohl.

His irritation vanished in his general excitement. "Animals that give electric shocks have been known on other worlds. But for Flashfever, biologists will have to establish whole new categories of plants! Plants!" He threw up his hands. "I see what you mean about the flexibility of reality. I'll bet Hitoshi Dan calls them plants because there isn't a GalLing' word that covers them. *I* don't know of any.

"Take the drunken dabblers, for instance—they grow in the middle of a fast-running stream and convert the energy of the water into electricity and use *that* for sugar conversion, cell-building, and so on! As common a weed as flashgrass has its own biological piezoelectric cells and uses wind power as an energy source."

"So that's why it's so thick in the vicinity of the hangar," Tocohl said.

"Right," said the Smith, "flashgrass gets on with daisy-clippers like ... you and Om im."

Tocohl grinned at the analogy. Om im said, matter-of-factly, "I'm the windy one."

With a chuckle and a sidelong glance at Kejesli, John the Smith went on. "All due deference to you, Captain, but I wish we'd put the camp beside a stand of lightning rods, just for the show."

"The tall black spines?" asked Tocohl. "I've only seen them from a distance. I admit the show's spectacular, but I side with the captain on this one—I'm not sure I'd want to be that close, either."

"Ah," said the Smith, "but they really *are* lightning rods. That's the beauty of the thing. They are that tall purposefully to catch the lightning they use for cell-building, energy, reproduction. They also channel the lightning's energy to the shorter, younger shoots in the stand; any excess beyond that, they bleed harmlessly into the ground."

In his enthusiasm, he rose from his chair to lean across the table, blind-siding Om im once more. This time was not as threatening from the Bluesippan's point of view, for both of the Sobolli's hands came down flat on the table. All to emphasize the authority of his conclusion...

"On this planet," John the Smith said, "the safest place to be during a thunderstorm is in a grove of lightning rods."

Tocohl inclined her head to the left to acknowledge. John the Smith eased back into his chair, adding, "That's theoretically speaking. Nobody's tried it, you understand, and I certainly wouldn't advise you to experiment."

Feeling it best to acknowledge that as well, Tocohl once again tilted her head left. "Don't worry," she said, "I don't plan to." She reached for her cup of winter-flame, found it empty, set it back down.

"Mine too," said John the Smith. "Refill?" A rumble of thunder drowned out her response but, reacting to the tilt of her head, he gathered both cups and headed for the dispenser.

Most of the other surveyors stood in small knots at various corners of the room, some in highly animated conversation. For the moment, John the Smith was alone at the dispenser, Tocohl said, "Excuse me, Captain," and rose. Motioning Om im to stay put, she strode across to join the Smith.

Quite deliberately, she came up on his left side, "outranking" him. In this matter, she was fully confident she deserved the position. Her spoken Sobolli was not the best, but it was more than adequate to make her point. "A word in your ear, John," she said, taking her cup nonchalantly from him. "High status to a Bluesippan is the reverse of yours. If you continue in this fashion, Om im will consider you a grov-eler of the worst sort, completely beneath contempt."

His upturned face went white. "Are you sure?"

"As sure as I'm standing here," she said. The reference to her high-status position was quite sufficient to reinforce her information.

"I didn't know ... !"

"Neither did your team's chamfer. You're hardly to be blamed for that. It's not your area of expertise."

"What should I do?"

"Approach him from the other side. Start now; you've a lot of damage to your image to repair."

"Thanks, I will."

CHAPTER 10

"Truthfully, *layli-layli*," Timosie Megeve urged, "do you really think the sprookjes murdered Oloitokitok?" Responding to her gesture, he touched the cadaver with obvious reluctance, grasped it by the shoulders, and helped her roll it into a prone position. He rubbed his hands against his thighs. "Isn't it more likely that he just blundered into an Eilo's-kiss or was hit by lightning?"

Layli-layli calulan prodded the body gently. If dealing with her late consort in this fashion bothered her, she was careful not to show it. Her plump hands stroked and probed with professional deftness. She said, "Blundered? Oloitokitok? Not likely. Think, Megeve: If you were a sprookje with no weaponry, but with a knowledge of the wildlife of this world, what would you turn against intruders? I admit only that there is a possibility of murder."

She looked momentarily away from her work to fix him with a firm stare. *"Possibility,"* she said, "is not *probability.*"

Her hands halted suddenly at the base of the neck. Although Oloitokitok had been wearing his 2nd skin, he had closed neither hood nor gloves; it was his face and hands the golden scoffers had scavenged. Here, however, the flesh showed only the effects of bacterial decay.

But *layli-layli calulan* leaned closer, pressed her fingers to the area, frowned slightly.

Megeve followed her gaze but could see nothing to warrant such attention. "What is it?" he asked, at last.

"I don't know," she said, "but I missed it the first time I examined—" Her voice broke off. She frowned a second time and turned to her comunit to address a spate of technical jargon to swift-Kalat.

Within minutes, swift-Kalat appeared at the door to the infirmary, with Alfvaen and the Hellspark's arachne at his heels, all three streaming rivulets of rainwater. *Layli-layli* gave them no greeting nor any chance to dry. Drawing swift-Kalat to the body, she indicated the base of the neck.

Wondering what had so excited the doctor, Megeve watched as swift-Kalat pressed gently at the indicated spot. Megeve turned away, unwilling to observe the ravagement done by the golden scoffers.

"What is it?" demanded Alfvaen impatiently. Trailed by the arachne, she moved forward for a closer look of her own.

"It appears that Oloitokitok was bitten by a sprookje," said swift-Kalat, "a second time, as you were, Alfvaen."

"So you know of nothing else that would make a similar mark?" *layli-layli* inquired.

"Nothing," said swift-Kalat, and *layli-layli calulan* continued, "The mark was made after his death."

"After his death," mused swift-Kalat. "If I theorize from the behavior of the crested sprookje I observed in proximity to the cadaver, I might deduce that the sprookje wished to investigate the changes that had occurred in the alien's metabolism."

"That doesn't account for the swelling," interrupted *layli-layli calulan*.

"Swelling?" Swift-Kalat touched the indicated spot a second time. Then he stepped back, lifting his hands. "My fingers aren't as sensitive as yours, *layli-layli*. I can't feel what you refer to."

"There is something beneath the skin at that point," the doctor explained, "something living." A flash of lightning whitened her face, solarized the scars across her cheek.

Megeve shivered in anger at the sight. *Barbarian*, he thought, then shook himself to relieve the sudden chill.

Layli-layli calulan had no such effect on swift-Kalat, for he merely said, "We have two alternatives. The first, to dissect; the second, to remove the cadaver from stasis to observe the results."

"Observe the results?" *Layli-layli calulan* frowned at the cadaver, then at swift-Kalat.

"I have just completed the dissection of two of the golden scoffers found near the cadaver and placed in stasis two days ago. Of the two, one had no unusual marks of any sort. The second, however, which I saw bitten twice by my own sprookje, now has garbage plants growing on it." His lips compressed. There was a soft chime from his silver bracelets as he reached out to touch *layli-layli's* arm with his fingertips. "I do not intend to cause pain," he said, "merely to convey information I think significant."

Layli-layli ran her palm lightly across his fingers. "I will bear the pain for the sake of the information," she said, then returning to the body, she added quietly, "Let us see."

Megeve, caught between his curiosity and his nausea, realized the *layli-layli* intended to dissect Oloitokitok's body. The sour feeling in the pit of his stomach became a hard knot. Without a word, he turned and left.

There had been a second turnover in the group that surrounded Tocohl. For the moment, only Om im and Rav Kejesli remained. The captain's gray eyes stared past Tocohl to the message board over her right shoulder, and Tocohl twisted in her seat for a look. Someone had scrawled: "Maybe they only talk to plants?" It was signed "Bezymianny." Beneath that, an "anonymous" couplet, in Bluesippan, read:

"I'm sorry I woke ya,
I'm only a sprookje ..."

Tocohl laughed aloud and grinned appreciatively at Om im, who feigned innocence with a complete lack of success. Kejesli scowled.

"No," said Tocohl, "it's nothing untoward. I'll translate the content, but I could never match that rhyme in Sheveschkem. It just isn't possible!"

Even as she translated, Tocohl realized that the few lines in an incomprehensible language could not have been responsible for Kejesli's scowl. Nor did it vanish when she'd finished.

Kejesli shrugged, Sheveschkem-style, and said, "You haven't asked about Oloitokitok, Hellspark. Shouldn't you be investigating his death as well as the sprookjes?"

"Tell me about Oloitokitok," Tocohl said, and Kejesli blinked as if caught completely off guard by the question. Om im raised his head slightly, about to speak, then glanced at his captain and held his tongue.

After a moment, Kejesli murmured, "I don't know. I—never knew him, not really. He was—" He stopped speaking abruptly, his hands worried the edge of the table. He looked away, his face darkening.

When he looked back again at Tocohl, he was angry: angry with himself. "He did his job and he never complained. I can't tell you anything more than that; you'll have to ask someone else."

"Ask Timosie Megeve," suggested Om im, "he and Oloitokitok seemed close. I'll give my views, but you'll have to bear in mind that"—he jerked his thumb back over his shoulder, a modified point that included Kejesli—"they're all crazy!"

Tocohl eyed him solemnly. "You're working in a madhouse," she said, then added to Kejesli, whose scowl had become still more pronounced, "Sometimes the only way to deal with other cultures is to assume they're harmless nuts—because they are, by your culture's standards."

"And you, Hellspark?" said Kejesli sharply.

Tocohl spread her hands grandly. "I am the maddest of all: I *shift* from culture to culture." She inclined her head slightly in expectation of applause.

"Charlatan," said Om im. "You Hellsparks are the wardens. All you do is humor the inmates and keep them from killing each other whenever possible."

"You," Tocohl said, "have an exaggerated esteem of Hellsparks that transcends all reason."

"Hardly that, Ish shan. I once saw a Hellspark drive a person to complete distraction by simply talking to him. Mind you, I understood the language they were speaking, and the content of the conversation gave me not a clue as to how the trick was done. But it was deliberate and we all appreciated it." To Kejesli, he said, "Havernan, remember?"

"I remember," Kejesli said grimly, "that unbelievably rude Katawn customs inspector."

Om im looked surprised. "I didn't think rude, so much as longwinded and boring." He turned back to Tocohl, "In any event, none of us liked him; all of us wished he would go away. It was at that point that the Hellspark breezed through. She had little patience for customs at best—none for the Katawn apparently. She talked to him for some fifteen minutes at most and the next thing we knew he was screaming at us all to get out and never come through his station again."

"I always thought she'd insulted him or blackmailed him in some fashion," Kejesli said.

"No," said Om im, "I assure you the conversation was completely innocuous. So what did she do, Ish shan, or is that a Hellspark state secret?"

Tocohl considered him. It was only a matter of idle curiosity that sparked his interest, but the feel of Kejesli's was something much stronger. How would you drive a Katawn to distraction, she thought. Then she had it.

"Think back, Om im," she said, "try to visualize it. As the Hellspark talked, did she keep walking?"

He obliged by closing his eyes. When he opened them again, he said, "Yes, she did. She picked up this and examined that and walked here and there..."

"Then I can tell you how she did it: by picking up this and examining that and walking here and there... Constantly moving as she spoke, right?"

"Yes," said Kejesli.

"It's simple. A Katawn can't hold a discussion with someone unless he's facing them, across a table or across a customs counter, for example. Or turned to face them"—she demonstrated by turning to address Om im face-to-face—"like this."

She grinned at the deviousness of that other Hellspark. "As long as that Hellspark kept moving the Katawn couldn't address her properly, and *he* had no sense of what was wrong. What sheer frustration that must have been for him!"

"You're right," said Kejesli, with a small sound akin to a gasp. "He kept trying to stop her, to get in front of her."

"Finally," Om im said, "he burst into tears and—as I said—screamed at us all to get out and never darken his customs office again." The small man gave her an almost proprietary look of admiration. "I had no idea, Ish shan, how easily you can manipulate people with language!"

"You do well enough in your own," Tocohl observed, and he arched a gilded brow in pleased acceptance of the compliment. Then he grunted and whipped his arm up sharply. (Watch out,) Maggy snapped simultaneously.

There was little need for the warning: Om im caught Kejesli's wrist against his own with a subdued crack that bespoke considerable force. Glaring at Kejesli, Om im reached for his dagger with his right hand.

Kejesli, totally stunned by the smaller man's reflex action, eased back into his chair. He splayed his hand at his throat. Om im returned the partially drawn dagger to its sheath.

The two continued to eye each other warily.

(Need the arachne?) Maggy asked. It was not as unlikely a query as it seemed; Maggy had already learned to use the arachne to trip Tocohl's opponents in a brawl.

(Thanks, no), Tocohl said, although she continued to eye the Sheveschkemen warily. Aloud she said, "Yes, Captain?"

Kejesli lowered his splayed hand to rub his bruised wrist, glaring at the two of them while he did so. Then he leaned forward once more, this time very slowly. "What are you *really* like, Hellspark?"

The intensity in his manner shocked her; she met it with curiosity of equal intensity. "I don't understand the question."

Still glaring, Kejesli said, "You charge into my quarters like Veschke herself; you kiss that hull-ripping Vyrnwyn's hand and that hull-ripping Vyrnwyn puts on hull-ripping boots!—Now you've got Om im acting like a maniac!"

Om im, now content to settle back and watch Kejesli with equal interest, said to Tocohl, "I told you, Ish shan. *They're* all crazy!" This time his thumb jabbed at his own chest.

"You change," said Kejesli. As he delivered it, the observation was an accusation.

"No," said Tocohl, "I don't. Not in the way I think you mean. You accuse me of changing my personality to suit the culture I'm dealing with?" Yes, from his reaction, that was what he was asking.

"Captain," she said, "what you saw in your quarters was ... the real Tocohl Susumo. I don't change personalities when I switch languages. Think of it as, well, like transposing a melody from key to key. It's still the same melody, right?"

He had stopped scowling, but the intensity of his interest remained. "Go on," he said.

"That's what I do when I switch from language to language: I transpose. That's all I do. I assure you Edge-of-Dark thinks me as flamboyant when I speak Vyrnwyn as you think me when I speak Sheveschkem. Or as Om im thinks me when I speak Bluesippan."

Kejesli looked unconvinced.

"Perhaps," Tocohl said thoughtfully, "it might be of some help to you if I spoke Hellspark?"

"Yes," he said, as if surprised by the suggestion. "It might at that. I've never heard Hellspark spoken; every Hellspark I ever met spoke Sheveschkem to me." The scowl returned briefly. "Or spoke some other language to someone else."

"It is considered the polite thing to do—use the language of the person you're speaking to, if at all possible," Tocohl pointed out.

"I know," Kejesli said curtly. His sweeping gesture disposed of politeness for the moment. "I've heard Hellspark was a manufactured language, like GalLing'. I've never heard it spoken and—yes—I'd like to very much."

"Then you will. First, though, I want to correct a popular misunderstanding. Yes, both GalLing' and Hellspark are artificial languages, but other than that, they bear no resemblance. In fact, they are diametrically opposed in intent. GalLing' was originally composed of all the sounds all the known human languages held in common, so that a speaker of any of the languages at that time could speak GalLing' without an accent. Oh, inflection gives you a clue, so does intonation, word choice, and so forth." She paused to drain her cup of winterflame and set it aside.

"Hellspark," Tocohl went on, "took the opposite route. It was originally composed to incorporate every known possibility of human language, all the sounds of all the various tongues, not to mention such refinements as inflection, tonal changes, proxemics and kinesics, as well."

Kejesli blinked, and Tocohl decided to leave well enough alone. She said, "Simply put, someone who speaks Hellspark can speak any of the known human languages without an accent. Nothing comes as a surprise. Where GalLing' was designed to exclude, Hellspark is inclusive."

Om im said, "Languages change too."

"They do. And every time a new possibility pops up, somebody very quickly coins a handful of new words to incorporate it. The words get flung like candy to the youngest kids, who tease us old-timers with them until we 'catch on.'" She grinned. "You wouldn't believe the word games that go on in a children's Babel."

"You're right," said Om im, "I wouldn't."

Tocohl turned back to Kejesli. "So, Captain Kejesli, what would you like to hear in Hellspark?"

"Veschke's Refusal," he said.

She began in almost a whisper, knowing he would hear her over the echoing rumbles of the storm. Like an incantation, the rhythms of her rising voice drew others from all corners of the common room. Although they did not understand the language, they knew a performance when they saw one. Intent on catching at least the flavor of the original, Tocohl saw them come only hazily. Again and again and again, she bade them "Strike! Strike!" Again and again and again, Veschke refused them coordinates of Sheveschke, and each time she bade them strike, Kejesli jerked in angry agreement. She paused a beat—the room grew utterly silent—

Dropping her voice, she delivered the words once more in a whisper: "Steel or fire, strike! *Strike!*"

A ripping crack of thunder split the air. Tocohl took a deep breath, grinned. Looking up, she said, "Couldn't have been too bad a translation. Thanks for the special effects, Veschke." With a swirl of her moss cloak, she sat down.

Someone had begun to snap his fingers, another clapped, a third stamped his feet in time. Startled, Tocohl looked around her—the first thing she thought was, I'm glad Buntec's not here to see that! The second...

"Veschke's sparks!" she said in GalLing'. "If you think that was good, you ought to hear the original the way Jassin does it!"

Om im said, "That's the best argument I ever heard for learning Sheveschkem."

"That's the best reason I know for learning any other language," Tocohl said. "Well, Captain, did I give you some idea?"

"What?"

Pretty potent stuff, Veschke's Refusal, even in my butchered translation, Tocohl thought. Aloud she said, "Have I given you some idea of the sound of Hellspark?"

Kejesli shook himself visibly. "Yes," he said, "yes. Thank you. I think even Jassin would have approved."

"That's high praise indeed! I cheated a bit here and there, using a word that wasn't exact but had the better sound. In translating something like that, accuracy in feel is more important than accuracy of phrase. I could give you something prosaic if you wish, handy phrases for the tourist, for example."

He stared at her, as if afraid she might conjure up typhoons with a "Where's the bathroom." "No," he said, "no thank you. My curiosity is more than satisfied."

"Fine, then we're back to the subject of the sprookjes."

Maggy pinged urgently for her attention. Tocohl thumbed her ear for silence, realized that only Kejesli would recognize the gesture, and said, "Just a moment."

(Yes, Maggy?)

Maggy's only reply was the scene flashed onto Tocohl's spectacles. Tocohl watched and listened, then whistled. "Captain? There's trouble in the infirmary. I think we'd better get there right away."

Feeling that the captain would wish to deal with the situation with as few complications as possible, Tocohl had spoken in Sheveschkem. Kejesli rose, this time answering in the same tongue, "Lead, I sail with your sparks."

She had him halfway across the compound, splattered in mud and drenched in rain, before she recognized that too as a line from the Epic of Veschke.

Om im, still at her right hand, reacted to her urgency by foregoing the politeness of a knock or a chime. He burst through the door to the infirmary, Tocohl and Kejesli at his heels. After that Tocohl had no time to consider poetry.

"Trouble" was the greatest of understatements: the wash of emotion within was almost physical.

Across the body of what must have once been Oloitokitok, Ruurd van Zoveel, gripping the edge of the table so fiercely that his veins stood out like rope, bellowed at Alfvaen and *layli-layli calulan*. Answering rage filled both their faces. Only swift-Kalat, seeming more concerned than angry, stepped forward to soothe the Zoveelian.

Alfvaen would not risk him. Taking two steps forward to swift-Kalat's one, she interposed herself between the two. "This-s is your choice, then! Look on me, child of fools!" Her arm snapped sharply across her chest in challenge. The fierce green glare she fixed on van Zoveel brought the enormous man to bay.

Maggy's arachne scuttled from beneath the table to position itself for a better view of the two. Behind Tocohl, Kejesli began, "What's all this bellowing? What's the hull-ripping matter?" At that point, he must have registered Alfvaen's threatening stance, for his voice dropped to a whisper in Tocohl's ear, "Tocohl—"

"Not now," she snapped. Across the room *layli-layli calulan*, never taking her dark eyes from van Zoveel's face, twisted the bluestone ring from her left index finger and slapped it down beside Oloitokitok's body. Tocohl heard a muted exclamation of horror from Om im.

Alfvaen would hold her pose until van Zoveel returned her challenge, but *layli-layli calulan* reached for the second ring, began to twist it off.

With a sharp intake of breath, Tocohl charged across the room. Vaulting table and body, she came down close enough to startle *layli-layli calulan* into a moment's pause. It was enough to let her press on. She grasped the shaman's wrists, attempting to part the hands with the ring still on her finger and praying inwardly that Veschke's blessings covered this. In Yn, she demanded, "Would you have it go astray?"

The plump woman did not struggle, she merely went back to what she had been doing before Tocohl's intervention.

"*Layli-layli calulan!*" said Tocohl. "You do not know his true name! Will you risk the death of one of these others, or your own?"

"You lie," said *layli-layli*, but her arms stilled in Tocohl's grasp, their motion uncompleted. Her black eyes burned into Tocohl's.

Tocohl held the gaze as she held *layli-layli's* wrists, summoning words. "I do not lie. *Think!* 'Van Zoveel' simply refers to his planet of origin, and 'Ruurd' is the commonest of male names on that world. Do you know his true name?"

The burning gaze dropped from Tocohl's face. *Layli-layli calulan* reached for the ring she had removed, and Tocohl released her wrists. The shaman's smoldering anger appeared to subside as she slid the bluestone ring back on her finger, but she said, "He's left his gods behind him, nor could they protect him if I knew his true name."

With that, she turned her back, consigning the group to non-existence.

Relief shivered along Tocohl's spine. When she rounded the table once more, this time to deal with the lesser problem of Alfvaen, she moved easily, with a ghost of a smile. Her incomprehensible exchange with *layli-layli calulan* had distracted the others enough to lessen their tension as well. Van Zoveel had stopped his bellowing to treat her to a puzzled look. Using that for a hook, she beckoned him with a conspiratorial jerk of the head, as if she might explain if he came closer. When he took the step, she caught him by the arm and tucked him away safely behind her, well beyond dueling range even if he knew the proper responses.

Om im slid silently into the space left vacant by van Zoveel. He said, "I am the fool, if Ruurd and Alfvaen will not clasp hands and drink together." It was in GalLing', but it was perfectly acceptable by Alfvaen's standards.

Maggy's arachne pricked its way closer and said politely, "May I watch, Alfvaen, Om im? I have never seen a real duel."

Still stiffly posed, Alfvaen said over her forearm. "I don't want to fight you, Om im. I was only trying to protect swift-Kalat." It was a break in the ritual, and a welcome one to both Tocohl and Om im.

"Duel?" said van Zoveel, taking a step forward to stare at the two of them in utter amazement. He spun on Tocohl, his ribbons fluttering nervously, "Are they crazy? Tocohl? I don't follow this one."

"You threatened swift-Kalat, Alfvaen challenged you, Om im appointed himself your champion," Tocohl said, summing it all up as briefly as possible. In Bluesippan she added, "Fool is right, Om im."

Om im answered in the same tongue, "I offered my blade; you accepted. Get her to fight on my terms and we'll both be fine."

Instead, Tocohl glanced at van Zoveel. "—Oh, if he's to save your life, van Zoveel, he *would* like to know just what this is all about."

For the first time, Tocohl saw fear in the Zoveelian's eyes. "I was angry," he said; with effort he kept his voice low and level, "I only spoke words, Tocohl. I have no actions to perform."

Tocohl raised her voice, "Alfvaen? He says he didn't mean it: he never intended harm. He'll clasp hands and drink with you and swift-Kalat"—she glared at van Zoveel—"right?"

"Yes, of course," he said, "with both of you, and Om im, and"—he glanced in *layli-layli calulan's* direction, set his features stubbornly—"with Alfvaen and swift-Kalat and Om im," he finished.

Alfvaen said, "And I with all of you." She lowered her arm. "No duel," she said firmly to Om im, who said, "Glad to hear it," and lowered his arm as well. Alfvaen smiled wanly and added, "Not even for Maggy's education."

"That's settled then," said Tocohl. "Sorry, Maggy."

"Maybe some other time?" The arachne took a hopeful step forward to tilt toward the two reconciled opponents. Alfvaen giggled.

Kejesli cleared his throat. "I want an explanation for this kind of behavior. You first, van Zoveel."

"They," van Zoveel began, and his gaze slipped away uneasily. He began again, "They wanted to cut up the body for no—" This time he stopped completely, and with a supplicatory gesture at Tocohl, he said, "She doesn't *care*. She never did."

Kejesli frowned but relinquished the floor once more to Tocohl who, understanding his anger at last, said quietly, "How much Yn do you understand, Ruurd?"

If the question surprised him, it also gave him a chance to collect himself. "I understood the words, but not the content, of what the two of you said before. I speak the female dialect but I know very little of the male." His palm brushed his sideburns. "Oloitokitok was teaching me ..." The hand came away abruptly, fell to his side.

Tocohl crossed the room to where *layli-layli calulan* stood, facing the wall, her koli thread flickering between her hands and her back as expressive of her anger as her threats had been. Placing an arm gently about the smaller woman's shoulders, Tocohl urged softly, in Yn, "Tell him: tell him who Oloitokitok was." She bent to look into the shaman's dark eyes. "He cared about Oloitokitok, too—that's why he's so upset. He thinks that you intend to deny Oloitokitok an afterlife."

The koli thread stopped its flicker, and *layli-layli* looked up skeptically. Tocohl said, "Yes, by his culture's standards: bad enough the golden scoffers damaged the body, but that you would ... ! Only someone who hated Oloitokitok would injure his chances further. Van Zoveel's gods only accept the beautiful, the *whole*, into their paradise."

"Is such cruelty possible?"

"Some gods are worse than others."

Layli-layli turned to fix the skeptical gaze on Ruurd van Zoveel. She said, defiantly, "Oloitokitok was my mate and my friend. How is it that you care, and yet you refuse us the right to learn the knots of his life?"

As Tocohl had expected, *layli-layli calulan* had used the pronoun meaning "related-to."

Van Zoveel not only heard the distinction but understood its significance. Deep sorrow lit his eyes; he turned his palms up and knelt. "Forgive me, *layli-layli calulan*, for not understanding the depth of your feelings."

"On my world, to—mutilate the remains of someone after death is the height of cruelty. As I listen to you now, I realize that your dream is strong enough to give meaning to your acts, no matter how they might have seemed to me in my ignorance." His manner was pure Zoveelian but his words were Yn; his contrition was equally comprehensible in either.

Maggy made a querying noise for Tocohl's ear only. Tocohl said, (He's so surprised she speaks of Oloitokitok as a person and not a piece of property he's willing to believe his gods will accept the impression Oloitokitok made on *layli-layli calulan* as evidence of beauty and let him into paradise.)

(I don't think that helps much,) Maggy said.

(I'll try to do better later. Meanwhile, just accept that *Homo sapiens* can get pretty weird.)

(I don't know what *normal* is for *Homo sapiens*,) Maggy said, with just the right touch of emphasis to make the observation a complaint.

Layli-layli calulan breathed deeply, and the bright pink drained slowly from her scars. Her face softened. Two steps brought her before van Zoveel who, though kneeling, was now of a height with her. She touched the heel of her hand to his forehead, then laid her hands gently in his. "We were both mistaken," she said in GalLing'. "Will you accept my apology as well?"

"Of course," Van Zoveel said earnestly, without hesitation, and *layli-layli* clasped his hands to draw him to his feet.

"Well," said Tocohl, "the storm has passed. If you'll excuse me, I'll go outside and see if I can find a sprookje or two." And before anyone could reply, she crossed the room and stepped into the clear, sharp air, still crackling with ozone, beneath a sky streaked with sunlight.

The sodden pennants that declared the shaman within slapped at the infirmary wall in the gusting wind; the sound made Tocohl jump. She shook her head, half to clear it, half to wonder at the extravagance of emotion Flashfever drew from them all—suddenly aware of an ache across her shoulders.

With what seemed extraordinary effort, she unclenched her hands. The tansy scent of bruised foliage filled the air about her as the moss cloak peeled moistly from her palms. Tocohl inhaled deeply, glad of a familiar scent to soften the sharp tang of Flashfever's air.

Maggy pinged softly, almost inaudibly.

(I'll be fine, Maggy,) she said, (give me a moment. Go talk to Alfvaen.)

A walk would ease her muscles of their tension-induced stiffness. She was down the infirmary steps and five strides into the compound's courtyard before she realized, from the soft squish of mud beside her, that Om im was still at her side. His tactful silence was the most likely cause of Maggy's softened ping.

Tocohl signed her appreciation and began a Methven calming, matching her stride to the rhythm of the ritual. Slowly she felt her panic fade. When the last vestiges of fear were gone, she found herself at the perimeter of the courtyard, looking out into the brilliant expanse of flashgrass. There she stopped. The Methven ritual, she noted with interest, seemed also to have eased her storm nerves. *Layli-layli calulan* was right about the ionization effect. Certainly she had been feeling it. Nobody in her right mind would have interfered...

Clicking her tongue at her own behavior, she turned to Om im and grinned wryly. "Still with me?" she asked.

He made the deepest, most flamboyant bow she had yet seen, came up grinning with relief. "I was about to ask you that same question," he said. "You pile risk on risk, Ish shan."

"Who accepted Alfvaen's challenge?"

In answer, he cocked his head and clapped a palm proudly to his chest. "That was only to distract her from poor old Ruurd. I was afraid he might know the ritual too and use it simply because that was the appropriate response, verbally speaking."

When she glanced at him in surprise, he gave her the Bluesippan thumbs-up yes. "I've seen him in an analogous situation. A rote inquiry in a little back street bar led him into a rote response that nearly got his head knocked off."

Tocohl laughed. She could think of any number of possibilities that could have led to the situation. Sobering, she said, "It's not likely that van Zoveel would have taken up Alfvaen's challenge though, *especially* as a rote response. He was so angry he was having trouble remembering his GalLing'—every third bellow was in Zoveelian and even that wasn't what I'd call articulate."

"It was *less* likely that Alfvaen would take me up on my offer. I've worked with her off and on for nearly twenty years total. I've seen her challenge more than once, but I've never seen her go through with it."

"She needs the proper responses," Tocohl said, "which *you* provided."

"I'm not from her culture: I don't know any better. She was looking for an excuse to break it off."

"How do you figure you rate if van Zoveel wouldn't?"

He chuckled. "Have you taken a good look at me lately, Ish shan? At my height, I'm visibly not Siveyn."

Puzzled, Tocohl eyed him askance.

His chuckle turned to a laugh. "No, no, Ish shan. You're looking with the wrong eye. Don't look at me in Bluesippan. Look at me in *Siveyn*."

She did her best to comply to his instructions—and saw precisely what he had intended her to see. Her laugh joined his.

Of *course* Alfvaen couldn't have gone through with the duel. Who in her right mind would think some alien midget an honorable opponent? Not Alfvaen—*especially* not Alfvaen, given her romantic bent. Van Zoveel, on the other hand, would not have been so lucky. Om im was right, there. Slipping back into Bluesippan, she turned up her thumbs to tell him so.

"You wouldn't have had that protection either, Ish shan," he added. He turned his face up and closed his eyes. "Ah, sun!" he said fervently. "You'll notice the rest of the team is beginning to turn out. You'll get your sprookjes soon."

"About time," Tocohl said.

He pointed to the perimeter fence at the opposite end of the compound where the flashwood crowded close, dripping water and reflected light. "They usually come out of the flashwood just about there."

Taking the pointed finger for an invitation, Tocohl started back across the compound.

"Risk upon risk," Om im said again as he fell in beside her. "The least I could do was handle Alfvaen. My blade was no help against *layli-layli calulan*. When she started to remove that second ring of hers..."

"Am I to understand you *credit* those bar stories about the Yn shaman's Death Curse?"

He stopped in his tracks, gave her a mocking look. "What, a cosmopolitan fellow like me believe bar stories? Let's be reasonable," he said. His face sobered and so did his tone. "I've seen *layli-layli calulan's* ability to speed the healing process with her touch and her rituals. What she can do for good, I have no doubt she can do for ill as well."

When she made no response, he went on, "At any rate, I'm in good company. I saw your face when you attempted to stop her from removing that second ring. I warned you about rash acts, Ish shan, but I had no idea how rash your acts could get!"

(I'll be fine, Maggy,) Tocohl said, (give me a moment. Go talk to Alfvaen.)

To judge from the readings Maggy was getting from the 2nd skin, Tocohl needed silence for a Methven ritual of calm. As Om im did not seem to distract Tocohl, Maggy felt no need to warn him to silence, so she headed the arachne back to Alfvaen.

She thought she understood most of what had transpired. It had taken a lot of file-searching though. The material on Yn shamans was purely non-experiential but there was a lot of it, especially what Tocohl tagged "bar stories." That would ordinarily have put it in the category of fiction but Maggy was still unsure of the differences between fiction and fact, despite Tocohl's attempted explanation. Listed as fact, she had several scientific papers on the shaman's ability to help or hinder another creature's bodily functions, which seemed to give credibility to several of the bar stories. She continued to search and compare, while she watched them and recorded everything. She was not about to miss a clue to the Yn shaman.

Layli-layli calulan was speaking to Kejesli: "Captain, I offer myself for disciplinary action. The fault was entirely mine. Ruurd van Zoveel has every right to ask for compensation."

Kejesli gave her what Maggy tentatively interpreted as a bewildered look. Maggy hoped *layli-layli* would explain, but van Zoveel gave her no chance. "Oh, no!" he said. "That's not necessary, *layli-layli*. We had a misunderstanding, that's all!"

If Maggy's information about the curses was fact, it had been a very dangerous misunderstanding.

"All right," said *layli-layli calulan*. (Except to note that she was no longer angry, Maggy was unable to categorize the shaman's expression.) She hesitated, then said, in the very gentle tone with which Maggy had heard parents address injured children, "Then swift-Kalat and I may return to our task?"

Van Zoveel opened his mouth to speak but nothing came out. He tried a second time. Maggy had to enhance his reply to hear it. "Yes," he said.

"Then you would be less distressed if you did not stay," *layli-layli calulan* told him, again in her very gentle tone.

"Yes," said van Zoveel. "I'll be outside. I'd better explain to Timosie, anyway—he was also very concerned."

That sent Maggy on another file search. She knew, from Tocohl's explanation to *layli-layli calulan*, why van Zoveel had been so angry. But Timosie Megeve was Maldeneantine, so she wanted to see if the same explanation applied.

Alfvaen leaned suddenly back against one of the infirmary beds. She looked very much like she had when Tocohl had asked Maggy to find a real doctor for her. Maggy wasn't sure if *layli-layli calulan* was to be considered a real doctor in Tocohl's use of the term but Maggy had enough points of congruence to assume a similar situation.

She sent the arachne a few steps closer to Alfvaen and said through its vocoder, "Psst, Alfvaen."

Alfvaen peered down at the arachne. "What is-s it, Maggy?"

Yes, she was having the same trouble focusing, Maggy saw, and the same speech difficulty. That was sufficient confirmation to act on.

On the theory that speaking of infirmities was to be done quietly, Maggy kept the vocoder low. "Perhaps you are in need of your medication, Alfvaen. Your speech has slurred and—"

"You're right. I am." Alfvaen drew the pill box from her pouch. Once again she had difficulty opening it, but Maggy couldn't help her as Tocohl had. The arachne was less adept at fine control than Alfvaen was at the moment. At last, Alfvaen managed to open the box; she took her pill. "Thank you, Maggy," she whispered, "I appreciate it. The worst part about Cana's disease is that your judgment gets bad just when you need it the most."

That seemed to call for a response, so Maggy said, "I think I understand."

During their exchange, van Zoveel had left. Now *layli-layli* bent swiftly to her task.

Alfvaen peered down again, then reached for the arachne and set it on the bed beside her, where the lens had an unobstructed view of the procedure.

Making a score of delicate incisions at the nape of Oloitokitok's neck, *layli-layli calulan* extracted samples of the tissue. These she inserted into—Maggy angled the arachne slightly—a machine which Maggy tentatively identified as a diagnostic of some sort.

While she waited, *layli-layli calulan* silently knotted and reknotted her koli thread. It served a purpose similar to that of the Methven ritual for calm, and Maggy noted with approval that the readings from Tocohl's 2nd skin were dropping to normal.

The machine chimed and issued a neatly racked series of slides. *Layli-layli calulan* pulled all the knots from her koli thread, wrapped it several times about her right wrist, then picked up the rack of slides. These she brought to Alfvaen.

Maggy projected that she intended to give them to Alfvaen for some reason but instead *layli-layli calulan* placed the rack carefully on the bed beside the arachne. Then she touched Alfvaen's chin to examine her eyes. "I believe you are in need of medication," she said, confirming Maggy's private approach to the suggestion.

"Yes," said Alfvaen, "I just took care of it. Maggy reminded me."

Layli-layli calulan turned her gaze on the arachne. "Thank you, *maggy-maggy*," she said.

"You're welcome," Maggy told her through the arachne's vocoder since she too seemed more comfortable addressing a discrete entity, "I am glad to have your confirmation."

Turning to meet Alfvaen's eyes once more, *layli-layli calulan* extended a hand to indicate the rack of slides. "Choose for me, please," she said.

From across the room, Kejesli said, "*Layli-layli calulan*, Alfvaen has Cana's di—"

The shaman ignored him. "Choose for me," she said again.

Kejesli made a noise that Maggy stored for later reference, while Alfvaen brushed her hand lightly across the edges of the slides, her face intent. Maggy focused the arachne's lens tightly on Alfvaen's face and hands, in the hope that she might record Alfvaen's serendipity at work.

"Try that one," Alfvaen said, indicating a slide. Maggy reran her tape twice; whatever Alfvaen had done, it wasn't on the record.

Swift-Kalat came forward to accept the slide from *layli-layli's* hand. He strode to the microscope, inserted it. Alfvaen picked up the arachne to follow him, holding it carefully before her as if the arachne were very delicate.

Layli-layli calulan and Kejesli joined them to watch without comment as swift-Kalat keyed the computer for display.

Images, some stored, some current, played across the screen as swift-Kalat examined and fined his examination with the use of various light sources and filters. At last the screen held a single image.

"Yes," he said, "if we were to leave the body out of stasis, these would become garbage plants."

"And what's the significance of that?" asked Kejesli, as if the question had been drawn from him by force.

Swift-Kalat sighed. "I don't know. All I can say is that, of all the dead creatures we picked up, only that"—he gestured at Oloitokitok's body—"and the golden scoffer I dissected the same day are growing garbage plants. They were both bitten by sprookjes. If the other golden scoffers have no sprookje bites and no garbage plants, then I would theorize that the sprookjes were responsible for the garbage plants."

"And what would be the significance of *that?*"

It was *layli-layli calulan* who answered: "If the sprookjes are responsible for the garbage plants, they may also have been responsible for Oloitokitok's death."

CHAPTER 11

"You'll see sprookjes any minute," Hitoshi Dan assured Tocohl, indicating with a wide-flung palm the same area of the perimeter fence Om im had.

His arrival precluded any further discussion of her rash acts but Tocohl knew this was only temporary; blade service gave Om im Chadeayne not only the right but the duty to reproach her for a risk such as she'd taken. Maggy would no doubt add a few words on the subject, as well. On her own part, Maggy minded redundancy not in the slightest. For the moment, Tocohl had a respite from both.

Respite from Flashfever's storms brought other surveyors out in number—how was it Om im had phrased it?—to dry their feathers. Tocohl watched as they formed small celebratory clusters, each a hodge-podge of style and manner. In all, the survey team was as diverse a group as she'd seen anywhere, no two from the same culture and most in worlds' motley.

"Yo, Hellspark!" came Buntec's bellow from across the compound. Tocohl turned, to see Buntec grab Edge-of-Dark by the hand and drag her along. The two arrived breathless with excitement, but before Tocohl could learn the reason behind it, Om im nudged her. "Sprookjes," he said.

Forgetting Buntec and Edge-of-Dark, Tocohl turned to stare into the brilliance of the flashwood. A handful of sprookjes, disturbingly dark amid the sparkle, pushed through the chattering, tinkling foliage. One by one, they squirmed cautiously through the great circles of barbed wire.

As each emerged and paused to preen the mud from its plumage, Om im named them, each in turn: "Bezymianny's sprookje, John the Smith's, Captain Kejesli's, Edge-of-Dark's, Hitoshi Dan's…"

He was quickly proven accurate. Those he had called Hitoshi Dan's and Edge-of-Dark's sprookjes made straight for Hitoshi Dan and Edge-of-Dark. The others passed on as if the little group of humans were invisible.

In turn, Om im ignored the sprookjes to pay court to Edge-of-Dark with a formal greeting.

Edge-of-Dark flushed pink from her hairline to the tops of her boots. "We're old friends, Om im! *You* don't have to do that!" The protest was echoed by the sprookje Om im had designated hers.

Casting a frown at the creature, she stiffened and went on, "We've got something important ..." So did the sprookje. Edge-of-Dark's frown turned to an open scowl and she jabbed both forefingers at the sprookje. "I can't stand talking when that thing is around! You tell them, Buntec."

"Botanic art," said Buntec, and looked furtively around her, to see if the other sprookje would mimic her. When it didn't, she went on to explain, in glowing terms, Edge-of-Dark's flower art.

Tocohl listened with interest but she kept her eye on the sprookjes. They were beautiful indeed, their sleek feathers beaded with drops of water that they shook away in tiny discrete spatters, rippling first one set of muscles, then another. Their control was so remarkable that Tocohl wondered if each feather might be moved separately. Their gold eyes were intent upon the humans, but neither gave any indication of so much as hearing Buntec.

Hitoshi Dan did, his eyes sparkled with excitement. His first few words proved that Om im had correctly identified the second sprookje. "If that's so," Hitoshi Dan said—and the sprookje's pace-keeping echo did nothing to dampen his enthusiasm—"how about land-scaping? That's a botanic art too! You use whole plants rather than cuttings and your arrangement is ... an artistically planned environment." His circled arms implied base camp in its entirety. "Better than mud," he and the sprookje said.

In concert, the two went on to explain landscaping at length. Buntec and Edge-of-Dark, neither of whom it seemed had encountered this art form, listened to their combined voices with growing wonder.

More sprookjes made their way through the barbed wire. Two more—Tocohl supposed them to be Om im's and Buntec's—joined the little group, as intent as the first and, for the moment, as silent as Buntec's.

Tocohl looked again from Buntec's sprookje to Hitoshi Dan's. There were subtle differences in marking. On the feathers of one the brocade held more gold than brown, on the feathers of the other the loops and scallops were deeper, more defined. Om im had a sharper eye than she, to be able to distinguish them at a glance, and at that distance—or his pattern recognition was better.

"I'm no expert on the subject," Hitoshi Dan finished, "but somebody on the team must know something about it—landscaping is an art common to many worlds."

"Hey!" said Om im sharply, and something behind Tocohl startled her forward by saying "Hey!" just as sharply and just as unexpectedly.

Tocohl spun at the warning. Her cloak swept a wide arc, caught suddenly as if snagged. Behind her, a startled sprookje let the edge of the moss cloak jerk from its fingers and backed hastily away.

(Sorry,) Maggy said, (your cloak's in the way. I didn't see it coming.)

"Speaking of botanic art," Om im continued, in a lighter tone, one of relief, "doesn't your cloak qualify?" He set his face, determined not to let the echo bother him, and waved off his echoing sprookje as it approached Tocohl from the other side. "That's the most interest they've shown in anything."

It was true, both sprookjes edged toward her and the other two showed signs of developing the same tendency. Keeping a wary eye on them, Tocohl held out her hand. "Lend me your knife, Om im."

There was a gasp of objection from Hitoshi Dan that sounded still more horrified in the beaked mouth of his sprookje. "Hellspark!" said Buntec. "I thought you, of all people—"

Om im laid the hilt of his knife in Tocohl's outstretched palm.

Buntec repeated, "You of all people," this time in quite a different tone. "Mighta known," she muttered at her sprookje, who agreed in an identical mutter, its cheek feathers puffing.

Tocohl lifted the edge of her cloak and slipped the knife through it, cutting four pieces. She flipped the knife first blade up, then blade down, and returned it to Om im with a generous bow.

That done, she held out the first bit of cloak to the sprookje she'd startled, Hitoshi Dan's. First in GalLing' and then Hitoshi Dan's language, she told the sprookje, "My name is Tocohl Susumo. Please accept this with my compliments."

The sprookje said nothing, to her great disappointment, but she continued to hold the bit of moss cloak extending from between her fingertips, so that the creature might touch it without touching her.

The puffed feathers along the sprookje's cheeks slowly deflated and the creature stepped cautiously forward to examine, then snatch, the piece of moss.

Tocohl watched as it stared (happily?) at its prize, then she turned to the second sprookje and repeated the process in Bluesippan. As before, the sprookje said nothing but accepted the tuft of moss from her fingers. Tocohl sighed and went doggedly on, in Vyrnwyn, in Jannisetti. Each time she met with the same result: a silent but accepting sprookje.

"They know it's a gift!" said Om im, voicing it for the rest. His sprookje echoed the words, giving Tocohl the impression that it too spoke for its companions. Om im gave the creature a sharp look but went on, "I don't know if that feather-puffing is sprookje-surprise or sprookje-pleasure, but—look!—they're each keeping the piece you gave them!" Then, with something like satisfaction in his voice, he added, "If they aren't intelligent, my blade has no edge!"

"I can vouch for the blade," said Tocohl. "You tried an exchange of gifts once before..."

"We did," said Hitoshi Dan (and sprookje), "and they ignored what we offered. Maybe they didn't recognize what we gave them."

"Perhaps they didn't," Tocohl agreed. To Buntec and Edge-of-Dark she added, "Now we have some new avenues to explore."

Buntec grinned at the Vyrnwyn. "Move ass, Edge-of-Dark," she said, "Let's get to it." Her sprookje repeated Buntec's command with the same emphasis; this time Buntec laughed. As she dragged Edge-of-Dark away, their sprookjes, tufts of moss still clutched in their hands, followed—one still echoing Buntec's laughter.

In the hour that followed, Tocohl, accompanied by Om im, van Zoveel, and their sprookjes, met and introduced herself to each of the sprookjes that came into the camp, with no success in any sense. Ruurd van Zoveel gave her a demonstration of his own sprookje's ability to mimic by running through twelve different languages. The sprookje had, without accent (or rather, with the *same* accent—that dictated by the sprookje's beaklike mouth), repeated every single one accurately. Yet when Tocohl tried the same thing the sprookje remained silent.

Most of the surveyors envied the silence, she discovered. Although Hitoshi Dan and swift-Kalat would speak in the presence of a repeating sprookje, the others would not except in necessity: the result was irritating as well as frustrating. Flashfever's irritation index was singularly high in more ways than one, Tocohl thought, as frustrated by the sprookjes' silence as the others were by their volubility.

Yet, as she sat in the misty sunlight and gazed into the flashwood, she felt the world had more than sufficient beauty to compensate for the trouble it caused.

Ruurd van Zoveel, Om im, and their respective sprookjes kept silent company beside her. Edge-of-Dark had vanished into the flashwood to pick leaves and flowers for a demonstration for the sprookjes, and Hitoshi Dan had appointed himself a delegation of one to find a surveyor who knew something about landscaping, so far without any luck.

She turned her attention back to the sprookjes, who watched their humans with proprietary interest, as if waiting for an opportunity to speak. Their feathers rippled with the intensity of their concentration.

Why do they never volunteer a word? Tocohl wondered. Maggy volunteers information to the point of distraction. She smiled to herself at the thought. New definition of sapient: that which gives unsought advice.

It struck her that Maggy had been uncharacteristically quiet. (What's swift-Kalat up to, Maggy?) she subvocalized.

(He is examining the golden scoffers found dead near Oloitokitok's body for sprookje bites and garbage plants.)

(What's a garbage plant?)

Maggy flashed a brief image on Tocohl's spectacles of a refuse heap. Long, silvery-gray filaments, like algae or seaweed, grew from it. (This,) she said, (swift-Kalat says to tell you,) and here the voice shifted to that of swift-Kalat himself, ("The common name is *garbage plant* because we have only found them growing on our refuse. Until Oloitokitok's death, that is. They take several components poisonous to the indigenous wildlife and break them down, rendering them harmless.")

There was a brief pause — Maggy was evidently putting together several bits of conversation rather than relaying one as it happened — then swift-Kalat's voice continued: ("So, if there are no sprookje bites, there are no garbage plants. If there are sprookje bites, as on Oloitokitok's body and on two of the golden scoffers, there *are* garbage plants. We may be able to verify that with a simple experiment. We give the sprookjes access to the remaining golden scoffers and we observe.")

This last remark was evidently a simultaneous transmission, for Alfvaen's wave caught Tocohl's eye, and Tocohl looked across the compound to see Alfvaen emerge from swift-Kalat's cabin. She placed a small table at the foot of the steps, then darted back up to sweep the membrane aside for swift-Kalat. His hands were full of stacked boxes which he carried down the steps to place on the table. Maggy's arachne squatted on the top step, ready and waiting to observe.

Alfvaen crossed to Tocohl who said, by way of greeting, "I know. Maggy's been keeping me posted."

"Now, if you could only teach her to scratch backs ..." said Alfvaen, grinning.

"Do you want your back scratched?" asked Maggy, from the hand-held on Alfvaen's belt. "I will send the arachne if you wish."

"Oh, no!" said Alfvaen, somewhat embarrassed. "My arm's not broken, Maggy. I was just making a joke." She canted an arm behind her and scratched self-consciously.

"I don't understand jokes very well," said Maggy, sounding apologetic. "Should I laugh?"

Tocohl cocked her head to one side and, after consideration, said, "No. Not now—the laughter has to come at a specific time to have the correct effect."

"Okay. Sorry, Alfvaen. I hope I will do better next time."

"No need for an apology, Maggy." Alfvaen looked around for something to smile at reassuringly, and settled for Tocohl's spectacles. Tocohl thought that an admirable choice.

Maggy said in her ear, (Will you explain later, please?)

(Yes,) said Tocohl. She watched inquiringly as Alfvaen reached again, apparently involuntarily, to scratch at her back.

Seeing the look, Alfvaen said, "It was seeing all those garbage plants, even though the ones on Oloitokitok hadn't broken through the skin yet—the whole idea makes me feel crawly all over."

Tocohl spread her hands in sympathy.

"Garbage plants?" said Om im and sprookje, and Tocohl let Alfvaen explain.

"Hey!" said Timosie Megeve. "What are you doing?"

Buntec looked up, unabashed, from the innards of the largest daisy-clipper, a smear of graphite across her face.

"I thought I'd give the Hellspark our grand tour, as long as I'm going out to look for evidence of grafting. You know as well as I do we've been up to our asses in equipment failures—no, no!—no reflection on you! I just thought I'd check things out beforehand as a precaution. Why take chances?" She closed the service panel with a snap, wiped her hands and—in response to Megeve's pointing finger—her face as well.

"Why the big one?" the Maldeneantine asked.

"Because I haven't flown the big one for weeks, and I want to give the flashgrass a thrill. Why *not* the big one? That's a gorgeous machine, you gotta admit." She patted it affectionately on the prow.

"True," said Megeve, "but I do wish you'd keep your fingers out of it … after all, that is supposed to be my job."

"I'll try," said Buntec seriously, "but it's not gonna be easy." She gave a wistful glance at the daisy-clipper and said, "See you later—I'm off to find the Hellspark before Flashfever comes up with another gully-washer."

She left him with a grin at his bewildered look and trotted happily back to the compound, where she found Tocohl trying once again to get Om im's sprookje to respond to Bluesippan—to no avail.

"How's about checking out the wild ones, Tocohl? I'm just about to go graft-hunting in some of the places we've seen the high-class sprookjes—you know, with the crests?" Her hand swept above her head in graphic explanation.

"It's worth a try," said Tocohl. "I don't seem to be having much luck here."

"Speaking of luck," said Buntec, "want to come, Alfvaen? You're a whole lot better at catching wild geese than I am."

"Jaef?" Alfvaen used swift-Kalat's soft-name as a full and complete query.

"Go with them," swift-Kalat told her, "I'll find someone else to hold the camera."

The arachne's legs telescoped to the fullest extent of their length, much as if Maggy wanted to make herself more noticeable. "I'll help you, swift-Kalat, if you like," said the voice from the vocoder.

He hesitated, considering the spidery mobile.

Maggy said, "I'll save everything."

Tocohl laughed. "She means that. She won't dump any data until you've told her to specifically, if that's what's worrying you." Snapping her wrist to give ring to her words, Tocohl added, "Her 'eye' is better than any camera, not only because it sees the full 360 degrees, but because she makes good choices as a rule. The fuller the information you give her, the better the choices. Just tell her what you want taped and why. At your leisure you can sort through what footage you wish to keep and she can transfer that to the survey computer."

"All right," said swift-Kalat to Tocohl. Then he appeared to think better of it and turned to the arachne, "Yes, Maggy. I'd appreciate the help."

"That's settled," said Buntec to Alfvaen, "you'll come?"

"Of course. If there's room."

"The more the merrier. Timosie's bugged that I want to use the big daisy-clipper. He'll feel better if I bring a crowd. Ruurd?"

"Thank you, but no," said van Zoveel, "not when Buntec's piloting."

"You don't know good when you see it, Ruurd," Om im and sprookje said. "Count me in, Tocohl." He rose to his feet and the sprookje followed suit.

Tocohl glanced from one to the other. "How do the sprookjes feel about the daisy-clippers?"

Om im and sprookje said, "Timosie shoos them away from 'his' equipment. He figures it's too dangerous to chance."

With a broad grin, Buntec said to the sprookje, "I know just how you feel; I got shooed away, too." To the humans, she said cheerfully, "Let's move — Dyxte will keep us posted on the weather, but we already know there's going to be another thunderstorm anytime now — there always *is*."

Leaving Ruurd and Maggy's arachne behind to keep swift-Kalat company, the five of them — Tocohl counted the sprookje — walked to the main gate of the compound. Just beyond it lay the makeshift hangar with its population of daisy-clippers, large and small. Beneath her feet, the flashgrass, which anchored itself with something like roots, was springy and glistening. After the mud of the compound, Tocohl delighted in the sensation.

Soon the flashgrass reached their knees and Tocohl lifted her cloak to prevent its being caught on the flickering wiry strands.

Timosie Megeve came around the largest daisy-clipper, shouted, and clapped his hands at a sprookje that stood before it. The sprookje moved off a short distance but no farther. Megeve appeared to find the distance acceptable and came from beneath the hangar to greet them.

A throat mike swung from his hand. "I thought, just as a precaution, Tocohl, you ought to be able to talk to Buntec when you're out of earshot."

At this distance, Megeve's sprookje didn't bother to echo him. "It's no good for long range, mind you—a mile is about the limit—but it might come in handy."

"It might at that," said Tocohl. "Thanks for thinking of it." She clasped the curve of plastic about her throat and put the tiny earplug in her ear; the weight was scarcely noticeable. As Buntec had taken an identical device from her overpocket and put it on, Tocohl said, experimentally, in Jannisetti, "How're you holding?"

"Just fine." Buntec's reply came as clearly through the earpiece as it did through the sparkling air of Flashfever. "Just fine," Tocohl repeated in GalLing' for Megeve's benefit. "Can you find us two more?"

Timosie Megeve frowned. "Two more?"

Indicating Om im, then Alfvaen, Buntec said, "Wouldn't dream of going out to hunt sprookjes without a serendipitist, or somebody with rocks in his head." Om im chuckled delightedly, but Megeve didn't share his amusement, merely looked stubborn.

"Don't be chintzy, Timosie," said Buntec. "It's not as if we're going to eat your equipment!"

"Or use it to hang pictures on," added Om im and his sprookje.

Buntec said, "*Please* stop talking until we get into the daisy-clipper and on our way—I can't stand it!"

"Then you'd better keep your mouth shut, too," said the small man affably. "Here comes your sprookje."

Having finished its echo, Om im's sprookje turned with the rest of them to see a third sprookje push its way through the flashgrass. Timosie Megeve muttered in despair and raised his hands to clap.

Tocohl caught his hands in midair. "*No!*" she said sharply but quietly. "I think it's got something in its hand. For Veschke's sake, don't do anything to scare it!"

She did not take her eyes from the arriving sprookje, but she felt Megeve's muscles relax and released his hands. Beside her, the others all turned cautiously to follow her gaze. Except for the sound of wind and distant thunder, everything was still as Buntec's sprookje pushed slowly toward them. (Maggy,) Tocohl said, (record this.)

The sprookje did indeed have something in its hand.

It stopped a scant two feet from Buntec and stared at her, its feathers ruffling in the wind. It seemed almost expectant. Then it came to Tocohl and, with a gesture identical to that with which Tocohl had passed out the bits of moss cloak, it stretched out its arm and offered her a tuft of something red and velvety-looking.

Praying that the fragile moment wouldn't break, that no one in the group would shout and frighten the sprookje away, Tocohl leaned forward, not daring to step closer, and reached out to take the gift. She turned it over slowly in her hands, allowing Maggy a good steady view through the spectacles, felt its texture. It was as velvety to the touch as it was to the eye, and it was not merely red, but patterned in shades of red. It was definitely vegetable matter.

Maggy said, (Nothing on it in the survey files; shall I ask swift-Kalat—)

(Later, Maggy,) said Tocohl. Aloud, she addressed the sprookje in Jannisetti. "Thank you," and on impulse, she held out her hand, just barely touching the feathery softness of the sprookje's wrist. The sprookje's cheek-feathers puffed slightly but it did not move away.

Tocohl drew her hand back and stroked the bit of mosslike substance, then, as slowly and carefully as she had done it the first time, she again reached out and touched the sprookje's wrist. This time she made a light stroking motion. The sprookje's cheek-feathers smoothed.

Grinning with excitement, Tocohl brought her hand back and made a great show, for the sprookje's benefit, of placing their gift into the pouch at her hip.

Very softly, she said, "Buntec, I'd like to try an experiment."

Buntec said in the same tone, "You name it; I'll do it," and her sprookje agreed.

"Your knife, please, Om im." Tocohl brought the knife up under the cloak, thrust it outward just beneath her chin, and made a long cut down the lay of the cloak's foliage to its now-ragged hem. A long narrow strip of moss peeled away into her hand. Its tansy scent spiced the air about her.

Cheek-feathers puffed on every sprookje face. Buntec said, interpreting the look, "You're a rotten person, Tocohl, cuttin' something beautiful like that." Again her sprookje echoed her words.

"You could be right, Buntec. I hope they'll forgive a bit of expediency."

Om im did, for he accepted the return of his knife without the customary ceremony.

Taking the long strip of moss by either end, Tocohl spread her hands and gave it a gentle tug to demonstrate its strength. Then she held out one end to the sprookje, who took it. Still holding the other end of the strip in her left hand, she reached out again with her right to stroke the sprookje's wrist. The strip looped between them and remained even when she withdrew her right hand.

After a moment, the sprookje's cheek-feathers relaxed. Tocohl said, in the same soft voice, "Now, very calmly, one at a time, I want you all to get into the daisy-clipper. Megeve, if you're not coming with us, please go back into the hangar, out of sight."

He stared at her aghast. In the same hushed tone, he said, "But you've got an exchange of gifts! You've got to tell the captain—that's more than we've gotten in these three years…" His sprookje too let its voice trail off as if in astonishment of its own.

"Good," Tocohl said, "but not enough, not for your captain."

"What more could you want?" Megeve and his sprookje demanded.

"Art, artifacts"—Tocohl glared at the sprookjes that refused to echo her and let the exasperation leak into her voice—"language. We're still going to look for those grafts, with a native guide if possible." She indicated the sprookje at the other end of the strip of moss with a twist of her head; her grin returned.

For a long moment, Megeve regarded her in shocked silence. At last he found his voice. "Crazy like a Hellspark," he said, and his sprookje thought so too. "You'll need those microphones. Don't worry, I won't do anything to frighten off your sprookjes."

The tableau held as Megeve stepped cautiously away. He was gone from sight for a few moments only, and his sprookje did not follow him, choosing to remain behind and watch with great golden eyes. It only backed slightly away when Megeve returned to distribute microphone necklaces to the others.

Om im took his with a very broad grin. "We'll leave you the pleasure of telling the captain of the Ish shan's first success, Timosie."

"I wouldn't dream of it," the Maldeneantine grinned back. "It will keep until you get back. Buntec would ... strip me naked and roll me through the razor-grass—" The sprookje paused on the same querying note, as Megeve glanced at Buntec, who doubled her fists and jerked her elbows back sharply to attest to the accuracy of his phrasing. "—If she missed seeing the expression on Kejesli's face," he finished.

"Absolutely," agreed Buntec and her sprookje. "And the minute we're gone he's gonna hightail it back to camp and shout his lungs out"—but despite her excitement, she kept her imaginary shout to a whisper—"The Hellspark swapped gifts! The Hellspark swapped gifts!" She exchanged a look with her sprookje and together they finished, "I know I would."

(He probably will,) Tocohl observed privately to Maggy. (If the arachne is available, try to record the expression on Kejesli's face for Buntec when he does.)

(It's important?)

(To Buntec, it is. Now, hush. I have to pay attention.)

"Please be careful," Megeve was saying, "I don't trust that thing around my machinery." His own thing voiced the identical sentiments. He glared at it. "If you must take one, take mine." Then he vanished, scowling, back into the hangar.

"Okay, Buntec," said Tocohl, "you first." And each of the others in turn climbed into the daisy-clipper, leaving Tocohl alone with the three sprookjes. Flashgrass danced and flickered around them.

She took a single step toward the daisy-clipper, allowing the strip of moss cloak to go taut, and then a second step. The sprookje let go.

Patiently, Tocohl picked up the fallen end of the strip and offered it again to the sprookje. The sprookje accepted it, and Tocohl took another step. This time the sprookje followed, although at the farthest extreme the length of moss permitted.

The other sprookjes came too, picking their way through the flashgrass warily, as if the strip of moss gave Buntec's sprookje a shield that they did not have.

The strip loosened as the sprookje quickened its steps to keep pace a foot or two behind her. When Tocohl reached the daisy-clipper, she played out another foot of moss and climbed in, sliding well over in the plush seat to allow sufficient room for the sprookje, and began to reel in the moss strip. The sprookje did not move; the strip went taut and Tocohl tugged gently. The sprookje let go. Tocohl slid to the door, picked up the end of the strip, and offered it again to the sprookje. But before Buntec's sprookje could accept, the second sprookje, Megeve's, grabbed for the trailing end and caught it. Startled, Buntec's sprookje skittered back a few feet.

Megeve's sprookje took a single step toward the daisy-clipper. Om im said quietly, "I think you've got a volunteer."

"We'll see," Tocohl said. With a slight frown of concentration, she slid back to her position next to Om im and, slowly but surely, began to reel in Megeve's sprookje.

And slowly but surely it followed. Through the door it came, its cheek-feathers fully puffed. Inside, it looked around slowly, taking everything in as carefully as Maggy's arachne might.

Its thigh-to-calf ratio was different from the human, but it sat, turning slightly to the side, to allow room for its knees. Aside from a few ruffled cheek-feathers, it did not look uncomfortable.

Tocohl fastened her seat belt with great deliberation, so the sprookje could see exactly what she was doing and how. She had hoped that the sprookje would follow suit, but she was disappointed. When the sprookje made no similar move, she leaned across it and, very gingerly, fastened its seat belt—snapped it open to reassure the creature— then fastened it again.

The sprookje watched her gravely, and snapped the seat belt open. "Okay," said Tocohl, "you've got that down."

When the sprookje made no further move, Tocohl patiently fastened its seat belt again, leaned farther across to close the door, and waited to see what the creature would do next. The sprookje looked at the seat belt, looked at the door, and sighed—as if resigned to its fate— and eased back into the seat.

"All right," said Tocohl, "now that we've got our trusty native guide, let's get this expedition off the ground, shall we?"

Buntec said, "I think you're crazy, Hellspark, but at least you picked one that doesn't talk back—not to us. You just made Timosie's day in more ways than one." She turned to her instruments, adding over her shoulder, "Give a holler if your fine feathered friend gets too hopped up. I'll take this as slow and easy as I can."

#

Swift-Kalat was pleased. Within minutes after he had removed the wrappings from the corpses of the golden scoffers, the first sprookje to see them—his own, in fact—had nipped each of them in turn. The first it had bitten twice, each of the others only once, as if extrapolating from the first.

He placed the bitten corpses into sterile boxes. In a few days, he'd know whether or not the sprookjes themselves were the source of the garbage plants. Whether or not that datum would make a difference to the survey team, he had no idea.

Layli-layli calulan's reasoning seemed farfetched but he was not one to ignore any theory without good cause. If the sprookjes were consciously injecting the garbage plants into all the human debris to cleanse their world of human-borne poisons, might they not also wish to cleanse their world of the human intruders as well?

Stacking the boxes, he paused to consider the sprookje and found it watching the arachne. The arachne, oddly enough, had skittered from one end of the table to the other. There it crouched, then suddenly shot up to its full height, crouched a second time, and skittered the length of the table once more. His first thought was that something had gone wrong with it but, no, its movements were too purposeful...

"Maggy ... ?" he began; so did the sprookje.

The arachne sprang once more to full height, startling the sprookje back in mid-query.

"I wanted to see if I could get it to notice the arachne." The voice from the vocoder sounded pleased. "It did."

Swift-Kalat suddenly regretted that he had not called another surveyor to record for him. However well Maggy recorded the sprookjes, the film would not include her own behavior which, to him, was equally intriguing. Then he remembered that Tocohl was in constant communication with Maggy through her implant. He and the sprookje asked "Did Tocohl suggest you try that?"

"No, she's busy. She told me to hush. I'll show her later." The arachne made another abrupt bob. This time the sprookje only blinked at it. "I deduce that it considers the arachne harmless," Maggy said.

"Yes," he said, the sprookje seconding him. He picked up the boxes to carry them inside the cabin, pausing on the threshold to scrape some of the mud from his feet. The arachne sprang from the table to follow him. The sprookje did not; perhaps, like most of the surveyors, it was drying its feathers.

There was an odd sound behind him. He turned to look and found the arachne scraping its legs one against the other in imitation.

"Shall I enter the material in your files?" Maggy asked.

"Yes, please, Maggy," he said. "You are very useful to have around."

The arachne bobbed a bow. "Thank you." It pricked its way on delicate feet to the console and stuck an adapter into one of the tiny receipt openings. The rest of its legs straightened to give it the height to reach the keyboard.

"Do you need help?" asked swift-Kalat, suddenly realizing how much he was taking for granted about the capabilities of this probe.

Implausibly, a chuckle came from the arachne. "No," it said, "my arm's not broken. —Did I say that correctly?"

Swift-Kalat laughed, as much from astonishment as from amusement. "Yes," he said, "I think so: you sounded very like Alfvaen."

"Good," said the arachne, setting about its task.

For a long moment, swift-Kalat watched; there was nothing to see. At last he remembered the sterile boxes he still held and crossed the room to put them in a safe place. When he returned, it was to draw up a chair and sit, his elbows on his knees, his chin in his hands, and the best possible view of the arachne. His bracelets clashed down his arm to his elbow.

His expertise, he found, was being challenged by more than the sprookjes. By definition, an extrapolative computer was not sapient but, by definition, neither were the sprookjes. The only difference seemed to be that Maggy responded to questioning.

When the arachne withdrew its adapter, he said, "Maggy, are you sapient?"

There was a long pause. Whether it indicated deep thought — and Maggy's deep thought would be faster than human — or was merely supplied for aesthetic reasons, swift-Kalat couldn't judge.

At last, Maggy said, "I don't know. From what Tocohl says, none of the definitions of sapience in my memory is true and sufficient to cover all cases. Legally speaking, however — no, I'm not sapient. Why do you ask?"

"In reaction to the extent of your curiosity."

"That's basic to an extrapolative computer. Curiosity is rather simple to program in: if the information I receive doesn't gibe with other information I have stored, I seek additional information; if I don't have enough information, I seek additional information. In me that's called programming. In a human, that's called curiosity."

"Again, a matter of definition," swift-Kalat pointed out.

"I see what you mean. Yes, a matter of definition."

Swift-Kalat fell silent. If he were asked, he wondered, would he be able to say, as he had with the sprookjes, that he deduced sapience in an extrapolative computer? The question brought him full circle to the legal definition: art, artifacts, language. Language, Maggy certainly had. Given the proper waldoes, he did not doubt that she could produce an artifact if she chose to.

The computer console chimed an interruption to his thoughts and he rose absently to answer it.

The caller was Kejesli. "Hello, swift-Kalat. Is Tocohl with you?"

"Buntec took her into the flashwood. I don't know how long they'll be gone."

"So she'll miss what she seems to have started. Well, you come then. It should be of interest to you as well: there'll be a brief lecture on landscaping in the common room starting about five minutes from now." With that, he signed off.

When swift-Kalat glanced down he saw that the arachne was already on its way. He followed. "Curious?" he asked.

"Curious," she agreed as the two of them started across the compound. "Besides," she added, "I want to see the look on Kejesli's face."

"I don't understand."

"Neither do I, but it's important to Buntec. If I record it for her, maybe she'll explain why," Maggy said, then added, "If she tells me, I'll tell you. I promise."

Edge-of-Dark skirted the barbed-wire perimeter to the main gate, her arms laden with stalks of flowers and leafy branches representing almost all of the local flora of the chlorophyll and rhodopsin families. She'd picked too many; she always did. Getting the gate open would probably require as much skill as arranging the flowers — and no less art.

She smiled to herself, thinking it wasn't often she'd been called upon to put her artistic talent to use on a survey. The chance gave her satisfaction of a kind she'd never before experienced.

The ground under the flashgrass became uneven. Not having a very good view, she slowed, stepped cautiously. The intermittent sight of the green boots brought a second smile to her face and shoulders. Amid the flicker of the flashgrass they were wonderfully aesthetic. Perhaps she had been going about her clothing incorrectly; perhaps it should be taken as a whole with its surroundings... What the Hellspark wore was in some peculiar way more fashionable for Flashfever than her own carefully chosen garb.

Guessing that she'd neared her destination, she halted to shift her still-dripping burden enough to look for the gate. To her relief, Timosie Megeve stood beside it, waiting to hold it open.

"Thank you, Megeve," she began, then she peered again through the foliage. She was no expert on Maldeneantine expressions, but he seemed agitated. "Is something wrong? You look like a womble about to bite someone."

Even as it left her mouth she realized he probably wouldn't understand the expression, but before she could explain he said, "Nothing's wrong, Edge-of-Dark. At least, I hope not. Hellsparks are crazy, that's all." He swung the gate wide and went on, "They took a sprookje along with them—in the daisy-clipper!"

"Who else went?" And when Megeve told her, she smiled as broad a smile as was possible with her arms full and, to reassure him, she added, "I wouldn't worry. With Buntec piloting and a serendipitist along, they can hardly get into trouble."

Megeve started. "I hadn't thought about the serendipitist. Do you believe in that sort of thing?"

"I believe in anything that works, I suppose."

A stalk of penny-Jannisett fell from the crook of her arm; Megeve stooped to retrieve it. He held it out to her, but realizing she had no free hand, he said, "Shall I carry some of that?"

"Just the one you've got. If I try to divide it up, I'll drop it all, I'm afraid. It would be gracious of you to help me into my cabin."

"Of course." He swung the gate shut behind her and took a few quick paces to lead the way. "What's all that for?"

"You missed our brilliant idea," she said, "*Buntec's* brilliant idea, in truth, although she is gracious enough to name me her collaborator..." And on the way to her cabin, she explained at length, her enthusiasm growing still more as she spoke.

"I see," he said, holding aside the membrane to her cabin to ease her entry. "It is a theory worth exploring, I suppose."

He watched as she maneuvered her plant cuttings onto a low table. When her hands were free, he held out the sprig of penny-Jannisett. "Edge-of-Dark," he said, "if you don't mind my asking—why did you start wearing boots all of a sudden?"

"Fashion," she said, over her shoulder. "Although I admit I have had some further thoughts on that subject." Deciding those would be of little interest to him—the Maldeneantine had no aesthetic sense that she had ever seen—she said simply, "You'll find a digital picture on the table by the console. The Hellspark tells me that's current fashion." She went from closet to closet to gather her working materials: scissors, wire, bowls, and vases.

To her deep regret, she had not been able to bring as large a selection of containers with her as she had wished. That was always true, but this time, the lack of choice frustrated her. Perhaps, she thought suddenly, she might ask the rest of the team. Who knows what sort of container Om im or even Kejesli might have brought, as art or as ritual item...

Megeve said, "I thought you were Vyrnwyn, Edge-of-Dark. Why should you be interested in Ringsilver fashion?"

It took her a moment to understand the implication of his question. "Ringsilver?" She strode across to stare at the picture over his shoulder. "Are you sure?"

"Of course I'm sure," he said. "I was there just a few years ago and they all dressed like that."

But Edge-of-Dark realized she had no need of his answer. Taking the picture from his hands, she stared at it. *"Ringsilver!"* she breathed, and promptly burst into laughter, fully expecting Megeve to follow suit. She looked up to find a scowl on his face.

Subduing her laughter, she raised her hand to splay fingers at her throat. "Your pardon, Megeve. It's not you I'm laughing at, it's me. Won't Om im love this! I have been—ever so graciously—tricked by that Hellspark of his!"

She flourished the picture at him and went on, "What a great deal of trouble to go to, to get me into boots for the sake of Buntec's sensibilities! What is it Buntec would say, 'Crazy like a Hellspark'? It's true, isn't it?"

"You mean she hoaxed you? And you're not angry about it?"

The question sobered her. She gave it the respect it was due and concluded, "No, I'm not angry. Consider for a moment: when I put on boots, I suddenly became human to Buntec. And Buntec reciprocated," she added, as the thought occurred to her, "by learning the Vyrnwyn formal greetings—so she became human to me."

Her long nails tapped the picture absently. "Almost like an equation. Edge-of-Dark plus boots equals human. Buntecreih plus formal greeting equals human. What do you suppose we have to add to the sprookjes to arrive at a similar result?" Thoughtful, she stared at Megeve without really seeing him.

"Well," she said, "perhaps it's flower art. If you'll help me carry out the table, we'll find out soon enough."

Megeve's only response was to bend to the task.

Outside, they placed the table in the mud. While Megeve leveled it with small flat stones, Edge-of-Dark settled herself on the bottom step, ignoring the damage the mud might do her clothes, and began laying out her tools and her bowls.

A sprookje, perhaps the one that mimicked her, approached, its golden eyes widening at the sight of the flowers. Although she admitted that might be nothing more than wishful thinking on her part, she vowed to do her best for this audience of one.

She began with the black lacquer bowl and reached for a stalk of tick-tick. As she brought the cutting upright, it began to chide gently. "For sound," she said happily, "I must choose them not just for sight, but for sound!" The sprookje agreed, but caught up in the wonder of her new creation, Edge-of-Dark scarcely heard the echo.

From the perch on which swift-Kalat had placed the arachne, Maggy had an unobstructed view of the whole of the common room, including Kejesli's face.

Hitoshi Dan waited for the small interested group to assemble and quiet, then he thrust Dyxte ti-Amax forward in a manner Tocohl would have called "showing him off." That might have been because his 2nd skin was elaborately patterned, in reds and blues, to resemble the anatomical pattern of human veins and arteries. Maggy, interested in defining Tocohl's concept of "beautiful," made a note to ask later, when Tocohl was no longer occupied, if she thought this beautiful as she had Geremy Kantyka's patterned 2nd skin.

There was a good deal more of interest. Dyxte was ti-Tobian. Maggy had already opened a file on another member of the team, Vielvoye ha-Somol, a ha-Tobian. Aside from a tourist guide which Tocohl had told her to tag superficial, Maggy had no information on either culture, and here was a chance to observe both.

Dyxte ti-Amax was also an expert at landscaping. The only thing Maggy knew about that subject was that Hitoshi Dan had categorized it as a botanical art form, so she was glad for his explanation, as brief as it was.

"Remember where we first met the sprookjes?" Dyxte asked, of no one in particular. "That entire area could easily have been a deliberate artistic effort." Maggy reviewed the tape she'd drawn from the survey computer. She didn't see what he meant, but then "artistic" gave her the same problem as Tocohl's "beautiful."

Dyxte went on, "Of course, their idea of aesthetics may differ entirely from ours—from mine." He drew a stubby forefinger along the vein in his arm from wrist to elbow. "Art comes from the heart, but the heart is instructed by the culture."

Now *that* information was useful, Maggy thought, and tagged it accordingly.

"The best way to find out," he said, "is to landscape an area of the compound." He laid a hand over his heart, tensed the muscles of his entire arm as if in reaction to pain. "I confess, I've been aching to do just that since our arrival, so it will be as much to my benefit as to the sprookjes'." Glancing at Kejesli, he said, "I see no reason to wait."

When Kejesli made no reply, Dyxte started for the door. Swift-Kalat paused to lift the arachne from its perch and place it on the ground beside him so Maggy might observe too. They were not the only ones to follow Dyxte outside; clearly a number of the surveyors were equally curious about this art form.

They watched in silence as Dyxte paced thoughtfully around the compound, stopping and turning at several of the cabins, now taking a step back for a better vantage point, now ignoring a cabin as if it did not exist.

At last he paused contemplatively before *layli-layli calulan*'s cabin, watching the white and gold pennants flap and spatter in the breeze. "Here," he said, and strode toward the door chime.

"No!" said Maggy; simultaneously Kejesli—and his sprookje echo—shouted, "Wait, Dyxte!"

Their warning was the louder. Dyxte ti-Amax halted, turned on his heels to give Kejesli his full attention. "Yes, Captain?" he and his sprookje said at once.

"You should have read your orders," Kejesli said. His sprookje echoed that, causing Kejesli to cast a scowl in its direction. "*Layli-layli calulan* is in mourning for Oloitokitok and can't be disturbed for"—he glanced at the display on his cuff—"another twenty hours unless it is a genuine emergency."

"Oh. Your pardon, sir." Dyxte turned to look once more at *layli-layli calulan*'s cabin. "Suppose I simply go ahead and do it without her permission? Does anyone know enough about Yn to tell me—?"

Maggy sent the arachne to his side. "I might be able to help," she said. "What would you like to know about the Yn?"

With no warning, Dyxte dropped to his knee to peer into the arachne's camera. "Extrapolative computer?" he asked; the question was as unexpected as his action had been.

Maggy considered her options. With swift-Kalat present she didn't think a lie advisable; but Tocohl had told her not to volunteer this information. Was answering a direct question volunteering? If she didn't answer, swift-Kalat would. He would *not* lie, not "too stupid to lie," like the survey computer, but definitely not programmed with the ability. Culture was like programming! She tagged that conclusion important.

As for Dyxte's question, Maggy decided to wait for Tocohl's advice. Meanwhile, her best course was to leave her options, and Tocohl's, open...

"Hellspark," she said, knowing Dyxte would perceive no delay between question and response, "at your service." She had the arachne bob a curtsey.

"How do Yn feel about plants?"

"Yn in general or Yn shamans?" she asked.

"*Layli-layli calulan*," said Dyxte.

That made the responsibility for discrimination hers. She searched her files on the Yn with particular attention to their shamans, to conclude, aloud: "There is an eighty percent chance that she will be very pleased to find her cabin surrounded by plants when she leaves her mourning."

"Maggy? Why an eighty percent chance?" swift-Kalat asked, sprookje-echoed.

"Because *layli-layli calulan* is an atypical Yn shaman," Maggy explained, "I can only extrapolate from the general behavior of Yn shamans."

"She does *like* the Flashfever wildlife," Hitoshi Dan observed.

Kejesli gave a one-handed shrug. "Go ahead, Dyxte," he and his sprookje said, "if that's the area that suits you. For safety's sake, I'll make that an order."

"No need of that," ti-Amax told him. "Eighty percent is high enough odds for any *ti*. Just let me get some scratch paper and start my planning."

A ruffled sprookje was either frightened or excited; perhaps both, thought Tocohl, as she kept a careful eye on the passenger beside her. And Megeve's sprookje was bristling all over, had been since the daisy-clipper lifted gently up and began its voyage into the depths of the flashwood.

To Tocohl's relief, however, the sprookje did not panic. It made no attempt to free itself from or to struggle against the seat belt that restrained it. The creature looked out the door for a moment, then turned deliberately away: the rushing ground beneath clearly made it more uncomfortable than did its human companions. It watched Tocohl with huge unblinking golden eyes.

Tocohl touched it gently on the wrist and it looked down at her hand but did not draw away. Tocohl stroked the ruffled feathers lightly, following the lay of the feathers, and hoping that the gesture might bring some reassurance. Evidently the hope was fulfilled, for the feathers began to subside slowly—first on the sprookje's extremities, then on the chest, and, at last, those on the sprookje's cheeks. Its fine gold and brown brocade pattern sparkled in the intermittent sun as Buntec steered the daisy-clipper deftly along the surface of a fast-moving stream.

Beyond the sprookje, Tocohl saw the surface of Flashfever un-roll—a sudden shattering brightness of frostwillows, a misty blue of monks-woodsmen, a squat stand of spit-outs—then the daisy-clipper dipped beneath the shadow of a cloud and the woods flashed brilliantly alight with spitfires and whirligigs. Tocohl blinked in wonder.

"Do you ever get used to it?" she breathed, to no one in particular. After a moment's pause, Om im tore his eyes away from his side of the daisy-clipper and said, "Hunh?"

"Never mind," said Tocohl, "you've answered my question." With a careful eye on the sprookje, Tocohl reached forward to tap Buntec on the shoulder. "How far out are we going?"

Buntec didn't take her eyes from the rushing view before her. "About twenty miles from here—take us about the same number of minutes. Riding the river may be the long way, but the ride is smoother and the view is better."

"Thanks," said Tocohl, "and thanks." Without reluctance, she centered her attention once more on the sprookje. "I am Tocohl Susumo," she began again, first in Maldeneantine, then in GalLing'. "I dub thee Sunchild until such time as thou wilt share thy name with me."

"Sunchild?" said Alfvaen.

Tocohl explained, "In the Zoveelian fairy tales, Sunchild was the bravest of all the sprookjes."

"Sounds good to me," said Buntec. "Fits."

Om im leaned across Tocohl and saluted the sprookje. "Sunchild," he acknowledged. "I wonder if I'd have the courage to climb into a daisy-clipper with four crazies."

"You did, didn't you?" Tocohl said with a grin.

The stream had broadened into a roaring expanse of river before them. Sunlight glinted off its churning waters, and along its torrent-swept banks, waterplants glittered and sparkled with a light that was their own. Sunchild, as if in affirmation of its name, cautiously turned to the door to look down at its brilliant world.

Buntec made a snapping motion at the control panel and grunted. Something in her tone raised the hair at the nape of Tocohl's neck. Two more snapping motions—then Buntec swung the daisy-clipper's joystick to the left. The craft did not respond.

"Won't slow," said Buntec sharply. "Won't turn, either."

Before them a stand of frostwillows rushed ominously closer. "Hold tight," commanded Buntec, "this is going to be rough!"

Alfvaen and Om im responded instantly, tucking their heads between their knees, sheltering in their hands. Tocohl grasped the sprookje's head, forced it down, sheltering it with her own shoulders.

The daisy-clipper slanted abruptly downward. For a long moment, Buntec fought it to a smooth glide, then the craft struck the surface of the river with a thunderclap. It lurched against the current like a skipping stone.

Tocohl gasped as the seat belt cut sharply into her flesh, and again as her shoulders smashed into the seat before her. The sprookje shivered in her sheltering arms but made no outcry.

Twice more the craft lurched forward, battering her against the seat back. Then, with a final screech of metal, it came to a shuddering halt amid a tangle of ripped and sparkling waterweeds.

"Abandon ship!" shouted Buntec. "I don't know how long this thing'll stay afloat—*no!* my side! You can't swim that white water, you barefoot fool!"

As Tocohl swiftly unsnapped the sprookje's safety belt to shove it through the door to safety, Buntec grabbed Alfvaen by the wrist and bodily drew her onto the bank of the river.

Om im scrambled across the seat. Tocohl, clinging to the frame of the door fairly threw him onto the slippery vegetation at the edge of the river. Buntec pulled Tocohl out of waist-deep water before Tocohl had fully realized she was in it.

The daisy-clipper, its crumpled prow snarled in the glittering weeds at the edge of the river, rocked lower and lower as water sprayed and pounded off its side. After a moment, it gave one last shudder and sank. Only the arc of its bubble cabin, spattering reflected light, showed above the dashing waters.

Buntec stamped her foot on the springy flashgrass of the bank. "Foot," she said in a matching torrent of Jannisetti curses, "Heel. Sole. Toes, *with green toenail polish!*"

That last refinement owed much to Edge-of-Dark, Tocohl noted absently, but did much to assure her that Buntec was unhurt. She looked around her. "Is everybody else okay?"

Alfvaen could not tear her stunned eyes from the daisy-clipper. "Alfvaen," Tocohl said sharply, and repeated the question in Siveyn.

"Yes," came the muted reply.

Om im said, "Fine," but there was a nasty-looking gash across his cheek. As he raised a hand to touch his face, his eyes widened and the color drained from his cheeks. He clamped the hand to the gash to stop the bleeding and sat down heavily.

Before Tocohl could reach his side, he gave her a wan imitation of his old grin and pointed instead to the sprookje. Like Buntec and Alfvaen, Sunchild was still watching what was left to be seen of the daisy-clipper. It looked dazed.

Worried about possible shock—she had no idea what a sprookje's metabolism was like—Tocohl took a stumbling step toward it. She was a little dazed herself. Catching her balance, she began a Methven ritual to right that as she walked unsteadily over to the sprookje.

She stroked its feathers. "I'm sorry, Sunchild," she said, keeping her voice as low and soothing as possible, "it's not supposed to do that." Alfvaen giggled, but Tocohl recognized the sound of relief rather than hysteria.

Tocohl watched Sunchild closely. On the off chance that warmth would counter shock in sprookje as in a human, Tocohl draped her cloak gently about the creature's shoulders, clasping it at the feathered throat. Sunchild's feathers ruffled the entire length of its arms. Tocohl gently smoothed the agitated feathers. After a long while, Sunchild seemed to become aware of her, then of the cloak. Its cheek-feathers puffed.

Buntec, her cursing finished for the moment, attended to the gash on Om im's cheek; Alfvaen scratched nervously as she looked on. "… Along to pick us up in no time," Buntec was saying, "I did manage to punch the emergency locator before we hit water."

"If the water didn't get into the transmitter, that is," said Om im.

"Right," agreed Buntec, with a glance at what remained visible of the daisy-clipper. "Hold still," she added sharply.

Alfvaen frowned at the small object in her hand; Tocohl recognized it as the ornate box in which she kept her medication. "I hope you're wrong, Om im, because the water did get into my pills." She held it where he was able to see the result without twisting away from Buntec's ministrations. "Nothing left but a s-single s-soggy lump. I'll just s-sit here and get drunk." Her free hand clawed at her back. "It is *s-safe* to sit here, isn't it?"

"As safe a place as you'll find on Flashfever," said Om im, "as long as a storm doesn't come up."

Not for Alfvaen, Tocohl suddenly realized; without medication, the alcohol level in her bloodstream could rise high enough to kill her. To Buntec, she said sharply, "How long before they come for us?"

"Twenty minutes, half an hour, depending on how long it takes them to pinpoint our location."

Tocohl whistled impatiently. Maggy would have pinpointed their location the moment Buntec signaled trouble with the daisy-clipper, but Alfvaen's pills were another matter. (Maggy,) she said, (have *layli-layli calulan* synthesize the proper medication for Alfvaen and send it *with* the rescue party.)

There was no response.

(Maggy!) she said again, this time with shocked urgency, *(Maggy!)* She left the sprookje's side, scrambling across the glittering grass to Alfvaen, to grab the hand-held from the Siveyn's belt. *"Maggy!"* she repeated aloud, "Maggy, what's *wrong?*"

But there was no response from that link either. Alfvaen stared at it and then at Tocohl with widening eyes.

Tocohl's shoulders ached suddenly with remembered pain ... the battering she had taken protecting Sunchild. "I should have realized," she said, "I took that much too hard!"

"Ish shan, are you all right?" All three of them stared at her with obvious concern.

She drew a deep breath. When she was sure she had her voice under control, she said, "I'm fine; Maggy isn't. Something's happened to her."

Shielding her eyes from the wan light of Flashfever's sun—because Maggy did not—Tocohl threw her head back to search the sky, hoping for a glimpse, a flicker of light to tell her that Maggy was still secure in her orbit. All she could see were gathering storm clouds.

For a time, swift-Kalat held the arachne where it might see both Kejesli's face and Dyxte's rapid sketches of the front of *layli-layli calulan's* cabin. But Dyxte was losing his audience to Edge-of-Dark.

When Kejesli and Dyxte's sprookje wandered away, Maggy said, "Do you think Tocohl would be more interested in the sprookjes than in the landscaping?"

"I am," swift-Kalat said, "I can't speak for Tocohl."

"That's confirmation enough. I want to see what Edge-of-Dark is doing."

Swift-Kalat set the arachne down and followed it.

Across the compound, at the foot of Edge-of-Dark's cabin, all of the camp sprookjes jostled and shuffled—each other, not daring to displace the humans—to see the flower art.

The intensity of their interest seemed to impress even Captain Kejesli, for he caught swift-Kalat's arm as he passed. Drawing him just out of echo-range, Kejesli said, "In Veschke's name, swift-Kalat, show me an artifact or a language!"

"I showed you an artifact," said swift-Kalat, with a snap of his forearm that made his bracelets clang with such authority that a dozen or more sprookjes and surveyors started and turned at the sound of it. For all the effect swift-Kalat's status had however, the captain might as well have been deaf. Releasing swift-Kalat's arm, he turned and stalked away, his beaded hair chattering at each angry step, to vanish into his quarters.

The crowd parted slightly to let Timosie Megeve ease his way from within. A wave of his pale hand encompassed sprookjes and humans alike. "I don't know what this proves," he said, "except that they're as bored as we are."

"Only that the sprookjes are interested in Edge-of-Dark's flower art. It does not prove they have a flower art of their own. Still, it means that we could be on the right track. It should be interesting to see what the sprookjes make of Dyxte's landscaping." Smiling slightly, swift-Kalat craned past Megeve's shoulder to watch as Maggy's arachne claimed Megeve's spot on the steps ... like a small child at a parade, he thought.

Megeve snorted. "And who's looking after the weather forecasting while Dyxte is messing around with sketches? We've got people out in the field."

"John the Smith. Meteorology is his—"

"*Swift-Kalat!*"

His head jerked up as he sought the source of the shout. The arachne stood at full stretch, a number of surveyors peering at it curiously. From Maggy ... ?

The arachne dashed down the steps and zigzagged through the crowd to splash to a stop before him. In a surprisingly sharp voice, it said, "I can't reach Tocohl. She doesn't answer—neither does Alfvaen!"

"What?" Megeve gaped at the arachne in astonishment.

Swift-Kalat knelt in the mud. "Repeat that please, Maggy."

"I can't reach Tocohl or Alfvaen," Maggy repeated. The sharpness was no illusion. "Something's happened to them."

"What was the last thing you saw?" asked Megeve, quite calmly now.

"Nothing dangerous. No crash, if that's what you mean. They were just flying along the river when the picture, the sound, everything, cut off." The anxious note was still in Maggy's voice, but swift-Kalat was reassured by her words.

"Swift-Kalat can tell you how much equipment failure we've had on this world," Megeve said. "It's probably only something gone awry with your receiver. Would you like me to take a look?"

As he stooped and reached, the arachne took a measured step back. "No!" it said. "Nobody touches my equipment except Tocohl!"

Megeve splayed a hand at his throat, rose. To swift-Kalat he said, "I wouldn't worry. They've got the transmitter in the daisy-clipper if it comes to that."

"You're sure? With both Tocohl's and Alfvaen's communication broken off simultaneously?"

"That's why I'm sure. Nothing could cut off both at the same time, except a defect in that"—he indicated the arachne with his toe, and it shied back a step farther—"or in the main part of the computer," Megeve finished.

"He's wrong," said the arachne. "I'm fine; Tocohl isn't."

"If it will reassure you, swift-Kalat," Megeve said, "we can contact them on the main transmitter."

"Yes, please," said swift-Kalat, and Maggy, sprookje-like, echoed the request. They trailed Megeve swiftly across the compound to the common room, where he seated himself at the console and punched the code for the daisy-clipper. After listening to the earpiece for a moment, Megeve took a flat case of tools from the pocket of his oversuit and began to dismantle the transceiver.

"Something's wrong with this one, too," he said disgustedly—and glanced at the arachne as if it were responsible. To swift-Kalat, he said, "And the fault is definitely with this equipment, swift-Kalat. Stop worrying; as soon as I get this back together, you can talk to your precious Siveyn and Hellspark."

"How long will it take?"

"I have no idea, but I can work faster if nobody's breathing down the back of my neck."

"I don't breathe," said the arachne, unmoving.

"I meant you, too," said Megeve, and Maggy's arachne—after a bob and a "Your pardon!"—followed swift-Kalat outside.

Swift-Kalat had intended to return to the sprookjes still crowded about Edge-of-Dark, but he found he could not keep his mind on them. The arachne, instead of resuming its place on the steps, stayed at his side. From that vantage point, it could see nothing but the backs of various legs.

Curious at her sudden apparent loss of interest, swift-Kalat wondered if Megeve might not be right. Perhaps some failure in the arachne ... ? "What are you doing, Maggy?" he asked.

"Thinking."

"Thinking about what?"

Tocohl's voice issued abruptly from the arachne's vocoder. "Once a thing happens twice, you must think about it three times." Then Maggy added in her own voice, "This has happened *three* times, to three separate communication devices. If Tocohl does not return in twenty minutes, we must search for her."

"Why twenty minutes?"

"Contact was broken when the daisy-clipper was twenty minutes from camp. Tocohl will discover the loss of contact and return here to see if anything is wrong with me. If she does not, she cannot."

"Are you sure of that?" swift-Kalat said. Not only could the question be asked in GalLing' without giving offense but often the question had to be asked in GalLing'.

Maggy answered it by repeating all of her previous statements in Jenji, assigning a degree of reliability to each. "If she does not, she cannot," Maggy finished; the arachne raised one spindly appendage and snapped it down.

The gesture was awkward—the arachne's joints were unsuited for it—but it gave the ring of authority to her words. There was nothing wrong with a computer capable of such reliability of speech.

Swift-Kalat stared thoughtfully at the reflection of his own status bracelets in the puddle of water at his feet. "I see," he said, and then fell silent. This has happened *three* times, she had said, assigning the statement to her own experience. In his experience ...

Four times. In his mind's eye, he watched as Timosie Megeve repaired the transceiver—not now, not today—but on the day Oloitokitok disappeared. There had been no locator signal, no emergency signal. Oloitokitok, so convinced of the sprookjes' sapience, had died. What then killed Oloitokitok?

To categorize two separate events as one as he did, perhaps improperly, would lead to deductions that, if false, were dangerous to speak. Yet he could not close his mind to the implications of the theory. He had to find a way to test it.

"Come, Maggy. We will not wait the twenty minutes," he said, and without waiting for a reply he started toward Kejesli's cabin.

They found Kejesli playing a somewhat reluctant host to Dyxte, who was saying, "But the penny-Jannisett that grows in the local flashwood isn't large enough. Now, if I take one of the daisy-clippers out into deep flashwood—it's only about a fifteen-minute trip—I can get the perfect plants!"

Beaded hair rattled in agitation against the backrest of Kejesli's chair. "No," he said, "you'll wait until Megeve has fixed the main transceiver. It's bad enough we've got one party out there unable to call in; I won't send a second one out until the communications are restored."

"The deep flashwood you're referring to, Dyxte," interjected swift-Kalat, "is that where we first found the sprookjes?"

"Yes," said Dyxte and swift-Kalat turned to the captain.

"That's where Tocohl's party was headed. Maggy"—he gestured at the arachne—"lost contact with them, too. She believes something has happened to the party. We must take one of the daisy-clippers and find them."

"Absolutely not." Again, the rattle of beads. Kejesli stubbornly gripped the edge of his desk. "Megeve tells me there's something wrong with that—thing. You know we have had a great deal of trouble with our probes, swift-Kalat, and that one has been poking around outside during a thunderstorm. I'm not surprised it's behaving oddly. You, and Dyxte, will wait until Megeve has the transceiver fixed." His gesture was one swift-Kalat had learned to interpret not only as final, but as a dismissal as well.

Swift-Kalat tried to frame the thoughts that concerned him into words, but found himself unable to do so without creating so frightening a truth that—with a shudder, he turned and left.

"Whew," said Dyxte when they were out of the captain's ear-shot. "He wasn't this bad on Inumaru! I wonder what's biting him?" Swift-Kalat darted a look at Dyxte, who added, "An expression, I didn't mean it literally. —Is it true that the arachne has lost touch with Buntec and the others?"

"Yes," said swift-Kalat. He wanted to say more; the possibility of misspeaking prevented him from doing so. The pennants that hung from *layli-layli calulan*'s cabin, dry for this brief moment, snapped gaily, caught his eye, and suggested a possible course of action.

Tocohl and *layli-layli calulan* had calmly called each other liars. A mistranslation only, Tocohl had assured him, yet if the Yn term included the Jenjin meaning of the word, then perhaps a shaman had the ability to deflect the danger of misspoken words.

It was the *only* course of action open to him. He would try speaking to *layli-layli calulan*.

A hand caught his elbow, brought him up short. "She's in mourn-ing, remember?" Dyxte said, having read his intent correctly. "We aren't supposed to interrupt her." Releasing his elbow, Dyxte thrust his hand straight into the air, as if to protect himself from some overhead threat. "Unless it's an emergency?" he said; the sudden concern in his voice made the gesture seem one of emphasis—or fear.

Swift-Kalat stared at him. Even that was beyond his power to voice. To claim an emergency might be to doom the party. *Alfvaen!* "I cannot say that."

"You *look* it," Dyxte said.

"Swift-Kalat ..." The arachne tapped at his calf delicately. "Will it help Tocohl if you speak to *layli-layli calulan*?"

"It might, Maggy. I don't know what else to try."

"Then I will arrange it."

"Wait!" said Dyxte. "You can't go in there either."

"Your pardon for the correction, Dyxte ti-Amax," Maggy said, "but your ignorance is no fault of your own. You were chamfered by a moron; everybody says so. I'm female. As such, I have sufficient status to call on *layli-layli calulan* even in her time of mourning." With that, the arachne darted off, sending up a shower of mud all the way across the compound, to stretch for the chimes at the entrance of *layli-layli calulan*'s cabin. A moment later, it disappeared inside.

#

As she paused on the threshold of *layli-layli calulan*'s cabin, Maggy checked it all through once more. She fervently wished that she had someone, Tocohl or even Alfvaen, to discuss it with—especially after Megeve's remarks about her sanity—but she could see no flaw in the plan.

She could not speak to swift-Kalat about it, that she knew. Swift-Kalat could not lie, Tocohl had said, and her memory banks backed up that statement; but she, Maggy, could lie for him. Hadn't Tocohl told her to lie to Kejesli? And didn't *layli-layli calulan* approve of lying?

Once again, she ran swiftly through all of her stores related to the Yn culture. The plan was eighty percent good. Given that *layli-layli calulan* was an atypical Yn shaman, that was the highest rating she could give it. If it would put her into contact with Tocohl again, it was worth the risk. Maggy had never before been out of touch with Tocohl for this long.

Maggy struck the chime.

Layli-layli calulan did not answer, but having made the decision, Maggy could not turn back. She pulled the membrane aside and stepped quietly into the cabin, relieved that she could find nothing in her data stores to indicate that a shaman's curse would work on a mechanical device.

As at the time Tocohl had first visited the cabin, the Yn shaman sat cross-legged on her blue mat. This time, however, a dozen jievnal sticks, set at precise intervals—precise for a human, Maggy corrected— around her burned dully. *Layli-layli*'s plump hands flashed and wove with the intricacies of the koli thread. Maggy read her moving lips without difficulty:

"... This for the love of woman to man"—her hands wove another knot—"this for the love of woman to woman"—still another, the thread shortened and twisted—"and this," she said, grasping the two tiny ends of thread that protruded from the glittering tangle, "is for death." She gave a slow, steady pull and all the apparent knots in the koli thread came inexorably unraveled, to leave nothing but the straight gold string to link her hands.

It was the death-song of a woman for a beloved sister whom she named Oloitokitok.

When *layli-layli calulan* looked up at last, Maggy raised two of the arachne's appendages and held them out before her. Despite its limited likeness to the human gesture, she hoped *layli-layli* would understand she meant to extend sympathy. Then, drawing the ritual words from a tragic drama of Yn origin, she said, "I must speak of one whose life is intertwined with mine. Let the dead be dead, and grant them the peace of tuli-tuli the beast."

The dark eyes were calm, the broad mouth turned up at the corners despite her mourning. *Layli-layli calulan* said, "I will speak to the living. What is the problem, *maggy-maggy lynn?*"

"Will you, *layli-layli calulan,* permit my sister to speak with you?"

"Who is your sister?"

"Her name is swift-Kalat twis Jalakat, and I claim her as my sister by right of the Hellspark ritual of change." There was Maggy's lie; no such ritual existed. She waited, observing *layli-layli calulan* carefully for change of manner that might suggest anger, a common reaction to an uncovered lie, or amusement, a less frequent but a possible response. While Maggy had seen both, she was not sure how either would appear in an Yn; she kept her Yn files active.

There was a pause, one that Tocohl would have categorized as thoughtful. Then *layli-layli calulan* said, "And her true name?"

The lie had passed for truth.

"Her true name is hers alone, not mine to give." That part was not a lie, thought Maggy—perhaps she should be amused—because she had heard swift-Kalat's soft-name but doubted that anyone in the survey knew it besides Alfvaen.

"You share the name of strength, *maggy-maggy lynn*. I will speak to your sister. Bring her to me."

Once more, Maggy held out the arachne's two appendages in sympathy. Then she sent it back to swift-Kalat at a run—for the second part of her lie.

Dyxte was still with him. Maggy checked through all the examples of lying she had and found Tocohl saying, "The fewer the witnesses the better..." It had been said with a smile, but Maggy knew Tocohl's smile did not always negate information. Besides, she had little enough to go on. "Please leave us, Dyxte," she said, "I must speak to swift-Kalat alone."

The look they gave the arachne she interpreted as puzzlement, but Dyxte said, "I'll speak to you later," and walked away. Swift-Kalat bent to listen.

Now, thought Maggy, something to satisfy swift-Kalat. "Hold out your hands," she instructed, and when he did, she placed two of the arachne's muddy extremities in them. "Please say the following after me ..."

Recalling a tape of a Ringsilver magician who, in Tocohl's frame of reference, could change a hard-boiled egg into a live bird, Maggy checked it through. Even knowing it to be illusion, Tocohl had been enchanted. Maggy hoped Tocohl would be as delighted with this illusion, so she said aloud, *"Hey, presto!"*

"Hey, presto!" repeated swift-Kalat. "What did *layli-layli calulan* say, Maggy, and what's this all about?" He wiped his muddy hands on his thighs.

"That was the Hellspark ritual of change," said Maggy, "that makes you, legally speaking, a woman. And *layli-layli calulan* is willing to speak to you now because you are my sister."

"Is that possible?" swift-Kalat squinted at the arachne.

"I just did it," said Maggy, in a tone she'd heard Tocohl use many a time for a *fait accompli*. "Come talk to *layli-layli*."

The arachne led the way to *layli-layli calulan's* cabin and entered behind him. The shaman looked up from her magically patterned mat and said, "You dream, swift-Kalat."

Swift-Kalat obviously recalled the exchange he'd seen between Tocohl and the shaman. He replied, "As do you."

"Be seated, sister and sister of my sister," the shaman said. Maggy folded the arachne's legs and placed the body on the floor where she could keep her camera eye on both; swift-Kalat knelt on his heels. "Now speak," *layli-layli calulan* said.

With great care, swift-Kalat chose the words to tell *layli-layli calulan* what had happened to Tocohl's party. To Maggy, it sounded completely reliable, even in GalLing', but it was not enough to explain swift-Kalat's sudden decision to begin the search immediately.

Layli-layli listened without comment until he had finished. After a moment's pause, she looked at him closely and said, "That is not all. If that were all, you would have waited the twenty minutes Maggy specified." When he didn't speak, she added, "Tell me what else is happening in the camp, or has happened, or will happen. You will not judge, but perhaps I will."

There was a brief jangle of bracelets. Without a downward glance, swift-Kalat jammed them to his elbow to silence them. "Oloitokitok died while Megeve repaired the transceiver. Megeve repairs the transceiver now, and Maggy cannot speak to Tocohl or to Alfvaen."

Maggy added that bit of information to stores and ran extrapolation on it. The results wouldn't have appealed to Tocohl, and they did not appeal to Maggy on the same grounds.

"I hear what you will not say," said *layli-layli calulan*.

Sweat beaded swift-Kalat's forehead. "Can you speak it without adding to the risk?"

"I can." *Layli-layli calulan* twisted the bluestone ring from her right forefinger. "With this hand, I will." She rose from the mat in a single smooth motion, gathered up the jievnal sticks. A rumble of distant thunder made her face suddenly passionate. "Hurry! We may already be too late!"

She sprang for the door and darted across the compound at so light and quick a pace that even swift-Kalat found it hard to match.

By the time the arachne caught up with them in Kejesli's quarters, Maggy found *layli-layli calulan* in the midst of an elaborate lie. Like Maggy, *layli-layli* took advantage of Kejesli's lack of knowledge of her culture, a lack Maggy did not share.

Nothing new in technique, Maggy noted, but she recorded it for her growing file on lying, for its style and for its purpose, which she hoped might become clear.

"The gods Hibok Hibok and Juffure," *layli-layli* was saying, "have sworn vengeance against our enterprise. The jievnal sticks"— she thrust them, smoking, before Kejesli's face—"tell me that only a red-haired woman can prevent disaster to us all."

Y herself was the only Yn god, and the jievnal sticks were not used for divination. Swift-Kalat was no likelier than Kejesli to be aware of that but for her to speak of disaster ... ! Didn't *layli-layli calulan* know what effect that would have on a Jenji?

Maggy searched the files, looking for a way to mitigate the damage, as, gasping, swift-Kalat flinched from *layli-layli calulan* to cradle his braceleted forearm as if he were in pain. Nothing, Maggy could find no precedent—

Hearing the gasp, *layli-layli calulan* glanced his way. Still holding the jievnal sticks inches from Kejesli's face, she stretched out her bare right hand to clasp it about swift-Kalat's wrist. "I speak a dream, swift-Kalat," she told him in a tone that commanded. "A dream can be turned."

Whether her words or her espabilities did the trick, Maggy couldn't tell, but swift-Kalat took a deep breath and said, "Do what you must."

Without releasing swift-Kalat's wrist, *layli-layli calulan* fixed her eyes once again on Kejesli. In the same tone of command, she said, "I invoke taboo."

Now Maggy understood the purpose of the lie. Only by claiming a taboo situation could *layli-layli calulan* force Kejesli to an action he had forbidden.

Kejesli, coughing from the smoke, braced a hand against the ceiling. "What is it you *need?*"

"A daisy-clipper and permission to take it out despite the broken transceiver," *layli-layli calulan* said, "nothing more."

Kejesli lowered his hand; halfway down, it bobbed once in a Sheveschkem shrug. Relief, Maggy decided, as Kejesli crossed to his computer console. He tapped a code and, even before a face appeared, demanded, "John, what are the weather conditions?"

It was Dyxte's face that sprang into view. "Captain, that storm is going to—be nasty—and we can't reach Buntec's party to let them know it's coming because—"

"The transceiver is out of commission," Kejesli finished for him. "Could we send a party in person?"

"If we do, *they'll* be caught in full storm on their return." Dyxte scrubbed his forehead as if to erase the deep lines etched above his brows. "We've got about ten minutes before the storm hits camp."

Kejesli broke contact without a further word and turned, his hand still clamped to the console's edge. "I can't let you go, *layli-layli,* no matter what your gods say." Shoulders gone taut, he stared past her. "They'll be all right, you know. Buntec will ground the daisy-clipper. As long as they stay inside, they'll be fine."

Layli-layli calulan held up a forefinger bare of its ring. "They had better be," she said quietly. On the roof above, rain began to drum.

CHAPTER 12

"You couldn't see the ship from here anyway," Buntec said, "much less tell if anything were wrong."

Tocohl brought her hand down, saw that it was shaking. "If it were dark ..."

"You said geosynchronous orbit. Even in the dark, you couldn't get a glimmer. Besides, this is Flashfever—stupid planet doesn't believe in dark any more than the Port of Delights." She thrust out a hand. "Let me have a look at that thing."

Tocohl passed her Maggy's hand-held. Buntec laid it on her knee while she prodded pockets; eventually she found what she had been looking for, some small implement adequate to open the back of the device. She glanced up in mid-examination to say, "Don't worry, Hellspark, I don't have the faintest intention of going after your implant. That could have been damaged when we got battered around. Are you hurtin' from it?"

"No," Tocohl said, rubbing the area. There was nothing to feel, neither bruise nor swelling. (Maggy?) she said; there was still no response. "No," Tocohl said again, "I lost contact with her before the crash—I'm sure of it. She's very protective. If she'd been in contact, I wouldn't have bruises."

Buntec snapped the hand-held shut. "Nothing wrong I can see but even looking's a bitch without the right tools. Well, even if the problem's at the source, the ship's in geosynchronous orbit..."

Meaning, Tocohl thought, the *ship* will be fine. She bit down hard on her anger, said only, "You mean a problem at the source can be repaired...yes. But, Buntec—the result might no longer be Maggy."

Her urgency was lost on Buntec. Tocohl should have expected as much. Buntec hadn't had the hour by hour contact with Maggy she'd had for so many years. Unable to explain, Tocohl lapsed into silence—and shivered at the depth of that silence.

Out of habit born of precaution, she manually ran spectacles and 2nd skin through their test modes: warmth, yes; heightened vision, yes; infrared vision, yes.

It was thornproof still and tougher in fact than the 2nd skins the rest of the party wore. The sensors on its surface made tiny patterns against the skin of her back and shoulders. Buntec was up and pacing, she realized, and realized as well that she could not have interpreted the patterns without hearing Buntec's actions.

(Oh, Maggy,) she said and then, into the silence, in Sheveschkem she added, (Veschke guide thee!) She took a deep breath. First things first: that meant Alfvaen. It might well be necessary to walk back to base camp. If only she had some better idea of Alfvaen's condition.

Alfvaen scratched furiously.

A sharp curse from Om im distracted them both, jerked them about to face the river.

A surge of water swelled the river and Buntec jumped back to avoid it. The swell splashed noisily against the hull of the daisy-clipper. With a hideous squeal of metal, the craft tore loose from the bank and rushed downstream like some ponderous underwater beast. Buntec howled with rage and stamped her foot obscenely after it.

Startled, the sprookje jumped to its feet and backed a dozen steps so quickly that the moss cloak closed, as if protectively, about it. Then its head snapped from the swollen river to the horizon. Its feathers bristled. Its beak jerked open, revealing a tongue that glowed the ominous red of a warning telltale.

It turned its head slowly and carefully, as if to display the tongue at its human companions. Like a deer flagging the white of its tail for danger, Tocohl thought. When Sunchild looked again to the horizon, she looked too.

"Eight-footed and bare-toed." That was the first understandable thing Buntec had said. "We'll have to follow that eight-footed — follow the daisy-clipper," Buntec went on, "Old Rattlebrain'll never find us unless we're sittin' right on top of it, twiddlin' our toes."

There was a grunt of firm assent from Om im, a "Yes" from Alfvaen.

But Tocohl did not take her eyes from the lowering line of sooty black clouds that moved toward them. More than the dramatic loss of the daisy-clipper, the approaching storm frightened the sprookje. And with good cause.

Now the thunderheads crackled with light. Tocohl shook off the hand Buntec laid on her arm, ignored Buntec's query—to count softly to herself.

At the low rumble of thunder, Tocohl turned to the rest and said, "There won't be a rescue team. That's over the camp now, and it's headed our direction. Rattle-brained Kejesli may be, but not rattle-brained enough to send anybody out in that."

Buntec said, "We're dead then, Hellspark. We might have made it in the daisy-clipper but—" Like reflected lightning, fear brightened her eyes; her voice was flat.

"John the Smith!" said Om im suddenly. Buntec stamped her foot at his apparent irrelevancy, but he went on. "Ish shan, John the Smith said to look for a stand of lightning rods. Theoretically we'd be safe in a stand of lightning rods."

"Theoretically," said Buntec; she stamped her foot again.

"Unless you've got a better idea," Om im told her.

A flash of warning red caught Tocohl's eye, brought the sprookje to her notice. She saw that it had walked some twenty feet in the direction of the flashwood. Now it stopped—facing them, displaying its tongue.

Feathers puffed with fear, it retraced its steps until it stood a pace or two from Tocohl. Again it displayed its tongue. Then it held out the edge of the moss cloak to her.

"*Where* do they go in thunderstorms?" Tocohl demanded suddenly. "Somewhere *safe!*"

"There's your better idea, Buntec," Om im said.

"Yes-s," Alfvaen agreed.

Buntec grumbled, "Better than sittin' in the wide open waitin' to be fried."

"Follow the native guide then," Tocohl said; she took the proffered edge of the cloak. The sprookje closed its mouth, turned about, and set off across the flashfield at a trot, the rest of the party close behind.

Within a few yards, Tocohl loosed the end of the moss cloak. Sunchild cast a brief glance backward to assure itself they were still following, then plunged on. A sudden gust of wind whipped alight the flashgrass, surrounding them with patterns now made ominous. With it came the first spatter of rain. The sprookje quickened its pace.

Thunder rumbled ever closer.

Flashfield gave way to flashwood. On its outer fringes stubby chuckling and ticking curiosities competed unsuccessfully with the sound of thunder. A head-high frostwillow, tossed by ever-stronger rain-laden gusts, shattered the air with the sound of a thousand crystal glasses breaking simultaneously. Om im shouted over it, "Heads up, Ish shan. Some of these plants are as deadly as the lightning we hope to avoid."

The sprookje glanced back again and, displaying a red tongue, made a wide path around a slender tree, notable only because it seemed pronged rather than branched.

Om im grasped Tocohl's wrist. "Eilo's-kiss," he supplied, "that's one of the nasty ones. Remember what it looks like—even the little ones can stun a human. The big ones can kill. Sprookjes too, it would seem." Before releasing her wrist he hopped a step forward to precede her. "Blade right," he said, then added without turning, "Buntec, you'd better guide Alfvaen."

Buntec reached for Alfvaen's hand. Tocohl acknowledged Om im's blade right with a raised and curled hand. She knew he saw nei-ther—his attention was fully on the path the sprookje broke.

They were headed away from the river, but Tocohl knew she'd be able to locate it again. Even without Maggy's assistance—Tocohl shivered at the harshness of the thought—Tocohl had a good sense of direction. Assuming they survived the storm, they could follow the river back to camp.

The thunder was closer now, and the sprookje quickened its step still faster. Om im, whose shorter legs needed three steps to her two, was forced into a run but did not appear wearied by the pace. Glancing up, the small man said, "Practice," and grinned as if he'd read her mind.

The sprookje wove through a thick wall of arabesque vine. Tocohl, following close behind Om im and the sprookje, did not look up until she had negotiated the fine but wiry barrier. "Lots of zap-mes," Om im warned as she freed Alfvaen and herself from the last of the tangle. They spent the next few moments avoiding a lashing from zap-mes of every conceivable size.

At last, the zap-mes seemed to subside to ankle-height new growth and Tocohl looked ahead. She drew in her breath involuntarily. Before her was the embodiment of the "blasted forest" of so many Zoveelian fairy tales.

Gaunt black spikes, trees unrelieved by branch or leaf, jabbed high into the blackened sky. Beneath them, and for a short distance beyond, nothing grew—but here and there the remains of something that looked charred. This was the stand of lightning rods. The sprookje stood before them, welcoming.

Well, she thought wryly, it's a suitable setting for a sprookje, I suppose. I hope it's as suitable for humans. The rain had turned earnest.

To Om im, she said aloud, "Looks like the native guide had the same idea you did. We didn't see this from the daisy-clipper. Sunchild must know the territory very well."

The sprookje picked its way warily into the recesses of the lightning rod stand.

"You couldn't have chosen a better guide," Om im said. "Now watch where I put my feet. Whatever energy the lightning rods don't need, they bleed off into the ground—once in a while there's a surface node that can give you a dangerous shock."

In cautious silence, the party continued its way to the heart of the shelter, where the sprookje sat waiting. Tocohl and the others followed suit as a gust of wind dashed water in their faces.

"Too bad we haven't time to build a shelter," Tocohl said.

"Oh, well, can't have everything," said Om im.

"Why not?" said Tocohl, and drew a grin from him.

Buntec settled Alfvaen, then herself. Curling up on her side, she threw an arm over her head and announced, "Nothing to do but sleep."

Lightning struck the tallest spikes of their shelter with an ear-splitting crack that brought Buntec bolt upright, staring wide-eyed and openmouthed. When the sound died away and their numbed ears could once again hear the shattering of frostwillows in the distance, Buntec said grimly, "Sleep, my foot."

Tocohl blinked away red Catherine wheels, turned her face into the rain to clear her eyes of the stinging tears the lightning flash had startled from them. The air seemed too full of rain to breathe, but she did not draw up the mask of her 2nd skin. It would only serve to remind her how much Maggy would have enjoyed this experience; few had ever sat amid lightning and lived to tell the tale.

She twisted her hair into a single mass to channel the water down her back, pocketed her spectacles. Enhanced vision was the last thing she needed at the moment, she thought, squeezing her eyes tight against a bolt of lightning so intense that even through closed lids it reddened her sight.

Wind tore through the empty spaces between the lightning rods, flinging leaves and bits of branch at them. Here and there a wet leaf struck one of the nodes Om im had warned her of—struck and struck sparks.

Thunder deafened and deadened their ears until they could no longer distinguish a silence from the thunder in their heads.

And through it all the sprookje, wrapped tightly in the moss cloak, left its own afterimage in Tocohl's eyes: a ghostly glowing image of regal unconcern.

After an eternity, the storm passed on...

Alfvaen, exhausted, had fallen into a fitful sleep. Wordlessly, for the words might not have been heard through still-ringing ears, the others agreed to rest; the run to shelter had exhausted their bodies, but the storm had exhausted their spirits as well. Buntec jerked in violent dreams.

Without knowing she had fallen asleep, Tocohl started awake at a tickling touch—Sunchild stroking her wrist. "I'm okay," she told it and was surprised to find that she could hear her own voice.

"That's good to hear, Ish shan," Om im said. He pounded the heel of his hand beside his ear, setting earpips a-jingle, and added, grinning, "In more ways than one."

"I know exactly what you mean," Tocohl assured him. Then she looked again at the sprookje. "From the way Sunchild's acting, I think it's safe to leave now. We'll have to make some decisions."

"Before we wake the others," he began—but a jerk of his thumb specified Alfvaen.

"You're worried about that scratching," Tocohl said. "So am I. Even if it's just a reaction to stress, I want to get her to *layli-layli calulan* as soon as possible."

"Yes," said Om im and woke the others gently. Buntec stretched luxuriously. "I think I'm alive," she said, taking obvious pleasure in the sound of each syllable. Alfvaen came to with a gasping sound, held her head.

"How do you feel?" Tocohl asked.

Alfvaen turned her head from side to side, gingerly testing the result. "Strange," she said, "so strange. Giddy, and"—she stood cautiously, as if unsure of the ground beneath her feet—"uncoordinated. I—" She took a deep breath and stared at Tocohl.

There had been no trace of slur in her speech.

"I can hear it," Tocohl said. "You should be drunker but you're not."

"I'm scared," said Alfvaen—and her lapse into Siveyn told Tocohl the depth of that fear.

Buntec had been speaking with Om im in low tones, now she said, "We haven't much choice but to walk home. Who knows where the daisy-clipper is by now, or if the locator is working. I say we head for the river and foot it," she finished, scowling deeply. It was agreed by all, right down to the obscenity.

Placing an arm around Alfvaen, Tocohl steadied her and said, in Siveyn, "My oath: that I will return you safely to swift-Kalat." She was rewarded by a lessening of fear in the sea-green eyes and she squeezed the Siveyn's arm. "Shall we go?" Tocohl offered her arm formally, and just as formally, Alfvaen accepted it.

The survey camp crackled with fears and rumors. The repaired transceiver had brought no response from Buntec's party and the storm, bringing forced inaction, heightened tension until it was as tangible as the stench of ozone. *Layli-layli calulan* kept her own counsel, but Maggy noted that the doctor scarcely let Timosie Megeve out of her sight. When she did, swift-Kalat followed after the Maldeneantine.

Maggy set the arachne following *layli-layli calulan*. When at last she reached the privacy of the empty infirmary, Maggy tilted the arachne, angling the camera up to observe the shaman's expression— an important part of any reply, Tocohl had told her—and asked, "Why should you and swift-Kalat find observing Megeve of such importance? I will help if I know what to look for. What dream have you?"

Sure she had phrased her query properly in Yn, Maggy found it surprising—yes, that was the term Tocohl would have used for a response so unexpected—when in response *layli-layli calulan* twisted her ring.

"Your pardon," Maggy said instantly. At the same time, noting shifting priorities, she drew the arachne back a few steps. Without it, she could know nothing of what had happened to Tocohl. She didn't wish to be impolite but she did want it out of range.

"No," said *layli-layli calulan*, reinforcing the word with the sharp upward jerk of the chin that said the same in Yn. "No dream. A nightmare rather."

Maggy waited, hoping she would explain. She wasn't sure it was safe to ask for further information, not the way *layli-layli* continued to twist her ring. Maggy moved the arachne a few steps farther away.

"Your pardon, *maggy-maggy*" — the shaman looked down at her hands — "I didn't mean to frighten you."

"Does that mean a shaman's curse *would* work on a mechanical device?"

"I don't know. I never had occasion to try. But it surely wouldn't work on you. I don't know your name."

"That's good," said Maggy, and she stepped the arachne back to its original position. "Then would you please explain what you meant about a nightmare? I want to help, but I can't when I don't understand."

Again *layli-layli calulan* surprised her, this time with a sudden smile, the first Maggy had ever recorded in her presence. Maggy suspected Tocohl would have termed it *quite* beautiful.

"How good is your Yn, *maggy-maggy*, or do you only understand specific phrases?"

"I have three Yn dictionaries, two grammars, and a library of fiction from which to draw analogy. I can puzzle out much."

"Then I have a task, one that only you can perform."

"Only me?"

"You are able to speak to Tocohl through an implant, just here." A be-ringed finger tapped the analogous spot below *layli-layli's* ear.

"But I can't contact her!"

"Not yet. However, the moment your contact is restored, I want you to deliver the following message verbatim to Tocohl and *to no one else*. Do you understand?"

"For Tocohl only," said the arachne, "so noted and tagged. There will be no unauthorized retrieval of this information." Lest that be insufficient, she added, less formally, "Don't worry, *layli-layli*, I'm good at keeping secrets. Tocohl taught me how."

Layli-layli calulan smiled a second time; this time the smile vanished as quickly as it had come. Face stern, finger touching ring, she spoke three sentences in soft, rhythmic Yn. Then she added a fourth in GalLing': "Remember, *maggy-maggy*, a textbook translation is not always an accurate translation."

But Maggy had already begun an exhaustive matching, not only of individual words with her dictionary stores, but of whole phrases with their context against her stores of Yn writings, fictional and nonfictional.

The result in Hellspark, the language Maggy knew best, was one sentence long: "Megeve may be responsible for the equipment failures."

A mistranslation? Maggy doubted it, so she sought information beyond her language banks for corroboration.

Item: swift-Kalat telling *layli-layli calulan*, "Oloitokitok died while Megeve repaired the transceiver."

Item: *layli-layli* responding instantly to this information, wishing to search immediately for Tocohl, willing to lie to do so.

No, thought Maggy, there was nothing wrong with her translation. But she had insufficient data to calculate the probability.

"Take me with you when you search for Tocohl," said the arachne; and *layli-layli calulan* said, "I was planning to."

The two rejoined the knot of surveyors that crowded about Dyxte in the common room, awaiting the primary meteorologist's pronouncements anxiously. Matching Megeve's expressions with what she had on tape in reference to Maldeneantine, Maggy concluded that he was abnormally nervous. In the light of the rest, John the Smith, Dyxte, swift-Kalat, Maggy found this inconclusive.

She let part of her system go on with its extrapolations even as swift-Kalat turned to her and said, "Where was the daisy-clipper when you lost communication with Tocohl?"

Maggy touched one of the arachne's appendages to the map on display. "There. I can be more specific if you have a more detailed map."

"No need," said Dyxte, "the storm has passed well beyond that." Swift-Kalat had already started for the door. Dyxte called out, "You've got about three hours, swift-Kalat, before that next storm hits. I'll keep you posted!"

"All right," said Kejesli, "start a standard search pattern for that daisy-clipper from that point outward. You know your positions. Do it now!"

Layli-layli calulan raised her hands, the gesture evocative of that she had used in claiming a taboo situation. "Shuffle the pattern to cover us," she said. "Swift-Kalat and I intend to let *maggy-maggy* lead us. Our pattern, as such, may be erratic."

Kejesli moved to object, but *layli-layli calulan* raised her hands a fraction higher and he said merely, "Take Megeve with you. I'll want a full report on the causes of the equipment failure."

The shaman's smile broadened. "Of course."

Moments later, a dozen daisy-clippers raced across the landscape of Flashfever toward the spot Maggy had indicated. "Buntec followed the river," said the arachne, from its precarious perch on *layli-layli calulan*'s knees.

"Yes," said swift-Kalat, who was at the controls of the daisy-clipper with Megeve at his left, "but this is quicker. We'll go straight to the spot you last saw them."

Megeve twisted about in his seat to peer at *layli-layli calulan*. "Do you really think that machine's trustworthy?" he said, jabbing a finger in the direction of the arachne. "It seems to me—"

Anxious to keep the arachne out of his clutches, Maggy flinched it deep into *layli-layli calulan*'s lap.

The shaman raised a protective arm between them. "It seems to me," she said, "that this machine is at least as trustworthy as *your* equipment."

"Still," said Megeve, "I'd feel better if you'd let me check out its circuits."

"I'd feel better if you'd keep your eye on the landscape," *layli-layli calulan* told him, and Maggy could hear the sharpness in her voice. "We are looking for a lost party. This time we intend to find them *before* they come to harm."

"Yes, of course," said Megeve. He turned his attention back to the search.

Free from the threat of his reaching fingers, Maggy telescoped the arachne's legs to give her, once more, a view of the passing scenery. The craft swerved to bypass a noisy grove of frostwillows—the wind had not yet died down—and *layli-layli calulan* grasped the arachne to keep it from tumbling from her lap.

Without warning, Maggy—high above the world of Flashfever—lost all contact with the arachne. It was as unexpected and as total as the initial loss of contact with Tocohl had been.

Now she had no way at all of helping to find Tocohl!

True, she had other mobiles, but none was sufficiently adept to handle a skiff. She tried reactivating the mobile that accompanied *layli-layli*, swift-Kalat, and Megeve at fifteen-second intervals; and, on the third try, she succeeded. Reassured, she ran a check, long-distance, on the mobile's circuitry and found everything in good working order. She began a read-through of all available literature to find out what might account for the arachne's lapse.

"I told you there was something wrong with it," Megeve was saying. "Now perhaps you'll believe me. Flashfever has been ruining all our equipment. Let me have a look."

Overlapping him, *layli-layli calulan* asked, "Are you all right? The arachne just suddenly collapsed." She held it firmly, well beyond Megeve's reach.

"I'm all right," Maggy said, produced a chuckle that seemed to reassure the shaman, and added, "it's the arachne I'm worried about. I can't account for the lapse."

"We're here," said swift-Kalat, and the arachne craned toward the door and looked down.

"Just a few feet upriver is the spot I lost their transmissions," it said. Within a few moments, all of the daisy-clippers were poised above the churning stream. A flock of golden scoffers screamed at them all in outrage.

Swift-Kalat coded to receive emergency transmissions and spoke into his throat mike, but said to the rest, "Nothing but the search parties answering." The other five daisy-clippers flashed away in the sunlight to weave a search pattern along either side of the river.

"You said we would not follow the search pattern, *layli-layli*," said swift-Kalat. "What would you have me do?"

"Maggy-maggy?"

Maggy decided that *layli-layli calulan* meant for her to answer swift-Kalat's query. "Continue to follow the river as Buntec did," she said, all too conscious of Megeve's muttered objection and of the arachne's inexplicable lapse.

"Slowly," added *layli-layli calulan*, and the craft glided forward, barely skimming the roaring waters.

They followed the river for another forty minutes, the silence within the daisy-clipper a sharp contrast to the clamor of their surroundings, until swift-Kalat said, "This is where Buntec habitually turned to cross land."

"When she went to look for wild sprookjes?"

"That's right, Maggy. Shall I follow her usual route?"

"Yes, please. Perhaps we will at least find evidence that they reached their intended destination."

"Don't count on it," said *layli-layli*. "The rains will have washed away most of the traces any party leaves."

"Not a grounded daisy-clipper," said swift-Kalat. "We have something large to look for," and he guided the daisy-clipper into the blazing cacophony of the flashwood.

The sprookje was barely visible as a dark patch moving through the undergrowth some twenty yards ahead. Sunchild seemed to have grasped the notion that they were headed back to the river and had taken the lead. As long as the sprookje was willing (and seemed to be tending in the right direction) Tocohl accepted the counsel; as Om im pointed out, it was more adept at spotting Flashfever hazards than the rest of them.

Om im led the human contingent, Tocohl and Alfvaen abreast of each other, with Buntec bringing up the rear. Om im and Buntec watched for hazards, Tocohl watched Alfvaen. They were traveling all too slowly for Tocohl's taste, but it couldn't be helped. The undergrowth was stubborn, dense.

Her eyes teared from the constant dazzle. Her ears, she was sure, had not yet stopped ringing from their assault by thunder. But she knew that the ringing was nothing more than background noise, Flashfever-standard. She ducked to follow Om im beneath a clamoring frostwillow.

Beyond was a thick stand of tick-ticks entangled in arabesque vines. Om im eased through—there were certain advantages to his size, Tocohl noted with envy. She leaned her weight against the nearest, to press them aside for Alfvaen. Sharp pain stung her, hip to ankle, and she jumped forward and spun. Nothing but a zap-me, she saw, hidden within the tick-ticks. "Just bruises," Tocohl said. "Serves me right for not looking. Could have been worse." She put her back to the task again, before the zap-me could reset its tendrils.

Alfvaen clicked her tongue, chiding Tocohl in imitation of the plant before she fought her way through. Her darting glance was bright, too bright to be set in a face as pale as that, thought Tocohl, following.

On the far side, Alfvaen paused to scrape furiously at her back, tangling the damp blue fringe of her bodice; then she pushed doggedly on. A swarm of vikries dislodged from stalks of tick-ticks, followed briefly along beside her. When she bent to drink water from the upcupped leaf of a green handplant, they scattered away.

(That thirst of hers worries me too) Tocohl had subvocalized the observation. Then, despite the lack of response, she went on doing it. (Maybe you can hear me, Maggy, and I just can't hear you...) Please let it be so, she thought.

(But I could use your expertise right now. Alfvaen no longer slurs her words. I'd say she was sobering—and the excessive thirst is a symptom of alcohol dehydration—but her behavior isn't right for sober either. Om im agrees, and he's seen her normal behavior. She looks like someone riding an oxygen high: too exhilarated for sense.

(And she's exhausted. We all are. But her exhilaration isn't Flashfever effect. I mean, not the same as the ionization high.)

The fallen trunk of something like a tree lay across their intended path. The sprookje waited atop it.

"We're coming," Om im told the creature. The words had no noticeable effect on Sunchild but the moment he began to clamber up, the sprookje vanished over the side. Tocohl made a knee for him, then waited in the same position, expecting Alfvaen to use the same step up.

Instead, Alfvaen glowered at her, took a running jump, and made the top. She overbalanced, toppled with a crash and an alarming series of squeals. "Alfvaen's okay," came Om im's voice, "she just landed in a pig thicket."

Tocohl hauled herself up, balanced on her chest, to see for herself. Bright-eyed and grumbling curses in Siveyn, Alfvaen stood methodically kicking at the edge of a waist-high clump of silver blue; each time she did, it let out another series of squeals. (Plant or no, that *sounds* like *la'ista*,) Tocohl said privately. (We must get her to *layli-layli calulan*! Soon!)

Tocohl reached down a hand to pull Buntec up. Together, the two of them slid over the obstructing trunk.

To this side was a small clearing, bright with penny-Jannisett and monkswoodsmen. Sunchild waited impatiently for the rest of them to regroup, and then set out again.

Tocohl held up her hand. "I think we all need a rest," she said. Om im glanced at Alfvaen, who was still tormenting the pig thicket, and sat down, pulling Buntec with him. "Alfvaen," he said, "sit down. You need the rest as much as I do."

The sprookje fixed its golden eyes on them, then stared up into the sky. Its cheek-feathers puffed. Openmouthed, warning tongue displayed, it again held out the edge of the moss cloak to Tocohl, who said, "No rest for the weary. Get up, everybody, and let's hope it isn't far to the next shelter."

"Someplace without a pig thicket, I hope," Buntec grumbled. She tapped Alfvaen's shoulder none too gently.

Startled, Alfvaen spun to face her. "Your pardon?" she said, for all the world as if returned to normal behavior. "We're going on? Why?"

"Because Sunchild gave a very expressive look at the sky," Om im told her.

"Oh," she said, forgetting the pig thicket to join him.

Once again the party set off to follow the sprookje to safety, but not before Tocohl and Om im had taken the opportunity to exchange worried glances.

The route brought them to a swollen stream that, no doubt, channeled into the river they sought. A happy chirring filled the air, grew louder and louder, until it almost drowned the sound of rushing water. "Drunken dabblers," Buntec shouted, over it all, "sound like good times and parties. Nothin' but plants."

Alfvaen glared at the two of them over her shoulder. A moment later, she let slip a branch which snapped and dashed a spate of cold water in Tocohl's face. The Siveyn had begun to speak softly to herself in her own tongue, so softly that Tocohl could not make out the words, not even when they had left the patch of drunken dabblers well behind.

They came to a bend in the stream and the ground rose slowly beneath their feet. Where the water tumbled swift about a bare and broken jut of rocks, tall weeds spaced themselves at neat intervals, flicking with the rapids. "Om im?" Tocohl pointed to them.

"Wave power," he said. "What you see in the water is a runner from these." he flicked a finger, in passing, at a black stem topped by a dull red gleam. "Any excess energy is bled off as light. They only glow like that when the stream is swollen—which means most of the time," he finished, with a wry smile.

"Wonderful!" said Tocohl, but Alfvaen growled in Siveyn, "Deathlight." She scratched and scowled, whether at the itch or the plants, Tocohl couldn't tell.

The sprookje turned opposite to the stream's bend to lead them back into deep flashwood. The ground rose steeply, so steeply in fact that they followed the sprookje's example and, whenever possible, drew themselves hand-over-hand along the arabesque and leatherstrap vines.

The wind picked up once again and with it the flashwood's noise. By the time they had clawed their way to the top of the small escarpment, rain was falling from the darkened sky. The sprookje had a fine sense of timing, there was no doubt about that. Tocohl, pausing while they caught their breaths from the climb, counted. The storm would be overhead in minutes. Already the lightning was close enough that she could scent burning vegetation on the wind after each strike.

To her right, low brush bent in the wind, aflame with its own internal light. Only a hundred yards beyond rose a second stand of lightning rods. The sprookje had already gone on. (It's sure we'll follow this time,) Tocohl commented, bit her lip at the silence that drowned out all of Flashfever's noise.

Follow they did, to the edge of the blackened patch that marked the stand's perimeter. Deep inside, the sprookje sat, waiting patiently for them to join it in shelter.

"Watch the ground and follow my lead," Buntec said; she reached to take Alfvaen's hand.

"No!" Alfvaen thrust her away with such force that Buntec stumbled two steps, three steps back.

Buntec caught her balance just in time to avoid falling onto the hazardous ground beneath the lightning rods. Cursing, she started for the smaller woman, this time with worried caution.

Alfvaen cut harshly through the Jannisetti curses: "No, Buntec. You must not interfere. I will not let this so-called Tocohl Susumo harm us further."

Buntec froze in her tracks, cast a swift glance of bewilderment at Tocohl, then a look of deep concern at Alfvaen.

"Alfvaen?" said Om im. "What are you talking about?"

"I speak of"—Alfvaen sought the word in GalLing', spoke it bitterly—"sorcery." And with fury rising in her eyes, she swung to face Tocohl.

Tocohl had seen that intensity, that ferocity only once before—on the face of a Siveyn about to issue a death challenge. Lightning ripped the air, striking the lightning rods, to give livid illumination to Alfvaen's anger.

"Don't touch her!" Tocohl snapped to the others. "Get into the lightning rods and stay there!"

"She's hallucinating!" Om im shouted over the dying thunder.

"I know what she sees," Tocohl said sharply. "Now get *back.*"

Alfvaen stepped toward Tocohl, fringe clinging sullenly as she raised her arm across her chest with stiff singleness of purpose.

A crawl of sensors along her arm told Tocohl that Om im was moving forward, not back, to blade right. Without taking her attention from Alfvaen, she shot a single word at him in Bluesippan, ordered him back by virtue of his blade service. The crawl of sensors told her he had obeyed.

"So, Haining Lefven!" The Siveyn took a second deliberate step forward, her green eyes fixed unwaveringly on Tocohl, and spoke again in cold, harsh tones, sharpening her native language to a gleaming point. "You spoke and spoke again, and each time your words were heard by earless folk. You danced before the sightless and they watched your every move. You drew sweet words from the speechless. But now there will be an end to magics—I, Tingling Alfvaen, offer you the justice of death."

Veschke's sparks, thought Tocohl, wouldn't Maggy love this! Straight out of the fictions the two of them were reading en route! And Tocohl chose her reply from the same fictions.

Stretching both arms before her, in the manner of a sleepwalker, Tocohl began, placatingly, "The sun shines on us both..." She turned her palms up. "The wind blows us both the scent of sea-jeme and sediji. The earth pulses beneath our feet its rush of life. I, Susumo Tocohl, have no quarrel with another child of Siveyn."

She let her hands fall to her sides, slowly, slowly.

But Tingling Alfvaen did not lower her hands. Rigid still with the anger of her own imaginings, she said, "This is your only choice, child of no one."

Tocohl said, "Alfvaen, it's me: Tocohl. You and I have no quarrel—at least none that won't wait until the storm passes. I vote the two of us get in out of the lightning before somebody gets fried."

"And I for life," said Alfvaen.

Veschke guide me, thought Tocohl, she's *hearing* the proper responses! What do I do now?

Lightning struck the lightning rods again; in its violent illumination, as she fought for vision, Tocohl saw Alfvaen blink. She's *hearing* the responses, but she saw the lightning flash! Maybe, just maybe, she's *seeing* what's real!

And with infinite slowness, Tocohl turned her back to Tinling Alfvaen. She blanked Flashfever from her consciousness, with all of its noises and glittering lights, and focused all of her attention on the sensors in her 2nd skin, which gave gross but tangible indication of Alfvaen's position.

To turn your back on a challenge was a strong indication of guiltlessness, but a death-challenge might not be so easily turned away. The challenger's desire to duel may outweigh the social strictures.

Tocohl's back crawled. Sweating, she waited out a heartbeat, then stepped aside — Alfvaen went headlong into the arabesque vines in front of which Tocohl had just been standing. Alfvaen turned swiftly.

Tocohl caught her by the kilt, heaved upward. The move misplaced a kick aimed at her heart; Tocohl took it stingingly in midchest, gasped, and kneed Alfvaen in the belly.

Not hard enough. Alfvaen, though twisted with pain, jabbed stiffened fingers sharply into Tocohl's side.

Still grasping the kilt, Tocohl swung Alfvaen bodily to the right, into a medium-sized zap-me. As the plant lashed with its several whips, Tocohl dropped the woman and threw a knuckle-blow, hard, at Alfvaen's temple. Alfvaen fell unconscious.

Tocohl dropped to her knees beside Alfvaen's still form. Her breath came in great rasps, aching through the injury to her side.

Had Alfvaen's reflexes not been crippled by her illness, or had Tocohl not taken advantage of Flashfever's traps — Tocohl shivered and blessed the pain in her side that confirmed her continued existence. Lightning and roaring thunder brought her to her senses. Rain poured down, drenching her.

Buntec pulled her gently erect, then bent to maneuver Alfvaen onto her broad shoulder. Om im slashed strips of arabesque vine. "We'll have to tie her up," he explained, "we can't risk that a second time."

Trailing vines, he led Tocohl to shelter, walking as slowly as she. She saw his concern, realized that she clutched at her side. "I think it's only a bruised rib. We'll find out when we get back to camp." She eased herself down on the blasted heath; letting the rain spill into her face, she began the quieting litany of Methven ritual against the counterpoint of thunder.

Buntec lay the unconscious Alfvaen beside her. Om im bound the Siveyn hand and foot.

"A waking nightmare," Tocohl said at last. "She didn't know what she was doing. Somehow, for some reason, she has sobered and her brain has a desperate need, waking or sleeping, for dreams."

"Then, if she sleeps, she'll be all right?" Buntec asked.

"She should be," Tocohl said, "once she's made up the lost dreaming."

"She may not," said Om im, a bitter tone to his voice that Tocohl had not previously heard. He brushed the blue fringe aside and laid a gentle hand on Alfvaen's back. "Look, Ish shan."

A flash of lightning showed them what he saw. Beneath the transparent 2nd skin, thin gray veining patterned Alfvaen's skin.

"Garbage plants," said Buntec, and her face paled. "No!"

Rain spattered them, but could not wash away the horror.

The storm had come up faster than expected, and Kejesli had ordered the searchers to return to base camp. They had worse news to report: the daisy-clipper had been found, some miles downriver. Save for a school of Flashfever streampuppies, it was empty.

"It crashed in the water and they had to abandon it." Edge-of-Dark leaned forward in her chair, poised as if to leap at them.

Kejesli tapped the Display: "Here."

"No bodies?" asked *layli-layli calulan.*

"No bodies," said Edge-of-Dark. "They may have been washed away by the storm surge."

With unexpected force, John the Smith slapped the table-top and said, *"No."* Then, more calmly, he added, "Suppose they got out safely—*assume* they did! A storm was coming up. Where would you go for shelter? Would you stay in the middle of a flashgrass savannah? Of course not, you'd head for the nearest lightning rod grove."

Kejesli grasped the straw. "Yes! Veschke light my way, that's just what I'd do! We'll check every grove of lightning rods that can be seen from the abandoned daisy-clipper!"

"We'll have to start farther back along the river," said *layli-layli.* "The daisy-clipper was found here, but Buntec would have turned across land *here*" — she indicated the spot — "so the daisy-clipper must have been washed downstream — and we have no idea how *far* downstream."

"Your pardon, *layli-layli calulan.*"

"Yes, Maggy?"

"May I be permitted to display my tapes? They may be of some service."

"Do it," said Kejesli, somewhat abruptly; and Maggy inserted the arachne's adapter into the console. A moment later, images of swift-Kalat's trip downriver flashed past, then froze, giving Kejesli an almost sickening jolt. The image expanded to show a detailed portion of the riverbank. The flashgrass was strewn with uprooted, tattered water-weeds, with chunks of mud so large they had not yet been washed away by the heavy rains ... all thrown onto the bank as if by great force.

Kejesli turned to swift-Kalat, who stared at the display hopefully. "Is there any animal that might make a mark like that?"

Swift-Kalat said, "Not to my knowledge. Maggy, can you pinpoint that spot on the map?"

The map reappeared instantly, but it was quite obviously Maggy's and not the display map. It was neatly marked with a series of bright red arrows, labeled, WRECKAGE OF DAISY-CLIPPER, BUNTEC'S TURNOFF, and POINT OF IMPACT?

"Shall I enter it into your computer?" said the arachne.

Kejesli looked to the others for advice. Megeve said, "That machine collapsed twice on us. It is without doubt faulty, perhaps dangerously so. I strongly advise against relying on it."

But *layli-layli calulan* seemed to speak for the rest, and her verdict was "Yes."

Like every other Hellspark Kejesli had ever met, this one had no respect for authority either. Maggy did not wait for his permission but went about her task on *layli-layli*'s word alone.

When *layli-layli calulan* withdrew to her cabin to wait out the storm, Maggy sent the arachne after her. Remembering her manners, she paused it on the threshold, tilting to observe *layli-layli.* "You may join me, *maggy-maggy lynn,*" she said, "but I prefer silence for some moments. I must think."

"Me too," Maggy assured her. She stopped the arachne just inside the door, squatted it; she did not want it to drip on the shaman's ritual mat.

She had run the most extensive diagnostic available to her, first on the arachne, then on her own hardware. She had found nothing physically wrong with either. Yet she had lost contact with the arachne twice—the second time, shorter than the first, as they raced the thunderstorm to camp.

Spurred by the message *layli-layli calulan* had given her for Tocohl only, she moved on to the possibility of sabotage, despite its low probability.

The search was a long one. She had very little in the way of files on sabotage *per se*. Making a note in her active file to stock up as soon as possible, for future reference, she moved on to the only other source available: fiction.

And there she found references to a number of devices that had the characteristics she sought. Each would jam not only an implanted transceiver but also the aural-visual transceivers that were critical components of hand-held, 2nd skin, and arachne.

She settled down to a closer examination of each. The first was the best match but she found she had appended to the story Tocohl's comment: "Oh, he *lies!!!* I don't believe a word of it, Maggy. He didn't do his homework." So, one could lie in the context of fiction. Well, that also confirmed that one could tell the truth in the context of fiction. She went on.

The next two were the inventions of cultures that Maggy could find no nonfiction reference to; in fact, as described, both the jamming devices contravened the laws of physics. Very unlikely, Maggy concluded, and tagged each with a comment of her own, the rude noise Tocohl had so appreciated.

Moving on to the next, she found a description and sketchy explanation of a device called an Hayashi jammer. The explanation was plausible, and the characteristics given were a very good match with those she sought. Did this author lie?

She cross-matched to nonfiction. There was indeed an Hayashi culture and much of what the fiction implied about it the nonfiction confirmed. So perhaps the Hayashi jammer exists, she decided. Now what?

Buntec had assumed that all the sprookjes' artifacts were biological, so she had suggested they look for grafts. And she had suggested that the sprookjes might have biological art as well. Tocohl had been willing to act on the assumption.

Right, Maggy told herself, sounding much like Tocohl to her inner ear, assume the Hayashi jammer exists. What follows logically?

Where is it? Not in camp, or she wouldn't have contact with the arachne at all. Not with the daisy-clipper. They had passed within the stated range of the device on their trip back to camp and the arachne had not collapsed.

With Tocohl! What if it were with Tocohl?

She hastily called up the map she had displayed for Kejesli. On it she plotted those points at which she had lost and regained contact with the arachne.

The range fitted. The second lapse had been of shorter duration but tallied nicely with the greater speed of their return trip. Two points do not make a graph, but she reached a 0.05 probability that Tocohl herself carried the Hayashi jammer and was moving upstream toward the camp.

Was there any way to confirm such a thing? Had it been done? Could it be done? No one on the survey team was Hayashi but—the team's records might show something…

Layli-layli calulan was lighting a jievnal stick. Maggy hesitated to interrupt her thinking, but with Tocohl and three others in danger, she could not ignore even so low a probability.

She brought the arachne to its feet. "Please, I'm sorry to interrupt, but may I use your console?" It was not polite, she knew, but she had already started the arachne toward it.

"Yes," said *layli-layli calulan,* after what seemed to Maggy a very long pause.

Maggy thrust the arachne's adapter into the console and searched for the team's personnel files. She met stubborn refusal. "As bad as Kejesli," she said. The computer was obviously keyed to hold certain information for authorized personnel only. She could break the coding but it would take time.

"What are you looking for, *maggy-maggy*?"

The question startled her, too much of her attention had been on the coding to notice that *layli-layli calulan* had moved to watch the display. Breaking codes on other computers was technically illegal. Maggy had no idea what *layli-layli* would think of it, so instead of volunteering any information, she answered the question as strictly as it had been phrased: "Further information about Timosie Megeve."

Without comment, *layli-layli calulan* touched the keyboard, then spoke aloud, *"Layli-layli calulan."* The records were obviously voice and fingerprint keyed. "It will oblige you now, Maggy."

"Thank you." The arachne touched the keyboard and watched the display, slowing it to human speed so that she did not offend *layli-layli*. The details of Megeve's training and employment inched by and probability took a jump upward: Megeve had trained in electronics *on Hayashi*.

"Will you help me to act on a probability of point-oh-six?"

"A hunch?" *Layli-layli calulan* knelt to look directly into the camera eye. "Yes—if you'll answer a question for me. Fair trade, Hellspark?"

"Fair trade," Maggy told her.

"Is there really a Hellspark ritual of change? The truth, *maggy-maggy*, in exchange for my help."

Now Maggy understood why Tocohl considered trading an art. That was a question she had not anticipated. She couldn't lie, having declared a fair trade; yet to admit that she had lied ... *Layli-layli calulan* had lied too—and there Maggy found a possible solution to the dilemma.

"There is now," Maggy said firmly. "The gods Hibok Hibok and Juffure have so decreed it."

Layli-layli calulan gave a shout of laughter. When she at last caught her breath, she said, "Now, tell me about your hunch, *maggy-maggy*."

Thunder jolted Tocohl to consciousness with a convulsive jerk that sent searing pain through her side. She gasped and pressed a hand to the pain's source, pushed herself to a sitting position with her free hand. The pain did not ease. The moss cloak whipped about her. Grateful for the distraction, she tucked its edges firmly beneath her thighs.

Moss cloak? she wondered suddenly, fingering it.

"The sprookje returned it while you were passed out," Om im shouted over the roar of rain. "Maybe Sunchild thinks the cloak is for injuries."

Tocohl glanced at the crumpled Alfvaen, whose face Buntec sheltered from the rain with Om im's cape. Why not Alfvaen then? Om im said something further.

"What?"

"I said," he repeated, "how are you feeling, Ish shan?"

"Blunt, rusted, nicked, and burred," she said. "Aside from that, I've never been better. How long have I been out?"

"Ten, twenty minutes. You're not holding us up, the storm is." He reached toward her, pried her crimped hand from her side. When she tried to resist, he said, "Ish shan, I've done enough fieldwork to have earned a degree in emergency medicine. It's blade right, and you know it."

She did; she let him probe the injury, gasping once or twice despite his gentleness. At last he sat back on his haunches. She could not see his expression but his tone was anything but relieved: "It could be broken, Ish shan. You can't travel: you risk puncturing a lung."

"Are you volunteering to carry me?" She kept her tone light but it was sufficient to silence any further warnings.

Lightning flickered, small stuff this time, but enough to light his face and let Tocohl see the depth of his concern for her. "Talk to me," she said, "I could use the distraction."

He gave her the Bluesippan thumbs-up yes and moved closer, just as another massive bolt of lightning struck not five feet above their heads. A great sheet of light enveloped them; at the periphery of their blasted heath, zap-mes lashed into action. An acrid smell, like that of burning insulation, assaulted Tocohl's nose. She gave a wan grin at Om im and observed, "Smells like one or two of those zap-mes overestimated their current requirements."

Om im batted at his ear. He had clearly not heard her over the still reverberating thunder.

Not willing to risk repeating that, Tocohl shouted, "I thought you said thunderstorms were a time for talking."

Om im shouted back, "Only for sprookjes!"—and pointed.

Twisting to look renewed the stabbing pain. More cautiously, Tocohl moved her whole body to face in the direction he'd pointed.

Two sprookjes kept each other company; their luminescent feathers, streaming with rain, shone in the gloom. Eerie light rippled along their bodies as the wind ruffled and twisted their feathers into pattern after pattern after pattern.

"To your left is Timosie's—Sunchild," Om im said next to her ear, "on the right is van Zoveel's."

Tocohl scrutinized the two. At last she said, "I don't know how you do it, Om im. I can't distinguish any difference in feather patterns—certainly not in this light!"

He was close enough that she could hear his chuckle over the sizzle of rain. "It's a gift, Ish shan—and it has nothing to do with the patterns on their feathers." He waited out a boom of thunder, then continued, "The same way I knew you were Hellspark."

"I assumed Buntec had told you—" Tocohl thought back. Om im had *not* been among those that Buntec had notified on their arrival. "How—?"

Om im spread his hands. "I honestly don't know. I've often been accused of an unusual espability but it can't be that because I can't tell the sprookjes apart if I can't see them."

"I'd hardly call *this* seeing," Tocohl said. A crackle of lightning whited out the gloom, in no way belying her comment. When she felt she could be heard again, she added in a shout, "Or think seeing the key component when you're seeing them from across the compound."

"There you're wrong, Ish shan. Across the compound or across the playground—I've been able to do this, whatever this is, since I was a kid."

He wiped rain from his face and went on, "I knew a pair of identical twins, only they weren't identical, not to me. Drove me crazy because everybody thought they were when I could see so clearly they weren't—even across the playground. When I objected, strongly, to everyone who called them identical, and proved that I could tell them apart even at a distance, I got run through the whole bank of espability tests as a reward."

Again he chuckled. "I shouldn't say that. What I got for reward was two of the best friends I've ever had. They were so pleased to have found someone who never once mistook the one for the other..."

"I think I can understand that. Even identical twins are different to themselves. Their voices are different: one hears the other through air but himself through bone conduction. The difference between how your voice normally sounds to you and how it sounds from a tape."

"I think it had more to do with my outrage. By my blade, Ish shan, to this day I still do not understand how anyone can mistake the two—they move differently. I could see it across a room! Why can't anyone else?"

A flash of lightning, this time farther away, lit and broke the scene into eerie segments like the flash of a strobe. Tocohl saw Megeve's sprookje shift and twist, saw its larynx bob. Neither sprookje blinked or winced at the ferocity of the skies.

She saw, in fact, something she should have seen on the tapes, had she not been distracted by the crests and yokes of the so-called wild sprookjes. Had she not been so *stupid!*

With a wrench that shot pain the length of her body, she turned to face Om im. Tears sprang to her eyes, to be washed away by the torrential rain. "Om im!" she said, gasping it past the pain in her chest. "The wild sprookjes! *They don't have a larynx!*" She tried to explain but found she had no breath to do so.

Alarmed, Om im caught her shoulders and firmly eased her to the ground. "Tell me later, Ish shan. Lie down. Lie down or, by my blade, I'll tie you down!"

She had no strength to fight and enough sense to obey. She let him stretch her out. Vaguely, she remembered the pain of a second probing of her injury, then she slipped into a fitful doze...

When she awoke, the storm had passed. She tried to rise, found her way barred by a firm but comforting arm across her shoulders.

At the sign of movement, Om im withdrew his arm. He brought his face into her line of sight, raised a gilded brow inquiringly.

"You can't handle me and Alfvaen," she said.

"I know. But—carefully, Ish shan."

She turned up her thumb in agreement. With his assistance, she eased herself to her feet. A trial step told her she could walk but that too would have to be carefully done or she would know the pain of it.

Alfvaen slept on; Buntec hoisted the Siveyn onto her shoulders as if she weighed little or nothing.

Sunchild—Tocohl saw that van Zoveel's sprookje had departed—but Megeve's had remained behind. To guide them. There was no longer any doubt of that in her mind. Sunchild rose too, ready to travel.

Following her glance, Om im said, "Now what was all that about sprookjes and larynxes?"

Tocohl smiled wanly and said, "Want to see a trick?" At his frown, she added, "That's not a non sequitur, I assure you. Want to see a trick you taught me?"

Without awaiting his answer, she fixed it firmly in her mind that this was Megeve's sprookje and that, like Megeve, it too spoke Maldeneantine. Walking gingerly, she approached the sprookje as she would have any Maldeneantine and, in that language, she said, "My name is Tocohl Susumo, and I greet you with a full heart."

Word for word, the sprookje echoed her.

This time, *layli-layli calulan's* search party consisted only of Maggy's arachne and swift-Kalat, a feat *layli-layli* had achieved by waving her "divination" sticks at Captain Kejesli and invoking no less than eight fictitious gods. John the Smith had been asked, in confidence, to remain behind and keep a watch on Megeve. There, *layli-layli* had simply invoked friendship.

While the other search parties followed up John the Smith's suggestion, that of checking every lightning rod stand in the immediate area of the downed daisy-clipper, swift-Kalat guided his upstream. From the shaman's capacious lap, the arachne recorded the passing flashwood.

When the arachne's joints buckled, *layli-layli calulan* said, "Stop here. If Maggy is right about the jammer and the range of it, Buntec's party is within a mile of us."

Swift-Kalat let the craft hover as he marked the spot on his computer-generated map, then guided the craft into the woods while *layli-layli calulan* watched the forest below.

They zigzagged for fifteen minutes, marking the spot each time Maggy's arachne came to or lapsed from consciousness, then they headed straight for the rough center of the disturbance.

"There!" *Layli-layli calulan* stabbed a be-ringed finger at a shimmering grove of frostwillows.

Swift-Kalat brought the daisy-clipper to an abrupt halt, swung it at right angles to its previous position, to peer in the direction indicated. "Only a sprookje," he said, not pausing to wonder at the disappointment where a day ago there would have been joy.

Then Buntec stepped from the cover of a monkswoodsman. Howling a greeting, she waved awkwardly from beneath her burden. Joy came and went, as swift-Kalat recognized that her burden was Alfvaen ... bound and unconscious!

Even before he could react and ground the daisy-clipper, *layli-layli calulan* had laid Maggy's arachne aside to transform the seat behind her into its emergency-bed mode. As the daisy-clipper settled into the groundcover, *layli-layli calulan* leapt out. Together, she and Buntec eased Alfvaen aboard where *layli-layli* began to check her over.

There was nothing swift-Kalat could do to assist *layli-layli calulan*, so he turned instead to the rest of the group that straggled from the flashwood. Om im bowed jauntily to Tocohl, took her hand, and laid it on his shoulder; she straightened—a brief spasm of pain crossed her face—and accepted the support, to walk the last few steps to the daisy-clipper, begrimed features held high and proud.

Om im said, "Take Alfvaen and Tocohl to camp. We'll wait here, Buntec and I, for the second lift."

But Tocohl had found the arachne. "Maggy!" she demanded—and the sprookje echoed her as if for emphasis—"What's happened to Maggy? Is she all right?" She lifted the arachne, wincing at the pain the action caused her, and shook it as if to bring it back to consciousness.

"Maggy's fine," said *layli-layli* from the rear of the daisy-clipper. She was stripping the 2nd skin from Alfvaen. "She told us how to find you. She thinks an Hayashi jammer's been planted on you—and the fact that we found you where she said we would bears that out. Check your throat mikes." *Layli-layli* ran her fingers lightly over Alfvaen's back; she drew in her breath.

Alarmed, swift-Kalat craned to look but only caught a glimpse of gray before Buntec shoved him aside to get at the daisy-clipper's tool kit. With the smallest screwdriver to hand, she attacked her own throat mike. "Nothing," she said after a moment's scrutiny—slammed the throat mike onto the daisy-clipper's floor and held out her hand for Tocohl's.

As Tocohl reached up to remove it, she gasped, causing *layli-layli* to look sharply in her direction. Tocohl snapped, "Nothing dangerous. Take care of Alfvaen," but she let swift-Kalat remove the mike from her neck and hand it to Buntec.

Om im said, "Possible broken rib, *layli-layli*," and earned himself a glare from the Hellspark.

"Never *mind* that," said Tocohl with an exasperated look, first at him, then at the sprookje. "I'm fine," she repeated with the sprookje still speaking emphasis, "take care of Alfvaen." Behind the exasperation, her face was ashen.

"Barefoot!" said Buntec; she reached into the exposed workings of the throat mike with a hemostat and withdrew a tiny object which she laid in the palm of her hand. "Maggy was right," she said curtly, holding it out for the others to inspect.

"Can you disable it?" Tocohl asked.

"Not without the proper tools," she gestured at what was available to her, "like working on a clipper engine with a sledgehammer."

Layli-layli calulan slid from the rear of the daisy-clipper. She handed Alfvaen's throat mike to Buntec, then climbed into the pilot's seat and strapped in. "I'll send someone for the rest of you as soon as I'm out of range of the jammer. Get in, Hellspark."

Buntec made a second dive into the interior of the daisy-clipper. "Emergency rations," she announced, "I'm famished." She tore into the box with fervor.

"Get in, Hellspark," *layli-layli calulan* repeated. This time Tocohl obeyed. Swift-Kalat helped her into the remaining empty seat, and seeing she was unable to reach the seat belt without renewed pain, he drew the strap and handed it across to *layli-layli* who snapped it shut for her.

"Take good care of Sunchild, Om im," Tocohl said and smiled wanly at the echoing sprookje.

Om im touched the hilt of his blade in acknowledgment.

Between bites, Buntec said, "Tocohl, *layli-layli*—don't mention the Hayashi jammer. Say we lost the throat mikes! Say anything, or nothing! I'll find a way to disable it without destroying the evidence. We'll see whoever planted them hung!"

"Yes," said Tocohl, and then she lapsed into silence. *Layli-layli calulan* turned the daisy-clipper back toward the river, traveling as swiftly as she dared.

Just as they reached the smoother surface of the river, the arachne stood up. Picking its way carefully onto the seat, its fragile legs straddling Tocohl, it tilted its camera eye up to scan her face anxiously. "Tocohl! Are you all right? *Tocohl!*"

"Let them sleep, *maggy-maggy*. They need the rest."

But Tocohl stirred and opened her eyes. Her words were barely audible but relief rang in them. "Maggy," she said, "you're all right!" Then she closed her eyes again. Some of the pain had left her face.

The arachne raised an extremity to touch Tocohl's cheek. Then it canted closer to speak in *layli-layli calulan*'s ear, "She may have a broken rib—"

"I know. Have a look at Alfvaen if you can manage it without waking them."

While *layli-layli calulan* reached for the comunit to report the location of the rest of the party, the arachne, balancing precariously, climbed the backrest to inspect Alfvaen.

Buntec brushed crumbs from her breast and said, "I have an idea that might work. Look around for a small Eilo's-kiss." She began to dismantle the two remaining throat mikes to check for additional jammers. "A good jolt of electricity should fuse the buggers solid. *Hah!*" She'd found a second jammer, which she handed delicately to swift-Kalat to hold with the first.

"Toes!" she continued, "what I wouldn't give for a look at the innards of that daisy-clipper that so conveniently crashed on us."

Swift-Kalat said, "You mean *it* might have been sabotaged?"

"I checked the engine before we left camp, swift-Kalat, and it was in perfect working order then! After which," she scowled, "I left it to the mercies of a Maldeneantine and a sprookje." This time, she turned the scowl on Sunchild.

"I found one," Om im announced. "A small Eilo's-kiss." He looked at swift-Kalat. "If it hadn't been for Buntec, we'd *all* be dead now: I know of only a dozen people who can handle a daisy-clipper that well and Buntec's the only one present on the expedition." He made a cheerful bow in her direction.

Grinning, Buntec returned the bow, and taking the two Hayashi jammers from swift-Kalat, she grasped them carefully between the jaws of a rubber-handled pliers from the tool kit. "Lead on," she said, and picked her way carefully through the glittering underbrush in Om im's wake.

She approached the Eilo's-kiss cautiously and began to stretch in its direction. "Wait, Buntec," said Om im.

"Rubber-handled pliers," said Buntec.

"I'm not worried. Sunchild is."

Buntec glanced at the sprookje. Its mouth was agape, displaying its red warning tongue. "Yeah, I know," she told it, sticking out her own tongue in imitation.

Then, with her free hand, she touched Sunchild on the wrist, stroked lightly as she'd seen Tocohl do. "Relax, friend—I don't plan to fry."

She touched the pliers to the Eilo's-kiss and was rewarded with a snap and a bright spark. Withdrawing her arm, she looked at the tip of the pliers. "Overzealous little bugger," she said, releasing the two jammers into her palm. "Ow!—but that should have fused them solid."

Buntec thrust the jammers into her pocket. Taking the remains of the throat mikes from swift-Kalat, she said, "May I have your attention for a moment?" Curious, he gave it—and Buntec flung the mikes deep into the flashwood, as far as they would go, where they disappeared in arabesque vine and squealing pig thicket.

"Oh, foot!" said Buntec, "I lost the throat mikes."

Swift-Kalat smiled; Buntec smiled back, pleased that he found her fiction acceptable by Jenji standards.

"And just in time." Om im grinned and pointed: two daisy-clippers emerged from the flashwood. Moments later, Hitoshi Dan was pounding backs all around, welcoming them like lost children. He was so happy to see them he gave the same welcome to swift-Kalat, who hadn't been lost. Buntec didn't begrudge it in the slightest.

On the skirt of the daisy-clipper, Om im paused and held out the edge of his cloak to Sunchild. The sprookje took it, loosed it, then turned and stepped into the flashwood, headed in the direction of base camp. "Thanks, but I'll walk," Om im interpreted with a grin. "After the last ride you had, I'm not at all surprised." He bounced aboard and gave Edge-of-Dark a flourish and a wave. Edge-of-Dark took his meaning; the daisy-clipper dashed for base.

CHAPTER 13

Everything reactivated simultaneously—from the arachne to Tocohl's 2nd skin and implant to Alfvaen's hand-held—and simultaneously Maggy assessed it all. The view from Tocohl's spectacles, though Maggy enhanced it, showed only the tuft of moss that the sprookje had given her; Tocohl had apparently put the spectacles in her pouch. From the arachne, Maggy saw Tocohl's still "booted" feet; the programming she'd read into the 2nd skin's local microprocessors had held even through the lapse of contact, she noted.

(Tocohl!) she said through the implant, *(Tocohl!)*

There was still no response. Maggy sent the arachne up for a better look while she checked the sensors in Tocohl's 2nd skin. Heart- and breath-rate close to normal—normal for unconsciousness, at any rate—but the swelling beneath Tocohl's skin at the third rib on the right spoke of injury.

Using the arachne's vocoder, she tried to rouse Tocohl to consciousness. She was somewhat surprised to realize that she would have *kept* trying, despite *layli-layli calulan's* injunction, had Tocohl not stirred and spoken. "Maggy, you're safe!"

(Veschke's sparks!) Maggy said. (You thought something had happened to *me?*) But Tocohl had lapsed back into unconsciousness and Maggy finished the thought to herself, Of course! All our contact had gone dead. You were as afraid for me as I was for you.

Having assessed the data from the 2nd skin, Maggy concluded a seventy percent chance Tocohl's rib was broken. Concluding as well that *layli-layli calulan* had little interest in probability by percentage, she said only, "She may have a broken rib—"

Layli-layli calulan, as Maggy had expected, already knew, but asked her to look at Alfvaen. Assuming Alfvaen still had the hand-held ... Maggy sent the arachne over the backrest of Tocohl's seat. It was no easy task manipulating the mobile in a moving vehicle, especially without stepping all over Tocohl. When she had at last landed and steadied it beside Alfvaen, she promptly switched a high proportion of her attention to the Siveyn.

While *layli-layli* notified base camp that Om im and Buntec were safe and gave the location where swift-Kalat waited with them, Maggy probed Alfvaen. "Asleep," she pronounced when her words would no longer be an interruption, "at least her heartbeat and respiration are the same as I noted when she slept normally."

"That's encouraging. Buntec says she seemed to sober, then began to hallucinate. She challenged Tocohl to a death duel, that's why she's tied. I can't tell you anything about those growths on her skin. They might be a symptom of Cana's disease that hasn't yet been noted, or they might be—" The daisy-clipper lurched slightly, *layli-layli calulan* did not finish the sentence.

She concentrated on piloting for a moment, then said, in a different tone, "Your last hunch was right: Buntec found an Hayashi jammer in Tocohl's throat mike. But that's a secret, you're not to tell anyone about that just yet."

"I will tell Tocohl."

"Of course. That was understood. But no one else."

Maggy scanned Alfvaen once more, considering as she did the state of Tocohl's rib and the fact that fiction had proved true in the case of the Hayashi jammer. She was silent for the remainder of the trip upriver as she recalled all the relevant Siveyn literature.

By the time they arrived within sight of base camp, Maggy had reached what she thought a good conclusion. "That must mean that Alfvaen and Tocohl are best friends," she said aloud.

"I beg your pardon?"

Layli-layli calulan sounded so puzzled that Maggy momentarily lost her certainty, until she recalled that *layli-layli calulan* simply didn't know the Siveyn as well as she did. "If Alfvaen challenged Tocohl to a death duel," Maggy said, "they must be best friends. I didn't know they were." She sought the analogous situation—midway through Alfvaen's favorite fiction—and found in Tocohl's gloss the comment: "Don't worry, Maggy. It'll all work out right. It always does in a case like this." Maggy knew from Tocohl's tone that this was intended to be reassuring, so she told *layli-layli calulan* precisely the same.

Whether it served to reassure *layli-layli* or not, Maggy couldn't tell. They had reached the base camp and the shaman shot over the barbed-wire perimeter to ground the daisy-clipper, with a jarring thump, directly in front of the infirmary. She exited shouting commands to those who waited with stretchers.

Maggy made sure the arachne got in no one's way, then sent it springing into the infirmary after them all.

Alfvaen and Tocohl had already been transferred from stretchers to beds. "Out," *layli-layli calulan* commanded, "that means everyone but you"—she pointed a finger stripped of its bluestone ring at Kejesli. Maggy ducked the arachne under a bed; she was not leaving Tocohl unobserved by any means at her disposal. "—And you," *layli-layli calulan* finished; she thrust her pointing finger under the edge of the bed in the general direction of the arachne.

Concluding that she meant to let the arachne stay, Maggy poked it hesitantly from concealment. *Layli-layli* scooped it and set it beside Alfvaen. "We'll get to Tocohl in a moment," she said, stripping the ring from her other hand, "but notify me if you sense any change in her condition." Tocohl seemed to be resting comfortably, so Maggy concentrated her attention on Alfvaen.

Layli-layli snipped through Alfvaen's bonds and, having shifted her to a more comfortable position, strapped her firmly to the cot, the catch-releases out of reach. Then she peeled back Alfvaen's 2nd skin, giving Maggy's camera eye a good look at the growths, and attached to her body various medical sensors. Next she took a sample of the gray filaments from Alfvaen's skin.

Behind her, Kejesli gasped. "Garbage plants!"

Without hesitation or a need to scan her Sheveschkem files, Maggy interpreted that tone as one of horror. She corrected him instantly: "No, they are not garbage plants. They bear only a superficial resemblance to the species I was shown."

"Good," said *layli-layli calulan*, "and thank you, *maggy-maggy*, that saves me a lot of time. —Captain, there are sedatives in the cabinet to your right if you need one." She set the diagnostic machine to its task of preparing slides of the sample.

Kejesli, as if exhausted, slumped suddenly into a chair, where he watched *layli-layli* with tired eyes. If such behavior did not worry *layli-layli calulan*, Maggy decided, it would not concern her either.

"While we're waiting for the slides ..." *Layli-layli* held out her arms, inviting the arachne into them. *Layli-layli* carried it across the room to place beside Tocohl.

Seeing she needed access to Tocohl's injury, Maggy provided it: the 2nd skin peeled away from Tocohl's ribcage in broad strips. *Layli-layli* first probed the swelling with gentle hands, then confirmed her shaman's diagnosis with a sounding scanner. "Yes, the rib's broken. No complications to that though. I'm giving her a local anesthetic, *maggy-maggy*"—she suited action to the words—"then we'll set the rib."

Once again she brought her fingertips to rest on the swelling. The reddening seemed to lessen. "You have more than average control, *maggy-maggy*. Is it fine enough to keep Tocohl's 2nd skin taut in this area only?"

"Tell me what to do," Maggy said, "and I'll do it."

"Good, she'll be more comfortable if I don't tape it." *Layli-layli calulan* smoothed the 2nd skin gently back over the injury where Maggy sealed it. "Be ready, I'm about to set the rib."

"Ready," Maggy said, set to record from both the arachne's lens and from the sensors in Tocohl's 2nd skin. The job was done in a single swift push ... then Maggy was drawing the 2nd skin tight in accord with *layli-layli*'s instructions.

"Fine, that's fine. You're to keep it that way until I tell you otherwise."

"Tocohl," Maggy began.

"Tocohl has no say in a medical matter. If she gives you any trouble, refer her to me. Or tell her it's that or taping." *Layli-layli calulan* directed a brief smile at the arachne. "And I'll give you one additional warning. She'll be in some pain when the anesthetic I gave her wears off. Do not be tempted to loosen the 2nd skin—"

Maggy had by this time been through her medical files. "I know," she said, risking the impoliteness of an interruption both to save *layli-layli calulan* the time and to assure her that she would take good care of Tocohl. "It might make the pain worse—and it could lead to internal damage. I'll tell her to do a Methven ritual for the pain instead."

"Suggest a Methven healing ritual as well. Between the two of us, we'll have her up and around in no time." She walked to the diagnostic machine, where her slides awaited, leaving the arachne one last instruction: "Tell me when she wakes."

Maggy sent the arachne bounding after her. At *layli-layli*'s glance of surprise, she explained, "I can tell through the 2nd skin when she wakes—and she'll want to see your results too. I'm recording for her."

"I see." *Layli-layli calulan* set about her work. When she had examined the slides—and given the arachne a chance to do so as well—she moved again to Alfvaen's side, placing the arachne at the head of the cot.

Again her fingers flickered lightly over the Siveyn's skin while her eyes scrutinized various monitors. Alfvaen moaned.

With a suddenness that made Maggy jump the arachne back, Alfvaen flailed against the straps that held her. Her eyes flashed open, fixed on the empty space between *layli-layli* and Kejesli. She began to speak, slowly at first, then building to the fever-pitch rapidity of terror.

"Alfvaen," Maggy said in Siveyn, trying to cut through the fear, "Alfvaen, there's nothing there! You're safe!"

Alfvaen did not hear her and went on as before. Maggy sent the arachne a cautious step forward to try again.

Layli-layli calulan laid her hand across Alfvaen's eyes: the Siveyn's violent struggles subsided to steady tension against the straps, her voice sank to a still-fearful whisper. "Can you translate for me, *maggy-maggy?*"

"Roughly, she says, 'They're coming! They're coming to get me! Let me go! The llistis are coming!'" That needed clarification. Maggy added, "The only reference I can find to llistis describes them as very ugly, very violent *mythical* creatures. No other match. She keeps saying it over and over again. I'm sorry, *layli-layli*, that's all I can tell you. I wish I knew more. That can't be right."

"I think your reference is probably correct. It fits with her medical condition and with what Buntec told me of Alfvaen's hallucinations." *Layli-layli calulan* brought her hands to either side of Alfvaen's temples and murmured softly. A moment later, Alfvaen relaxed back onto the cot, fell silent; a moment after that, she was asleep—to all appearances, peacefully.

"I don't understand," Maggy said, taking care to keep the vocoder low.

Layli-layli calulan answered in quiet calm. "You won't find it under Cana's disease, but elsewhere... Look at the monitors. Those growths are not obstructing her circulation; what's more, the blood monitor shows no indication of alcohol in Alfvaen's system."

That was so, Maggy had to admit, but ... "I still don't understand."

"You'll find the information under *delirium tremens*. To be healthy, a human being *needs* to dream. Alcohol disrupts the ability to do so. Now that the alcohol is gone from her system, Alfvaen's mind and body seek instinctively to... catch up on dreaming. Awake or asleep, she dreams—sometimes of duels, sometimes of Ilistis."

She strode to a cabinet, brought out a small blue container, strode back to Kejesli. Shaking a pill into his hand, she commanded, "Take that."

Kejesli obeyed listlessly, bringing the pill to his mouth, swallowing a number of times. At last, he looked up at *layli-layli calulan*. "Can't you do something to get those *things* off her?"

Having by this time reviewed all available information on the effect of alcohol on the human body, Maggy was surprised to hear in Kejesli's voice the same horror it had held when he had mistaken the growths for garbage plants. Didn't he understand ... ?

Layli-layli calulan explained it for him, simply and firmly: "Those *things*, Captain Kejesli, are healing her."

"Healing her?" swift-Kalat said, when *layli-layli calulan* repeated her statement for him half an hour later. He bent beside Alfvaen and stroked her temple gently. "Are you sure?"

"As sure as I can be with an unknown life-form. Check the slides yourself—you'll see the structure is similar to, but does not match, the garbage plants." Turning to draw him with her to the display screen, *layli-layli calulan* was forced to an abrupt halt to avoid a collision with Kejesli.

He attempted to move out of her way but his grip on the edge of Alfvaen's cot prevented him from backing the necessary distance. Startled, he glanced down at his hands as if he had not seen them before—or as if he had no control over what they were doing, Maggy thought. With obvious effort he removed, first one to splay it at his throat, then the other. This time he stepped out of her way.

"No offense given, Captain," *layli-layli calulan* said patiently, "but I would prefer that you wait outside until I have finished checking Buntec and Om im for injury. Your debriefing can wait that long..."

Kejesli splayed his hand a second time at his throat. Without a further word, he walked unsteadily—as if the infirmary floor heaved beneath him, disturbing his balance—to the door and vanished through it.

While swift-Kalat pulled a chair to the display screen to do as *layli-layli* suggested, the shaman retrieved her sounding scanner. Om im, standing over Tocohl, glanced up at her approach. "That's not really necessary, *layli-layli*," he began.

"Humor me," said the shaman. "It gives us the opportunity to speak of things among ourselves that we might not speak of to Kejesli."

More secrets, Maggy decided, and realized abruptly that she had not given Tocohl the message she held from *layli-layli*. Finding Tocohl alive though injured had drawn from her an unusual response: without any deliberation, her priorities had shifted. She shifted them back; when Tocohl awoke, she was to receive *layli-layli calulan*'s message before Maggy said anything else.

Om im waved aside *layli-layli*'s invitation to lie down, choosing instead to draw a chair to Tocohl's side, blade right. With a look Maggy interpreted as resignation, *layli-layli* scanned him where he sat, taking care to approach him from the politic side.

Buntec, who had been silently observing Alfvaen, now turned and strode across to them. For a long moment, she gave Tocohl the same scrutiny. Then she said, "It's too bad we haven't the equipment to salvage that daisy-clipper"—she punched her palm—"I'd give an arm to see that engine."

"I'd give Megeve's arm to see that engine," Om im said.

"You don't know it was Megeve," she countered. "Anybody had the chance to plant those jammers. And we don't know the clipper was sabotaged."

Om im eyed Buntec for a long moment, then, tilting the chair back, he drew his blade and began to hone it. *Layli-layli calulan* stepped back, gave him a look that Maggy could neither see nor interpret from the position of the arachne. "Sorry," he said, sheathing the blade and bringing the chair upright with a thump, "I didn't mean to disrupt your examination."

Layli-layli calulan said nothing, only stepped forward again to draw her fingers lightly down his body. Maggy angled the arachne for a better look and discovered that she did not actually touch him except once. "Just a bruise," Om im said, having noticed the arachne's interest. "Buntec, show Maggy those gadgets. You were right, Maggy, about the Hayashi jammers. Buntec's got them in her pocket."

Never having actually seen an Hayashi jammer, Maggy sent the arachne skirting Tocohl's head in order to record this for future reference. Buntec reached into her overpocket. (Maggy? *Maggy?*) Though the words were soft and urgent, Tocohl's voice rang through their private channel. (Are you all right, Maggy?)

Instantly, Maggy split her attention. Halting the arachne where it could show her both the palmful of tiny electronic parts Buntec held out for inspection and Tocohl, she said, in what she judged from *layli-layli's* usage to be a reassuring tone, (I'm fine. You have a broken rib though. *Layli-layli calulan* told me to suggest you perform a Methven healing ritual.)

Tocohl's eyes did not open. (Healing ritual it is. —I'm glad you're safe, Maggy. It got awfully lonely without you.) Her voice fell silent but Maggy could tell from the sensors in her 2nd skin that she had begun the ritual.

Through the arachne, Maggy said softly, "Tocohl is awake now and has begun the Methven ritual you required."

Just as softly, *layli-layli calulan* told the others, "Quiet, please." She moved to Tocohl's side; placing her fingertips on Tocohl's injured ribs, she too fell silent, as if in ritual of her own.

There went the priorities again, Maggy realized. She did not understand why that was happening. Forgetting priorities—forgetting to deliver messages one had been told were important—that was something that happened often in fiction, but it had never before happened to her. She ran a diagnostic.

A moment later; Tocohl opened her eyes and said wanly, "Hi, how's Alfvaen?"

Layli-layli calulan repeated her diagnosis for the third time. While she spoke, she took Buntec firmly by the shoulders, sat her on the edge of Tocohl's cot, and ran the sounding scanner over her. Laying aside the scanner, she finished her account with the command, "Another moment of quiet, please."

Priorities, thought Maggy. She pinged privately for Tocohl's attention, but before she could speak, *layli-layli calulan* said, "That means you too, *maggy-maggy*." A finger, bereft of its ring, pointed at the arachne. Maggy dropped the arachne into a crouch; if the pointed finger was aimed, she could at least keep the arachne from being a direct target.

Layli-layli calulan smiled. "I only meant, don't be distracting, *maggy-maggy*. I had no intention of quieting anyone permanently." Tocohl twisted her head to give *layli-layli* a puzzled look, then twisted farther to take in the crouched arachne. Understanding lit her tired face and she smiled reassuringly into the arachne's camera eye. Maggy kept quiet: she was taking no chances.

When *layli-layli calulan* had finished treating Buntec's handful of bruises, Tocohl said thoughtfully, "The sprookje... suppose it identified the toxin in her system? You did dub that a 'sample tooth,' Buntec; maybe the description is more apt than anyone thought. That second bite it gave Alfvaen might have been what it considered ... well, an antidote."

"As a hypothesis," said swift-Kalat—he had finished his examination of the slides *layli-layli calulan* had prepared and come to stand behind Om im—"that's safe to say."

Taking into account what was "safe to say" in Jenji, Maggy knew he was not nearly as sure of that as Tocohl, but that he wished it so and could speak it without fear.

Buntec shifted on the edge of the cot—with great care—to face Tocohl directly. "Not much we can do for her if it's wrong," she pointed out. "Next question: What'll we tell Old Rattlebrain—about the jammers, I mean?"

"Unless you know for sure who planted them ..." Tocohl began. It was more question than statement: Buntec punched her palm again, Om im grunted. Tocohl took both for answer and went on, "Let's not tell him anything just yet. At the moment, we're the only ones who know they existed."

"And the person who planted them," Om im said, scowling.

"That could work out to our advantage," Tocohl finished.

"Meaning he doesn't know we're on to him." Buntec spread flattened hands, narrowly missing *layli-layli calulan* with the broadness of the gesture. In Jannisetti, it signified clearing the table to deal afresh with a problem.

Raising her voice, Buntec announced, "Swift-Kalat, I'm speaking in GalLing' only, and it's hypothesis. I'm just gonna tell Tocohl how it seems to me and I don't wanna worry about the words, so don't get all sweated up about reliability, okay? The truth is what we're trying to get at." Swift-Kalat took a deep breath, obviously preparing himself. "Go ahead," he said, and Buntec launched into a rapid-fire summary of their suspicions, adding not a few of her own.

"So," she finished at last, "if—and only if—the daisy-clipper was sabotaged, then Timosie Megeve did it. He was the only one who had the chance."

"The sprookjes—" Tocohl began.

"You don't believe that and neither do I. The sprookjes may have had the chance but they don't have the know-how."

Tocohl shifted to address the arachne. "On the available evidence, Maggy, what's the probability that Megeve planted those jammers?"

"Roughly twenty-five percent."

"Not high enough," said Tocohl.

"High enough for me," Om im said; drawing his knife, he began to hone it again.

"Not good enough for Buntec, or she'd have rammed it down Kejesli's throat the moment she saw him," Tocohl pointed out. "And you, swift-Kalat, could you speak of Megeve's treachery?"

"I could not," swift-Kalat said. "*Someone* attempted to isolate the four of you from contact with base camp, but I do not know who or to what purpose. Megeve had the knowledge and the opportunity, but every member of the team also had the opportunity. Perhaps others had the knowledge."

"Maggy?" said Tocohl.

Maggy recognized this as Tocohl's shorthand way of requesting further information. "According to the personnel records, three other members of the survey team have also spent time on Hayashi: Hitoshi Dan, Edge-of-Dark, and Om im."

The rasping noise from the side of the cot stopped abruptly. "Count me out, Maggy. Suicidal I'm not; if the daisy-clipper was sabotaged I was meant to go down with the rest of you."

That made sense and made Maggy reexamine the evidence. "Then if the daisy-clipper was sabotaged," she concluded aloud, "there is a thirty-three percent probability that Megeve planted the jammers. Would that be high enough?"

"Wait up, kid," said Buntec firmly, "you're doin' this wrong."

"Tocohl?" Maggy said.

"Let Buntec tell you, Maggy. I'm too tired."

Buntec turned to the arachne. "*I've* been on Hayashi—tearin' up the local Port of Delights with an old buddy isn't the kind of thing Old Rattlebrain or the Older Rattlebrains that tell him when to wipe his nose would care about. What's more, I've seen those jammers sold on a half-dozen other worlds. You can't just go by that. Not enough info."

"Oh," said Maggy, revising her tactics. Now, it seemed, she had no way of estimating the probability.

Buntec punched her palm, twice, with force. "If only I could eyeball the innards of that daisy-clipper ... Toes, and toes again."

"Mind your language, Buntec," commanded *layli-layli calulan*.

That surprised Maggy who knew perfectly well that toes were not obscene to an Yn. From Buntec's expression, it surprised her as well, but grudgingly she said, "Yeah, right. Not in front of the kid."

"Not in front of my patients. They need calm and rest, all of them." *Layli-layli calulan* touched Buntec gently at the right temple, so Maggy knew that one of the patients referred to was Buntec herself. The shaman went on, "Using language you consider obscene is far from calming." She spoke quietly to Buntec for a few moments longer.

The words she spoke did not seem as important as her soothing tone and her soothing touch, but when she had finished Buntec's face had lost some of its anger. Even her voice was calm. "Thanks, *layli-layli*. Lot more shaken up than I realized—lightning blastin' away no more'n an inch from my face! You wouldn't believe ... !"

"I believe it will make a good story," *layli-layli calulan* said, drawing a rich chuckle from Om im.

A broad grin spread slowly across Buntec's dark face. "Oh, will it *ever!*" she agreed.

"Then stick to that," Tocohl said. "Save the jammers for the sequel. We still have to know more." The sensors in the 2nd skin told Maggy how tired she was; drooping eyelids confirmed that.

Tocohl forced her eyes open; with effort she raised a hand to stop Buntec from rising. "Give Old Rattlebrain a real teaser, Buntec"—a hint of smile touched the corners of her mouth—"tell Old Rattlebrain I'll be out to talk to his sprookjes as soon as I've had my nap."

She grinned at the astonished faces looking down at her and added, "And if Alfvaen wakes before I do, please tell her that her serendipity is unrivaled."

#

The room was quiet. Buntec and Om im had gone to make their abridged report to Kejesli; *layli-layli* and swift-Kalat bent over Alfvaen, taking further readings and speaking in whispers so soft Maggy had to enhance to understand them.

Tocohl's eyes were closed but Maggy knew from her sensors that she was not asleep. Maggy settled the arachne beside her pillow to keep watch. Then she recalled the priorities ... she pinged furiously for attention, before the odd lapse could occur again.

"What is it, Maggy?"

(Just for you,) Maggy said, (*Layli-layli calulan* said I was to tell you—*only* you—the first time we renewed contact. I'm sorry I didn't; I don't understand why; I ran a diagnostic—)

(You'd better get on with it then.)

Maggy relayed *layli-layli calulan*'s message in the shaman's own voice, using her taped recording of it. Then she added, (In Hellspark, that would be, 'Megeve may be responsible for the equipment failures,' right?)

(Right.) There was a pause, a long one by human standards. (So *layli-layli* thinks Megeve may have had something to do with Oloitokitok's death too,) Tocohl said at last. (What led up to that, Maggy—any idea?)

(What swift-Kalat told her, I think. I'm not sure.)

(Show me.) She opened her eyes.

That meant picture as well. Maggy obliged with the arachne's eyeview of the exchange between swift-Kalat and *layli-layli calulan* that her lie had brought about.

When the tape was finished. Tocohl said, (I see. Megeve "fixed" the transceiver while we were missing, just as he fixed it while Oloitokitok was missing. Neither swift-Kalat nor *layli-layli* likes the coincidence. I see the point, too. An Hayashi jammer doesn't affect anything out of its range. It wouldn't have affected the transceiver at this end and Kejesli would have known something was wrong at our end. He'd have sent out a search party immediately.)

(He wanted to fix the arachne too,) Maggy said. (I wouldn't let him. Neither would *layli-layli*.)

(Good thing, too, under the circumstances.) Again she paused. (But what would he stand to gain by killing us? Even if we assume he's an Inheritor of God, that the Inheritors want this world...) The sensors in her 2nd skin spiked suddenly. (Maggy! Did Megeve tell Kejesli about the gift the sprookje gave me?)

(No. Buntec will be pleased: she can still see the look on Kejesli's face. Should I tell her?)

(Buntec will be far from pleased, Maggy, and I'm an idiot for not thinking of it. With the four of us dead, Megeve was the only witness to the exchange of gifts—and he told no one!)

(A gift is evidence of sapience?)

(Not evidence, no, but strongly suggestive. Even Kejesli would have held his report on the strength of that.)

(Then, by killing the four of you, Megeve would gain nothing. I recorded the event.)

(Ah, but he didn't know that, Maggy. I'm not sure he knows that even now. Perhaps he was only casting doubts on the arachne's reliability because you were so adamant that something had happened to us.)

(Or perhaps he was right to cast doubts on my reliability,) Maggy said.

The sensors spiked again. (What's wrong, Maggy?)

(Nothing that I can find on a diagnostic but—)

(But what?)

Maggy explained about the shifting priorities that had prevented her from carrying out *layli-layli calulan*'s instructions.

When she was done, Tocohl said thoughtfully, (The message wasn't delayed long enough to do any harm, if that's what's worrying you. That your priorities shifted without your being aware of the shift is a little surprising, Maggy. It's worth investigating certainly. But ... I did the same thing myself—I had to know *first* if you were safe. Everything else was secondary.)

(There's something else.)

(Tell me.)

(I acted on probabilities lower than those I've ascribed to Megeve.) Maggy could tell from Tocohl's expression that she did not understand, so she explained, (I could accept the high probability that you were dead and do nothing, or I could accept the low probability that you were being jammed and act. *Layli-layli calulan* was also willing to accept the low probability. She called it a "hunch"; is that correct usage?)

(Absolutely.) A slow smile spread across Tocohl's face; the sensors in her 2nd skin told Maggy that she had calmed as if no longer worried. *(And,* please note, that's absolutely consistent with your shifted priorities. You were right about the jammers. Stop worrying.)

(Yes, in this case the low probability was the true one. So—in the future, how should I assign priorities?)

(Like the rest of us. It's something you learn by doing. I will say, however, that it always seems to help to have someone else to talk it over with—even if you don't take their advice once you've done it.)

(With you,) said Maggy. (*Layli-layli calulan* comes.)

Through Tocohl's spectacles Maggy watched *layli-layli calulan* approach. The shaman, her broad mouth stretched broader in the smile Maggy had recorded only once before, bent over Tocohl. (Beautiful smile,) Tocohl said drowsily; and Maggy was careful to note that she had correctly anticipated Tocohl's reaction.

"You're disturbing my patient, *maggy-maggy.* She does need the nap she spoke about."

The arachne bobbed apology. "Your pardon," Maggy told her through its vocoder.

The shaman's fingertips brushed Tocohl's temples; she murmured words incomprehensible to Maggy. The readings from the 2nd skin began to resemble those of Tocohl when she was drowsy, a comfortable, easeful drowsiness.

For a brief moment, Tocohl struggled to rouse herself. (With me, Maggy,) she agreed, and then she let *layli-layli calulan's* touch draw her into sleep.

Tocohl woke to the sound of distant thunder and an urgent voice: (Danger, Tocohl! Wake up! *Danger!)*

The infirmary was dark, silent. Maggy pushed the spectacles for available light without waiting to be told; in the brightening, Tocohl saw Timosie Megeve start across the room on silent feet.

She waited, tensed but unmoving: in the darkness he perceived, Megeve could not know she was awake. (Record this, Maggy.)

(I am,) came the response, audible only to her.

Layli-layli calulan was nowhere in evidence. At Alfvaen's bedside, swift-Kalat had fallen asleep in his chair, his head pillowed on his arm, his fingers brushing her face.

Megeve paused as he neared the two.

Under the circumstances, the pause seemed too ominous to chance. "Sssh," Tocohl said softly into the darkness, "and don't turn on the light. *Layli-layli calulan* says Alfvaen needs as much sleep as she can get." She was rewarded by seeing Megeve jump as if she'd struck him.

He recovered quickly, counting on the darkness to keep his reactions from her, and in a quiet, controlled voice he said, "Sorry to wake you, Tocohl Susumo. I thought I'd drop by and see how you and the serendipitist were doing."

(Maggy, I want the arachne in tripping range.) Aloud, covering the faint thump and scuttle of the arachne, Tocohl said, "Oh, we're fine. Nothing a little sleep won't cure, according to *layli-layli*." She raised herself on one elbow, felt the stab of pain, and knew she was at a disadvantage. She let out a hiss of breath, eased herself back down. He doesn't know we suspect him, she reminded herself, let's keep it that way. "You didn't wake me, the storm did. Come tell me what's been happening. I seem to have missed a great deal."

Megeve lifted a chair and brought it silently to the bedside. A soft clicking dogged his heels but he did not seem to notice. "Nothing much," he said as he sat beside her. "Is it true you can speak to the sprookjes?"

(So that's what this is about!) "Only partially true, I'm afraid," she said, and saw him relax ever so slightly. "I can get your sprookje to echo me. It's a step in the right direction"—*there's* an accurate phrase, she thought—"but hardly enough to satisfy the legal requirements. I'm sorry. I know how much it means to you, especially because of Oloitokitok."

"Yes," he said, his voice rough with emotion. But, at the far end of the tunnel of light her spectacles provided, she saw his expression: relief.

Tocohl waited a moment, as if allowing him to get a grip on himself, then she said. "*Nothing much* happened here?! *Layli-layli calulan* broke mourning to look for us." It startled her as she said it, for she had only now realized that Maggy's tape had shown the shaman in the midst of deep mourning. How had swift-Kalat gained access to her? "And that means you had as much trouble as we did, or more. You weren't joking about the equipment failures … !"

The cabin's membrane was flung open, startling them both. Om im and *layli-layli calulan* spattered water on the threshold; both had been running hard. Om im, Tocohl saw, carried the hand-held Maggy had given Alfvaen. (Thanks, Maggy. I didn't realize you were in touch with them.)

"Hi," said Tocohl cheerfully. "You needn't put on the light, *layli-layli*"—recognition gave nothing away: *layli-layli* was recognizable even in the light available to Megeve—"Timosie was just keeping me from getting bored."

Layli-layli calulan took the hint. As if nothing at all were amiss, she said, "Will the light disturb you, Tocohl? I came to change Alfvaen's IV. It will just be a moment."

"No, the light won't disturb me," Tocohl answered; in fact, as *layli-layli calulan* raised the light, Maggy adjusted her spectacles accordingly.

Layli-layli set about changing Alfvaen's IV—she was alternating glucose with saline evidently—careful to wake neither Alfvaen nor swift-Kalat. That was a nice touch, Tocohl noted with appreciation, as was Om im's pause for a brief glance at Alfvaen before he continued on toward Tocohl.

Tocohl turned to look again at Megeve. "Tell me," she said, "what was the problem with the transceiver? Since it almost killed me, I'd like to know the cause."

"You're not the only one," Om im said. He moved smoothly to blade right of her, deftly interposing himself between Megeve and Tocohl without any hint of rudeness.

The Maldeneantine twisted his hand down his wrist, then leaned back and said, "There's not much to tell: it was the usual for Flashfever. —Do you know much about electronics?"

"Not a lot," Tocohl said, omitting to mention that Maggy's data stores made her an expert on the subject, "but tell me anyway. I'm always willing to learn."

Megeve explained in technical terms and then said, "All of which, in simple terms, means we had fungi growing on the 'plate. It cooked and shorted out one of the freeloader diodes. Until I found which one, cleaned up the fungus so it couldn't happen again, and replaced it, you were all on your own."

Maggy pinged and pinged again.

"I see, I guess." Tocohl said, careful to imply that she had no idea what he was talking about, then she gave a yawn that cracked her jaw. "Sorry, I'm drowsing off again. Thanks for the company, Timosie," she added, "but now if you'll forgive me ... ?" She yawned again.

"Oh, of course!" Megeve took it as a dismissal, rose so hastily the chair tipped behind him. Om im caught it, drew it to him; bowing deeply to Tocohl he said, "I'll keep silent company, I promise, until you wake. A bored Hellspark is a blot on my honor as a Bluesippan." The grin he gave her was pure deceit: he sat blade right.

Megeve glanced frowning from one to the other but could clearly see no cause for alarm. To all appearances, Om im was merely in one of his gallant moods. Megeve said a few polite good-byes and started for the door.

Tocohl left him to the wary eyes of Om im and *layli-layli*. (What is it, Maggy?)

(Probability of sabotage now ninety-nine percent; equal probability that Megeve is responsible.)

That was as high a probability as Maggy would ever commit herself to, and Tocohl said, (What caused the jump?)

In her spectacles, Tocohl saw Megeve open the transceiver. The image froze abruptly, then expanded, until she could see an area of the 'plate in microscopic detail. (That,) said Maggy, adding an indicator arrow to the still, (is the diode he spoke of. There is no evidence of fungus, no evidence of a short.)

(You're sure?) said Tocohl, knowing that it was unnecessary to ask.

(I'm sure,) said Maggy, just as unnecessarily. She added, replacing the first image with another, (This is what a shorted freeloader diode looks like. It's unmistakable.)

(I'd have said spectacular—but unmistakable it certainly is. I grant you the rise in probability.)

Maggy said aloud, "Om im, you're going to cut yourself if you're not careful." Her inflection made it as much a question as a statement.

Tocohl turned her head to look—Maggy cleared the taped images from her spectacles—and saw that Om im pressed the hilt of his blade to his forehead. His hand grasped the blade so tightly that he was, as Maggy warned, close to letting his own blood.

"Don't you dare," Tocohl snapped in GalLing', then instantly followed it up with the proper phrase in Bluesippan: "I have need of that hand, undamaged."

By degrees, Om im loosened his hold on the blade. At last he turned it in his fingertips and sheathed it. Tocohl breathed a sigh of relief.

"Buntec thought to search the daisy-clipper hangar," he said. "I stood watch for her. I'm sorry to say she found nothing of interest." The knife was out abruptly, once more he touched the hilt to his forehead in apology; this time Tocohl had no fear that he would cut himself for penance.

"If you want to sleep," he went on, "I pledge to stand watch myself. We left John the Smith to watch Megeve—he was the one who warned *layli-layli*—and swift-Kalat was here…"

"*Maggy* was here," Tocohl said, eyeing the handheld at his belt meaningfully. "She waked and warned me—and called on you for assistance, as you expected her to, or you wouldn't have taken the handheld."

"Yes."

"Then you can hardly claim to have left me without a watch. Maggy never sleeps—for which I am very grateful, because she now gives a ninety-nine percent probability that Megeve tried to kill us once already."

His gilded brows shot up. "How … ?" He glanced at the arachne to address the question in retrospect to Maggy herself.

Tocohl said, "Let's get it all over with at once." Painfully, she eased herself to a sitting position. "Would you mind lending a shoulder, Om im? Now we have something specific to tell Kejesli."

From across the room, *layli-layli calulan* said. "Lie down, Tocohl; you're still under my care. Kejesli can perfectly well come to you. *He* has no broken rib." It was mildly said but the look which accompanied it was a command.

Tocohl inclined her head, acquiescing, but remained erect. In response to Om im's worried look, she drew her legs to one side to favor her injured rib. His look did not change—but Tocohl had to be able to see, to speak face-to-face with Kejesli.

Passing to the comunit, *layli-layli* paused once, to touch her fingertips to swift-Kalat's temples. His eyes came open and he rose to scan the room, as if seeking to learn what had startled him awake. Finding nothing but *layli-layli* at her comunit coding a call, he returned his attention to Alfvaen.

"Captain," said *layli-layli calulan*, "you wished to speak to Tocohl. You may do so in the infirmary. She is awake now." She broke the connection, then made two more calls in swift succession, to ask both Buntec and John the Smith to join them in the infirmary as well. To Tocohl, she explained, "We may have need of some we trust."

Tocohl, as *layli-layli* drew near, saw her features set in disapproval and set her own in stubborn opposition. The threatened chiding never reached the shaman's lips; in its stead, a smile of resignation turned the corners of the broad mouth wryly up. Without a word, *layli-layli calulan* laid a gentle hand against Tocohl's injured side. Realizing the *layli-layli* meant to ease her pain, Tocohl closed her eyes and did what little she could to help herself, a Methven ritual against the sharpness in her chest. After a moment, breathing seemed less difficult.

She opened her eyes, only to find them caught and held by the dark intensity in *layli-layli calulan*'s own.

The shaman's voice was no less intense: "Will you pronounce judgment on Megeve?"

Tocohl had forgotten that complication. Looking at the faces around her, she realized that swift-Kalat had joined the group as well. The phrasing reliability demanded was expedient to her own purposes as well. "No," she said, "I would not. I have good reason to believe that he disabled the transceiver to keep you from contacting us, yes—but *Alfvaen* tried to kill me."

Before swift-Kalat could begin to object to her phrasing, she went on. "There was a physiological reason for that. I'd ask no judgment on her, nor offer one. Perhaps Megeve is the same; perhaps the stress of the ionization ..." She fixed her gaze on *layli-layli*, attempting to match the shaman's intensity.

"Yes, perhaps. We have, none of us, been behaving normally." *Layli-layli calulan* lowered her eyes to study her hands, still bare of rings. "Even I—"

She did not finish, but Tocohl knew she meant her attempt to curse van Zoveel. "Even you," Tocohl agreed quietly. It was not accusation, only a statement of fact.

The Yn shaman was quiet for a long moment, then she turned her dark gaze on the arachne. "*Maggy-maggy* ... what is the probability that Megeve sabotaged Oloitokitok's equipment as well?"

Alarmed. Tocohl began, (Ma—) She had no chance to complete her intended warning. "I'm still gathering data," Maggy said without hesitation. "The probability is insignificant without sufficient information."

Tocohl, who had been about to instruct Maggy to say just that, whatever the truth might be, was startled. (True, Maggy?) she demanded privately.

(Yes and no,) Maggy said, in the same mode, (did I do right?)

(Yes! Oh, yes!)

Kejesli burst dripping into the infirmary, braids a-chatter. He reached for the roof, found none, and lurched toward them. Behind him followed Buntec and John the Smith. "So what's up?" said Buntec.

(—Later,) Tocohl added, and silently blessed Maggy's understanding of verbal shorthand. Aloud she said, "Give me a hand to the console. —Maggy, bring the arachne. We have something we need your opinion on, Buntec."

The arachne scurried past. By the time Buntec and John the Smith had helped Tocohl to the console and eased her into the chair Om im brought, the arachne was ready to display. To the arachne's right, Om im placed a second chair. Tocohl patted it. "Sit, Captain. It's a long story and you'll need a surface to clutch."

He sat and gripped the edge of the console. "You've found a language … ?"

"That I'm still working on. This is somewhat more pressing a problem."

His face darkened. Tightening his grip until Tocohl could almost count his pulse in the risen veins, he said, "Tell me." The rest crowded in to watch over their shoulders, John the Smith carefully choosing the "high status" side of Om im.

"Maggy, we'll start with Timosie Megeve's explanation of the transceiver failure."

Maggy obliged with the tape she'd recorded from Tocohl's spectacles, adjusting it slightly to avoid the usual distracting jumpiness caused by minute movements of Tocohl's head. Megeve's image was only halfway through the technical part of his explanation when Buntec grunted and muttered something under her breath.

(Should I stop?) Maggy asked.

(No, go on.) Tocohl sat, patient against the ache in her side. Having finished that tape, Maggy said, (Now the tape of the transceiver, right?)

For the benefit of Kejesli and the rest, Tocohl answered aloud: "Now the tape you made when Megeve tried to contact us because you and swift-Kalat were concerned about our safety." She watched again as Megeve tried the transceiver, claimed it did not work, opened the service panel—

Buntec stamped her foot, and pushing between Tocohl and Kejesli to address the screen over the arachne, she began, "You barefoot—"

Layli-layli's plump hand caught her shoulder in so firm a grasp that Buntec stopped in mid-bellow. "Curse all you want, Buntec, but do it quietly. Remember Alfvaen." Buntec resumed her cursing in a fierce whisper.

As she had done for Tocohl, Maggy froze the image of the 'plate and enlarged it. "He lied!" said John the Smith, then immediately repeated it in a harsh whisper.

For a brief moment, everyone muttered and whispered at everyone else simultaneously; then, as one, they deferred to Buntec for an explanation of what they were seeing.

Buntec gave it, right down to the polished toenails. Then she leaned toward the screen. "Maggy, can you run the tape back to where Megeve 'tried' to contact us? —Yes, there," she said as Maggy obliged. "Now give me a close-up of his hands." Maggy did just as she was instructed. Buntec stamped her foot—but quietly.

"I don't understand," Maggy said.

"It's a kid's trick, Maggy. Watch carefully. He's got a strip of plastic, he edges it under before he switches on. It looks like the transceiver's switched on, but the contact isn't made."

Kejesli stood so abruptly that his chair struck Buntec's shin.

Buntec grunted but caught his elbow. "There's more," she said, grimly; she reached into her overpocket with her free hand. Still gripping his elbow, she turned him face on, opened her palm scant inches from his nose to display the Hayashi jammers. Well past obscenity, she told him only what they were and how they had been used.

As if to test its reality, Kejesli plucked one of the jammers from Buntec's palm and squeezed it. His face turned grim. Dropping the jammer back into her palm, he brought his hand sharply up to the pin of remembrance he wore on his vest.

Then he spun and punched at the console's keyboard. Maggy released it to him immediately. Edge-of-Dark appeared on the display. "Get Dyxte," Kejesli snapped at her. "The two of you draw weapons from supplies and report to the infirmary at once. Not a word to anyone else."

As shocked as she was, Edge-of-Dark snapped back, "We're on our way," and was gone.

Kejesli, gripping the console, turned on Tocohl. "Why?" he demanded. "Why would he do it?"

Tocohl laid her pouch across her thigh and drew it open. The piece of moss—still a vivid red—curled within like some small comfortable animal. "For this, I think," Tocohl said, taking it gently in her hand to lay it on the table before him. "Megeve's sprookje gave me this just before we set out: the four of us—and Megeve—were the only witnesses."

"That's what *he* thought," Maggy said.

"Said with just the right emphasis," Tocohl told her. "Why don't you show the captain *that* bit of tape."

The display remained blank. "You've seen it, Tocohl, or you can watch it on your spectacles—but you shouldn't be sitting up. It hurts you to sit up. If you'll go back to bed, I'll show Kejesli the tape. Fair trade?"

Tocohl stared down at the arachne. "No," she said, "it's pure, unadulterated blackmail, but you've got yourself a deal." When she held out an arm for assistance, she found John the Smith ready and waiting.

"Wait," said Kejesli. "A gift? This?" He brushed the tuft of moss.

"Looked like more of a trade, actually," Om im said. "Megeve's sprookje was hoping for a piece of Tocohl's cloak in return."

"But to keep the sprookjes from being found sapient—"

Tocohl rose to her feet; pain that had gone unnoticed in the excitement returned to drain the blood from her face. "The Inheritors of God want this world, Captain. I don't know why. You'll have to ask one. And I'd say Megeve's a likely candidate."

"*Waster!*" Kejesli spat the word, so angry he lapsed into Sheveschkem, "So you'd burn Veschke, would you, waster—"

Tocohl, who had never heard a Sheveschkemen use that strongest of all condemnations, started so violently that it brought her a stab of pain. She pressed her hand to her side; Maggy stiffened the 2nd skin against her.

Kejesli's eyes widened. "My lady—" he began, still in Sheveschkem. Then he shook himself and splayed his fingers at his throat. In GalLing', he said, more gently, "Get her to bed; let me see this tape." He seated himself once more before the console.

By the time John the Smith had eased Tocohl down onto her cot—Om im keeping close behind to assure himself the Smith would handle the task correctly—Kejesli was already concentrating on the tape. A lightning flash illuminated two shapes making toward the infirmary door, distorted beyond recognition by torrential rain. Buntec stamped across the room to peel back the membrane and peer into the downpour. She stiffened momentarily. Then, with an air of courtliness quite unlike her, she drew aside the membrane to allow the two newcomers entry and in a tone of astonishing sweetness she said, "Do come in, Timosie. We were just speaking about you."

Maggy withdrew the arachne's adaptor from the console, stepped it back. Kejesli rose to his feet. Om im was halfway across the room, aimed like a thrown blade at the door. John the Smith stepped forward as well, blocking Tocohl's view. She attempted to rise but *layli-layli calulan* pressed her firmly back onto the bed—and pushed John the Smith to one side so Tocohl might see from where she was.

Hitoshi Dan began, "Timosie here tells me—" He got no further. Taking in Kejesli, he took an instinctive step backward, and then, just as instinctively, turned to look at the object of Kejesli's fury. Bewilderment crossed his face when he found only Megeve; he turned back to Kejesli, his expression clearly seeking explanation.

"One death on this world was not enough for you, dastagh!" The captain took a single step toward the Maldeneantine. "You needed four more!"

Megeve paled. For a brief moment, Tocohl thought he might turn and flee. But there was nowhere to run to. As if he had read the thought, Megeve put his hand to his belt—a cocky sort of gesture, but surprising under the circumstances.

He pushed past Hitoshi Dan and advanced toward her. "What have you done, Hellspark?" he demanded. "Months of work ruined; sacrifices made in vain."

Matching his anger, Tocohl said, "What work? What sacrifices? The four of us? The sprookjes?"

That he did not answer. Instead he began to chant in a language Tocohl did not, for all her experience, recognize. (Maggy, record.)

(I am.)

Megeve continued toward her, his steps timed to the rhythm of the chant, all expression draining from his face.

As he reached the center of the room, Tocohl stretched out her hand to warn him.

Too late, she saw him blindside Om im. The result was almost too fast for the eye to follow. Om im's blade flashed out and up. Megeve screamed in anguish, his hand spattering an arc of blood as he jerked out of the small man's reach.

The knife flashed a second time. Tocohl had barely enough time to gasp as it struck Megeve's side, ripped upward. Megeve's belt clattered to the floor where Om im kicked it deftly across to John the Smith. "Put a foot on that, John," Om im commanded, "and don't let it up until I'm done."

To Megeve, who nursed his injured hand, Om im went on, "Move an inch, Megeve, and you're dead." His glance flicked the length of the Maldeneantine. "I won't bother with a body blow—your 2nd skin would deflect it—I'll go straight for your throat."

Timosie Megeve froze, good hand gripping injured. The grip was tight enough to whiten his knuckles but insufficient to stop the steady drip of blood.

Even Kejesli was stunned into inaction. Thus the tableau held—until the arrival of Dyxte and Edge-of-Dark. Om im, still seeming the only one of them capable of action, said, "Target Megeve. If he moves so much as a hair, stun him."

Dyxte, bewildered, glanced at Kejesli. "Do it," Kejesli said, and the two obeyed. With a sigh of relief, Om im wiped and sheathed his knife. Then he crossed to John the Smith, where he bent to pick up Megeve's belt.

"You look puzzled, Ish shan." He grinned, a strained expression more of relief than humor. "Could it be that your education is sadly lacking?"

"It could be," Tocohl said; attempting to match the lightness of his tone, she succeeded only in matching its forced quality.

"Watch and learn." He bowed, added a flourish of cloak. Then he strode a few steps from them, raised the belt to shoulder height—

There was a sharp spitting sound, followed almost immediately by a rasp of metal on metal. A small but deadly looking dart embedded itself in the infirmary wall. Buntec whistled.

Maggy said, (You didn't have your hood up, Tocohl. He could have killed you with that!)

"I'm sorry, *layli-layli calulan*," said Om im, staring at the dart. "I didn't think it was that powerful."

Kejesli looked from the dart to Megeve. "Strip him down. I want his 2nd skin. We don't know what else he might be carrying."

Under the watchful eyes of Dyxte and Edge-of-Dark, Megeve was stripped and marched across the courtyard where a cell was hastily improvised from a section of the supply room.

Tocohl could hear Kejesli's shouted orders even over the rumble of the passing storm. Then she turned to face the small man who stood patiently beside her bed. "I live," she said in Bluesippan, "I thank the sharpness of your blade."

He grinned; this time the grin was genuine. "Ish shan," he said, in passable Hellspark, "everybody needs a friend, some time or other, even a legend."

He turned the belt over in his hands. "I saw a weapon much like this used when I was on Hayashi, but it never occurred to me that Megeve—" He met her eyes ruefully. "I didn't even think of it—until he made that move." Flawlessly, he reproduced Megeve's cocky gesture.

"To arm the weapon then," Tocohl said. "May I see?" She held out her hand toward the belt, but Om im drew it from her reach. Mildly puzzled, she said, "How can it hurt me? The one he intended for me is there." Her glance flicked to the wall where swift-Kalat held the arachne up for a close look at the imbedded dart.

Om im called out, "Don't touch it, swift-Kalat. If the barbs are sprung within the wall, it will be safe; but it may not have penetrated far enough, in which case you could get your fingers rather nastily sliced. And Megeve seems capable of having poisoned the dart, too."

To Tocohl, he explained, "The standard model carries four darts. Let me disarm it for you." He made a swift motion, then aimed it again at the wall, well away from swift-Kalat; this time nothing happened. He handed the object to Tocohl to examine to her and Maggy's satisfaction.

As Tocohl turned it over wonderingly in her hands, she asked aloud, "Why? Why should he try to kill me? It's too late."

Om im looked at her in surprise. "You of all people, Ish shan, should know that even gods take vengeance on those who thwart them."

#

Tocohl slept again; *layli-layli calulan* had seen to that, and Maggy rather wished she could understand how the trick was done. She wondered if it weren't simply a matter of perception, much like the difference between her perception of the Ringsilver magician and Tocohl's. She tagged the matter for further investigation.

Meanwhile, with a camera eye recording those events in which Tocohl would most likely have an interest, she sent the arachne after Kejesli who was still in the storeroom interrogating Megeve.

"Worryin' a wound," Buntec called it, in a tone Maggy interpreted as acid. "Don't know what he thinks he'll hear. He hasn't liked any of Megeve's answers so far." She pounded the side of the storeroom and bellowed, "Maggy's comin' in with me to eyeball the little b.f.f."

Dyxte opened the door to them. "Just don't get between me and the target, Buntec."

"Hah. Where's he gonna run?"

"He was ready to kill Tocohl," Kejesli snapped back, "I won't give him another chance—at any of us." Edge-of-Dark's weapon never left its target and, as Maggy's arachne scuttled by, Dyxte retrained his gun in the same direction. "Okay," said Buntec, "I take your point. Get anything out of the waster yet?"

"You call me a waster," Megeve said suddenly, "what do you see here? *Nothing*. No communications, no homes, no farms. They waste the resources of an entire world. —Even if they are sapient, the sprookjes don't deserve this world. What have they done with it? *Nothing!*" Despite the emphasis, he spoke calmly, as if he might convince them of the justice of his actions.

Kejesli's scowl deepened—Maggy had no trouble interpreting that expression. In a voice that sounded to Maggy carefully controlled, deliberately even, he said, "It's a lousy planet. There's too much rain, too much lightning. Even in sunshine the air stinks of storm. But if the sprookjes are sapient, it's theirs—and I'd burn beside Veschke before I'd let you take it from them."

"You still don't understand—" Lifting his hands, Megeve took a step forward. Dyxte and Edge-of-Dark dropped to firing position.

"Then explain it to me," Kejesli said.

Warily Megeve lowered his hands, clenching them into fists. "The world's too valuable for sprookjes," he began.

With a snort of disgust, Kejesli turned his back on the Maldeneantine and strode for the door.

Megeve called hastily after him: "Listen to me, Captain—the lightning rods! They're biological superconductors!"

Buntec gave a grunt of surprise; interest took her a step closer to Megeve, who immediately turned to address her. "Buntec," he said, "you understand, don't you? Superconductors that don't require an entire advanced technology to produce. Superconductors that don't need to be artificially maintained by cooling!" Kejesli had turned back to stare at Megeve with widening eyes.

"Yes," said Megeve. He was smiling now, and Tocohl would have called his tone triumphant. "Forests full of superconductors! Now you see why Flashfever is too valuable for sprookjes. Give it even a moment's thought and you'll admit I'm right."

Maggy was thinking indeed; she knew precisely what that would mean, to her and to Tocohl, if what he claimed about the lightning rods were true. "Cheap memory!" she said to Buntec. "Do you think the sprookjes would trade for moss cloaks?"

A short, sharp laugh answered her; there was no warmth in the sound. "There, Megeve," Buntec said, "even the kid knows better." Looking down at the arachne, she went on, her voice gaining warmth as she spoke, "They'll trade for something, Maggy; and I'd trust a Hellspark to find out what every time. Don't you worry—if you can't figure out a fair trade, Tocohl will."

"Good," said Maggy. She split her attention at once, setting a part to work on possible trade goods for the sprookjes. Given their reaction to Alfvaen's blood sample, wine would not be high on the list of probabilities. Biologicals—like Tocohl's moss cloak—there was the place to start.

The rest she devoted to Megeve. His smile had gone. Again he tried to back away, as if Kejesli's look were as dangerous as *layli-layli calulan*'s curse. Already backed against the wall, he sank instead, sliding his shoulders down until his knees suddenly buckled and he sat on the floor, dropping his head between them.

It didn't seem an opportune time to ask for further information, but Maggy wasn't sure when she'd have another chance. And Megeve had seemed willing to talk just a moment ago. "I don't understand," she said. "Why would that make Flashfever 'too valuable for sprookjes'?"

When Megeve made no answer, Maggy said, "Buntec?"

"C'mon, kid," Buntec said, "let's get you out of here. He's what my momma would have called a bad influence. And Tocohl wouldn't like you hangin' around him. *Neither* of us should be hangin' around 'im." She started for the door, clearly expecting the arachne to follow.

"Bad influence?"

"Somebody you shouldn't imitate if you want to grow up to be a human being."

Maggy was not sure that applied to her, but since Buntec seemed to mean it sincerely, she decided to go along with it, and with Buntec — at least until she had a chance to talk the matter over with Tocohl. She sent the arachne trotting after Buntec.

Once outside, she found the two of them momentarily alone. Rain still battered the arachne; she did not, however, expend the energy needed to compensate for the distortion it caused the arachne's eye. Instead she sent the arachne at full speed after Buntec. "Buntec, wait!"

Buntec splashed to a halt in mid-puddle. Hands sheltering her eyes and face, she bent to the arachne.

"Buntec, I don't understand. And it's secret so I can't ask anywhere else. I'm not a kid, I'm an extrapolative computer, and I don't understand why Tocohl wouldn't want me 'hangin' around 'im.' "

"You may be a computer, kid, but *that*" — a sharp jerk of her elbow toward the storeroom made Megeve the referent — "*that* is a villain, and nobody's momma wants her kid hangin' around villains. You got it now?"

"Yes," said Maggy, for that one word, villain, explained it all. "I've got it now. Thank you!"

"You're welcome — now let's get the hell out of the rain before we both get zapped."

CHAPTER 14

Maggy had much to think over—so much, in fact, that she spent most of the night swapping data from active files to inactive and back again, cross-referencing wherever she saw the need. She regretted that not all of her memory could be active simultaneously. Still, she supposed this to be what Tocohl called "concentrating on one thing at a time." If it didn't hurt Tocohl's thinking, Maggy saw no reason it should hurt hers.

Even in the infirmary the sound of thunder could be startlingly loud. Alfvaen had awakened to it twice; each time, *layli-layli* called on Maggy to interpret. Maggy did the best she could but Alfvaen still made little sense. As *layli-layli* did not seem disturbed by this, Maggy was content to wait and watch through the arachne at her side. Swift-Kalat did the same, although Maggy would hardly have described him as content.

Tocohl slept on, stirring only slightly at the sound of thunder. Maggy kept an active watch on the 2nd skin sensors. The normalcy of the readings reassured her, as did the fact that Buntec and Om im took turns guarding the infirmary throughout the night.

Morning came but the sky remained a dark patchwork of clouds, stitched with flashes of lightning. Despite all the questions, cued and waiting to be asked, Maggy did not wake Tocohl at the customary time. Rest, *layli-layli* had assured her, was what Tocohl needed most to heal. As long as there were no sprookjes in the camp, there was little for Tocohl to do but heal.

Still, questions were the next highest priority. Maggy sent the arachne across the room to peer up at Om im. "Will you tell me what I missed?" she asked, phrasing the question as Tocohl would have. Om im gave a sidelong glance at the sleeping Tocohl. Maggy said, "If the thunder doesn't wake her, we're not likely to."

"True," he said. He reached down and lifted the arachne to place it on the edge of Tocohl's cot, the camera eye at a level with his own. "Where shall I start?"

"Where the daisy-clipper went down," Maggy said, and settled the arachne to record it all. The account was far more interesting than Maggy had expected: not only did it differ in detail from Buntec's account of the same circumstances, but it differed in style of delivery a well. Om im's words were gentler, his gestures more extravagant—as if to compensate for the softness of his voice.

From time to time Tocohl stirred. Maggy's readings showed her close to consciousness—then, as if soothed by the sound of their voices, she would drift back into sleep. *Layli-layli calulan* woke to find Om im describing the duel between Alfvaen and Tocohl. To Maggy's surprise, she did not interrupt. Without a word, she joined them—to the proper side of Om im—and lightly touched first Tocohl's rib, then her temples. What she found seemed to satisfy her, for she smiled and said only, "Good morning," before she moved on to check Alfvaen.

Maggy was glad *layli-layli* had not felt it necessary to interrupt. Maggy was disappointed that she had not seen the duel between Tocohl and Alfvaen for herself, but Om im's account was considerably better than Buntec's. Trained in a different form of dueling, he was a better observer of both the movements and formalities involved.

He was in the midst of demonstrating those movements for her when van Zoveel burst into the infirmary, flinging droplets of water from the end of every ribbon on his tunic. As if it had been a planned part of the demonstration, Om im crossed to intercept him.

Not, Maggy was sure, that he thought van Zoveel any threat to Tocohl; he simply did not want van Zoveel to wake her. Enhanced sound confirmed this. Keeping his voice very low, Om im said, "Not yet, Ruurd. *Layli-layli calulan* says she needs the sleep."

Van Zoveel fairly stamped with impatience but he too kept his voice low. "You don't understand," he said, "Captain Kejesli said she had gotten Megeve's sprookje to echo her. I must know how. There's a clue that I'm missing."

"You'll learn soon enough," *layli-layli calulan* said, joining the two. "Give her a few more hours of healing."

"I don't need her for heavy lifting, *layli-layli*. I need her for talking."

"Not now," said *layli-layli calulan*.

"I waited all night..."

"Then you've had practice. You can wait out the storm. I won't have her disturbed until there's a reason for it, and she can hardly demonstrate without a sprookje to echo her."

Glaring, van Zoveel started once more toward Tocohl but Om im spread his hands in the Bluesippan shrug, discreetly cutting off his approach. "We'll both have to wait for our answers," said Om im.

"You will wait elsewhere," *layli-layli* told van Zoveel. Maggy watched as the two of them glared at each other for a long moment, then van Zoveel gave way, and stamped back to the door. "If she wakes ..." he began.

"If she wakes, she'll have breakfast," *layli-layli calulan* told him, "and then I'll notify you."

Van Zoveel muttered a word under his breath that Maggy had been taught was impolite to say aloud in Zoveelian society, but he left nonetheless. Neither of the others took offense; clearly they did not recognize that any had been given. Maggy wondered if she should explain it to them but decided against it. All but a handful of times that Tocohl had been in an analogous situation, Tocohl had said nothing. Maggy settled on adding that query to her growing list.

She wanted Tocohl awake as much as van Zoveel did, she found. Experimentally, she rocked the arachne from side to side, imitating to the best of its ability his impatient stamp, to see if that had any effect on the matter. It did nothing to help, except obliquely — for Tocohl came awake.

"Your pardon, Tocohl. I did not mean to wake you. I was only experimenting."

Tocohl blinked puzzled eyes at the arachne. "Experimenting at what?"

Showing her the bit of tape of van Zoveel, Maggy explained. By the time she was done, both Om im and *layli-layli calulan* had joined them and were watching the arachne with thoughtful looks. "It doesn't do anything," Maggy concluded, "I guess that means it's a null gesture?"

With a glance at *layli-layli calulan*, who smiled in return, Tocohl corrected, "I'd say it worked, Maggy. That's an unconscious attention-getting device. You used it correctly, and for you, it worked. You have my attention."

"But I didn't mean to wake you. *Layli-layli calulan* said you needed the rest. That's why she told van Zoveel to go away." As the possibility had just now occurred to her, she added, "Now she'll make me go away too!"

"No," said *layli-layli calulan* with another smile—this one directed at the arachne. "You can stay, Maggy; talking to you comforts Tocohl. Read your sensors: they're steady."

What she said was true, Maggy saw, although how *layli-layli calulan* could tell she did not know. Again, the ability must have something to do with the shaman's different perception.

Once more, a figure burst through the door. This time *layli-layli calulan's* response was quite different. "Ah," she said, "John." It was as if she used the name as greeting. She turned to Om im and said, "John the Smith will keep watch for a while. It's time you had a chance to clean up." Om im glanced at Tocohl, but *layli-layli calulan* went on, "Go. I'll see she gets breakfast."

Tocohl said, "Go ahead, Om im. I'll be fine."

Maggy considered the stubborn set of Om im's face and said, "I'll call you if there's trouble."

That seemed to reassure him. He woke Buntec and together they plunged into the courtyard, lost to sight in the downpour even before the door membrane slapped shut. Thunder rattled the room.

Approaching *layli-layli calulan* on the side which gave him high status, John the Smith said something into her ear which Maggy couldn't make out; enhancing only enhanced the sound of thunder. The Smith looked serious and seemed surprised when *layli-layli calulan* answered him only with her most beautiful smile.

(Tocohl?) Maggy asked.

(I'm sure we'll find out,) Tocohl said. The sensors in her 2nd skin showed that she was not disturbed. Maggy folded the arachne's legs and settled it beside Tocohl as *layli-layli calulan* approached the cot once more.

For a long moment, *layli-layli calulan* looked down at Tocohl and at the arachne. At last she said, "Hitoshi Dan believes that *maggy-maggy* is an extrapolative computer."

"He's right," Tocohl said. She glanced across the room, pointed a polite little finger. "Swift-Kalat would tell you the same."

Layli-layli calulan smiled beautifully once again. "I do not think so, *tocohli*, not in Jenji."

That sent spikes through all the sensors in Tocohl's 2nd skin. "What do you mean?"

The smile went from *layli-layli calulan's* face. "Have you

thought what the Hellspark ritual of change might mean on some worlds?" Sensors spiked again, this time higher than the first, but no change showed on Tocohl's face. Tilting her head to the side, she said, "No, I can't say that I have."

"I thought as much. You and *maggy-maggy* have much to discuss. I'll see to Alfvaen and then to your breakfast. Think over what I've said." One last time, she gave Tocohl her most beautiful smile, then she turned and walked away.

(Maggy? I hope you know something about this "Hellspark ritual of change" business?)

(I lied to swift-Kalat. I would have asked you, Tocohl, but I couldn't.)

(Don't get excited. Just tell me what happened.) She shifted in the cot—getting comfortable as she called it. Something she did before someone began a long report.

Maggy took this to mean she wanted the full story. She began at the point where she had lost contact with Tocohl, and because she needed Tocohl's advice, she explained her own actions as she went along. At the "Hey, presto!" Tocohl laughed aloud and said, (Oh, Maggy, that was *perfect!*)

Tocohl's laugh alleviated any further worry: the reasoning that had led Maggy to use the "Hey, presto!" as she had was sound.

(So, that's how swift-Kalat got to see *layli-layli* when she was in deep mourning,) Tocohl said, (I'd been meaning to ask you about that.)

Still smiling, Tocohl closed her eyes, and Maggy could tell from the sensors that she was getting tired again. *Layli-layli calulan* was right: healing required rest.

(You should sleep again,) Maggy said, and seeing *layli-layli* approach with a tray, she repeated it aloud, "She should sleep again, *layli-layli calulan*."

"She should eat first."

Maggy checked the sensors again. "She's very tired."

"Maggy," said Tocohl firmly, "that's nothing compared to how hungry I am. Which doesn't show on your sensors, so you know absolutely nothing about it. Greed you've a fair grasp of; hunger, no. Let me eat." Tocohl eased herself cautiously into a sitting position—Maggy was pleased to note that the action no longer made her sensors spike as emphatically as it had the previous day—and accepted the tray from *layli-layli calulan*.

"Thank you," said Tocohl. She gave a sidelong glance at the arachne, which seemed to imply that she thanked the shaman for something other than the meal. With a similar glance at the arachne, *layli-layli calulan* said, "You are quite welcome."

Their manner gave Maggy cause for concern. When *layli-layli calulan* returned to Alfvaen's side to wake swift-Kalat, Maggy said, (Did I do right? You told me I could lie.)

(You did right, Maggy,) Tocohl said, around a mouthful of food. (I hadn't intended to grant you blanket permission, but you seem to use discretion—and since it saved me a long, painful walk through the flashwood out there, I can scarcely complain.)

(I won't lie to you.)

(I won't lie to you, either. Between friends, it's not good policy.)

That brought a sudden sense of conflict. (Is swift-Kalat my friend?)

Tocohl stopped eating. (I think he'd be able to say so.)

(But then I shouldn't have lied to him. Lying causes him distress, even when a stranger only mentions it.)

(Maggy, I don't think he'll hold it against you. Even Jenji permits the establishing—the creating—of a useful ritual. If I put it to him that you did not lie, but rather created what was needed to suit the circumstances, he won't be distressed. Any more than he'd be distressed if someone in the camp had built a machine that overrode the Hayashi jammers and allowed him to find us safely. Do you see the distinction I'm making?)

(I think so. I'm not sure.)

(Well, let me assure you the ritual you created is useful, and will be used in the future. *Layli-layli calulan* has plans for it already. And I know a dozen traders who'll be very happy to turn it to their advantage: all of them male and all of them, up to now, unable to trade successfully with the Yn.)

Maggy skimmed her files on the Yn one more time. (You mean, if you make Geremy your sister, he could deal with the Yn female to female?)

(Compared to some of the other male traders, Geremy has done pretty well. He's always had the advantage of his sharpness, and of his name. If we make him our sister, he'll—)

Sensors in the 2nd skin spiked; this time pain was not the cause. Maggy said, (What is it?)

Instead of answering directly, Tocohl frowned at the tray of food. Maggy judged that she was thinking something over and waited politely, not wishing to distract her. She was pleased that Tocohl ate while thinking—that, at least, meant she could rest as soon as she was done. Meanwhile she took the opportunity to update her files on lying.

She found herself at once faced with another dilemma. While *layli-layli calulan* approved of lying, and did it well herself, she also fell into the category of friend. Maggy knew that friend overrode a great many other priorities, both behavioral and cultural. Tocohl had approved of her action at the time, but Maggy needed to know why, in order to know whether the same approval was still operative. The question was imperative, worth distracting Tocohl to ask. (Tocohl?)

(Um?)

(Should I tell *layli-layli calulan* the truth?)

Tocohl laid the tray aside. (The truth about what, Maggy?) she asked as she eased herself down.

Maggy replayed the bit of tape. Once again, *layli-layli calulan* asked what was the probability that Megeve had killed Oloitokitok. Once again, Maggy answered that her information was insufficient.

(Stick to your story, Maggy. I'd have asked you to lie in that case anyway. I'd like to hear your reasoning, though.)

(*Layli-layli calulan* intended to kill van Zoveel because of Oloitokitok's body. The probability—do you wish the figures?—is extremely high that she would kill a man she thought responsible for Oloitokitok's death. While the odds that Megeve was responsible are low, perhaps due to insufficient information, *layli-layli calulan* acted upon lower odds when she followed the search technique I suggested to look for you.)

(Maggy, I'm proud of you. Your reasoning is impeccable. —Now, add this to information about Megeve, if it isn't already in your stores. In Yn, the sound *ee* has strong meaning. Do you understand that, in some cultures, specific words are thought to have power beyond their simple communicative use?)

(Sympathetic magic,) Maggy said. (When you feed a code word into a computer, it brings an entire program into being. Is that the derivation of the idea in human context?)

Tocohl grinned. (I rather doubt it: there were humans and sympathetic magic long before there were computers, but that's a good analogy.)

She went on, (All right. *Y* is the name of *layli-layli*'s world, that world being the source of all life and, hence, the greatest, most potent magic of all.

(Please remember, I'm describing a cultural attitude, not a fact. — The title laylee-laylee calulan also indicates a power, the doubling of the term expressing her espabilities.)

Maggy saw what she was getting at and interrupted to save her further explanation: (So Geremy and Timosie and *maggy-maggy* are all names of power!)

(That's it! Not as potent, perhaps, as *layli-layli calulan*, especially now that she knows you're an extrapolative computer, but your name might be sufficient to give your words more weight with *layli-layli* than anyone else's.)

She twisted to address the arachne directly. Clearly, she used the arachne as a focus sometimes, too; Maggy moved it to a position that did not require her to turn.

(Thanks,) said Tocohl, (I see I'm falling into that little habit, too. You shouldn't have bounced it on the bed; it *did* get my attention, in more ways than one.) She was silent for a long moment, then she went on, (I'm thinking that the *ee* in *Timosie Megeve* might have been very important in all this...)

(I don't understand.)

(I'm thinking that Timosie's very name might have given his words more weight to Oloitokitok. Suppose Megeve suggested to Oloitokitok that no one would believe, for instance, that the two of them had seen the sprookjes behaving in a sapient fashion.) She focused her eyes at some point beyond the arachne. (Or suppose ... Maggy, Sunchild was Megeve's sprookje! She was willing to chance a ride in a daisy-clipper! The equipment failures ... Megeve's acting as if the sprookjes would mess with his equipment! Suppose the sprookjes did mess with the equipment. Suppose ...)

(Too many supposes,) Maggy interrupted. (I can't give an accurate probability on any one of them. I'm not sure I even follow your line of thinking.)

(Why would Megeve want Oloitokitok dead?)

(Well,) said Maggy, knowing that aesthetically such an important question required a pause before the answer, (he wanted you dead, if I understand this correctly, because he thought the four of you were the only witnesses to the sprookje's gift.)

(Yes. Suppose there had been an earlier gift, one only Megeve and Oloitokitok witnessed.)

(Why wouldn't Oloitokitok tell everyone about the gift?)

(That's where the name Timosie comes in. If someone named John the Smith had said, "They won't believe us. Let's wait until we can get some real proof," Oloitokitok would have said, "There are two of us. We've both seen it. Let's tell everyone and they'll help us look for real proof." But if Timosie said the very same thing, Oloitokitok would have said, "All right, let's wait until we can get some real proof.")

(Tocohl, that's *silly*.)

Tocohl laughed. (I never said it wasn't. But I've seen it happen. Geremy—because of the *ee* in his name—does a rousing business trading with Yn males. They think he's special and important.)

Only one response seemed appropriate. Maggy made the rude noise.

Tocohl laughed again. (Agreed,) she said, (but that doesn't change the possibility. I never said human beings were logical, or reasonable, or even sane.)

(I know,) said Maggy. (But they are very confusing.)

(Admit it: we keep you from being bored.) Tocohl flashed a smile at the arachne that Maggy judged every bit as beautiful as *layli-layli calulan*'s.

(Yes,) Maggy said, (you keep me from being bored.)

(Good. Now think about this. Megeve never took you into account as a possible witness. There was someone else he never took into account as well...)

(The sprookjes.)

(That's right. If only we can find the words to ask, Sunchild may be able to tell us what happened to Oloitokitok. In the meantime, I agree with you: it's safer not to give *layli-layli* any odds at all that might make her do something rash.)

Through the arachne's eye, Maggy saw *layli-layli calulan* approach long before Tocohl reacted to her footsteps and turned. Tocohl began to rise, but *layli-layli* said, "This is only a lull between storms, Dyxte tells me. There'll be no sprookjes for several hours, assuming the next is the day's last."

"So Tocohl should sleep," Maggy said aloud.

"Yes." *Layli-layli calulan* stripped her rings from her fingers and laid them beside the arachne, giving Maggy an excellent chance to observe them closely. To Maggy's disappointment, they seemed to be ordinary bluestone, so she recorded the movements of *layli-layli*'s hands instead, first as they touched the injured rib. Maggy could tell from the sensors that Tocohl was reinforcing her healing ritual simultaneously. Then, as *layli-layli*'s fingertips brushed Tocohl's temples, the same sensors began to indicate drowsiness.

Tocohl sighed and sank farther into the cot. Her eyelids parted ever so slightly. (Maggy,) she said, glancing sleepily up at the infirmary roof, (where are you?)

It took Maggy only a split second to weigh the pros and cons. Then she formed the image of the Flashfever starfield Tocohl would have seen from her position had the roof and light pollution of Flashfever not intervened. She hesitated a moment—Flashfever had no constellations she knew of so there were no established groupings of stars. That made the task more difficult, but at long last she decided upon an aesthetic place to put the glittering point that would represent herself. She added an indicatory arrow and projected the resulting image onto Tocohl's spectacles, all before Tocohl had drawn another breath.

And when she drew it, it was a sudden, sharp intake... Maggy knew a sound of delight when she heard it from Tocohl, and the slow, drowsy smile that followed merely confirmed Maggy's assessment.

(I missed you, Maggy,) Tocohl said, very softly.

(I missed you too,) Maggy said; then she was silent, letting Tocohl drift into sleep.

All in all, Maggy concluded, she had done right. Tocohl knew that she could not see the ship from here, so Maggy had not lied to a friend. She had told a pleasing story, and she was very proud of her new ability.

The storms continued throughout the day and into the night, but morning at last brought to the skies a clear pale-blue stillness. A fresh wind swept the last tang of ozone from the camp. Buntec took a deep contented breath of it, scrambled into her boots, and skipped down the steps of her quarters into the first pale rays of sunlight.

She was the first. If there had been a gong to ring to wake the other members of the team, she'd have rung it. But there wasn't—and for the moment, she could not bring herself to venture into shadow long enough to knock at various doors.

The stillness was loud enough to wake others. One by one, the surveyors stumbled out, blinking up into the sky, and smiled. Buntec waved at Edge-of-Dark who waved back, glanced down at her own bare feet, reddened, and darted back inside.

It took Buntec a second or two to realize just what sequence of events had sent Edge-of-Dark back into shadow. Once she had, she was spurred into action without any further thought.

She splashed across the compound, raced up the steps of Edge-of-Dark's quarters, and stuck her head in, uninvited. "Don't," she said, "don't, Edge-of-Dark. I can stand your f-feet"—though the word *was* hard to get out when it wasn't an obscenity, when she didn't *mean* it as an obscenity, she managed to say it and go on to the important part of her objection: "Don't miss the sun just because of me!!!"

Edge-of-Dark paused in the midst of pulling on her second boot. Her jaw dropped, then closed abruptly to draw her mouth into a brilliant smile. "Buntec," she said, "you are one of the nicest people I've ever met. That makes up for any sunshine I missed for these!" She pulled the boot to, tapped it with a long green nail.

Embarrassed, Buntec ducked her head. "I wish," she said, "there weren't so many traps between us. I like you too, Edge-of-Dark. I like you a lot. I don't know how to get from here to there"—she gestured at the expanse of floor that separated them and found she knew the perfect expression—"without, as the Trethowan say, putting *my* f-foot in it." It was minimally easier to speak the word the second time—and Edge-of-Dark's peal of delighted laughter made it worth every bit of the effort.

Still laughing, Edge-of-Dark stood and straightened. "I will close the distance, too. If we warn each other, look out for each other, we will make it."

"Yes," said Buntec, lifting her head and grinning. For a long moment, the two of them simply stood there grinning at each other across the small separating distance, then Buntec said, "Sunshine!"

"Yes," agreed Edge-of-Dark. "Would you give me a hand with my table and bowls, Buntec? The sprookjes need help across a distance too."

The two of them carried the small table down the steps to set it in the sunlight. Edge-of-Dark made a quick trip back for bowls and scissors and the rest of her odd paraphernalia.

Buntec leaned back, stretched her legs. When she sat up again, she caught movement at the edge of camp. "Your sprookjes are coming," she called up to Edge-of-Dark. There was no response. Well, it required none, thought Buntec, and settled in to watch the sprookjes appear in the flashwood and start to work their way through the fence.

She blinked suddenly and rose to her full height, shading her eyes and squinting. Surely she was imagining it—but she hoped she wasn't.

Those surveyors closest to the sprookjes turned, gave excited exclamations, tapped others. No, not imagining things. "Edge-of-Dark, get out here!"

Beside her, Edge-of-Dark responded only to her urgency of tone. "I'm here," she said, then absently, "I'll need to pick flowers. Would you like to come with me?"

Buntec dragged her eyes away from the sprookjes to glance down. Edge-of-Dark was contemplating her paraphernalia. Buntec caught her by the shoulders, turned her to face the sprookjes. "Tell me," Buntec demanded, "tell me if you see what I see! Look at the sprookjes and then tell me if you need to pick flowers!"

And in Edge-of-Dark's widening eyes, Buntec found all the confirmation she needed. She turned again to the perimeter fence.

A dozen sprookjes were cautiously assisting each other through the barbed-wire barrier—and each carried an armload of brilliant blooms and leaves of all sizes and shapes.

Edge-of-Dark started forward, as if drawn by all that color and noise, but Buntec caught her shoulder. "Stay here. Stay here. They know where to find you." She stared again at the approaching sprookjes, sure beyond dispute that all would come straight to Edge-of-Dark. She sprang from the steps. "I'm gonna get Maggy. She should be taping this."

Dazed, still caught up in the sight, Edge-of-Dark sat abruptly. "Yes," she said, "I should stay." She managed to tear her eyes away to look momentarily at Buntec. "They're coming! They've brought flowers!"

Buntec could feel her own fierce grin. "*Your* art they recognize," she said, for the pleasure of putting it into words. Then, still grinning, she started for the infirmary.

#

"I don't care," Maggy said, *"I'm* going to wake her. She'll want to see this." The emphasis was so startling that Tocohl at first thought herself in the midst of a particularly vivid dream, then waking and simultaneously catching the sense of the distantly heard words she realized she was hearing Maggy's voice relayed through her implant.

Buntec's voice, seeming equally astonished by the emphasis Maggy had put on the *I,* said, "Whatever you want, kid. Make your own decisions, take your own lumps."

"Lumps?"

There was a pause as Buntec sought a way to explain. "Take the consequences, good or bad. Tocohl might not take kindly to being kicked awake, not even for this."

(Maggy?) Tocohl asked. (What's going on?)

An image of Om im looking up flashed briefly onto her spectacles; from the angle, someone tall must have been holding the arachne above his head. "She's awake," Maggy told him, and rather smugly. I bet *I* sound like that when *I* deliver a *fait accompli,* Tocohl thought.

(Look,) Maggy said and showed her a crowd of surveyors and sprookjes, all jostling about in front of Edge-of-Dark's cabin. (The sprookjes brought flowers for Edge-of-Dark.)

Despite the irrationality of the act, Tocohl sat up for a better view, noting with relief that at least sitting was no longer painful.

(Was I wrong to wake you?) Maggy asked, the smugness gone from her voice.

(No, Maggy. You did just right,) Tocohl told her and couldn't resist adding, (No lumps.)

The smugness returned. "No lumps," Maggy informed Buntec.

In Tocohl's spectacles, a sprookje, cheek-feathers puffing, seemed to battle with itself, torn between careful handling of its bouquet and direct contact with Edge-of-Dark.

Edge-of-Dark watched it struggle for a moment only, then, with a sweep of her arm, cleared a space on the surface of her table and took a step away, giving enough ground to tell the sprookje she would not attack it. The sprookje's cheek-feathers settled a little. Settled enough, Tocohl saw, for it laid its bouquet carefully onto the table and stepped hastily back.

The second sprookje did likewise. The third looked at the table, looked at Edge-of-Dark, and, fluffing all its feathers to twice normal size, it stretched out its arms to offer its bouquet directly to Edge-of-Dark.

Edge-of-Dark inched forward to take the gift, holding the chattering sprays as delicately as the sprookje had.

"Good for you," said Buntec—it was obviously she who held Maggy's arachne—and the sprookje echoed her. "How about that," Buntec went on, sounding twice as pleased, "you may be a pain in the butt, but at least you're not chicken-shit."

Buntec's words and echo seemed to reassure the others as well: each of the remaining sprookjes delivered its burden directly into Edge-of-Dark's arms, as if the act were a matter of pure course. Edge-of-Dark, dazed and grinning from behind her armload of sprigs and vines and stalks, began to look like an artistic composition of her own design.

A hand touched Tocohl's shoulder, her spectacles cleared, and she smiled back at Om im.

"Megeve couldn't have stopped it," he said with enormous satisfaction. "He couldn't have killed enough of us to stop it."

"So I see." Tocohl tapped the frame of her spectacles with a fingertip. "But I'd like a closer look." The spectacles instantly provided a close-up of Edge-of-Dark. "Thanks but no, Maggy, I mean I'm coming out."

Om im offered his shoulder for support. As Tocohl got to her feet, *layli-layli calulan* said, "I suppose there's no point in arguing with you?"

"None at all," Tocohl assured her, "but"—she reacted to the twinge in her side as she straightened—"I will take it easy."

"I think she means it," said Om im, lifting a brow at Tocohl in surprise. "That's less of an argument than we got from Maggy on the subject of waking you."

"Maggy doesn't have a pain in her side." But Tocohl released his shoulder and walked slowly to the doorway on her own. The pain was there but no longer so bad she would be unable to function.

Om im thrust aside the membrane and bowed her into the sunlight, where she stood, dazzled by the confusion.

The sprookjes had been granted front row center at two separate shows. Edge-of-Dark made art of the plants they'd brought her, and beside *layli-layli calulan*'s cabin, Dyxte was up to his elbows in the red mud, planting a stand of tick-ticks. Sprookjes gathered around both, paying such rapt attention that their echoing was only haphazard and intermittent.

Around each crowd of sprookjes, small knots of surveyors watched and recorded, trying for all their excitement not to startle or to distract the sprookjes.

In the hush their gestures and their movements shrieked cacophony. Buntec, now holding the arachne at waist-height, grinned from ear to ear, while Hitoshi Dan's grin began at the tips of his toes, shot his eyebrows up, and ran out his extended arms to spread the fingers of both hands wide. Kejesli shrugged one-handed. Van Zoveel first turned out his thumbs in puzzlement, then shrugged back at Kejesli with a down-turned palm. John the Smith jockeyed for position with Tryn Ilan of Dusty Sunday—who was only trying to find a better camera angle, not assert authority.

Tocohl closed her eyes, made momentarily giddy from the sudden full impact of it all. Her hand reached out, found Om im's shoulder beneath it.

"Ish shan? Are you all right?"

She opened her eyes. "For a fool, I'm fine." Grinning down at him, she added. "I know your secret. And I'll bet you can't tell the sprookjes apart right now."

He obliged her by looking, first at one group, then the second, then up again at her, perplexed. "You're right. They all look alike."

"They're too interested in Edge-of-Dark and Dyxte to worry about their toes."

"That's not much of an explanation."

"I know. But I've got to find Megeve's sprookje before I can give you a better one."

He looked again. "I can't help you."

Having finished planting his tick-ticks, Dyxte rose and came toward them, trailing his collection of sprookjes. "Good," he said to Tocohl, warming the perfunctory GalLing' with a thump of his fist to his heart, "you're awake. Would you be willing to sacrifice that cloak of yours in a good cause?" His sprookje echoed his request.

"For art's sake?" Tocohl said. She sighed. "There's not much left of it, but you're welcome to the remnants. —Inside."

He thanked her with a spread palm and slipped past Om im, who turned out two fingers and said, in surprise, "That's Megeve's sprookje, Ish shan, but it didn't echo you!"

"It doesn't recognize me in all this noise," she said, adding to herself, at least, *I hope that's the explanation.* This would take conscious effort, she saw, and again she released Om im's shoulder. Taking a step toward the sprookje the Bluesippan had indicated, she told herself, *You're talking to a Maldeneantine: be polite.* "Sunchild?" she asked.

"Sunchild?" said the sprookje, its voice overlapping hers.

"Thank Veschke," said Tocohl, and the sprookje, ruffling, echoed all the feeling she'd put into the phrase. Without considering the action, she reached out a hand to smooth down the risen feathers.

The sprookje's head dipped suddenly, beak flashing sharply down toward her hand. Tocohl felt the prick of its "sample tooth." When it raised its head again, its feathers had already begun to subside, laying back smoothly against the body in long rippling waves. "You just wanted to make sure I was all right," she said and was echoed.

(It talked to you!) said Maggy.

(Not yet. So far that's just echo. Bring the arachne over if you will: I'd like to have as much tape on this as possible.)

"Now how did you do that?" Om im said. Then, in a tone of admiration, "Never mind. Don't tell me. It'd be like asking a magician where the doves came from. Go on," he urged, "I'll just stand here and appreciate the results."

"Don't go overboard," Tocohl and Sunchild said, "I haven't got *anything* yet—except a damn echo I could well do without."

Om im laughed. "You're never satisfied. First you're unhappy that it won't talk, now you're unhappy because it will."

She eyed him wickedly. "Let's try a second experiment, shall we?" Sunchild agreed vocally. "Let's see what happens when I go from Maldeneantine"—and here she shifted stance and position—"to Bluesippan ... and keep on talking."

For the first time, she heard a catch of hesitation in the sprookje's echo—just at the moment she shifted from accommodating a speaker of Maldeneantine to a speaker of Bluesippan. "Now," she and sprookje said together, "go ahead. Say something, Om im, I dare you."

"Dare me ..." he began, completely puzzled. Then his mouth snapped shut as he realized Sunchild had echoed him as well. "By my blade," the two of them said together, "what have you done to me?"

"Not me," Tocohl assured him, reassured to find the sprookje still echoing her as well, "Sunchild." She grinned at the sprookje, feeling as ruffled in her excitement as Sunchild so obviously was. "You catch on quick," they said, as if to each other.

Dyxte, trailing the moss cloak, paused on the threshold to look down at them. "It talks to you!"

Sunchild did not echo him. Tocohl frowned at the sprookje, waited until Dyxte had reached the bottom step, and shifted into ti-Tobian. Sunchild's eyes widened. "Yes," said Tocohl as Sunchild and a second sprookje—Dyxte's—both echoed her, "but you see how complicated this echo business can get."

"You've got *two* echoing you now!" Dyxte said, then threw a protective arm across his face at the realization that the same two had echoed him as well. "Oh, no!"

Om im glanced up at her, clearly wondering what would happen if he spoke. With the touch of a finger to the tip of her nose, she urged him to try. "Testing," he said cautiously, "one, two ..." The same two sprookjes echoed him. "Now you've really done it, Ish shan," all three said accusingly.

"I'm afraid so," Tocohl admitted. Behind her a chorus of sprookjes sounded the same regret. "Let's see if we can get Sunchild inside"—she winced at the amount of echo as another sprookje joined the chorus—"where I'll have only one to deal with."

Dyxte, with a wild look at her, bundled the cloak under his arm and made for *layli-layli calulan*'s cabin. Two of the sprookjes hesitated only a moment before following him. Sunchild remained, still staring solemnly.

It turned at the arrival of Buntec, Maggy's arachne, and van Zoveel, and its eyes widened. "Veschke's sparks." said Tocohl, seeing the look—attention drawn back, the sprookje echoed her—"I wish you wouldn't!"

"It's true!" said van Zoveel. "It echoes you!"

To her relief, it didn't echo van Zoveel. "Inside," she said and Sunchild seconded that.

Buntec set the arachne on the infirmary's bottom step, where it immediately skittered up to the door and rocked impatiently. "Lumps," said Buntec, clenching a fist in its direction, "you're about to learn the literal meaning of lumps."

The arachne stopped its rocking instantly and bobbed deferentially. "Your pardon, Buntec," Maggy began.

"Don't worry about it. Just don't do it. It drives me up a wall."

Maggy lowered the arachne a fraction of an inch, just enough to appear greatly interested, and said, "Really?"

Buntec rolled her eyes at Tocohl, sighed, and said, "Kids." She climbed the steps and held the door, toeing the arachne inside. Tocohl made the various shooing motions that gestured first Bluesippan, then Zoveelian in.

Then she took a deep breath and, hoping Sunchild would remember, held out to the sprookje an imaginary length of moss cloak. The sprookje came forward, took the imaginary end, and followed her to the threshold.

There it stood, feathers ruffling. Om im said, "This isn't a daisy-clipper, Sunchild. By my blade, I swear it won't crash." Echoing his words, Sunchild entered the infirmary.

"It echoed you too!" van Zoveel said. "How…! *How…?*" He rocked impatiently at her side.

"Lumps?" said Maggy, directing her query to Buntec.

"Probably," said Buntec, with a glare at van Zoveel, "in about three minutes if he doesn't cut it out. I've warned him about it…"

As if fascinated, the arachne trotted a yard or so away, the better to get a full-figure view of van Zoveel and Buntec. The movement drew a surprised glance from van Zoveel. "She's waiting for me to deck you," Buntec explained. "She wants to record it for her files."

Van Zoveel stopped his rocking abruptly. With visible effort, he held his body still, but the ribbons on his tunic still fluttered his excitement. "Tocohl," he began.

"No lumps?" Maggy sounded disappointed, and knowing how unusual it was for her to interrupt, Tocohl decided that was an indication of how disappointed.

"Some other time," Buntec said, "I'm sure."

That was enough to satisfy Maggy. To satisfy van Zoveel would not be so easy. She stood quietly for a long moment, then she turned and greeted him, with Sunchild repeating each word, in Zoveelian: "May the sun warm you in the cold wind."

Ruurd van Zoveel responded automatically: "May the wind cool you in the hot sun." This time the sprookje echoed him.

With a whoop of delight, Buntec clapped van Zoveel on the shoulder. "Now you've got two, Ruurd!" In her burst of enthusiasm, she added, "Make it do me, Tocohl."

Tocohl grinned. "Are you sure?" The sprookje echoed her. "It's more trouble than it's worth."

But Buntec was caught by the enthusiasm of the moment. "I don't mind! Do it!" she said, clapping her hands together in her excitement, so Tocohl grinned again and, shifting her stance, mimicked the gesture. "Now talk," Tocohl and the sprookje invited.

"Hiya, Sunchild!" Buntec said, and when Sunchild repeated her words, she clapped van Zoveel on the shoulder a second time, crowing her delight.

Perhaps, thought Tocohl, overkill is the way to go. A moment later she had the sprookje echoing both *layli-layli calulan* and swift-Kalat as well.

Maggy rocked the arachne. "Me, too. Make it do me, too!" but before she had completed the sentence, Sunchild had joined in as well. Maggy stopped the rocking, as if in surprise. "What did I do?" she and her echo asked.

"You just proved," Tocohl said, with Sunchild picking her up, "that you're definitely Hellspark."

In the momentary clamor of voices that followed, Sunchild tried valiantly to echo them all, even as they interrupted and overlapped each other's words. But it could manage only a phrase here and a phrase there, and its feathers began to fluff in its distress.

"That echo," Tocohl announced—so loudly that it was her voice the sprookje followed—"has got to go."

Silence ensued as Tocohl considered the sprookje. "All right," they said together, "everyone keep quiet for a moment." Tocohl stroked the feathers at Sunchild's wrist until they subsided. Then, keeping a careful eye on them for any renewed sign of alarm, she slowly raised both hands to the level of its head. Curling the fingers of her right hand very loosely, she circled Sunchild's beak. Her left hand she brought to the level of its larynx, an inch away from the feathery length of its throat.

"You must not," she began—as it tried to echo her the opening beak touched her encircling fingertips; simultaneously, she pressed the feathers over its larynx—"speak aloud." The sprookje, surprised at the contact, snapped its beak shut, leaving her sentence unfinished.

As slowly as she had raised them, she drew her hands away. "Don't speak," she repeated. It started to but she raised her hands as if to circle and press again and the sprookje closed its beak with an audible snap. "Got that?" This time it made no attempt to mimic her words and she smiled in satisfaction. "Yes, I see you have."

Turning to Om im, she said, "I wonder if it's all or nothing. — Say something, Om im."

He grinned up at her. "I'm humbled before you, Ish shan," he said, his words belied by the cock of his head and the tilt of his brow.

The sprookje remained silent.

"Good," said Tocohl. She turned back to face the sprookje. "Now all I have to do is convince you you've got to shout to make me understand."

"Shout?" said van Zoveel.

"Figuratively speaking," said Tocohl, still absorbed in the task. "Om im, I need your help."

"Name it."

"If Sunchild follows me, I want you to come along too." At his thumbs-out agreement, she said again to the sprookje, "Let's try this. You understood this before." Once again she held out an imaginary length of cloak. Once again the sprookje reached for the nonexistent other end.

When Tocohl walked the few steps toward the cot where Alfvaen lay sleeping, Sunchild followed with Om im at its heels. Tocohl stopped, turned her thumbs out.

Om im turned his own out in jubilant approval.

The sprookje stared, first at one, then at the other. Then, slowly, as if questioningly, it too turned its thumbs out. Tocohl jabbed hers out a second time, hardly able to constrain her excitement. "Yes! Om im, tell it yes!" Om im laughed and jabbed his thumbs out a second time as well.

The sprookje mimicked the gesture, this time with ruffling feathers and the same flamboyance Om im brought to it.

Now Tocohl "extended the cloak" and both followed her until she stood over Alfvaen. Remembering the bright warning tongue the sprookje had used to indicate danger, she touched Alfvaen's shoulder and stuck out her tongue. *Layli-layli calulan* moved closer, to watch the sprookje's reaction.

But there was none that Tocohl could see. She tried again: this time lifting one hand to her face to mimic the puffing of cheek-feathers as she touched Alfvaen's shoulder. The sprookje's cheek-feathers fluffed. It leaned forward, glancing from Alfvaen to Tocohl, and nipped Alfvaen's hand.

When it straightened, its cheek-feathers subsided. Reaching across to Tocohl, it stroked Tocohl's wrist reassuringly until Tocohl drew her hand from her face. "It's not worried about Alfvaen, *layli-layli*," Tocohl said, "at least, I think not."

"Ask about the filaments, if you can."

"I can try." Tocohl tucked her fingers gently beneath the long gray threads that covered Alfvaen's shoulder and raised them slightly. Once again she mimed sprookje-alarm.

The sprookje turned out its thumbs with authority.

Startled, Tocohl commented, "Oh, I guess it means 'I understand.'"

The sprookje bent again to Alfvaen. Using both hands, it began to stroke Alfvaen's shoulders briskly. The gray filaments crumbled beneath its fingers, and the sprookje held out a handful of fragments to Tocohl.

She cupped her hands to receive and the sprookje tipped the fragments onto her palms. In turn, she offered them to *layli-layli calulan*. "Now you know as much as I do," she said.

Layli-layli calulan smiled. "More. The plants are dying, Tocohl. It means that when the alcohol is gone from Alfvaen's system, the plants die. They intended that to restore Alfvaen to what they considered human-normal." The shaman looked across at the sprookje and, very deliberately, turned her thumbs out. "I understand," she said, "thank you."

The sprookje stared at *layli-layli calulan* as if seeing her for the first time, then it turned its thumbs out—at *layli-layli*, at Om im, at Tocohl. Om im returned the gesture just as vigorously; *layli-layli*, smiling, did the same. Tocohl brushed the crumbled fragments from her palms and tipped her own thumbs out jauntily.

"Yes," Tocohl said, reinforcing each word with a jab, "yes, we understand. You understand."

"I *don't* understand." Van Zoveel, silent all this time, pushed toward the little group. "It mimicked our gestures before, but never as if it understood them!"

"Because it *didn't* understand them. Right now, it understands less than a handful: 'follow'—" She demonstrated by leading the sprookje away from Alfvaen with her imaginary cloak. "I wonder if that includes 'follow suit'?" Pulling up a chair, she sat, grateful for the moment's respite, and repeated the gesture. It worked: the sprookje followed suit—pulling up a chair and sitting, albeit somewhat uncomfortably, to face her. Tocohl thumbed approval. "You too, van Zoveel," she said, making the same gesture at him, "follow suit."

He hesitated, and Tocohl said patiently, "Thumbs out to show you understand, then follow suit." This time he obeyed.

The sprookje enthusiastically jabbed its thumbs for him as well. "How ... ?" said van Zoveel.

"The answer's been staring us in the face all this time. Om im was the only one who saw it."

Om im, standing blade right of her chair, jerked his head to stare at her with surprise. "Me?" he demanded.

"You. How did you know I was Hellspark?"

He shrugged, shoulders high, hands drawn back in fists. "I don't know. As I said, you looked Hellspark."

"And each sprookje looked individual to you—like the team member it mimicked." She settled back, to find a position which lessened the ache in her side. Across from her, the sprookje shifted as well, seeking its own comfort in a chair unsuited to its physique. Tocohl thumbed approval at it and it thumbed back.

"To tell it from the beginning," Tocohl went on, "I should have seen it in your tapes of the so-called 'wild sprookjes.' *They* haven't any larynxes—but our feathered friend here has a very visible one."

Van Zoveel's ribbons fluttered as he leaned toward the sprookje, as if to check. The sprookje's larynx obligingly bobbed. "The wild sprookjes simply have no visible larynxes, Tocohl. Yours is scarcely apparent, after all. I do—I *did* see the difference at the time the brown sprookjes moved into camp—but it's as insignificant as the crests and colored yokes."

"I'm sorry, but you're wrong. It's not a matter of visible or hidden. The wild sprookjes have no larynxes."

"Oh, but they must!" van Zoveel said, glaring sidelong at the sprookje. "How else could they talk?"

"They don't. Not audibly." Tocohl grinned. "You try to talk in a stand of lightning rods with a storm directly over your head. That's where the sprookjes go during a storm, swift-Kalat—"

"Yes, so I would deduce from what Buntec and Om im told me of your experiences," swift-Kalat said.

"Sunchild didn't even react to the thunder. She's got ears but I'll bet she shuts them down for the length of the storm. Why waste a perfectly good social occasion simply because you can't hear one another?"

Swift-Kalat moved closer to the sprookje, bending down to examine the side of its head. The sprookje turned to watch him, making the examination impossible. Straightening, swift-Kalat said, "The only simple test I can devise at the moment requires loud noises. I'd rather not frighten it, unless ..."

"I'd rather you didn't either," Tocohl said

Swift-Kalat stepped back, letting the sprookje settle again, and Tocohl went on, "Now, about two years after you got bitten by the first wild sprookje, van Zoveel, the camp sprookjes showed up. I theorize that it took them that long to analyze your gene pattern, to compromise between it and the sprookje's pattern, and to give the sprookjes what they felt they lacked—a larynx, for example."

"Get serious, Tocohl," Buntec interrupted. "That's too much credit. You're sayin' they can muck around with their genes just for the hell of it?"

"For swift-Kalat's sake, I posit it as a theory. But—look at what we've seen them do, Buntec. Swift-Kalat's sprookje nipped Alfvaen and, in the space of a few moments, analyzed the sample, judged it abnormal, and prepared a living antidote, which it then injected."

Buntec whistled. The sprookje turned its head to stare at her. "Yeah, Sunchild, I'm impressed," Buntec told it. To Tocohl she added, "We're talking smart cookies here."

"Smart enough," Tocohl said, "to have decided that you were sapient long before you so much as suspected they were."

"None of which explains the parroting," van Zoveel said.

"I'm coming to that. The compromise sprookjes arrive in camp—bear in mind that they may never have heard audible speech before—and they look over the survey team, and what do they find? Every member of the survey team speaks a different language!"

"We all speak GalLing'," van Zoveel said.

"Audibly, yes," Tocohl said, "visually, no. Your pardon, van Zoveel, but no matter what language you speak audibly, your body speaks Zoveelian—every gesture, every stance you take, even the way you position yourself to speak is Zoveelian." Swift-Kalat made a sharp questioning noise and Tocohl cocked her head at him. "Yes, that's why you feel uncomfortable around van Zoveel. He may speak Jenji without an accent, but his movements are wrong. Wrong only in the sense that they are not Jenjin, which is quite sufficient to disconcert you unless he's sitting down."

The arachne straightened to full height. "Proxemics and kinesics!" Maggy said.

Tocohl grinned at it. "Right you are. The moment I danced Maldeneantine at Sunchild, Sunchild saw me. From then on, I could get her to notice anyone else simply by switching from the proxemics and kinesics of one language to another in mid-sentence."

"So if Alfvaen learned her lessons right, swift-Kalat's sprookje will echo her!" The arachne stepped closer to the sprookje. "But why did Sunchild echo me, Tocohl?"

Tocohl grinned. "For the same reason Buntec threatened to give you lumps ... I'd gotten Sunchild to see van Zoveel, and you imitated him by rocking the arachne. That was apparently sufficient evidence of your sapience for Sunchild to follow up."

"Oh." The arachne pricked delicately forward, its every step watched closely by the sprookje. When it was directly in front of Sunchild, Maggy had the arachne extrude both adaptors, twisting them outward in awkward imitation of the thumbs-out Tocohl had used.

It was good enough for Sunchild, who thumbed back at the arachne enthusiastically. A crow of delight—obviously adapted from Buntec's—came from the arachne's vocoder. Then Maggy added, "I think it's going to be tough to talk to her, Tocohl, for me anyhow."

"Not just for you," Tocohl said, "for now I'll settle for a pidgin. I think she's finally getting the idea that she has to shout—make broad gestures—to make me understand. I suspect her language is all in the position of the feathers. I'm no more equipped for that than you are."

"Proxemics and kinesics," van Zoveel said slowly. "The schools I studied in never gave more than a theoretical course in either." He glanced sharply at swift-Kalat. "Is that really why you always seem so uncomfortable when we speak Jenji? Because I move wrong?" He slapped his hands despairingly together. "I am a dangerous fool, Tocohl—"

"Don't castigate yourself, van Zoveel. I fell into the same trap. If I hadn't been automatically compromising my movements and stance to accommodate a mixed group of languages, to avoid offending anyone, one of those sprookjes would have parroted me the first time I opened my mouth to speak Jenji or Siveyn or Bluesippan."

Van Zoveel frowned. "What about *layli-layli calulan* and—your pardon, *layli-layli*—Oloitokitok? Oh!" His shoulders relaxed and he went on to answer his own question, "Then the Yn must have different proxemics and kinesics for male and female, just as they have different spoken dialects for male and female."

"Exactly," Tocohl said, "likewise your two Sheveschkemen: one from the south, one from the north. Two different languages in *all* aspects." She glanced down at the arachne. "As Maggy said though, swift-Kalat's sprookje would have echoed Alfvaen the first time she got her Jenji right in front of it. She would have too, and fairly soon. That makes me feel a little better: I had her serendipity for backup if I blew it."

She shifted again, made more uncomfortable by the thought than by her injury, and finished, "I'm *looking* for it, van Zoveel, and all I've caught so far is the cheek-puffing business! Om im's been seeing it all along without knowing what it was he saw, so I think we'd both better apply to him for assistance."

"You keep saying that, Ish shan, but I haven't the vaguest idea what you're talking about."

"You said I looked like a Hellspark. I'm betting you watched me come into the common room and greet three people in three different languages."

"Yes, but I couldn't hear you over that crowd."

"You said 'looked like'—when I greet someone for the first time, I *do* stick to that culture's kinesics and proxemics. It makes a better first impression. You saw the shift, just as you can see the different stance each sprookje takes to accommodate to the language of its respective human. Just as you saw that your twin friends held themselves differently, *moved* differently, Om im. Without the proper words to describe what you were seeing, you couldn't tell me—but you saw it."

Om im cocked his head to one side. "Then you'll teach me the words, Ish shan, so next time I can tell you what I see. How can I help in the meantime?"

"As I said, the best we can do for the moment is a pidgin. If you'll pick up and use the same broad gestures I use, I think Sunchild will understand that we have a language in common."

"I am in your service," he said, touching the hilt of his blade to remind her that this was literally true. The sprookje did likewise.

"Yes," Tocohl agreed, "but try to avoid extraneous gestures like that one. We've just confused Sunchild... Don't worry: This is as good a time as any to establish a *no.*"

It took her some few moments of silent gesturing but she accomplished it to her satisfaction: for *no,* fingers scraped emphatically against the thumb as if to rid the hand of something at once noxious and sticky. Sunchild mimicked her with the same enthusiasm it had given the thumbs-out *yes.*

"Why so broad a gesture?" swift-Kalat asked. "Sunchild can apparently distinguish very subtle movements."

"I can't," said Tocohl, "I need movement to attract my eye and remind me to look instead of listen. And a *no* or a *yes* I want to be able to see at a distance." She rose. "Now let's see if we can get the other sprookjes to understand as much as Sunchild." Signing for Sunchild to follow, she headed for the door.

Instantly Sunchild rose. So did Om im, causing the sprookje to thumb yes so vigorously it nearly jabbed Om im in its excitement. "Outside is a good idea," Om im observed aloud. "We're definitely running out of room for all this enthusiastic communication!"

Tocohl laughed and led the entire troupe, thumbs out triumphant, back into the sunlight.

Once outside, however, the sprookje's triumph turned abruptly to distress. Its gold eyes darted from group to group of the surveyors and its feathers bristled.

Tocohl, having had the same experience only a short time before, knew the source of the trouble: the utter confusion of languages it saw danced. Turning Sunchild gently but inexorably to face her, she stroked the sprookje's wrist feathers. "Don't panic," she said, "watch me," and she brought both hands, flat and crossed, to her chest. "Follow"—again she extended the imaginary cloak—"me"—again she brought her hands to her chest.

Yes, thumbed Sunchild, its feathers subsiding.

Very deliberately, inviting her to do the same, it turned its attention on Dyxte who, having just finished draping streamers of Tocohl's moss cloak from a dozen places on *layli-layli calulan*'s cabin, now stood back to admire his work. Obviously pleased, he turned and sought others to admire his work as well. The sprookjes surrounding him, as excited as they might be, did not serve; nor did the handful of surveyors—all of whom were too intent on observing the sprookjes' behavior to notice Dyxte's.

Tocohl drew her party to his side. "Nicely done," she said and a second sprookje, Dyxte's, echoed her approving words.

"Thank you," said Dyxte, echoed himself. Then he crooked a finger to indicate his sprookje. "It's still parroting us both," the two of them went on. "I'm not sure—"

But as he spoke, Tocohl raised her hands to his sprookje's beak and larynx, as she'd done earlier to quiet Sunchild. Dyxte's sprookje stopped speaking, leaving Dyxte to finish his sentence alone. "—You accomplished much—"

Dyxte stopped to stare, first at Tocohl, then at his sprookje, in astonishment. "It stopped echoing me," he said. "You did it!"

"I don't think so." Tocohl eyed Sunchild suspiciously. "I think Sunchild translated for me." (Maggy, let me see what Sunchild did while I signed at Dyxte's sprookje.)

The requested image flashed on Tocohl's spectacles. Watching carefully, she caught the movement she had seen only peripherally as she had gestured to Dyxte's sprookje. (Again, Maggy, more slowly.) This time she saw clearly the ripple of feathers along Sunchild's thigh, the minute shift of stance.

"This," said Tocohl aloud, "is not going to be easy. But I'll be burned if *I'll* settle for a pidgin. Obviously, I need feathers. No—stripes! Maggy, stripe my 2nd skin—make it brown, dark brown, and gold."

The stripes began at the tops of her "boots" and raced upward to vanish into the folds of her collar. Sunchild watched their progress with startled interest. Sure of the sprookje's attention, Tocohl said, (Maggy, I want you to imitate that feather ripple by distorting the stripes. Now!); and Maggy obliged.

Sunchild's eyes widened still farther. It rippled feathers identically, then thumbed a vigorous *yes.*

"Got it," said Tocohl triumphantly, and she and the sprookje thumbed happy *yeses* at each other. "Now wait here," she went on, "I've got to see if it works on the rest of your people as well." She signed *follow* and flicked *no.*

Leaving all but Maggy behind, Tocohl crossed the courtyard and plunged into the excited crowd at the steps of Edge-of-Dark's cabin to find Kejesli. Her presence sparked a babble of greeting and echoed greeting.

"Veschke's sparks, Tocohl," Kejesli—and his sprookje—shouted to make themselves heard, "your rib!" With three peremptory shoves he gave her breathing space in the crowd. "Why are you out of bed . . ?" he said, and his sprookje echoed his concern.

She grinned and shouted back, "Because I've got a word to say to your sprookje!"

(Again, Maggy. Ripple for *quiet*,) Tocohl said, and the stripes on her 2nd skin flashed into motion.

"You can talk to them? You can really talk to them?" Kejesli said, and this time he spoke without accompaniment. "They told me you'd gotten one to echo you but—" He broke off suddenly, shutting his mouth with almost as audible a snap as the sprookje's. "It stopped echoing me! What did you *do?*" he said, staring at the silent creature beside him as if it were about to bite.

"I told it to shut up," said Tocohl. "That's the only phrase I know in sprookje so far—but that's not a bad start for learning a language without words."

CHAPTER 15

By the time the sprookjes had begun once again to look at darkening skies and to flash their tongues in warning, Tocohl had established some fifty gestures, all broad, in pidgin, and with Maggy's help she could recognize and imitate five—tentatively—in the more subtle and infinitely more difficult language of the sprookjes themselves. Quite enough for one day, she decided, as she watched them vanish into the flashwood at the edge of camp.

(You *should* be resting now. I've got sensors spiking all over the place.)

Tocohl stared thoughtfully down at the arachne. (I see you've been spending a lot of your time with Buntec.)

The arachne tilted upward, much as if startled. (Yeah. How did you know? Did I do wrong?)

(No, no, not wrong. And I can tell because you're picking up her phrasing. Just take care to use it appropriately. Bear in mind that Buntec is considered coarse and vulgar by about half the surveyors, even though she's very refined by her own standards.)

(Okay,) said Maggy, then through the arachne's vocoder, she said, "Om im, Tocohl's going to rest now."

"Good idea." He patted his shoulder, offering it for her support. "Ish shan?" She accepted his aid and found Buntec supporting her from the other side, gently urging her toward the infirmary as the first spatters of rain began to strike. Maggy trotted the arachne along beside them.

"One moment."

It was the first time Tocohl had heard true command in Kejesli's voice. Buntec jerked to a halt, her surprise confirming Tocohl's. Om im raised a gilded brow and turned as well.

Hands on hips, Kejesli waited until he had the full attention of his troop of surveyors. "We've wasted enough time on this world already. I want your revised reports tonight: the message capsule goes tomorrow morning..." A cheer rippled through the crowd, forcing him to pause momentarily. When it subsided, Kejesli's manner softened. Smiling at Tocohl, he finished, "At that time, Flashfever passes from our jurisdiction to that of the Hellsparks who, I'm sure, are more than ably represented already."

His hand sought the pin of remembrance at his lapel. In Sheveschkem, he added. "Veschke guide you, Tocohl Susumo."

Tocohl responded in the same language, "Veschke got me here ... and she's not one to strand a trader."

As she touched her pin of high-change, Maggy said, (Yeah, but how is she on people who impersonate byworld judges?)

(I don't even want to think about it,) Tocohl said as she let Om im and Buntec lead her back to the infirmary.

(I do,) said Maggy, and her *I* had become a thing of wonder.

Too exhausted to do more than note the fact, Tocohl said only, (Then do it quietly,) and, to her relief, Maggy obliged. Blessing the respite, Tocohl settled into her cot and slept. For the next three hours not even the thunder was able to wake her.

When she did awake, it was not to an ear-splitting crash of thunder, but rather to the smallest of protests—an outraged, bewildered, "Hey!" in a voice that was unmistakably Alfvaen's and it brought Tocohl fully awake by the time Alfvaen had finished her complaint, "I'm all strapped down!"

Tocohl sat upright. Beside her, Om im chuckled and called out, "We thought we'd give our Hellspark a chance to recuperate before you broke her other ribs, Alfvaen."

"Don't confuse her," said *layli-layli calulan* firmly. Just as firmly, she pushed swift-Kalat aside—he was attempting to hug Alfvaen where she lay—to loosen the straps and free her. She sat up into swift-Kalat's embrace, and for a moment, there was appreciative silence on all sides. Then the two shyly released each other.

Alfvaen stretched and scratched and said, with a sigh, "That's *better*." As she addressed the remark to swift-Kalat, Tocohl suspected she referred to the embrace as well.

A sound very like a crow issued from the arachne's vocoder. "The books were right! *I* was right!" The arachne, sprang for the edge of the cot, clung precariously by three of its forward appendages until swift-Kalat boosted it onto the bed beside Alfvaen, where it tilted to peer at her. "But you were supposed to win the duel, weren't you? How are you?" she demanded, rocking the arachne from side to side.

Alfvaen, still bemused, said, "You're all right, Maggy. I'm so glad. Tocohl was worried!"

"You," Maggy repeated, doubling the frequency of her rocking, "how are you?"

Alfvaen looked at the arachne and then all about her in wonder. "I feel ... fine?" Puzzling over her own sensations, she frowned down at her hands, as if checking their condition might tell her the state of the rest of her body. "The last thing I remember, we were following a sprookje and I was ... I was *sobering*—without my medication. I feel ... *sober*, Maggy, for the first time in years!"

She turned a wide-eyed stare on *layli-layli* who said, "Yes, although I'd prefer to make a few confirming tests."

"Oh, of course! The others who have Cana's disease! Can they be helped too, *layli-layli*?"

"I believe so. If the sprookjes are willing." She glanced across the room at Tocohl. "I agree with Tocohl's assessment: your serendipity is beyond question." Then she busied herself with her instruments, checking monitors, and interrupting only to draw another blood sample from the Siveyn while Om im told Alfvaen what had happened since her last clear memory, that of the vanishing daisy-clipper.

Waiting until *layli-layli calulan* had finished her tests, Tocohl rose and crossed the room to perch on the edge of Alfvaen's cot. Hand, palm up in the crook of her elbow, she greeted Alfvaen formally.

"From what Om im tells me," Alfvaen said, "I slept through all the excitement."

Om im laughed, startling Alfvaen. Tocohl, smiling, said, "Hardly that. In fact, you were a major portion of it yourself."

"What do you mean?"

With a gesture, Tocohl deferred to Om im: "His version is the most colorful one that retains some accuracy." Buntec's version had grown to epic proportion in the retelling, to the point that it embarrassed Tocohl.

Om im touched the hilt of his knife and recounted the duel between the two. He had only begun when a look of horror came into the Siveyn's green eyes. Surprisingly, her first action was to jerk her head at the arachne. "Oh, Maggy. That's what you meant! I thought—I thought I dreamed it!"

Splaying her fingers at her throat, she turned again to Tocohl. "I dreamed so many terrible things! I thought that was only one more! *Your pardon*, Tocohl!"

"You did dream it," Tocohl said easily. "And like a dream, it's forgotten on waking. Just don't do it again—I only lived through it by trickery."

"But why? Why would I challenge you, and to death? That doesn't make sense. What grievance did I claim?" She laid her hand on Tocohl's wrist. "Please," she urged, "tell me. I only recall something nightmarish, something about you that terrified me..."

"It's not important," Tocohl began. In retrospect, it would only serve to embarrass Alfvaen further: her "grievance" had been downright silly.

But *layli-layli calulan* said, "Tell her, *tocohli*. It is part of the healing." So Tocohl described the incident, repeating Alfvaen's challenge and her own responses verbatim.

Alfvaen gasped, but Tocohl said, *"Now* I've forgotten it."

"I haven't," said Maggy, "I remember the words but I don't understand them."

Alfvaen looked at the arachne unhappily. "I accused her of *glamour*, of influencing someone's emotions"—her eyes glanced at swift-Kalat, slipped away in embarrassment—"by unnatural means: psi powers, love philters. It's a terrible crime on my world. Fortunately it doesn't happen very often."

"But it does," Maggy said. "In the books, it does."

"But those are only fiction. —And Tocohl replied that she was as natural as I, and took a terrible chance turning her back on me! You know how dangerous that was, don't you, Tocohl?"

"Believe me, I know it. I can still feel the hair on the back of my neck rising. But I could *feel* your position on my 2nd skin, so I knew when you rushed me. That and the zap-me probably saved my life."

"I didn't get to watch," said Maggy, something almost petulant in her voice. "When you duel again, may I watch?"

Tocohl smiled again and took Alfvaen's hand in her own. "As I said, just don't do it again. If Maggy were there, you wouldn't stand a chance against us."

"I could stay out of it," suggested Maggy hopefully. "After all, two against one isn't polite. And Alfvaen was *supposed* to win."

Swift-Kalat said, "I don't understand what this is about."

"My low taste in reading matter," Alfvaen said. "Maggy expects us to do certain things because of the books she and I read."

Patiently, Tocohl said, "Maggy, fiction and reality often reinforce one another, but fiction can't be counted on to give you a pattern for reality. Alfvaen's nightmares took the form they did because of what she reads. Yes, she's my friend, and yes, we fought a duel over swift-Kalat, but that's where it stops. That's as far as we'll take the pattern."

"Oh," said Maggy, again injecting a note of disappointment into the vocoder's phrasing, "you mean she *doesn't* love swift-Kalat?"

Om im dropped forward, hiding his face in his hands, while his shoulders shook in suppressed laughter. Tocohl closed her eyes and sighed, then she opened them again and looked at the reddening Alfvaen. "Do you want to answer that one, Alfvaen? I don't see how we can make it any worse than it already is."

Scarlet-faced, Alfvaen tilted her head up to face swift-Kalat. In perfect Jenji, she told him not only that she loved him, but precisely how sure she was of her truth, and that was very sure indeed. Swift-Kalat replied in kind, stroking her cheek to seal the bargain.

"She says," Maggy began to Om im, "she—"

"Not necessary, Maggy," said Om im, still shaking with laughter. "For some things no translation is needed."

"But you see," said Maggy, "that's right, too. And the fiction told me how to find Tocohl, so why *aren't* you going to fight a duel properly?"

"Because I don't *want* to fight a duel with Alfvaen," Tocohl said firmly.

Alfvaen drew her glance away from swift-Kalat, took in the glare with which Tocohl favored the arachne, and said, matching Tocohl's firmness, "And I don't want to fight a duel with Tocohl either, Maggy."

"Oh," said Maggy, this time in quite a different tone, "you don't *want* to. Why didn't you say so in the first place?"

This set Om im laughing again, and Tocohl nearly bit her lip in two trying not to join him.

"Alfvaen," Maggy went on, "do you wish me to forget the duel you and Tocohl already had?"

Tocohl gasped out, "Alfvaen, she means that literally. She'll wipe her records of it if you ask her to."

"I see." Alfvaen looked thoughtfully at the arachne. "No, Maggy, don't forget it. You need it to remind you that fiction doesn't tell you the whole story."

"Thank you." The arachne bobbed slightly.

Alfvaen continued to watch it for a moment, then she said, "If you like, Maggy, when *layli-layli calulan* says I'm healthy enough to release from custody, I could demonstrate the standard dueling techniques for you..."

"Oh, yes. I'd like that very much!" The arachne suddenly contracted.

"Maggy?" said Tocohl, worried by the abruptness of the movement.

The arachne unfolded and pricked gingerly across Alfvaen to stare upward at Tocohl. "Tocohl?"—the voice held puzzled surprise—"I know what 'like' means!"

Tocohl could feel the smile spread from her toes to her scalp. In deep satisfaction, she said, "And about time, too. Good for you, Maggy! I like you very much."

Maggy made no reply. In fact, for the next several hours, she was remarkably quiet. To Tocohl, it was clear that Maggy needed some time to herself, to think things out. So Tocohl took the opportunity to catch the rest she still needed.

At long last, she was awakened by Maggy's urgent pinging, and by the more urgent rocking of the arachne at her side.

(What is it, Maggy?)

(They're here.)

(They made good time. That's a lot sooner than I'd expected.) Tocohl sighed. Rubbing her hands over her face, she tried to compose herself. When simply waking didn't achieve that end, she began a Methven ritual.

Maggy, uncharacteristically, interrupted. (Tocohl,) she said, in what would have been exasperation in anyone else's voice, (we could skip. I can have the skiff in and out before they can get Kejesli's permission to land.)

A flash of lightning lit the door membrane to an eerie glow. Tocohl pointed an elbow. (In that?)

(I'll risk it.)

(There's no need. I told you before, Maggy: I pay my debts.)

(Yes, but—)

(No buts.) She looked fondly at the arachne. (But I appreciate the offer.)

Again Maggy made no reply. Then she said, (I like you too, Tocohl—very much.)

In response, Tocohl laid her hand on the fat body of the arachne, caressing it lightly.

(Why did you do that?)

Tocohl glanced at her hand, drew it away. (Hellspark gestural reflex,) she said, (affectionate feelings expressed in touch.)

(Like you hug Geremy when you see him?)

(Just so.)

(Put up your hood.)

Tocohl cocked her head to look inquiringly at the arachne. (Why?)

(It's a surprise,) said Maggy. (Put up your hood.)

Puzzled, Tocohl did so. A second or so later, when the hood had molded to her face and sealed itself, Tocohl felt a phantom weight on her lap. She glanced down, aware that the sensation was Maggy manipulating the 2nd skin but wondering at the purpose of it. The phantom, very gingerly, leaned against her.

Laughing, Tocohl closed her eyes and concentrated on the feel of it: a small form had perched itself on her lap and leaned fondly against her. Small arms encircled her waist, careful to avoid the injured rib, a head leaned against her cheek—a head complete to tickling curls. The phantom gave her a shy, childlike hug.

(Oh, Maggy,) she said. Even in subvocalization, it came out a husky whisper. Then in reflex, her arms closed around the phantom—to find, to the doubling of her surprise, that Maggy had thought of that too. Her 2nd skin limited her movement to where the child's body would have been. Her arms found small sharp child shoulders to hug in return. The illusion was broken only by the lack of sensation in her bare hands. That, she ignored; concentrating on the presence, she gave a second hug.

Then the weight was abruptly gone. Tocohl opened her eyes to find them stinging with the start of tears. Her lap was, as she had known all along, empty.

The soft voice in her implant said, (Did I do right?)

(Yes,) said Tocohl, unable to say more.

(The sensors said so but—Are you going to cry?)

Tocohl grinned. (Actually, I'm not sure. But it's nothing to worry about if I do. It's a normal reaction to strong emotion, even strong positive emotion. No, in fact, I have this horrible feeling I'm going to start giggling.)

(That would be better.)

And that did it: Tocohl did indeed start giggling. (Maggy, why in the world did you opt for a child-sized impression?)

(You said I was three, and Buntec calls me "kid.")

(Ah, that makes perfect sense then.) Tocohl grinned foolishly at the arachne. (For a kid, you're something special.)

(Thank you,) said Maggy, and her tone retained little of her previous primness.

A shout from the door startled them both. Tocohl's hands dropped to her lap, the arachne hopped to the side where it could see beyond her. *Layli-layli calulan* gave Kejesli a fierce look of remonstrance, cutting off a second shout.

He charged across the room, clearly agitated, and skidded to a halt beside her. "Tocohl. This place has suddenly become like festival. I have six Hellsparks waiting in orbit for permission to land, one of them a byworld judge by the name of Nevelen Darragh, who says you sent for them."

Despite the fact that he had kept his voice low, Alfvaen had awakened and heard it all. She sat up in her cot, wide-eyed and openmouthed, using both hands to fend off *layli-layli*'s attentions.

Tocohl met her eyes, glanced away. To Kejesli, she said, "I did."

"All right then," said Kejesli, "I'll grant them permission to land."

Alfvaen slid off her cot to intercept him before he could reach the comunit. "Wait, Captain. I want to know—" She did not complete the thought. Eyes narrowing, she moved to Tocohl's side with quick, cautious steps; Kejesli followed, drawn by her manner. "Tocohl," she began.

"Yes," Tocohl said, "it's me they've come to judge."

"Then you're not a judge after all."

Tocohl glanced at swift-Kalat just in time to watch a look of horror spread across his face. To him, she said, "If you'll recall our conversations, neither you nor I ever said I was a byworld judge, swift-Kalat." The slight emphasis she placed on his status made him jerk reflexively. "You accused the sprookjes of the murder of Oloitokitok;

you asked me to judge the matter. In my judgment, the sprookjes are innocent of blame. *Your* reliability is not in question."

He gave the matter careful thought, clearly turning over their several conversations on the subject in his mind. At last he said, "Neither is yours."

That drew a laugh from Tocohl. "My reliability in Jenji may be fine, but in Hellspark I'm in serious trouble."

Kejesli, recovering at last from his gape, said, "What I choose to believe in Veschke's honor, Tocohl, is no reflection on your integrity." He glared about him as if expecting dissent, looked relieved when he received none, and went on, "You came at swift-Kalat's request to learn the sprookjes' language. Nothing more need be said on the subject."

"That's also true," Tocohl said. "Those judges are here at my request. They already know what I did; I told them."

"You *told* them?" Kejesli gaped again. "But why?"

Drawing the arachne up to its full height, Maggy answered for her. "We pay our debts."

It fell to swift-Kalat and Buntec to ferry the newcomers into camp. "Byworld judges?" she demanded as she strode toward the hangar. "You expect me to believe Tocohl needed help? Why'd she send for more byworld judges?"

Swift-Kalat didn't answer. Phrasing a reliable response to that was more than he cared to risk; he had no intention of causing Tocohl Susumo more trouble than she had caused herself. Two steps later, he ran full-tilt into Buntec. He took a step backward, excused himself for having been so absorbed as to blunder into her.

Hands on hips, she said, "Swift-Kalat." In tone, it implied some sort of warning, as did her glare. But before swift-Kalat could repeat his apology, the glare turned thoughtful. "Okay," said Buntec, "let me see if I can phrase this right. Swift-Kalat, is there something going on here that I should know about?"

That he could answer. "Yes."

She made an odd gesture with her fingertips, perhaps coaxing, perhaps only an expression of impatience. "Give me a hint."

"Tocohl never said she was a judge." That had to be said first, for the sake of reliability, but having said it, he had no idea how to continue.

Buntec's eyes narrowed, then widened. Without warning, she let out an ear-splitting whoop, simultaneously slapping him on the shoulder. Startled, he drew back. "Buntec …"

But she was laughing. Wiping her eyes with her fist, she took a deep breath, sobered. "Ringsilver boots," she said, "I mighta known." Once more she planted her fists on her hips, glared back in the direction of camp. "So Old Rattlebrain found out and turned her in, did he?"

It took swift-Kalat a moment to decipher this. "No," he said, "Tocohl sent for the judges."

"She turned herself in?" In the distance, a single trader put down in the flashfield. Watching it land, Buntec said, absently, "That'd account for their timing. If she'd sent a message capsule just after she arrived."

Once again she slapped him amiably on the shoulder. "Well," she said, "let me see what I can do." Without explaining, she started for the hangar at a trot.

Swift-Kalat hurried after her. As she threw open the hangar doors, she said, "D'ya know *why* we need byworld judges?" Not giving him a chance to consider this, she answered her own question: "Context. We're bloody well gonna see that they get all the context they can handle, and then some!"

Her daisy-clipper was first out of the hangar. As she passed, swift-Kalat could see that she was speaking into the comunit. He hoped whatever she intended was clearer to her current listener. He hoped, as well, that whatever she intended would be of some help.

He guided the daisy-clipper toward the trader to ground it just behind Buntec's craft—he hadn't the skill to hover at the hatch the way she did—and slid from it to help his passengers with their gear.

From the amount of it, they intended something of a stay. For some reason he could not identify, this gave him a sense of relief—as if this implied deep consideration rather than hasty judgment.

Their introductions doubled this sense of relief. Nevelen Darragh had the white hair and lines of great age—something one seldom accrued without accruing experience to match—and piercing blue eyes that would miss nothing.

Geremy Kantyka looked mournful, as if he would have preferred to be elsewhere, although the design on his 2nd skin seemed to have been chosen to suit Flashfever. "I'm here as an onlooker," he explained in Jenji, "I'm an old friend of Tocohl's." Which, thought swift-Kalat, went a long way in explaining his mournful expression.

The third was a puzzle: there was something familiar about her but he could place neither her face nor her name, Bayd. The familiar was her stare of wonder at her surroundings. Geremy Kantyka had to nudge her twice before she took formal notice of swift-Kalat. "Bayd," said Kantyka once again.

"Sorry," she said, but her gaze was abruptly caught by the flashgrass. "Is it always like this?"

"It's more impressive during a storm," swift-Kalat said. "This is a lull—for safety's sake, we should be going."

"Yes." Again the words were abstract in her wonder. Geremy punched her this time, causing Nevelen Darragh to laugh and say, "The woman who forgets her manners is Bayd Shandon, swift-Kalat. *Not* a byworld judge." For some reason, this drew a laugh from Bayd Shandon.

"No," she agreed. "Not a judge. I'm here as a glossi"—swift-Kalat frowned at the unfamiliar term—"an expert in languages." Her forearm shot sharply down, proving the reliability of her statement.

She hefted her gear into the daisy-clipper and followed it, sliding to the far window to continue her gaping. The other two seated themselves in the back, and swift-Kalat climbed in beside Bayd Shandon with a renewed sense of relief. All three were Hellspark; all three spoke his language as if they had been born to it. That meant he could explain what had happened in Jenji. In Jenji, they could find no fault with Tocohl's actions or words.

The daisy-clipper rose from the flashgrass, drawing a wordless exclamation of delight from the woman beside him. As he aimed the craft back to base camp, he glanced briefly at her. Her hand shot up to point: in the distance, lightning crackled into a stand of lightning rods—most likely, the one in which the sprookjes waited out the storm.

"Tocohl Susumo has made a start at establishing a pidgin to enable us to communicate with the sprookjes."

"A pidgin?" Bayd Shandon sounded astonished, as if he had somehow called into question Tocohl's reliability.

Swift-Kalat realized the implication. "The sprookjes," he explained, "communicate by ruffling their feathers. Tocohl and Maggy, between them, have developed a way to respond in kind, but the rest of us will have to make do."

"Ah," said Bayd, "that's better."

"Ruffles her feathers," said Geremy from behind him. His tone made it sound dire. "The talent runs in the family, Bayd."

"Which one, Geremy?"

When Geremy only grunted in reply, Bayd laughed again. And this time swift-Kalat took his eyes from the terrain long enough to have a closer look at her: the same red hair, the same gold eyes, the same chiseled features—though in Bayd they were sharpened as if an abstraction of Tocohl's.

"You are a relative of Tocohl Susumo?"

Bayd grinned at him, leaving no doubt. "Her mother," she said and in response to another grunt from Geremy, she added, "Don't let Geremy disconcert you. He would sound the same if he were being awarded his fifteenth status bracelet." She snapped her wrist down, and her laughter passed for the ring of authority.

Maneuvering the daisy-clipper into its hangar took his full attention for the moment, but once it was grounded and stilled, he turned to Bayd Shandon. "The presence of byworld judges may call into question your daughter's reliability. I assure you *I* have no such doubts." He brought his wrist down, letting his bracelets speak for him. In the confinement of the daisy-clipper, the sound was shattering.

When the last of it had died away, Nevelen Darragh said, "This gets more interesting by the moment. I look forward to hearing your account, swift-Kalat."

For once, swift-Kalat wished she had spoken in GalLing'. Unlike his own language, GalLing' would have made a clear distinction between an informal telling and the testimony of a trial. Not that he would have spoken differently in either case but in GalLing' her choice of word would have given him an indication of her intentions. To ask her to repeat herself in GalLing' might imply that her Jenji was inadequate and he had no wish to impugn her reliability. Regretfully he let the matter go and led the three through the gusting rain and into base camp.

He paused for a moment at the perimeter fence, wondering where to take them. He decided against the infirmary. Then, seeing Buntec urge her party into the common room, he followed, hastening his steps as the rain quickened.

He ushered them in and found them towels.

"... That's right," Buntec was saying to her charges, "I'm not giving formal evidence so you're not listening, but that's not going to stop me from saying it anyhow." She glared at Kejesli, set her fists at her hips, and raising her voice so that it carried to Darragh and Kantyka and Shandon as well, she went on, "If you find Tocohl guilty of impersonating a byworld judge, when she risked her ass to give the sprookjes a fightin' chance, then you don't deserve the title yourselves."

"Buntec," snapped Kejesli, half rising from the table at which he sat, his knuckles blotched from the effort of gripping its edge, "that's enough."

Buntec glared back. "That's Kejesli," she said, half introduction, half insult. Under the heat of her glare, something softened in Kejesli's face, although his hands remained tense. "For now," he added.

"Then I'll save the story of Edge-of-Dark's boots for later," Buntec said, her own tension gone as quickly as it had come. Turning back to the newcomers, she invited inquiry with a tap to the top of her boot and a broad grin. An answering grin from one of the newcomers told swift-Kalat she'd found a listener. He was curious himself, although he knew Buntec's accounts were more fiction than truth, however careful she was in his presence.

"Swift-Kalat," said Buntec—again her manner of delivery made it something more than an introduction—"who will tell you true whether you hear it or not." It was some form of challenge she leveled at the newcomers. "He was the one who told us the sprookjes were sapient. Not his fault we were too stupid to listen and too bone-lazy to check it out."

She swung her hand to indicate the others. "Yannick Windhoek. Harle Jad-Ing. Mirrrit."

Yannick Windhoek was a sour-faced man. He scowled at Buntec, scowled at swift-Kalat, then greeted swift-Kalat in lightly accented Jenji. Zoveelian, like Ruurd, thought swift-Kalat, but, unlike Ruurd, this man was trained in what Tocohl called "the dance." His movements caused no discomfort; it was only his grim demeanor that worried swift-Kalat.

The other two were more reassuring. They held hands like a couple of courting ten-year-olds. Hellspark both, they greeted him in perfect Jenji. Mirrrit, the woman, was tall and slim and elegant, with penetrating brown eyes. Harle Jad-Ing—he was Buntec's listener-to-be—was small, bright-faced, eager.

Still such impressions gave swift-Kalat nothing he could speak of reliably. He laid them aside, awaiting further information, to introduce the three who had come with him. And then was forced to repeat himself as John the Smith, Hitoshi Dan, and Vielvoye—a glance at Buntec's welcoming grin led him to believe she had been the one to notify them—entered and gathered, still dripping, to examine the newcomers.

For a moment, the crowd held a festive air, as if it were nothing more than the excitement of new faces after three years of the same. Then Kejesli pushed himself forward. "Tocohl Susumo is recuperating in our infirmary," he said, taking Darragh for senior, possibly because of her apparent age, and addressing his edict to her. "You will see her when *layli-layli calulan*, our team's physician, so permits."

Geremy Kantyka's morose expression took a sudden turn for the worse. Bayd Shandon frowned, made as if to speak, but was pre-empted by Nevelen Darragh, who spread her hands and said, "As you wish, Captain, although it was she who called us here."

"What's more," said Tocohl's voice from somewhere at the rear of the crowd, "now that they're here they won't mind a few weeks waiting. It's the trip that's costly, not the time spent on Flashfever."

Hitoshi Dan and John the Smith parted, then pushed farther to each side, to allow passage to Tocohl, with Om im at her right. Tocohl's face brightened. "Hi, Mom! What did they catch you at?"

"Curiosity." Bayd grinned back, mirroring her daughter's manner. "Geremy told me. I thought I'd come along and see just what sort of trouble you've made this time." She looked thoughtfully at Om im, seeing something that swift-Kalat could not. "Is that necessary, Om im?"

It was Tocohl who answered: "It was, for one cut." And Bayd frowned sidelong at Kejesli. "I heard you were recuperating, but I assumed Captain Kejesli ..."

"Captain Kejesli wasn't entirely." Tocohl touched her side. "Broken rib. Maggy's holding me together with baling wire."

From behind her, Maggy corrected, "I tightened the 2nd skin where *layli-layli calulan* told me to tighten it. She should be lying down." Nudging its way past John the Smith, the arachne stepped warily to the fore, as if to defend Tocohl, then said, "Geremy!" and darted forward to stop at the woeful man's feet. "Tell Tocohl to sit down, at least, then introduce me to Judge Darragh before Tocohl forgets again. Hi, Bayd! Long time no see!"

"Veschke's sparks, Tocohl—sit down before you fall down—what have you been feeding her?" Geremy picked up the arachne to set it on a table, drew a chair for Tocohl, looking hangdog at first one, then the other. Tocohl sat, Om im still at her right hand.

Maggy said, "I don't eat."

"Ha!" said Buntec. "You scarf up everything in sight, kid. You eat info the way a Jannisetti hog eats hogchow."

"I don't get it."

"We feed 'em by the shovelful," Buntec said, "they suck it up the same way."

Bayd said to Geremy, "I think you just had your question answered: a diet of pure Jannisetti. Long time no see to you too, Maggy—and this is Judge Darragh." This time Bayd Shandon made the introductions all around.

When she had finished, the arachne settled in the circle of Tocohl's arms, tilted upward, and said, "Are they *real* judges, Tocohl?"

Buntec guffawed, along with two or three others, notably Bayd and Om im. The rest, swift-Kalat included, stiffened, not appreciating the implications of the question. But Tocohl laughed too, long and hard, until she had to bring up a hand to press against her side.

"Was that funny?" Maggy demanded.

"The emphasis was," Tocohl said, wiping tears from her eyes. "And how would I know? You're the one with a list of byworld judges."

"Could be their fathers."

To this Tocohl seemed to have no reply. It was Nevelen Darragh who leaned forward and said, "Would your list have voice signatures, Maggy?"

A rude noise issued from the arachne's vocoder and to it Maggy added, "*I* can match any voice signature, without half trying."

Tocohl eyed Darragh with a look that was clearly sympathy. "Nice try," she said.

"Only one way to tell, Maggy," Buntec said. "There's an old Jannisetti proverb—" She fixed Darragh with a gimlet eye. "If it looks like a judge and it acts like a judge, then it *is* a judge."

"Oh," said Maggy, "but what does a judge look like?"

Buntec spread her hand. "Take a good long look at Tocohl," she said. "Now you know as much as I do."

The arachne tilted up at Tocohl once more, as if to indicate that Maggy was doing precisely as instructed. "I rather think," Tocohl said, "it's not that simple." Laying a hand on the fat body of the arachne, Tocohl raised her eyes to meet Darragh's. "Might as well finish what you started," she said, then tensing, "I come for judgment—"

Yannick Windhoek snorted. "Damned overeager kids," he said, scowling fiercely, and Tocohl turned to look at him, startled. He went on, "I haven't even had my lunch yet, and she wants a judgment. Never give a judgment on an empty stomach, child. It's the surest way to make mistakes."

Nevelen Darragh glanced sidelong at Windhoek—from his vantage point, swift-Kalat thought he saw the corner of an amused smile but couldn't be sure—and then she turned to face Tocohl again. "As you so rightly pointed out," she said, "the trip is costly. Once here, however, we are hardly pressed for time. Give us a few weeks to acquaint ourselves with this world before you make demands of us."

"Yes, of course," said Tocohl, seeming chastened but no less tense for the temporary reprieve.

"Oh, good," said Maggy, "that means you can go back to bed and heal some more. Make her go back to bed, Bayd."

"What makes you think I have any more influence than you do, Maggy?"

"Geremy then," Maggy said, "he can check her rib."

"Don't tell me the doctor here is a quack!" Geremy said.

"*Layli-layli calulan* is an Yn shaman," Maggy corrected, reverting momentarily to her previous prim tone. "Honestly, Tocohl, I don't know where he gets these words."

Geremy Kantyka stared at the arachne, his eyes wide with astonishment. Tocohl burst into laughter and swift-Kalat could almost see some of the tension drain from her frame.

"Oh, good," said Maggy. "It was a joke. I thought so."

When Tocohl had at last caught her breath, it was to say, "I'm proud of you, Maggy."

The arachne tilted upward. "I'm proud of me, too." Unfolding the arachne, Maggy stepped it to the edge of the table. "C'mon, Geremy, make yourself useful. If you check her rib, at least she's gotta lie down *that* long."

279

"Go on," said Buntec, elbowing Geremy in amiable fashion, "make the kid happy."

Geremy, looking ever more woebegone for the elbowing, said nothing but moved to help Tocohl to her feet. Om im rose as she did, and Bayd Shandon followed. Maggy settled the arachne once more on the table. "Maggy?" Tocohl questioned over her shoulder.

"I wanta watch here too," Maggy said. "Somebody's gotta make sure they don't steal the silverware."

Darragh eyed the arachne. "Pretty cocky for somebody who's already tried to rifle my computer," she said, surprising swift-Kalat with her use of Jannisetti phrasing.

"Maggy!" This time Tocohl's voice mingled surprise and disapproval.

The arachne hunched down. "Did I do wrong?"

"What did I tell you about going through swift-Kalat's cupboards?"

"It's impolite—at least in public." The arachne sank lower. "I'm sorry, Tocohl. I didn't think it was in public."

Tocohl splayed her hand at her throat. "My apologies, Judge Darragh. The fault is mine, not Maggy's. I set her a bad example."

"No offense taken. I had expected you to try."

"But Tocohl didn't—" Maggy began.

Still looking at Tocohl, Darragh finished, "I had not expected Maggy to try."

"You don't know me very well," said Maggy.

"So I see." But it was Tocohl that Darragh continued to watch. Tocohl flushed under her scrutiny and, at last, reached for the arachne. "Let her stay," said Darragh.

"All right," Tocohl said reluctantly. "Maggy, mind your manners. If you give them any trouble, they have my permission to kick the arachne out."

"What about mine?" said Maggy, imitating to perfection the tone of challenge that swift-Kalat had heard only once or twice from Tocohl.

Tocohl sighed. Pressing a hand to her injured rib, she said, "Maggy, do you want me to go back to bed or not?"

"Pure blackmail," said Maggy, "I set you a bad example too. Okay, if they say get out, I get the arachne out, I promise. Now go back to bed."

Swift-Kalat was still observing the arachne as Tocohl left, taking with her Om im, Bayd, and Geremy. The light touch of a hand on his arm was sufficient to startle him. He jerked to look, first at the hand, then into Darragh's seamed face.

"Come," she invited in Jenji, "sit with us while we eat. Your words on Tocohl Susumo's behalf have intrigued me. I wish to hear your account of her actions with no further delay."

This time swift-Kalat was not sorry she had spoken in Jenji: the word GalLing' translated as "intrigued" was, in his language, the indication of a thirst for knowledge so strong that by her use of it he knew her to be a seeker after truth. And if the truth were spoken of Tocohl, she had nothing to fear. "Yes," he said, "I too wish you to hear my account."

But before he could follow her to the gathering of judges, she paused to narrow her eyes at the arachne that Maggy now bounced from side to side, dangerously risking it at the very edge of the table on which it stood.

What was the term Tocohl had used? "Kinesics," he explained to Darragh. "She uses van Zoveel's kinesics to express impatience or to obtain attention." He addressed the arachne: "What is it, Maggy?"

"I too wish to hear your account."

"I will speak in Jenji," he told her, by way of warning her of the difficulties she might face in understanding.

"Good, then I can practice my Jenji. What I do not understand, I will ask you to explain later." When neither of them spoke, she added, "I *am* polite," bringing a smile to Darragh's face.

Although Maggy had spoken in Jenji, swift-Kalat knew that, like any youngster, her reliability was not high in that language, either in the speaking or in the hearing. To Darragh, he said, "She is three years old, but as she says, she is polite. I will explain to her later."

Again Darragh smiled; this time swift-Kalat saw the thoughtful look that accompanied it. "Then she may accompany us," she said, and swift-Kalat held out his arms to offer Maggy transport for the arachne.

When he set it down in front of the other judges, Yannick Windhoek scowled at it once, then resumed eating. Harle Jad-Ing and Mirrrit smiled at each other. "A spy in our midst!" said Mirrrit, peering with exaggerated concern at the arachne. As she spoke in GalLing' and her manner so strongly suggested Buntec's, swift-Kalat did not bridle as he might have once.

The arachne did. Standing it to full height, Maggy said, "I'm not a spy. I can keep secrets. Ask *layli-layli calulan* if I can't. She'll tell you." Then the body tilted abruptly upward at Darragh. "I won't keep secrets from Tocohl, if that's what she means. Do you want to kick me out?"

Mirrrit looked startled. Even Yannick Windhoek glanced up again. "No," said Darragh. "Maggy, we have no intention of keeping this a secret from Tocohl. We simply want to know what happened here. Mirrrit was making a joke."

"Yes," said Mirrrit, splaying a hand at her throat, "it was intended as a joke."

Maggy reversed the tilt on the arachne. "You're not much better at jokes than I am," she observed, and Harle Jad-Ing, laughing, said, "Perhaps, but she needs the practice or she'll never be good at it." Mirrrit punched him amiably in the shoulder.

"Oh," Maggy said. "We could practice on each other, Mirrrit, if you like."

Once again swift-Kalat saw the sudden sharpening of interest, this time Mirrrit's, as she glanced from Jad-Ing to the arachne. "Yes," she said, "I'd like that, Maggy."

"Fine," said Darragh, "that's settled then." Swift-Kalat was momentarily distressed to hear her speaking in GalLing', but she raised her voice to take in the rest of the surveyors who made no attempt to hide their interest: "We beg your indulgence. We have need to speak and to listen in Jenji for the sake of clarity."

The announcement drew a number of hostile glares from various members of the survey team, many of them directed at swift-Kalat, but Buntec grinned. "Tell 'em straight, swift-Kalat," she charged him; to the rest she said, "Maggy'll tell us all later—right, kid?"

"Bet your ass, I will," said Maggy, flawlessly matching Buntec's brash good humor, then adding, "Did I say that right?"

"Bet your ass, you did," Buntec assured her. And in that brief exchange, swift-Kalat saw the hostility of the others fade as quickly as it had come, leaving in its absence only an intense curiosity.

He turned again to Darragh, and without waiting to be asked a second time, he began his account by quoting his own note. If they could hear and understand its import in Jenji, then they would be capable of hearing and understanding what he had to say about Tocohl.

Behind him, Vielvoye hovered closer, as if proximity might make the words comprehensible; when it did not, he moved to the opposite side of the table where he might watch swift-Kalat's face, and squinted with effort. But the judges—all four of them—could hear what swift-Kalat had said. With a clash of bracelets to emphasize his reliability, he settled in to tell it all.

When he came to account how Maggy had invoked the Hellspark ritual of change to make him her sister so that he might speak to *layli-layli calulan*, Windhoek stopped eating to stare at Darragh. It was so sharp a change in manner—from all of them—that swift-Kalat immediately splayed his hand before his throat. "I intended no offense," he said. "If I have, in ignorance, broken a taboo by speaking of this matter ..." The arachne rose and he ended his appeal directly to Maggy. "You said nothing of taboo."

"If you will permit me to speak, Judge Darragh," Maggy said, "I believe *I* may speak most reliably on this matter."

"Please do."

"Swift-Kalat, before that day, the Hellspark ritual of change did not exist. I invented it to enable you to speak to *layli-layli calulan*. It was dream, not lie, and *layli-layli calulan* will tell you that the Hellspark ritual of change will serve the Hellsparks well on her world." The arachne mimed a wrist-snap of authority that was all the more compelling for its awkwardness.

Mirrrit said, "Veschke's sparks, but that's brilliant! Think of it, Harle, think what you could do as my sister!"

Harle grinned at her and said, "That's positively insidious. From second-class citizen to first in one 'Hey, presto!'"

"It won't work that well in practice," Windhoek pointed out.

"Oh, I know that," Harle said, his grin only fractionally lessened by Windhoek's scowl, "but think of the wonderful little seeds of doubt that plants."

Swift-Kalat might, at some other time, have been fascinated by this exchange, but the arachne's silence told him that it was his assessment Maggy awaited. He said what he would have said to any child: "Think carefully. Have you spoken reliably? Such an invention would seem more characteristic of Tocohl—"

"Oh!" said Maggy, stepping the arachne closer. "I did not mean to imply that Tocohl was not capable of inventing the Hellspark ritual of change. Tocohl's *very* inventive." There was a grunt of assent from someone, but swift-Kalat did not take his eyes from the arachne. Maggy went on, "I'm sure she would have invented it, or something that would do, if she had been in my situation. But I couldn't even talk to her, swift-Kalat. I had to do something! Did I do wrong?"

"No, Maggy," he said firmly, "you did the right thing. I do not question your reliability." With that he brought down his wrist for emphasis. In the clash of bracelets he thought: She has language and she created what is surely an artifact—she fulfills two of the three prerequisites for the legal definition of sapience.

When the sound of his bracelets had died away, Maggy said, "I'm glad. I'm sorry for the interruption, Judge Darragh." Once again she folded the arachne's legs and settled it to watch. "Go ahead with your account, swift-Kalat; I will not distract you any further."

Swift-Kalat took up his account where he had left it, without comment. Had he commented, he would have been forced to call the reliability of her final statement into doubt. Her very presence was a distraction, as absorbing a distraction as the sprookjes. Even as he told the four judges of the first hint of Megeve's treachery, a portion of his mind was planning to speak to Tocohl about Maggy as soon as he had finished here. If Tocohl could speak of art, then the opportunity to bring Maggy to the attention of four byworld judges should not be passed by. There would be no survey team to make such a judgment, rightly or wrongly, in the case of an extrapolative computer.

As reluctant as she might be to admit it with any more than a small sigh of content, Tocohl was grateful to be off her feet again. *Layli-layli calulan* said, "You will someday outgrow that streak of stubbornness and settle into comfort."

The thought startled Tocohl briefly upright, shock spreading across her face. "Veschke's sparks, I hope not!"

"Then learn to apply it where it will do good instead of damage." *Layli-layli* pushed her gently down and touched fingertips to her ribcage. The rest kept silent while the Yn shaman applied her own good.

When she had finished, Tocohl introduced to her *the bayd shandoni* and "my sister, by the Hellspark ritual of change, *the geremy kantyka.*"

Having been introduced as her sister, Geremy greeted the Yn shaman in Yn-female without a single misstep; nor did he flinch, as many would have, under the scrutiny that resulted. "Yes," said *layli-layli* at last, "it will help. Not as much as I had hoped but … it will help."

"Maggy will be pleased to hear that," Tocohl said, knowing that the mention of her name was sufficient to call Maggy's attention to the tribute. "And before you ask too: She's not a byworld judge, *layli-layli.*"

Layli-layli calulan's small hand closed tightly around her bluestone rings, her eyes shifted to Bayd. "Nor is Bayd," Tocohl said.

Frowning, *layli-layli calulan* said, "Then I shall seek someone who is. There is, still, the matter of Oloitokitok to be judged."

Tocohl reached up to clasp her wrists in sympathy. "Seek Nevelen Darragh," she said. "She will satisfy you. She dreams and her dreams have strength."

"She's in the common room with the others," Om im put in. "Put your rings back on, *layli-layli*. They're discussing Tocohl's fate in there and tempers could be running a bit high by now."

Layli-layli calulan glanced down at her clenched fist. "Yes," she said softly. It took visible effort to open her hand; the rings had left small distorted ovals in her flesh. With great deliberation, she replaced the rings on her fingers, then she turned toward the door. Abruptly, she turned back, concern mingled with the suppressed anger in her face. "Om im," she said.

His concern mirroring *layli-layli*'s, Om im touched the hilt of his knife and glanced inquiringly at Tocohl who said, "My knife is yours, *layli-layli*—but he serves only as a reminder. He will not intervene to his own risk."

"I need only the reminder, *tocohli*. That I swear."

Satisfied, Tocohl turned her thumb up to Om im. He rose to join *layli-layli calulan*, and in a moment the two of them had vanished into a smear of gray rain.

"That's a useful man to have around," Tocohl said, settling her head on her good arm.

"That he is," said Bayd, grinning. "I'll tell you my story if you'll tell me yours."

"Done," said Tocohl, with the snap of her fingers that sealed a bargain between Hellspark traders. Then she sighed her relief and said, "Veschke's sparks but I'm glad to see you, Bayd. I was scared to death

I'd have to leave Maggy in the hands of a novice, however useful he may be under other circumstances. I'm happier to have her looked after by someone who's had considerable experience in such matters."

Geremy glanced in the direction Om im had gone. "Not a pilot, I take it!"

In spite of herself, Tocohl grinned. "Not a parent," she corrected. "Bayd, on the other hand, has not only raised a passel of children, but I can vouch for how well she's done it. I trust her to do as well by another one."

Bayd was silent for a long moment. At last she said, "Then you were right. It's happened."

"I think so, yes." To Geremy, who gaped, she added, "I told you Garbo wouldn't be so dumb if you'd put a little money into memory for her." She turned her attention back to Bayd. Bayd's own ship was older, no less treasured than Tocohl's as a craft—but its computer was not an extrapolative computer and could not hold the same promise as Geremy's Garbo.

From the regret on Bayd's face, Tocohl knew she was thinking along the same line. "I'll look after Maggy, Tocohl, if for any reason you can't..."

"You know the reason, Bayd. The penalty for impersonating a byworld judge is restriction to one world for life. Maggy'd go crazy restricted like that; she's not meant for it." Frowning, she added, "Neither am I, if I spoke in Jenji, but I knew that. As long as you'll look after Maggy, I'll have one less worry."

Bayd snapped her fingers; the sound was loud in the stillness between thunderclaps.

"Thanks, Mom."

With effort, Tocohl produced a wry smile. "You'll have to look after the sprookjes, too. You'll need Maggy's help for that. Did they tell you anything about the sprookjes' language?"

"Only that they ruffle their feathers."

"That they do." This time Tocohl's smile was genuine. "You'll love it. Do you know *I* almost missed it? Let me tell you—Wait, let me *show* you as well." (Maggy?)

(You're supposed to be resting.)

(I am resting. I can rest and talk at the same time.)

(Oh. Would you like to watch?)

(No, I want to brief Bayd on the sprookjes' language. Can you link up with her spectacles too? And Geremy's.)

(Bet your ass. Better I show her than you get up and demonstrate.)

(Cheeky,) said Tocohl.

(Yeah,) Maggy agreed, and she sounded very pleased with herself. Tocohl smiled and got on with the business at hand. With the help of Maggy's tapes, she'd need only a few hours to teach Bayd everything she'd learned of the sprookjes' language and the pidgin they'd been creating as well.

They were well into it—Bayd had spotted two sprookje "expressions" from the tapes alone—when Maggy cleared Tocohl's spectacles. She must have simultaneously done the same for Bayd and Geremy as well, for they both raised their heads to query Tocohl.

"Swift-Kalat wants to talk to you, Tocohl," said Maggy, and this time the voice issued from the arachne's vocoder. The three Hellsparks turned: swift-Kalat stood at the doorway, toweling off the dripping arachne. "He said I should bring the arachne because it's easier for him to talk to me this way."

"All right," said Tocohl. "What is this about, swift-Kalat?"

"It's about Maggy." He strode toward them, wiping rain from his arms as he came. The arachne scuttled along at his heels.

"About me?" Maggy asked, putting just the proper amount of surprise into her phrasing.

Draping the towel around his neck, swift-Kalat watched the arachne for a moment. Maggy, not receiving an answer to her question, trotted the arachne around to tug at Geremy's ankle. Geremy bent to lift it onto the bed, where Maggy sent it—delicately—the length of Tocohl's body to stare up at swift-Kalat. "About me?" she repeated and began to rock the arachne.

Tocohl pointed a long finger, knowing Maggy could see equally well from the rear of the arachne, and said, "Stop that." The arachne stopped instantly. "What about Maggy, swift-Kalat?"

He frowned, first at her and then at the arachne. Bayd said, in Jenji, "Would you find it more appropriate to speak your own language?"

His frown deepened. "No," he said at last, "Maggy must understand what I say."

"I speak Jenji," Maggy said, sounding offended.

"He means no offense, Maggy," Tocohl said. "He means to make things easier for you. He's being polite. Your Jenji really isn't good enough to handle complex ideas."

"If you say so," Maggy said. "No offense taken, swift-Kalat."

"I can translate for you, if you like," Tocohl said. Again he hesitated. Then he looked down at the arachne. "Maggy, are you sapient?"

Maggy gave the question her due-consideration pause, then she said, "Not legally."

"Yes, not legally," swift-Kalat said, "but without reference to legalities, Maggy—are you sapient?"

Tocohl, who had been hoping the question wouldn't be raised publicly, frowned at the arachne. "Just a moment, Maggy. Geremy, watch the door; warn us if anyone comes." When Geremy was in position, Tocohl said, "All right, Maggy. I'd like to hear your answer to that too."

"Yes," said Maggy, then, "Yes! Yes!" and the arachne bounced to her excitement. This time Tocohl did nothing to inhibit the arachne's display. In a moment, it stopped rocking of its own accord, ran the length of Tocohl's body—not nearly as delicately as it had the first time—to peer at her from her pillow. "You're not surprised," Maggy said, accusingly. "Not a single sensor's worth!" There was a pause as if she were double-checking. "You're worried." The arachne hunched, reflecting that worry.

Tocohl laid a hand on its side. "A gesture meant to reassure," she explained. "You haven't done anything wrong, Maggy, but yes, I'm worried." She cocked her head to look at swift-Kalat, considering him carefully. "I should have expected swift-Kalat to notice."

"You mean you're not surprised because you knew?"

"Exactly. Ask Bayd and Geremy if you don't believe me."

"She's been expecting it for some time," Bayd said; she too kept her eyes on swift-Kalat.

"Then why are you worried? I don't understand."

"Because swift-Kalat expects me to take your case to the byworld judges—there are four of them. That was your thought, wasn't it, swift-Kalat?"

"Yes, of course." He looked puzzled. "If you can prove the three legal requisites, Tocohl. No one could deny her ability to use language, and she invented the Hellspark ritual of change."

Tocohl raised an eyebrow. "Perhaps I told her to say that," she suggested.

(You *lie!*) said Maggy, but she kept her outrage private.

(Please wait, Maggy. I promise I'll explain.)

(You'd better,) Maggy replied, a touch of warning in her voice.

Swift-Kalat frowned at Tocohl. "You were not in contact with her at the time."

"True, but perhaps I left her with the idea in case of an emergency."

"And told her to claim responsibility as well?"

"Why not?"

Swift-Kalat jammed his bracelets against his elbow. "I see: that is the argument the judges will take." Abruptly, he switched to Jenji, *"Did* you invent the Hellspark ritual of change?"

"No," answered Tocohl in the same language, "I did not. Maggy did."

"Tocohl, the judges all speak and understand Jenji reliably." He snapped his forearm and his bracelets dislodged to clash authoritatively. In GalLing', he went on, "There remains only art to prove her legal sapience."

In spite of herself, Tocohl chuckled. "Oh, swift-Kalat—forgive me for saying so, but you did not hear the full import of Maggy's ritual of change."

"What have I missed?"

"She might, very simply, have said: You're now my sister, swift-Kalat. She didn't. She added, 'Hey, presto!'—and that, in no uncertain terms, is art."

"Yes! Yes, of course!" Swift-Kalat smiled broadly. "You *can* prove her sapience to the judges!"

"No."

The word came out more sharply than she'd intended, and swift-Kalat stiffened, his smile shifting and setting into a frown of distaste that verged on anger.

"Wait, swift-Kalat. Hear me out. I have good reason not to bring Maggy before a panel of judges."

He folded his arms across his chest. He would wait, the gesture signified, and he would wait patiently.

Tocohl, without turning, reached out to the arachne once again. "Maggy, please bear with me. I *will* explain."

"Okay," said Maggy and settled the arachne in the curve of her arm. Its metal shell seemed to warm to her touch as Maggy adjusted the temperature of her 2nd skin to compensate for its coolness.

"How old is Maggy, swift-Kalat?"

"Three years old, by her own count. Although I believe that was your estimate."

"Yes. Now, if you were to assume a human being were directing all of her actions, what age would you assume that human being to be? I'm asking a rough estimate only."

"A very bright seven-year-old, I'd say."

Tocohl glanced at the arachne. "Your reliability in Jenji is higher than I thought. Sorry, Maggy, I'll keep that in mind in the future." Turning back to swift-Kalat, she said, "Is a seven-year-old sapient?"

"Tocohl—" he began, astonished.

Tocohl spread her hands. "Without reference to legalities and *in Jenji*, swift-Kalat, is a seven-year-old sapient?" She was cheating ever so slightly by forcing him into Jenji and she was well aware of it, but he would understand her point quite clearly as a result.

In Jenji, there was only one possible answer to her question and, reluctantly, he gave it: "No. A seven-year-old is not sapient."

"Not?" said Maggy, lifting the arachne to its full height to stare at him.

"In Jenji," Tocohl explained, "the term for sapience carries a connotation it lacks in GalLing'—only an adult who is sound of mind can be sapient. A child lacks the responsibility." She gathered the arachne into her arm and said, gently, "You know a great deal, Maggy, but you haven't had enough experience to go with it. You still have trouble sorting fact and fiction, for example."

"I'm learning."

"I know you are. The point is, you don't know enough yet. Let me put it this way: Would you like to go off on your own now?"

The arachne hunched. Tocohl saw herself reflected in the ebony eye of its lens. "Do you mean without you?"

"Yes, that's exactly what I mean."

"I wouldn't like that at all. Who'd explain things to me? Who would I talk to?" The arachne began to rock. "You wouldn't make me go away without you, would you, Tocohl? Say you wouldn't. Say it in Jenji."

Tocohl pressed a hand to her side. The ache was not physical. "That's something I can't say in Jenji, Maggy. You know the penalty for impersonating a byworld judge as well as I do. But Bayd will look after you—she'll be there to talk to and she'll explain things to you and, believe me, she's very good at it. She looked after me until I was old enough to look after myself."

"But she's *not* you!"

"I know—but she likes you and you like her. That's the important thing."

"I *told* you we should have skipped out."

"Yes, and I told you—"

"We pay our debts," said Maggy. She made a rude noise, drawing it out longer than a human would have been capable of, and settled the arachne once more in the crook of Tocohl's arm.

Tocohl looked up at swift-Kalat. "I trust I've made my point?"

"With one minor exception: byworld judges can declare a species sapient. That does not interfere with the raising of that species' young."

"To my knowledge, Maggy is the only one of her kind. Geremy's Garbo is exactly the same model of extrapolative computer but Garbo isn't sapient, at least not yet. The judges would be forced to decide on Maggy and on Maggy alone. I won't risk that—I'd rather trust her to Bayd until she's grown up enough to take care of herself."

"I understand," said swift-Kalat. "I will not raise the question before the judges. But, in five years' time, I will come to Hellspark to inquire into Maggy's status."

"In five years' time, go to the Festival of Ste. Veschke on Sheveschke. Bayd and Maggy will both be there, along with sufficient judges to satisfy anybody. And make sure Geremy's treating Garbo right, too."

The arachne tilted slightly. "Garbo's dumb," said Maggy, "not as dumb as Kejesli's computer, but dumb enough not to care *how* Geremy treats her."

From across the room, Geremy said defensively, "Garbo's a baby. And I didn't know she was a baby, Maggy. If she can learn the way you have, I'll see that she has the chance."

"Maybe you can advise him, Maggy," Bayd put in. "Your experience might help him teach Garbo."

"Really?"

"Really. Older children are often a great help with younger children—they remember what it's like."

"All right, I'll help." And from the vocoder came the sound of snapped fingers. "Get her *lots* of memory, Geremy."

"There goes the new artwork for my 2nd skin," said Geremy mournfully. "Ah, well. I think I'd rather have the company."

"Geremy, if it makes you feel any better, Maggy offered to duplicate your Ribeiro for me, and she can do it too."

"You said he wouldn't like knowing that!" Maggy exclaimed. "Why are you telling him now?"

"Because *now* he will like knowing that. Situations change, and when they do, a human's reactions will too."

"Do you really like knowing that now, Geremy?"

Geremy laughed. "Yes, I guess I do."

"And before? Would you have liked knowing that at the Festival of Ste. Veschke?"

"I wouldn't have liked it a bit at the Festival of Ste. Veschke," he assured her.

"I don't get it," said Maggy.

Bayd laughed. "Then make him explain it, Maggy. It will be good practice for him—it'll help him when Garbo starts asking questions like that."

"Geremy? Will you explain—"

"Later, Maggy," said Geremy. He left the door and strolled toward them. "Om im and *layli-layli* are back."

Maggy, for once, was not to be put off. Thrusting the arachne to its full height, she sent it stalking toward him. "Later!" she said. "That's all anybody ever tells me. Why does everybody say 'Later, Maggy'"—she used a clip of Geremy's voice and then followed it with a clip of Tocohl's—"'Later, Maggy.' And then they don't even remember when it's later. Later, my ass."

This last was delivered in Buntec's phrasing but it was Maggy's voice. And the stalking tirade had brought the arachne to the foot of the bed at the same moment as *layli-layli* and Om im reached it.

Only Tocohl saw that the expression on *layli-layli calulan*'s face was not the result of Maggy's speech. Maggy bobbed the arachne hastily. "Your pardon, *layli-layli*," she said. "Om im, you were supposed to remind her about the rings."

Layli-layli calulan, who had been twisting her right ring angrily, dropped her hands to her sides and forced a smile. "I was only twisting, Maggy. I had no intention of taking it off. Certainly not as a result of anything you said." She scowled, and it was as startling as her smile could be. "I agree with your sentiments. But bear in mind that Tocohl was told 'Later' by the judges—and so was I."

Tocohl raised a brow in surprise. "So," she said, "we all get to stew in our own juices." The realization brought all the tension back to her frame and Maggy, reacting no doubt to the sensors, brought the arachne back to her arm as if to comfort her by its physical presence. Well, yes, Tocohl thought, glancing aside at it; I just taught her that and it *does* work. She bent her arm protectively about the arachne.

(Tocohl,) said Maggy privately, (I have to say something now, not later.) Tocohl gave her full attention. (I don't like this,) Maggy went on. (This feels the way it felt when I couldn't contact you.)

(I know, Maggy. I'm scared too—but at least we can talk to each other this time. That makes it easier to live with.)

There was a pause of consideration. (Yes,) said Maggy at last. (At least until the judges decide about you. And I'm very scared about that.)

For all that happened in the days that followed, they seemed to Tocohl to pass with painful slowness. Maggy's behavior had taken an uncharacteristic turn—not surprising, Tocohl supposed, in light of the attitudes the survey team brought to bear on the panel of judges—but Tocohl took it as evidence that Maggy was as frightened as she professed to be.

When Nevelen Darragh requested Tocohl's tapes, Maggy stalked the arachne away. Her voice sulky, imitative of the tone Kejesli had taken to using with the judges, she said, "Get stuffed. You wouldn't let me see *your* files."

Shocked, Tocohl dropped to one knee beside the arachne. "Your pardon," she said to Darragh hastily. "Maggy," she began, not quite knowing what to say beyond that.

Darragh's eyes crinkled. Smiling reassurance, she too dropped to her knee to face the camera eye directly. "Then I propose a trade, Maggy."

"Forget it," said Maggy, "I don't do business with—"

"Maggy." Tocohl had no idea how that sentence would have ended and didn't want to know. "In the first place, showing Nevelen what happened in context certainly won't hurt. In the second place" — she touched the arachne lightly — "I trust you'll make a canny trade and get something useful to both of us from it."

"Like what?" This time Maggy sounded interested.

Tocohl spread her hands. "I leave that to you. It will be good practice."

"You want me to? You're sure?"

"Context always matters, Maggy. In Darragh's position I'd want it very badly."

"Okay, if you say so. But if she wants it badly, I'm gonna deal high."

"Good for you." And Tocohl found herself exchanging a smile with Nevelen Darragh as Maggy stepped the arachne forward to indicate her willingness to accompany the judge.

Tocohl did not kibitz Maggy's negotiations; she would have to learn sometime. To her surprise, Maggy did not volunteer any information about them beyond the observation, "Nevelen Darragh is a mean trader."

"Then I hope you learned a few things from the experience."

"Yes," said Maggy. But from then on she kept the arachne close by Tocohl's side, dogging her heels even when there was no need for a separate presence.

A long series of thunderstorms kept meetings with the sprookjes brief and intermittent, but with Tocohl and Bayd working in silent concert knowledge of the language had progressed to primitive sentences in both Tocohl's pidgin and the sprookjes' own native language. Darragh, it turned out, was as good as Tocohl or Bayd, once she dealt with an established language. Learning that reassured Tocohl: Darragh would be more than competent to handle any need for judgment that might arise between the sprookjes and their newfound neighbors.

"Better a judge that speaks the language than one who relies on a translator, even if the translator is Bayd," Tocohl observed to Om im as they waited out yet another storm in his cabin.

The judges had taken up residence in the common room, and by unspoken agreement, the surveyors socialized elsewhere — generally in the infirmary, with *layli-layli calulan*'s blessing. Rib healed, Tocohl had long since decided she'd get more sleep on the cot Om im offered, even though her feet hung off the end of it.

Alfvaen thrust her head in and said, without preamble, "Maggy, Bayd arranged it for us to spend the storm in the lightning rods with LightningStruck." That, they had learned, was the name of the sprookje Tocohl had dubbed Sunchild; it carried more a sense of "reckless" than "brave" and suited her admirably. "If you want to join us, come now."

"No," said Maggy, without hesitation, "but thank you."

Alfvaen frowned briefly at Tocohl and then, after a quick glance over her shoulder at swift-Kalat's eagerness, she shrugged after her own fashion and vanished.

Tocohl said, "I'm surprised at you, Maggy. You won't miss a thing here if you send out the arachne..."

"I want to see you. I can't see you through your spectacles."

Om im leaned to one side to consider the arachne. "Stubborn," he said. "I'll bet I know where she gets it, Ish shan." To Maggy, he added, "It seems to me you might be interested in the activities of the judges."

"Buntec says they're doing exactly what Tocohl did when we first arrived: reading the files, watching the tapes, asking questions. She's waiting for them to con Edge-of-Dark, she says."

Om im laughed. "Maybe they have and Edge-of-Dark hasn't caught on yet. John the Smith still hasn't touched his blade to how Tocohl trained him to stand on my safe side." At Tocohl's look of inquiry, he added, "I asked Bayd; she asked Maggy."

"You didn't tell John the Smith."

"Of course not," said Maggy primly, then giving credit where credit was due, she added, "Bayd and Om im didn't think that would be a good idea."

"I agree. Better he thinks it a matter of prestige than one of hazard. We wouldn't want Om im to get an undeserved reputation for violence."

"By all means," Om im said, "let's keep it to a deserved reputation for violence."

Maggy stepped the arachne closer. "Was that a joke?"

"A small joke, but what else would you expect from someone my size? And you both need a little cheering." He brought his gaze level to meet Tocohl's. "Stewing in your own juices is one thing, but with four judges stirring the pot and Buntec throwing in spice by the handful—"

"Buntec? Have I missed something?"

"Maggy may have missed something: she can't tape visuals for you from a hand-held like this one." He gestured just enough to remind her that Maggy's hand-held was still at his belt. "Buntec told Windhoek—the one who looks like he's sucking a lemon?—Buntec told him that to charge you he'd have to charge the entire survey team for contributory negligence and creating a public hazard."

"Oh, Veschke's sparks," said Tocohl and laughed in spite of herself. "She didn't really?"

"She did. And Edge-of-Dark backed her up. I wish you could have seen Windhoek's expression; it went well past the sucking a lemon stage."

"You want to see?" Maggy said. "I didn't miss it. I was watching with Geremy and Garbo. I didn't know it was funny though."

"By all means, let me see." And when Maggy had played through the sequence for her, she laughed loud and long. Windhoek's expression was all that Om im had promised. "Buntec chooses her targets well," she said, when at last she had caught her breath.

"That was funnier the second time," Maggy said. "Most things aren't. Why is that one?"

Tocohl gave this the consideration it deserved. "Part of it was actually seeing Windhoek's expression. Part of it was relief—Maggy, I was afraid you'd stopped socializing altogether. I was worried about you."

"Oh," said Maggy, "because I keep the arachne here?"

"It hasn't left my side for five days. *Have* you been talking with Geremy and Garbo all this time?"

"Since yesterday."

"At least to members of the survey team and to Bayd and Geremy," Om im confirmed. "As for the judges"—he grinned—"well, she used a spate of Sheveschkem on Windhoek that turned Captain Kejesli a remarkable shade of green. He's been muttering the same words under his breath for a week. Maggy may not have been talking, but she's certainly been listening."

"It was her not talking that concerned me. Even insults are something of a relief." She eyed the arachne sternly and added, in warning, "As long as you don't make a habit of it."

CHAPTER 16

The storm raged through the night but it was not the storm that kept Tocohl awake. Bayd had accompanied the party and she put the time to good use, conferring with Tocohl through Maggy. Tocohl had the easier time of it, for Maggy screened out most of the blinding light and the deafening thunder to convey only the sprookjes and Bayd's commentary.

"I'll take the next storm watch," Tocohl said. "I wish I'd thought of that sooner; it would have saved us a lot of time."

There was a pause as Bayd waited out the thunder. "It's hardly a matter of neglect. This is not something I'd volunteer for more than once. If there is a next storm watch, you've surely got it. Most of us are only here because we wanted to see if it lived up to Buntec's lurid description."

"And?" Tocohl prompted, amused.

"Buntec didn't tell the half of it."

Again there was a momentary silence from Tocohl's vantage point; again Tocohl knew from the sharp reactions of those nearest Bayd—Nevelen Darragh and swift-Kalat—that Maggy had blotted out another thunderclap. The sprookjes sat content, excited only by Bayd's questions and answers. They had already learned that thunder and lightning distracted her, although neither Bayd nor Tocohl could tell if they understood why.

Given the ruffling of their feathers, Tocohl thought there was a good chance they were speculating on the subject among themselves. She could only make out a phrase here and there, and the one that recurred most often was "strange sprookje."

When the sound faded back in, Alfvaen—Tocohl saw her at Bayd's glance in her direction—said, "Bayd, I'm just curious, but do they have any trouble telling you from the other Hellsparks? When they talk about me, Om im says, he can always tell because they look like me for just a moment."

"No, they can tell us apart better than we can them. They've had to give us names, though, which they continue to use. Random syllables don't translate well into sprookje, and Tocohl and I decided it was safer for us to learn sprookje before we confuse the issue again by trying to teach them a purely verbal language like GalLing'."

"What sort of names?" The voice was swift-Kalat's.

Bayd turned to give Tocohl a view of him through dimming rain and said, "Remember that they weren't aware each of you was from a different culture. When they discussed you among themselves they referred to you with a proxemic and kinesic overlay that defined each of you unmistakably; in practice, you were 'the Jenji,' Kejesli is 'the northern Sheveschke,' Dyxte 'the ti-Tobian,' and so forth."

"Oh, is that all," said Alfvaen, sounding disappointed.

For Bayd's ear, Tocohl said, "She was hoping for something more romantic."

Bayd took the cue and said, "You got an actual name, Alfvaen. You, they call 'One-Who-Was-Poisoned.' It took us three days to puzzle that one out. We kept being distracted by the Siveyn overlay they used and didn't realize they were being more specific than that."

Alfvaen looked from Bayd to LightningStruck, suddenly embarrassed. "Oh. Bayd! Can you tell LightningStruck that I didn't mean to hurt Tocohl, so she won't be afraid of me?"

"She's not afraid of you," Nevelen Darragh said, in such a way that Alfvaen was fully reassured by the sound of the statement alone, and once again Tocohl too was somehow reassured by the judge's perspicacity.

"How about you?" Alfvaen asked. "If I understand this correctly, Tocohl simply would have been 'the Hellspark.' But so are you and Bayd and—"

Bayd laughed. "What they use to signify Hellspark is any behavior that compromises between two or more cultures. Tocohl is now officially known as Strange-Sprookje-Hellspark-With-A-Crest-Like-The-Sun-On-Penny-Jannisett, and I got dubbed all of that plus 'Newly-Arrived.'"

Alfvaen turned widening eyes on Darragh who smiled and, making the Siveyn gesture of formal self-introduction, said, "Strange-Sprookje-With-A-Crest-Like-Frostwillow, at your service."

Alfvaen began a smile—but it froze and faded. Crossing up-turned arms at her wrists, she said only, "I understand." The gesture said in no uncertain terms that the two of them were barely on speaking terms but that Alfvaen would be civil.

Bayd turned swiftly, granting Tocohl a view of Darragh's re-action: a swift upcurling of both hands that said, Give me time to prove myself.

"The best she could do, under the circumstances," Tocohl com-mented, for Bayd and Maggy only. It was not sufficient to soothe Alfvaen; Tocohl could see that rigid control set in muscle by muscle. "Bayd," she said in warning, "remind her that I called in the byworld judges myself."

That had the effect Tocohl expected. Alfvaen frowned but her limbs loosened, her shoulders sagged. "She didn't have to do it, Bayd. Why did she?"

"But she did have to do it!" Darragh said in surprise. "I thought you understood that."

"I don't," snapped Alfvaen, and swift-Kalat said, "To speak re-liably in Hellspark, you mean."

Darragh looked from one to the other in astonishment. Bayd said, "I think you'd better explain it to them, Nevelen. They apparently haven't thought it through."

"She had to do it for the sprookjes' sakes," Darragh said. "The moment she decided they were worth the risk, she doubled their chances of safety. Your accusation of murder would have held up Kejesli's re-port for a time, swift-Kalat, but for how long? Suppose Tocohl hadn't found the language. What then?"

He snapped his wrist, startling even Tocohl with the sound. "Then," he said, "I'd have made an official request for a panel of byworld judges—" In midsentence, he stopped and stared at Nevelen Darragh.

"Which would have taken months to clear through channels," she said, "That's what happens when you make an *official* request through a bureaucracy. And meanwhile, the chances are good that MGE would have sold the planet, the Inheritors of God would have taken posses-sion, and the sprookjes would have been in very great danger, if what happened to Alfvaen more than once is any indication."

She shifted to take in Alfvaen and went on, "It takes precisely the same number of byworld judges to try someone for posing as an official of the Comity—or as a byworld judge. And it gets an instant response if it goes to the right recipient."

"Which it did," said Alfvaen.

"Which it did."

Maggy's soundproofing went briefly into operation. Tocohl saw the others flinch but Alfvaen, thoughtful now, kept her eyes on Darragh. When the sound returned, it was only the sound of rain. Without a word, Alfvaen turned her left hand palm-up, curling the fingers as if to enclose something very fragile. It was fragile, indeed, for it was the beginning of renewed trust she offered to Nevelen Darragh.

Beyond her, LightningStruck curled her hand in imitation of the gesture. Bayd said, "Veschke's sparks, Alfvaen. That's going to take me a month to explain!" and started in.

Tocohl and Bayd worked through the night. When the sky cleared briefly as the sun rose, LightningStruck escorted Bayd and the others back to base camp. After a few clear signs that they all needed sleep, the sprookje disappeared once more into the flashwood. No others came.

"Do you suppose they have some way of communicating with each other by long distance?" Tocohl said, stifling a yawn.

"On this world," said Om im, "it's probably by grapevine."

With so little sleep, this reduced Tocohl to a fit of giggles. "Definitely a botanical artifact," she agreed, explaining the joke for Maggy's benefit. "Go away," she added to both of them, "let me sleep." But as she dozed off, she was well aware that neither Maggy nor Om im obeyed, and she slept more soundly for that.

When she awoke, it was to Om im's light hand on her face. "Ish shan, we've a full day of sun ahead of us—and the sprookjes have brought you a royal visitor." She blinked at him. "You slept through the night," he explained, "and there's a crested sprookje in camp."

That brought her fully awake and to her feet. She bounded down the cabin steps, Maggy at her heels, and followed Om im to the little garden Dyxte had planted in front of *layli-layli calulan*'s cabin. Dyxte's plants luxuriated in the pale sunlight and, in the midst of them, stood a brilliantly crested sprookje.

A sharp smell assaulted her nostrils. Under her breath, she said, "Veschke's sparks—is it injured?" She could see nothing apparent wrong with it but the smell was that of infected flesh.

"No, no, Ish shan!" Om im was laughing but trying as well not to breathe in; it gave his laugh a curious quality. "The mystery of the torn-up thousand-day-blue is solved. That's what you're smelling." He pointed to a small plant that swelled purplish-blue through the compound's red mud.

The crested sprookje ruffled at the small group of brown sprookjes. No, thought Tocohl, watching more carefully—the crested sprookje bristled. The brown sprookjes picked through Dyxte's garden, pulling out the thousand-day-blues and tossing them aside into a pile.

A knot of surveyors watched this all, cameras taping furiously. Tocohl stopped beside Dyxte, who gave her a full-body smile and said, "Graffiti. One of the camp sprookjes planted thousand-day-blues in my landscape."

"Watch," said Bayd, "the brown ones think it's funny."

Bayd was right, to judge from the feather rufflings. Despite the smell, the brown sprookjes cheerfully went about ripping out the thousand-day-blues. When they had found them all, one of the brown sprookjes gathered them into a bundle and walked toward the flashwood, holding them at arm's length all the while. This sent the rest of the brown sprookjes into ripplings of delight.

"Children!" said Tocohl. "The brown sprookjes are youngsters!"

"I think so," said Bayd.

As the smell dissipated, the crested sprookje stood off to examine Dyxte's work with what seemed to Tocohl a practiced eye. Then it stepped in for a closer look at *layli-layli calulan*'s pennants and the tattered festoons of Tocohl's moss cloak. Judging from its stance, it was very pleased with the effect.

Tocohl stepped forward, Maggy rippling the stripes in her 2nd skin in the most formal greeting they knew in sprookje. The crested sprookje ruffled its feathers in the same pattern; simultaneously, its crest rose. (Veschke's sparks, Maggy. How are we going to answer that one?)

(We're not,) said Maggy.

(All right. But let's tell His Nibs we're not physically capable.)

This they managed with some effort. The crested sprookje came closer, examining Tocohl as carefully as it had the moss cloak, even to running a gentle finger along her arm—and puffing in surprise to learn she was not feathered. It drew her hand upward to scrutinize. Tocohl winced in anticipation of a nip but it did no such thing: instead it drew her hand gently along its own feathers, spreading them to display the skin underneath.

"Did you get that, Maggy? Bayd? I think we just got words for 'skin' and 'feathers.'"

The crested sprookje let her hand drop. From its own vibrantly colored yoke, it tugged a feather and gave it to her. Feathers are good, it told her silently, try them.

Tocohl bit her lip to keep from laughing and translated this, adding, "Get swift-Kalat." Swift-Kalat pushed through the crowd to join her.

"Feathers are good for sprookjes," she told it, translating aloud in GalLing' as she went along. "Skin is good for strange-sprookjes. I give feather to the Jenji to examine." She was forced to lapse into her created pidgin—as yet they hadn't the sprookje word for "examine." In pidgin, it was the nipping motion with which everyone in camp had been examined.

"Keep your eyes open, Bayd. He—"

"She," corrected swift-Kalat.

"—She wants LightningStruck to translate that."

"Got it."

(Got it,) agreed Maggy, and together they repeated Tocohl's phrase, this time ending it with the sprookje's own term.

The crested sprookje turned his attention on swift-Kalat. "You examine?" Tocohl translated for him. Swift-Kalat turned his thumbs up. The crested sprookje looked first at LightningStruck and then at Tocohl for confirmation. "Yes," they both told her.

"Give feather," the crested sprookje agreed. "Feathers are good." Then she stepped back to indicate the garden.

"She wants to know if you made that," Tocohl said.

Swift-Kalat flicked his fingers *no*. At the same time, Tocohl expressed the sprookje negative. Reaching into the crowd, she brought Dyxte forward. "The ti-Tobian made that." And she translated the crested sprookje's response for Dyxte: "Her Nibs says it's very good. Different and strange, but very good. It's what she came to see, if I got that right."

"Thank her for me, Tocohl. Ask if she does landscaping, if you can." That wasn't easy, but Tocohl managed it.

"Yes," came the answer, "I will show you—" Tocohl broke off her translation. "Did you get that last, Bayd?"

"I think it's a time referent. See if she'll explain it. We need time referents desperately—I can't even sort out their tenses, if they've got them."

There was a flurry of activity and a flutter of feathers involving all five sprookjes, three Hellsparks, and van Zoveel. At the end of it, they were forced to agree that both sides would wait for understanding. And that Dyxte would wait to see the crested sprookje's work.

By then, most of the surveyors had trickled away to let the glossis get on with their work. Swift-Kalat had gone to examine the feather. Only van Zoveel and Alfvaen remained. It was Alfvaen who next attracted the crested sprookje's attention. "I examine One-Who-Was-Poisoned," Tocohl translated, adding, "She means to nip you again, I think. So be forewarned, Alfvaen."

"Yes," said Alfvaen, and she held out her hand, flinching only slightly when the expected nip came.

Having taken her sample, the crested sprookje turned to Leaper, the brown sprookje that had been swift-Kalat's shadow, the first Tocohl and Alfvaen had seen. The crested sprookje ruffled its feathers and raised its crest. "Good work," translated Tocohl for Alfvaen's benefit, "with a raised-crest fillip."

"Perhaps it's a superlative," Nevelen Darragh suggested. Tocohl raised a brow. Darragh smiled and went on, "Perhaps youngsters don't rate a use of the superlative."

"Anything's possible."

"Let's find out if they are youngsters," Bayd said. "Good timing," she said as Om im brought tarps and spread them on the muddy ground. Bayd sat, inviting the crested sprookje to join her.

Tocohl watched the two, but she found herself increasingly distracted by some elusive thought she could not quite touch a blade to. Her glance kept returning to Alfvaen: the Siveyn shared a tarp with LightningStruck.

"Yes," Bayd confirmed, "the brown sprookjes are youngsters. It was a matter of the larynxes. I can't quite make it out. And the fact that youngsters are more flexible in a new situation. FineGarden—that's the best I can do on Her Nibs's name—FineGarden wants to know if we are too. I told her no. We think a strange land is too dangerous for youngsters."

Tocohl waited for the rippled reply. FineGarden seemed to say that strange sprookjes could be dangerous too. Tocohl's eyes widened. There it was: the strange sprookje that could be dangerous was Maldeneantine—Timosie Megeve!

She looked again at LightningStruck, completely at ease beside Alfvaen even though she had seen Alfvaen at her most violent. And she remembered seeing the sprookjes back away from Megeve.

"They're afraid of Megeve but not of Alfvaen!" she said aloud—and it was to Byworld Judge Nevelen Darragh that she spoke. "Perhaps one of them saw something!"

For answer, Darragh stood to tap the chimes at the entrance to *layli-layli calulan*'s cabin. When *layli-layli* appeared at the entrance, Nevelen Darragh turned again to Tocohl. "Ask them," she said, "ask them about Oloitokitok."

"I'll try," said Tocohl. To *layli-layli*, she added carefully, "I can't promise anything." Frowning in thought, she rose to her feet and shifted her body as if she were about to speak in the Yn male dialect.

LightningStruck looked startled, then rose. Shifting to match her kinesics to Tocohl's, she riffled her feathers in alarm and opened her mouth to display a tongue warning. The feathers settled as quickly as they had risen, to indicate to Tocohl that she must wait. All this Tocohl translated for *layli-layli calulan*, while LightningStruck held a hurried consultation with FineGarden.

Tocohl was unable to follow this, except for LightningStruck's quick shift into Yn-male (again signifying Oloitokitok?) and back to sprookje. FineGarden replied just as rapidly and just as incomprehensibly—then addressed herself to Tocohl.

"We wait," Tocohl interpreted, "LightningStruck will ask—or possibly will get—Vikry. Vikry?" FineGarden shifted to Yn-male. "Oh, yes. I understand," Tocohl said. "Vikry is Oloitokitok's sprookje."

"Do you think Vikry can tell us what happened to Oloitokitok?" Alfvaen said as LightningStruck hurried off into the flashwood. Tocohl gave her Kejesli's one-hand shrug. FineGarden, who seemed enchanted by the gesture, drew her into a lengthy discussion that passed the time until LightningStruck returned.

With her was a sprookje Tocohl had not seen before.

(This could be tricky, Maggy,) Tocohl said privately. (We've got to get this just right. Tell me if the arachne spots anything I miss.)

(Right,) said Maggy, moving the arachne to one side for a clearer view of the new arrival. (Vikry is carrying what appears to be a short length of cable.)

That was curious. Tocohl craned for a look, but the object was obscured by the sprookje's feathers. (What kind of cable?) (I can't tell from this angle. I'll let you know in a moment.) The arachne moved slowly, angling closer to the sprookje.

Knowing how capable Maggy was of splitting her attention, Tocohl went on to greet Vikry and to introduce herself. Her 2nd skin rippled stripes in several different areas.

"I'm asking what they know of Oloitokitok," she added, "I'm telling Vikry that you were very close to Oloitokitok, *layli-layli*, and we want Vikry to tell you about him." Brown and gold stripes rippled at Tocohl's wrists. "And I will speak for you to understand."

For a long moment, Vikry turned his enormous gold eyes on *layli-layli calulan*, his feathers a jumble of activity.

Tocohl would have reached to smooth the feathers but she did not know if Vikry was familiar with the pidgin and she had no sprookje for reassurance. LightningStruck did it for her, adding the pidgin gesture as well, with a glance at Tocohl to see if she understood. Tocohl turned her thumbs up and simultaneously had Maggy ripple a yes.

Hesitantly, Vikry moved toward *layli-layli calulan*. "Oloitokitok good," Tocohl interpreted, "Oloitokitok *very* good."

"Yes," said *layli-layli calulan*, turning her thumbs up in agreement with the sprookje.

"Oloitokitok gave Vikry this," Tocohl went on, still translating, as Vikry held out the short length of cable to *layli-layli*.

(It's a piece of superconducting cable,) Maggy put in privately. (Expensive gift!)

(Thanks,) said Tocohl, and she continued aloud, "He wants to know if you want it back, *layli-layli*."

"Tell him if Oloitokitok wanted him to have it, then I want him to have it," said *layli-layli calulan*, motioning in pidgin that the length of cable was his. Tocohl did the best she could in sprookje, but she was glad to see Vikry had already gotten the idea.

Vikry went on, in both pidgin and sprookje simultaneously. "Oloitokitok good," Tocohl translated again, "Vikry thanks you. Vikry gave—I wish we had some idea of tenses—yes, *gave* Oloitokitok some-thing—something like cable? I didn't get that. Did you, Bayd?"

"No, I didn't." With Maggy's assistance, Bayd rippled green and gold stripes asking Vikry to repeat himself.

Superconducting cable, Tocohl thought as she watched. They gave me moss for moss—

"I still don't understand," Bayd said, signing it as well.

"LightningStruck," said Tocohl, in GalLing' and sprookje si-multaneously, "you and I spent two storms in good/safe plants. Tall plants. What do you call them?"

LightningStruck made the same riffling of feathers that Vikry had made. "You've got it!" Bayd said.

With Maggy repeating the riffle, Tocohl asked Vikry, "Oloitokitok gave you the cable, and you gave Oloitokitok lightning rod?"

Thumbs up and another riffling, this time across the chest. "Lightning rod and cable—the same!" Tocohl translated triumphantly.

Thumbs went up all around, everyone happy to have gotten that straight, but Tocohl felt a chill run up her spine. (Odds on Megeve jumped again,) Maggy reported.

(I know. Now we ask a few nasty questions.)

She addressed herself to Vikry again, translating as she went. "Oloitokitok good. Oloitokitok give you cable, you give Oloitokitok lightning rod." Thumbs up on each. Inexorably, Tocohl went on. "Megeve see you give Oloitokitok lightning rod?"

Vikry again turned thumbs up. Om im growled in Bluesippan, touching the hilt of his knife. *Layli-layli calulan's* face turned grim. A handful of the other surveyors, catching on to the implications of Vikry's report, stirred restlessly.

"Go on," Tocohl said to the sprookje, "then what happened?"

She'd gotten the idea of continuation across, for Vikry picked up the story from there. "All excited," Tocohl translated, "Megeve and Oloitokitok make ... beak flaps with ... no, I don't ..."

Seeing her confusion, LightningStruck stepped in and demon-strated, by parroting Tocohl's last few words. Then she repeated the feather rufflings that were, unmistakably, the sprookje for "verbal speech."

"Beak flaps with safe thunder," Bayd said. "Ah! Distant enough thunder that you needn't worry about lightning and needn't shut down your ears!"

(What is it?) Maggy asked. (You just spiked on every sensor. Are you all right?)

(Help me out, Maggy. I'm going to make another guess.) Tocohl touched Vikry gently on the wrist to make sure of her attention. Speaking aloud as she went along, Tocohl began, "Vikry. Oloitokitok gave you cable. You gave Oloitokitok lightning rod. Megeve saw. Megeve and Oloitokitok very excited. You show me Megeve and Oloitokitok."

LightningStruck riffled her feathers to sign that she did not understand.

"You give Oloitokitok lightning rod." Tocohl shifted to a stance that mimicked Vikry's and made her an imaginary gift. "What do Oloitokitok and Megeve do? How do they move? Vikry show me Oloitokitok. LightningStruck show me Megeve."

The two younger sprookjes riffled at FineGarden. Tocohl couldn't tell if they were asking FineGarden's permission or if they were asking her to explain Tocohl's request. Whichever it was, Vikry at least turned back and turned her thumbs up.

"Good," signed Tocohl. "You show us Megeve and Oloitokitok." (Tape this, Maggy.)

(You think I'm as dumb as Garbo?) Maggy had already moved the arachne to a position that afforded her an unobstructed view of the two sprookjes.

(Sorry, Maggy,) Tocohl said. (If this works, we can't afford to miss the chance to record the result.)

The two sprookjes made a fine show of smoothing their feathers and readying themselves, then once more Vikry turned her thumbs up.

(It might *not* work,) Maggy began — but the two sprookjes had already changed manner. Vikry took on the proxemics and kinesics of an Yn male with an accuracy that would have astonished even a native dancer of the language. From *layli-layli calulan*'s whitening face, Tocohl knew that the sprookje had caught much of Oloitokitok's individual manner as well.

LightningStruck — too slender, too small — was nonetheless the image of Megeve in every movement.

The sprookjes clacked their beaks, apparently in imitation of the two humans speaking to each other. No sound came out — Tocohl had expected none — but she could read the sequence of events in their movements.

Oloitokitok waved something triumphantly in his hand. He started for ... yes, he must have started for base camp, urging Megeve to follow quickly.

Megeve—angry and fearful—caught him by the tips of his feathers. His excitement barely controlled, Oloitokitok turned to face Megeve. Megeve made beak flaps. Oloitokitok watched him, his great gold eyes widening. Megeve made more beak flaps. Oloitokitok quieted, deflated, then sagged—into a posture that shrieked humiliation. As Megeve made yet more beak flaps, Oloitokitok resigned himself to failure.

To Tocohl, they might just as well have spoken the words: Megeve had convinced Oloitokitok that their evidence would not be accepted.

She was not the only one who understood. Beside her, Om im spat out a curse in Bluesippan and grasped the hilt of his knife. Tocohl gripped his shoulder and he quieted, but the hand on his hilt did not loosen.

In silent anger, they watched the remainder of the sprookjes' dumb show, fighting to comprehend the sense beneath the movement.

At last, Megeve made beak flaps at Oloitokitok that buoyed his spirits. Together the two of them set off for base camp: Megeve still angry but no longer so fearful, Oloitokitok in anticipation.

"That was how he seemed," said *layli-layli calulan*, "the day before he d-disappeared." Her scars of office stood out against the pallor of her cheek. "Ask them what happened next."

"What then?" Tocohl signed, but both sprookjes had already returned to their own individual stances.

In sprookje, Vikry explained that they had seen nothing more that day. A storm had forced them to take shelter for the evening. The next day, when the weather was safe, they returned to the camp. LightningStruck followed Megeve out to the hangar but Megeve had— here LightningStruck ran out of understandable signs and showed them— Megeve had raised something heavy to threaten her with it. "Megeve not safe," she signed again, showing the red warning of a thrust-out tongue for emphasis.

Vikry agreed. When he had followed Oloitokitok out to the hangar shortly thereafter, Megeve had frightened him away too.

The sprookjes could show little more. From a distance, they had seen Megeve give something to Oloitokitok. Then two daisy-clippers had left together. That was all.

"No more beak flaps from Oloitokitok," Vikry finished.

"No," said Tocohl, her hand still clenched on Om im's shoulder. "That was the last anyone heard from him."

There was a long grim silence that was broken at last by Nevelen Darragh. "You have your witnesses, *layli-layli calulan*."

Layli-layli calulan, with the calm of an empty suit of iron armor, said only, "Yes."

"Tocohl, may I borrow your blade?"

It took Tocohl a moment to realize that Darragh was referring to Om im. "Of course," she said, relinquishing her grip on the Bluesippan's shoulder. Her hand ached. "Your pardon, Om im," she muttered hastily. She got a brief glancing smile in return as he stepped forward to bow to Darragh.

Darragh smiled at him. "You know the drill, Om im. Call court in the common room in"—she consulted her own computer briefly—"one hour. Any cases dealing with the world known as Flashfever may be presented at that time."

"And presiding?" Om im asked.

"Byworld Judge Tocohl Susumo."

Tocohl opened her mouth but nothing came out. Across the way, *layli-layli calulan* met her eyes, and gave a crisp, satisfied jerk of her head.

"S-*su*sumo?" Tocohl said, her voice harsh with the effort.

"*Su*sumo, it is. I heard it, too, Ish shan—and you'll remember that I *can* hear the difference." Om im made her a sweeping bow, looking up from the very bottom of it to raise a gilded brow at her impishly. When he straightened, he called out in ringing tones: "Court called. Court called. One hour from now in the common room. All cases dealing with the world known as Flashfever may at that time be presented. Byworld Judge Tocohl Susumo presiding." With a final flip of the eyebrow, he strode away jauntily to deliver his message to the rest of the camp.

Stunned, Tocohl could say nothing to the queries of those around her. She noted only in an absent fashion that Alfvaen, fierce but proud, turned them all away. Standing frozen in an eddy of movement, Tocohl said to Maggy, (But I'm *not*—I *never* wanted to be a byworld judge.)

(I don't understand,) said Maggy, (you were willing to let them *think* you were.)

And at last Tocohl understood. It was at that moment that Nevelen Darragh stepped to face her and Tocohl said, "Yes, I do understand. You mean to make me pay the debt."

"You cannot be a byworld judge in name only. One way or the other, you must take the responsibility as well."

Tocohl's glance followed Darragh's to rest on the arachne, Maggy's only visible presence. "The choice is yours," Darragh said.

There was no choice. If four byworld judges found her an acceptable colleague, then only her own lack of willingness stood in the way. To turn down that responsibility was to deny her responsibility to Maggy, which she could not do.

"I pay my debts," said Tocohl.

"I'm glad to hear it," Darragh said with a smile, "though I expected no less." She laid a comforting hand on Tocohl's arm. "We do give advice to our younger judges, you know. If you need any assistance in this matter, any of us will be glad to help."

"Thank you," said Tocohl, as relieved as Darragh had intended her to be. "You can give me a hand with the sprookjes, then. It's not going to be easy, explaining to them what we're doing."

"Tocohl?" It was Alfvaen. Still puzzled by it all, she frowned slightly and said, "I don't understand. Are you a judge or aren't you?"

"I am now."

"Oh!" Maggy spoke up at last through the arachne at her feet. "I understand! You *invented* Byworld Judge Tocohl Susumo!"

"It would seem so." Tocohl smiled at Darragh, then knelt to face the arachne. "Do you understand what that means?"

"I'm not sure…"

"It means you and I stay together," Tocohl said, and from the arachne Maggy let out an ear-splitting whoop of joy.

CHAPTER 17

The common room was once more filled to capacity when Tocohl arrived at the appointed hour. This time the tables had been pushed aside in favor of loose ranks of chairs, all facing a single table at the end, behind which was one last chair. Beside that stood Om im—dressed, she realized, in the finest of his finery. Bracketing him, but at a discreet distance, were four other empty chairs.

As she followed Maggy's arachne in, Om im touched the hilt of his knife to her and said, loudly enough to make himself heard over the general tumult, "Court called on Flashfever. Byworld Judge Tocohl Susumo presiding."

Tocohl felt her face grow hot as the surveyors turned en masse to stare at her. Behind her Harl Jad-Ing said softly in Hellspark, "Courage, Tocohl. The hardest walk is the length of the room."

"Besides," Mirrrit added, "you brought it off the last time. It *ought* to be easier now that it's official."

The crowd, murmuring noisily, parted in waves to let them through—Maggy's arachne, Tocohl, and the four judges behind her, legitimizing her by their presence. "See here, Tocohl," Kejesli began as she reached a point almost to the fore. "I demand to know what this is all about. As captain of the survey, I have a right to—"

Yannick Windhoek, as sour-faced as ever, said, "Tocohl Susumo, fourteen years an apprentice, has risen to judgment on Flashfever. May she fly with Veschke's sparks." He touched the pin of Veschke at his breast and, mouth agape, Kejesli touched his own in response and fell back silent.

Without thinking, Tocohl too touched the pin of high-change in the folds of her hood, only then realizing its significance. (That'll teach me to take risks with religions,) she said to Maggy.

(We took the risk,) Maggy reminded her, using the Hellspark *tight-we* for emphasis.

(Yes, and look what happened to you!)

She had reached the fore. Om im swept her a low bow and drew the chair for her; when she and the other four were seated, he once again said, in ringing tones, "Court called on Flashfever. Byworld Judge Tocohl Susumo presiding."

Under cover of the sound of some forty people jostling to settle, Tocohl said in protest, "You needn't overdo it."

"I like the sound of it," he said, grinning. "I think I'll do it again."

"No," she said, and he touched his hilt, suppressing his grin to a small quirk at one corner of his mouth.

Layli-layli calulan stood and the last few mutters of the crowd died instantly away. The shaman's face was once more serene. "I come for judgment," she said. "I accuse Timosie Megeve of Maldeneant of the premeditated murder of Oloitokitok of Y, and of the attempted genocide of the species known as the sprookjes of Flashfever. Will you judge?"

Tocohl took a deep breath, let it out slowly. "Yes," she said, "I will judge." And with that, Megeve's trial began.

The trial was swift. The sprookjes had little to add beyond identifying the item ("same/like") that Megeve had given to Oloitokitok—before the two of them had taken daisy-clippers into the flashwood—as a locator. To that, Buntec could only say that it would have been possible to rig a locator to deliver the shock that killed Oloitokitok. She could not prove it had been done, although there was no doubt in her mind that it had.

Confronting Megeve brought only a repeated indictment of the sprookjes, for "wasting" the world of Flashfever.

Tocohl heard them all out. At last, she said, "Before I begin my deliberations, does anyone else have anything further to add?"

Yannick Windhoek stood. "Yes. The doctor *layli-layli calulan,* who is also an Yn shaman, has explained to me that constant exposure to heavily ionized air has caused many members of the survey team to behave in an abnormal fashion."

"I'm aware of the effect," Tocohl said.

"Then I ask that you take it into account when you judge Timosie Megeve's actions."

"I intend to," Tocohl said. She scanned the room, awaiting further comments or suggestions. There were none. "That's it?" she asked, her glance resting on Nevelen Darragh. Darragh merely directed her own glance at Om im, so Tocohl turned to him and said, "That's it. Get them out of here, Om im. I need time to think."

Om im did; in a matter of minutes he had, by voice alone, cleared the room of all except Bayd and the other judges.

Bayd laid her hands on Tocohl's shoulders and gave her a comforting squeeze. "Megeve has plenty of judges to appeal to, you know."

"I know. That makes it no less my responsibility."

"Do what's right—for all of us." Bayd gave her a smile and a second squeeze, then turned to leave with Windhoek and Jad-Ing and Mirrrit.

Maggy's arachne trotted along behind her. "Maggy," Tocohl said, "you don't have to go."

"I know," said Maggy happily, "I'm *staying* with you." The arachne followed Bayd out into the courtyard.

A cheerful laugh beside her reminded Tocohl that Nevelen Darragh was still present. She turned, suddenly afraid, and Darragh said, "Shall I stay?"

When Tocohl hesitated, Darragh said, "I assure you Om im is quite as good as sounding board or as silent support."

Tocohl blinked down at Om im, who raised a brow at her. "She'd feel more secure if you stayed, Nevelen. After all, you're an old hand at this."

"Stay," said Tocohl to Darragh. She spoke in panic, but once the word was out, she found herself oddly calm and accepting.

"What did I tell you?" Om im said. After a bow to each, he strode the length of the room, pausing at the door to call out, "Now you'll see what it's like from the other side, Nevelen. I'll be right outside, Tocohl." Then he was gone from sight.

"He will be too," Nevelen Darragh observed as she gestured Tocohl into a chair and drew a second up beside it for herself, "even if it takes you three days to reach a decision."

To reach a decision, Tocohl thought, and once again heard the echo of Bayd's words: "Do what's right."

For Tocohl, that meant to begin with the Methven ritual for calm, and then to turn and examine the evidence against Megeve in her mind one final time, setting it deep in the context of Flashfever. When she was done she thought, with bitter amusement, so being a judge means that your choices are restricted...

There was only one verdict she could give; and as she looked up at last into Darragh's eyes, she met sympathetic understanding—and agreement. "Tell Om im I'm ready," she said.

"Yes," said Darragh, rising, "you are."

As Darragh walked the length of the hall, Tocohl herself rose, discovering only then that her muscles ached with stiffness. (Maggy? How long—?) (About two hours.) Tension then, not length of time. She stretched to work out such of the ache as she could.

The common room filled in minutes. None of the surveyors had gone far, that much was clear. Again, Timosie Megeve was brought; again, Om im called court for her. This time the quiet was instant and absolute.

At the front of the room, Tocohl perched on the edge of the table. Cribbing formal words from a handful of byworld trials she witnessed, Tocohl said, "In the matter of Timosie Megeve of Maldeneant:

"I find the evidence connecting him to the death of Oloitokitok of Y to be insufficient and circumstantial." She met *layli-layli calulan's* eyes; the effort of doing so chilled her. "We could not prove it," she said with emphasis. *Layli-layli calulan* dropped her eyes under the scrutiny, an admission that even she could not deny the truth of that.

"However," Tocohl went on, "the charge of attempted genocide is quite another matter. There we can prove that Timosie Megeve consistently, and with forethought, concealed information that would have enabled this survey team to make a clear evaluation of the sprookjes' intelligence. We *can* see the same pattern in his attempts to disrupt the survey team itself, which also lessened the team's ability to make such an evaluation."

Turning to face Yannick Windhoek, she said, "As for the effects of the ionization, we must—as you say—take into account the abnormal behavior of other members of the survey team.

"Kejesli acted hastily in the matter of the sprookjes, yes, but he was willing to give them a last chance by taking swift-Kalat's charge of murder against them seriously." She smiled briefly at Kejesli; "Seriously *enough,* at any rate," she pointed out.

"In like manner, *layli-layli calulan,* although prepared to curse Ruurd van Zoveel, allowed herself to be stopped by a ruse." At that, Windhoek's eyes widened; he glanced at *layli-layli* who gave him silent thumbs-up confirmation. Tocohl went on, "And she never bothered to check the survey computer to learn van Zoveel's true name. Even Edge-of-Dark was glad of a chance to do right, rather than angry that she'd been conned... All any of the rest needed was a little push in the right direction.

"Yet Timosie Megeve remained unmovable. Worse, he was pushing in the wrong direction. He admits that he thought the sprookjes sapient; yet everything he did was an attempt to convince others they were not. He did not actually commit genocide, yet his actions might, in the end, have resulted in genocide."

Tocohl slid from her perch and turned to face Timosie Megeve. "You found the sprookjes so unlike you in spirit that you judged them unworthy of human rights; in like manner, I judge you. Timosie Megeve of Maldeneant, I find you guilty of attempted genocide. How do you choose, Megeve: death or restriction?"

"I appeal."

"That is your right," said Tocohl. She stepped back. "Address your appeal to another judge."

Timosie Megeve raised his hand. In a defiant voice, he said, "Yannick Windhoek, will you judge an appeal?"

"I will judge," said Windhoek, his voice as cold with finality as his face: "No appeal. The judgment stands."

Timosie Megeve whitened, and Tocohl had no choice but to repeat her query, as if she were caught in its relentless rhythm: "How do you choose: death or restriction?"

"I accept my role," he said, "I choose death."

The option was always given; it was seldom taken. Silence fell heavily. Tocohl stiffened. "Very well," she said as, one by one, the members of the survey team raised their hands to shoulder height— each signifying his or her unwillingness to perform the deed.

Layli-layli calulan rose, twisting the bluestone rings from her fingers as she stepped forward. "Pattern demands that I fulfill it," she said, holding out her rings to Tocohl.

Tocohl raised her palm and the rings dropped into it. "Death," she said softly, "at the hands of *layli-layli calulan* of Y. Let it be so." And to *layli-layli calulan*, she said, "You have his true name."

"Death," said Timosie Megeve scornfully, "at the hands of this barbarian. Do you expect me to believe in your death curse?" He began to laugh. *Layli-layli calulan* raised her hands, touched him ever so gently, and spoke a few grim words against the harsh, rasping sound of his disbelief.

Two days later, Timosie Megeve died, laughing no longer. At the end, he had no choice but to believe.

Windhoek, who was heading in the direction of MGE's main center, might have carried the final survey report, but Kejesli preferred to waste MGE's money. A message capsule went instead, and with all due ceremony, as subdued and formal as it was under the circumstances.

Tocohl felt odd. There was no triumph, only a sense of relief that it was over at last. She felt drained—worse, she had no sense of expectation.

Mirrrit and Jad-Ing, with Maggy's assistance, had put together a program that enabled anyone whose 2nd skin had graphics display to reproduce the sprookjes' feather-ruffling; and Bayd had, quite pointedly, taken over the job of learning the sprookjes' language.

Alfvaen would return with the survey team. Kejesli meant to restore her reputation with MGE but Alfvaen would have gone anywhere to be with swift-Kalat, much to Maggy's embarrassingly outspoken satisfaction.

But all this only served to leave Tocohl at loose ends. Spatters of rain began to fall, sending the last few onlookers scurrying for shelter, but Tocohl felt no need to hurry.

"Tocohl?" A hand caught her elbow. It was Nevelen Darragh. "I'd like a word with you in private." And the hand at her elbow swept her along. "Om im volunteered his quarters."

Tocohl was inside almost before she realized what was happening. When she did, it was with great surprise to see Windhoek, Harl Jad-Ing, and Mirrrit. Maggy's arachne squatted on the table, chatting happily with Om im and Mirrrit.

"Sit down," Darragh said and Tocohl obeyed, curious at last. Darragh went on, "You have a panel of four judges at your service, quite enough for a judgment of sapience."

Tocohl turned to stare at her. It was Maggy's sapience they meant—they *knew*, all of them. She opened her mouth to protest.

"Just a moment," Darragh said. "I do understand your reasons for not wishing such a judgment made—but we would be prepared to grant you Maggy's guardianship at the same time. Kids need looking after."

"I—Nevelen, as far as I know, Maggy's the only one of her kind as *yet*. I won't have her ... growing up under intense scrutiny. Being treated as a freak or a curiosity wouldn't be good for her."

"Then the judgment will he held closed, reported only to other byworld judges." Darragh watched her carefully. "Give it thought before you answer, Tocohl. Such a decision would set a precedent that would be of great advantage to others like Maggy as they arise, and it would alert the rest of the byworld judges to look for them as well."

Darragh was right, Tocohl knew, it would help the others, but Maggy was her first concern. "Maggy, what do you think?"

"Would we stay together?"

"We'd stay together."

"Then whatever you decide is fine with me."

Tocohl took a deep breath. "All right, Nevelen, as long as I'm her guardian and the judgment is closed. I won't have her treated as a freak," she said again.

Moments later, it was official: the extrapolative computer known as Margaret Lord Lynn of Hellspark had been declared a sapient child, Tocohl her guardian, and the proceedings had been declared For Judges' Ears Only.

Tocohl shivered. To Om im, she said wryly, "So you told them about her. I didn't think you knew." But his sudden look of surprise told her she was completely wrong. She turned to Darragh, hoping for an explanation.

The one she got was not the one she expected. Darragh said, "Om im was our backup. If you hadn't asked for a sapience judgment on Maggy, he'd have asked for one on the sprookjes."

"But that was already decided..."

"Not as far as the government knows. And since we all traveled here for a sapience hearing"—a wave of her hand ran the range, from the smiling Mirrrit to scowling Windhoek—"the government pays our travel expenses, not you."

"Oh," said Maggy, "that's good! That means we have lots of money left over for more memory!"

Darragh laughed and Tocohl laughed along with her. "As for who told me," Darragh said "it was Maggy herself. It was clear from her behavior that she'd gone well beyond what we normally think of as standard behavior, even for an extrapolative computer. I asked her for the details."

"I told you she was a mean trader," Maggy volunteered.

Tocohl eyed the arachne curiously. "And what did you get in return?"

"Nothing," said Maggy, hunching the arachne, "unless you count the experience."

"Taking advantage of children, Nevelen?" said Om im. "I'm surprised at you."

"So am I," said Tocohl. "Maggy, what exactly was the deal?"

"I wanted to know what had happened to other people who had claimed to be byworld judges. She offered to trade a complete file on judges and judgments for information about me—but she said I couldn't open it until after the four of them had judged you. And they didn't so I can't and I got nothing, and I promise you, Tocohl, I'll know better next time."

Darragh wiped a hand across her face, her shoulders shaking.

"Maggy," said Tocohl, "they did judge me. You have every right to open that file."

"I do?"

Tocohl looked pointedly at Darragh who said, "Yes, Maggy, you do."

"Oh, good," said Maggy, "then I'm not such a bad trader after all!" She fell silent, probably to examine the information Darragh had given her.

"I have one last message, Tocohl," Darragh said. "Your father invites you to join him for a little 'on the job training.' I suggest you take him up on the offer. The talent may run in family, but experience always fines it. I'm headed that way myself. Perhaps you and Maggy would like to tag along?"

"Yes," said Tocohl, "I think that's a fine idea."

"Me too," said Maggy, emerging from her studies momentarily. "We didn't see Tocohl Sisumo at the Festival of Ste. Veschke." And, mirroring Tocohl's sentiments exactly, she added, "I miss him."

Tocohl and Maggy made their good-byes. Alfvaen returned them in perfect Jenji. Bayd grinned and promised to keep up her lessons, at least until the team's pickup arrived, and sent Tocohl off with a pile of tapes for Sisumo.

Somehow Tocohl found it was hardest to take leave of *layli-layli calulan*, who had lost so much on Flashfever. But the shaman smiled her brilliant smile. "May the threads of our lives twist together again and again," she said, "and may the two of you always dream as well as you did here."

Then Tocohl gestured Darragh and Geremy into Maggy's skiff. "We have as usual, a storm to run," she reminded them.

Om im stopped her with a gesture. "There's nothing more I can do here, Ish shan," he said. "Do you have an opening for a seasoned judge's aide?"

The question surprised her but not greatly. At last, she said, "Om im, I'd like that very much, but not just yet. Maggy and I have a great deal to work out between us and I think — I know — you'd be something of a distraction."

He laughed and bowed. "I understand. And I heard the 'not just yet.' I'll see you at the Festival of Ste. Veschke in a few years, Ish shan, and I'll ask you again."

"Done." Tocohl snapped her fingers and climbed in, glancing back for one last sight of the merry eyes that glittered beneath gilded brows. She found herself still chuckling after she had delivered Geremy and Darragh to their respective ships.

Then all three were on their way and there was nothing much to do except to consider all that had happened. Once again, Om im's impish cheer sprang to her mind.

A seasoned judge's aide! she thought suddenly.

"Maggy," she said, "I think I've been had."

"You?" said Maggy. Tocohl looked down: the arachne sat at her heels, still activated.

"Me," said Tocohl. "I think I may just have been thrown in that situation deliberately — to see what I would do. I don't know the extent of the setup involved, but I'm going to find out."

"I can't tell from Judge Darragh's files but maybe you could," Maggy offered.

"Good idea, Maggy. What would I do without you?"

"You'd be bored," Maggy said authoritatively, as she presented an index on the spectacles for Tocohl to examine.

Tocohl laughed. "Much better that I be in trouble?" she suggested.

Maggy gave a thoughtful pause. "Well, as long as we're *both* in trouble, I suppose that's all right."

"Yes," Tocohl said. "That's very much all right."

Afterword, *Long* After
by Janet Kagan

Words fail me, and when they do, they often do so spectacularly. HELLSPARK was my second novel. (No, Gentle Reader, my first novel was not the one you think; see the afterword after this.) I spent five years writing and re-writing each line of this book over and over and over again. I wanted this one to be perfect.

Perfect, hah! Just as the book went into the final stages of editing, I made a horrifying discovery: Tocohl *nodded*. Riffling through the rest of the ms., I found Om im *nodding,* too, and half a dozen characters shaking their heads to mean "no."

Even here on Earth, a nod doesn't always mean "yes" and a shake doesn't always mean "no." I'd undercut my own premise.

If Ricky hadn't gotten me and HELLSPARK onto a computer, I'd never have lived through that week. I couldn't do a global search and replace—it wasn't that simple—but I could let the computer search out any and all nods and shakes so I could rewrite each individually. "'Yes,' she said."

By then I was down to the wire; I had about a week to turn in the finished ms.

Finished, hah! Nancy Weisenfeld, the copy-editor on HELLSPARK, was the only one to notice that I had somehow managed to rename a character in mid-stream (almost literally). Global search and replace? Oh, no—it wasn't that simple—because I'd renamed him, he'd wound up in conversation with himself! (I don't mind a character who talks to himself, but this one did it from two different bodies. That's another sf story altogether.) Always remember: the copy-editor is there to save your butt. She caught it and I managed to fix it.

Those two experiences, however, left me sweating and anxious and wanting to rewrite the whole damn thing at least three more times. In the end, my editor, David Hartwell, had to resort to blackmail to pry the final rewrite out of my clutching fingers: he threatened to publish the draft he had in his hands "as is."

"As is" was awash in nods and shakes and had a character talking to himself. I couldn't let him publish *that!* I relinquished/surrendered/gave up, and HELLSPARK went to print.

Shortly after the book hit the bookstores, I ran into a friend at a convention. She'd read HELLSPARK, she said, and she'd loved it. She was even willing to back that up in specifics. In the midst of all her specifics, however, she said, "By the way, so you know for next time, every time you said *sentient*, you meant *sapient*." Then she went back to what she'd loved about the book.

Half an hour later, I managed to find a copy in the huxter room. Sure enough, I had missed the nose on my face: every time I'd meant *sapient,* I'd written *sentient;* when I meant non-*sapience*, I'd written non-*sentience*. I was embarrassed beyond belief. If Tor had gone to a second edition, I'd have paid *them* to have the type reset, to have the glaring error repaired.

...All that was way the hell back in 1987.

#

Last year Stephe Pagel phoned to tell me his brand-new publishing company was ready to do a new edition of HELLSPARK. As he always does when he talks about HELLSPARK, Stephe managed to refer to the title twice, once as "Hell's-park" and once as "Hell-spark."

If I look blank and boggled when somebody does this for me, Gentle Reader, it's because I can't do it. You'll notice I didn't do it throughout the book. (In fact, I still have the note Nancy Weisenfeld appended to the ms. page where Tocohl explains the Hellspark "state secret" of alternating the pronounciation; it reads simply: "Thank you for not doing this." Cracks me up every time I see it—I could have driven *both* of us stark, staring bonkers.)

I may not be able to hellspark the pronounciation myself, but I gotta tell you I get a kick out of hearing it done. HELLSPARK is in print again because Stephe *can* alternate the pronounciation and because he gets a kick out of doing it.

Having made my day, Stephe went on to discuss technical aspects of the new edition. Last, but not least, he said, "And, oh, by the way, if there's anything you always wanted to change...?"

#

I've thought about this long and hard. Here's my decision.... Yeah, there were a couple of typoes in the Tor edition I'd like fixed.

As much as Megeve's "*wind*-colored" outfit tickled me, I think I'll save that for another story, so I've asked Stephe to make that "*wine*-colored," as it was in the ms.

Then there were the four-hundred-some hyphens Tor cut from my ms. When I learned to spell, *co-operation* had a hyphen, anything that began with *non-* did, too. Spelling has changed; nowadays I can read the word *cooperation* without thinking of chickens. So I passed on restoring those four-hundred-some hyphens...all but two of them.

My current dictionary tells me the hyphens are gone from the two words in question. I don't care; I put 'em back in.

No, I'm not going to tell you which two words. Without their hyphens, I puzzle over them. Now you can puzzle over them.

As for my glaring, horribly embarrassing misuse of *sentient* for *sapient*.... *Sapience* and *sentience* are often used interchangeably in modern day colloquial speech, but the two words are not interchangeable.

I've decided to leave the decision up to the sapient Stephe. Only as I began to write this afterword did I realize why: I have a brand-new superstition. I can laugh about it, I can recognize it for the superstition it is, but that doesn't stop me from sweating blood at the thought.

Here's my superstition: If Stephe corrects that glaring error, sure as shootin', some brand new reader will come up to me at a convention, hellsparking the title all the way, to tell me how much he loves the book and, in the midst of all the specific loves, he'll say, "Oh, by the way—" and tell me about something WORSE that I didn't catch.

No book is ever perfect, no book is ever even finished. For you to read HELLSPARK, I had to stop writing it. I had to give it up to put it into your hands.

HELLSPARK is no longer my elaborate, private daydream— HELLSPARK is yours now. Flaws and all, I hope you like it.

Thanks for listening.

AFTERWORD TO UHURA'S SONG

I never intended to write a *Star Trek* novel. The thought never even crossed my mind: I had (and still have) a head full of worlds of my own.

Then our house caught fire. For an endless time, we lived in a trailer in the driveway while the house was stripped and repaired. My manuscripts survived, kind friends actually got my computer working ("Okay, stand back, Janet. We're gonna plug it in now—"), even the disks for HELLSPARK survived, which should have made it that much easier...but I couldn't write a word.

All too aware of our financial straits, I began to consider getting a real job. "Before you do that," Ricky said, "call Hartwell. He's been asking to see your writing—let him."

At the time, Hartwell was the editor of the *Timescape* sf line at Pocket Books, the line which included *Star Trek* novels. I'd met him at sf conventions and he'd bummed cigarets from me; that didn't give me leave to call him. To give measure to my desperation, I *did* call Hartwell.

I explained the circumstances and the writer's block and asked him, in so many words, if he'd read a work in progress and tell me if I should go back to being a secretary. (Helluva thing to lay on somebody, now that I think of it!)

"Do you want to send it to my home or to my office?"

In for a penny, in for a pound. "I might as well make it official—your office." I wrapped up a clean copy of the current draft, mailed it off and went back to cleaning smoked books.

Time passed. Ricky and I decided we needed a convention and off we went to PhilCon. Hartwell was there, but Ricky assured me he wouldn't talk to me about my book at a convention and, besides, I managed to avoid him all day....

Until about two in the morning at somebody's room party, when I turned and found him at my side. "Got a cigaret, Janet?" "Sure," I said, relieved at the normalcy of the request. I gave him a cigaret, loaned him matches. He lit up, handed back the pack of matches. "Thanks," he said, then, "Come into my office." Taking me by the elbow, he steered me into the adjoining (empty) room.

As he settled in the easy chair and I settled onto the floor where I could share the ashtray, Norman Spinrad came in. (Thank god, I thought, maybe I can make a break for it while he's talking to a Filthy Pro.) Norman said, "David—"

"Go away, Norman"—David made shooing motions—"I'm talking to Janet about her first novel."

Norman didn't shoo. Instead, Norman Spinrad knelt down, looked straight at me, and pointed at David. "This man," he said, "is an *editor.*" (He said it the way most people say *mass murderer.*) "Do you have an agent or would you like me to introduce you to mine?"

Norman Spinrad was, even then, one of the finest writers of social and political satire I've ever read. He was a very Big Name Writer, not to mention president of SFWA. He didn't know me except in passing and I didn't know him except to envy his work. (God, those kick-in-the-head short stories of his!) *Norman Spinrad* wanted to know if I had an agent.

"Uh," I said. "Yes, I have an agent."

That was a start, but that wasn't good enough for Norman. He knelt there and laid it out in no uncertain terms: I was not to agree to *anything* Hartwell proposed without running it past my agent first. I nodded solemnly and said I knew the drill, but Norman made me *promise.*

I *promised.*

Only then did Norman get to his feet. Giving David the hard eye, he said, *"Now* you can talk to her about her first novel," and he shooed.

I lit a cigaret, only to discover I had one already burning in the ashtray. I handed the fresh one to David and took a swig from my beer. I steeled myself. "Okay," I said, meaning, Okay, you can tell me to go back to being a secretary now. I've had Norman Spinrad talk to me like a Dutch uncle...anything else is superfluous.

"I love your manuscript," said David. And he went on at great length about how *much* he loved my manuscript and in such detail that I finally understood that he'd actually *read* my manuscript!

Surprise! That wasn't superfluous! For the second time that evening, I was bowled over. He liked my book. He wasn't telling me to get a real job after all! I think I managed to say, "Uh...thanks."

David waited patiently. When he was sure I'd heard him and understood the message, he went on, "I'd love to publish your manuscript, but right now I'm not allowed to publish first novels. The only first novels I can publish are first *Star Trek* novels—"

He let it hang there.

I had not been able to write a word for close to nine months. It was three in the morning, I'd had two beers, Norman Spinrad at my feet, and here was an editor who wanted to publish my first novel but could only publish first *Star Trek* novels—

To this day, I swear I had nothing to do with this. After all that had happened, I couldn't have said a word. Into that long silence, I heard my subconscious say, "Hey, you want a *Star Trek* novel? I'll write you a *Star Trek* novel!"

Without so much as a pause, David Hartwell said: "Thirty page sample, ten page outline. I need it next week."

"Okay," said my mouth.

#

I got home, I slept till noon, I panicked. Monday afternoon, I phoned Hartwell: "Uh, what *exactly* did I promise you?"

"A thirty-page sample, a ten-page outline. I need it next week."

"That's what I was afraid of," I said. "Okay."

After due consideration, I decided it was okay: I could have fun with this, secure in the knowledge that nobody but my mom (the real *Star Trek* fan in the family) would ever see it.

That thirty-page sample was the first thing I'd written since the house fire; it broke the log-jam.

Good thing it did, because the next thing I knew, Hartwell wanted the book—in three months, no less!

I was half-way through my final draft—and explaining to a friend how I'd come to be writing UHURA'S SONG—when, at long last, I realized I was writing a *Star Trek* novel because I'd been conned into it by an *editor.* (I use a tone normally reserved for *mass murderer.*)

Oh, god! I thought Norman meant, Don't agree to any terms on HELLSPARK. Norman meant, Don't agree to *anything!*

I swear it wasn't me, Norman; my subconscious made me do it. And, in defense of the *editor*, my subconscious was right to agree. Writing UHURA'S SONG was just what the doctor ordered. I'll never forget the months I spent trekkin' with the crew of the *Enterprise*—for all the sheer terror of having to write at warp nine, I had a *ball.*

Mom loved it—that's what author's mothers are for, of course—but other people's moms wrote to tell me they loved it, too, and other mom's kids. Thanks for making a new kid feel so welcome. I'll always be grateful: your kindness and your generosity and your encouragement made all my other books and stories possible. Thank you, one and all. As Spock would never say, May you love long and prosper.

#

Now I'd like to take this opportunity to answer the three questions about UHURA'S SONG that I get asked most often.

Q: Who is Evan Wilson?

A: I think of her as Tail-Kinker, myself. I'm glad you liked her. So did I: she was my mom. (Yes, she was the champion tree-climber in the neighborhood.) She claimed never to see the resemblance, but anybody who knew her recognized her instantly.

Q: Are you writing another *Star Trek* novel?

A: No. Pocket turned down my outline for a sequel to UHURA'S SONG, and it'd be no fun without Mom.

Q: Where do you come up with this stuff?

A: There I was writing like crazy to meet Hartwell's outrageous deadline.... We'd moved back into the house. My computer was on the floor and I was working cross-legged on the floor in front of it. I'd gotten to the part where the First Walk party has to cross the hanging bridge over the raging flood waters.

Bigfoot (then No. 2 cat in the household and desperate to be No. 1) was curled contentedly in my lap.

I was anything but content. I couldn't get Brightspot onto that bridge.

I tried having Kirk cajole her across. That didn't work: she couldn't hear him over the roar of the water. I tried shoving her. That didn't work either. If you've ever tried shoving a cat off a table, you'll know about those invisible sucker pads cats have on their paws and bottoms.... *Nothing* I tried worked.

Elijah sauntered in from his rounds. Elijah was No. 1 cat; ordinarily, he sat in my lap while I worked. What was a second-rate cat like Bigfoot doing in my lap when Elijah rated first? He stared at Bigfoot in sheer disbelief.

Bigfoot ignored him. This compounded the audacity, and Elijah glared. Still Bigfoot made no move to give up my lap to Elijah. Elijah stepped gingerly forward and sniffed an ear, as if to confirm he was actually seeing what he thought he was seeing. Yes, it was so: Bigfoot had taken Elijah's spot.

I went on pounding my forehead against the wall. I could not think of a way to get Brightspot onto that bridge. Maybe I should skip that bit and come back to it....

Now, Elijah knew I didn't appreciate fighting in the house. He'd let Bigfoot push the limits for weeks at a time before he was (with deep apologies to me) *forced* to beat the bejeezus out of Bigfoot. So, when Elijah walked around to the other side of me to sniff Bigfoot's tail, I didn't think anything of it. I thought Elijah meant to curl up *next* to me.

Instead, he stretched his neck and sniffed Bigfoot's tail a second time. Confirming again: yes, that is Bigfoot; yes, the uppity so-and-so is in my spot; no, he still hasn't given way graciously.

Without malice (or warning), Elijah *chomped* the tip of Bigfoot's tail.

Bigfoot levitated five feet across the room and landed fully bristled and ready to defend himself to the death.

Without so much as a glance in Bigfoot's direction, Elijah stepped delicately into my (now-empty) lap. Rubbing and purring his hellos, Elijah turned his back to Bigfoot.

When I finally stopped laughing, Elijah settled in, Bigfoot stalked off in a huff, all injured dignity...and I wrote the scene that got Brightspot onto that hanging bridge.

How do I come up with this stuff? I dunno, unless you ask me about something specific...then, you may get a very specific answer.

Ask me sometime who I stole Spock's best lines from....

ADDITIONAL READING FOR HELLSPARK AND UHURA'S SONG

For various reasons, my additional reading lists didn't make it into either of my first two published books. As the the two were written (in some ways) simultaneously, they share very similar concerns. Both grew out of the reading I was doing at the time. So I'm going to give you the combined reading list here. These were the keepers. I hope they're still in print; they all deserve to be.

Ardrey, Robert: *The Territorial Imperative*.
If you don't know about blue male satin bower birds, you must read this. I'm still arguing with some of Ardrey's conclusions, but that just means I still have more stories to write.

Farb, Peter: Word Play: *What Happens When People Talk*.
Pure fun. Anybody who likes words and playing with words will have a ball reading this. If you've gotten this far, this means you.

Hall, Edward T.: *The Silent Language*.
Hall, Edward T.: *The Hidden Dimension*.
Edward T. Hall is the man who taught the Hellsparks everything they know about proxemics and kinesics. (All errors and misunderstandings are my fault purely.) These were only the first of his books I'd come across; I've since collected everything he's written. His work is always a delight to read and always inspiring. (Writers take note: *The Silent Language* contains "A map of culture" that I now use *every* time I build a culture. I consider it an invaluable spur to the imagination.) It's time I reread them all again.

McNeill, William H.: *Plagues and Peoples*.
How plagues have changed the course human history. Scary book, and you'll come away from it changed, too. (I'd intended UHURA'S SONG to be a first-contact story; *Plagues and Peoples* turned it into a second-contact story.)

Lopez, Barry: *Giving Birth to Thunder, Sleeping with His Daughter: Coyote Builds North America.*

I'm addicted to Trickster stories and, of all the collections I've read, this is my favorite. The tales are grand and the writing is purely lovely.

I learned wonderful things from these writers. HELLSPARK and UHURA'S SONG are fan letters to them.

If you're looking for sense of wonder, look to them—and then look at the world around you with bright new eyes.

Meisha Merlin Publishers, Inc proudly announce the return of Storm Constantine to America!

Herald: an official messenger, a forerunner, or to proclaim the approach of.

Storm Constantine, best known for her Wraeththu series from TOR, is back. We are proud to announce the first of our Storm Constantine short story collections. *Three Heralds of the Storm* contains three short stories by this peerless fabulist. This chapbook marks the first publication anywhere of *Such a Nice Girl*, and the first U. S. appearances of *Last Come Assimilation* and *How Enlightenment Came to the Tower*.

"Storm Constantine is a myth-making Gothic queen, whose lush tales are compulsive reading. Her stories are poetic, involving, delightful, and depraved. I wouldn't swap her for a dozen Anne Rices."   Neil Gaiman

"Storm Constantine is a literary fantast of outstanding power and originality. Her work is rich, idiosyncratic, and completely engaging. Her themes, constantly explored and re-examined through her novels, have much in common with those of Philip K. Dick—the nature of identity, the nature of reality, the creative power of the human imagination—while her sensibility reminds me of Angela Carter at her most inventive."
Michael Moorcock

Three Heralds of the Storm by Storm Constantine
64 pages, chapbook, acid-free paper, $5.00

BloodWalk by Lee Killough
456 pages, trade format, acid-free paper, $14.00

Hellspark by Janet Kagan
336 pages, trade format, acid-free paper, $12.00

To order your copies, please fill out the order form below and return it with your payment, check or money order payable in US funds, to Meisha Merlin Publishers, Inc., PO Box 7, Decatur, GA 30031. Please allow 4-6 weeks for delivery.

NAME_____

ADDRESS_____

CITY_____ STATE_____

ZIP_____ COUNTRY_____

HERALDS COPIES _____ X $5.00 = _____

$0.50 per book S&H _____ X $0.50 = _____

BLOODWALK COPIES _____ X $14.00 = _____

$3.00 per book S&H _____ X $3.00 = _____

HELLSPARK COPIES _____ X $12.00 = _____

$2.00 per book S&H _____ X $2.00 = _____

TOTAL _____

Dealer inquiries are welcome.